stone soul

Born in Derry, Northern Ireland, Peter J Merrigan was first published at the age of 17 in the Simon & Schuster anthology *Children of the Troubles*, edited by Laurel Holliday. His first novel was *The Camel Trail*.

Following a Bachelor of Arts in Writing and English from London, Peter spent nineteen years in England as a marketing and advertising professional before returning to his native town. He lives with his husband in Co. Tyrone.

Find Peter online at peterjmerrigan.com

ALSO BY PETER J MERRIGAN

THE AILIGH WARS SAGA
Stone Heart
Stone Forged
Stone Soul
Stone Fall

THE RIDER SERIES
Rider
Lynch

STANDALONE NOVELS
The Camel Trail

STONE SOUL

PETER J MERRIGAN

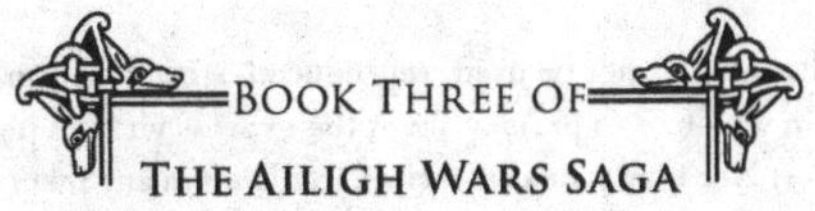

Nightsgale Books

1 3 5 7 9 10 8 6 4 2

First published in 2021 by
Nightsgale Books, Co. Tyrone, Northern Ireland

ISBN 978 1 9163838 1 4

Cover by Nightsgale Books

A CIP catalogue record of this book
is available from the British Library and the
Library of Trinity College Dublin

Typeset in Perpetua by Nightsgale Books

For my family

Ní scarfainn leis ar ór na cruinne.

N
Thúr Rí
Northern Druids (Doagh)
Grianán Ailigh
Knockdhu
¥ Uí Ultan Stronghold
Giant's Ring
Carrowmore
Emain Macha
Tomb of Maeve
Mac Dalaigh Stronghold §
Ó Nallon Stronghold
Cruachan
Castlestrange Stone
Teamhair (Hill of Tara)
Clonycavan
Poulnabrone
Baurnadomeeny
Ó Hargon Stronghold
Ardgroom
Drombeg
¥ Áed's birthplace
§ Rónán's birthplace
ÉIRINN
50 miles

Pronunciation Guide

Achall	*ackal*
Áed	*aid*
Ailigh	*ay-lick*
Breasal	*bressel*
Cáer	*care*
Cormac	*cormack*
Ethal Anbuail	*ethal an-bwale*
Fionn	*finn*
Gallen	*gaylen*
Grainne	*grawnya*
Grianán	*greenan*
Mogh Roith	*mog roth*
Mordha	*mora*
Muirgel	*murg-ell*
Orlaith	*orla*
Rónán	*rownan*
Teamhair	*tah-war* (modern day Tara)
Thúr Rí	*tur-ree*

Chapter 1

She stood on top of the black basalt columns of the ancient stone causeway and held her hair back from her face as a fierce wind drew tears from her eyes. Foaming spray kicked up a short distance beneath her and the roiling waves of the sea were black with doubt. She had cast the bones earlier that evening and the omens were laced with dread. Her horses, tethered to the carbad on which they arrived before sunset, whinnied on the landward side of the causeway, stomping their hooves in the browning grasses.

'He's late,' Gallen said.

Grainne nodded. In the dark of a harvest evening, two weeks before the festival of Samhain, Gallen was an anchor at her side. He had been training under her guidance for five years now and, by the Yule, he would be ready for the first ceremony of his druidship. Where once there was an ill-tempered boy who could not control his fists, there now stood a man, confident of mind and body. She was thankful that he insisted on journeying with her.

Grainne watched the choppy waves whose seafoam licked over the rocks beneath their feet like many hungry tongues. That her old mentor would be rowing a small curragh under these treacherous conditions meant his news would be grave.

Although the moon had been masked by the autumn-bronzed clouds, she tracked its position by its luminous sheen. Dawn was close.

Her grey horses cried for her attention again and she gave a prayer to her most gracious lady Cáer to ease the geldings' fears. They would be back on the road by dawn and the storm clouds would have dissipated by then. She would ease the horses in a slow canter until their panic subsided.

A sheet of lightning dazzled the clouds and the roll of thunder that followed cracked against the stone columns of the causeway.

Gallen winced. 'The gods are angry.'

The rain softened to a drizzle, but their robes and winter cloaks were saturated. They made a sign with their fingers to ward off the gods' fury.

Their journey from Grianán Ailigh took them two nights along the coast, weaving the carbad through dense forestry and dismounting for the rocky terrain that saw Gallen leading the geldings through twisted pathways. The young messenger, who had arrived at Ailigh to inform Grainne of her old mentor's request to meet her here, would say nothing of Cathal's reasons, and he hurried away as fast as he came. Grainne's fear rose with every passing moment.

'Where are you, Cathal?' she asked the ocean.

Gallen pointed.

In the distance, a small stain rose in and out of view over the waves. Grainne pulled her hood up against the wind and stepped towards the rocky shoreline to greet her mentor. As the small hide-skinned boat drew close, she could see his face was wet with sea-rain and his cloak was soaked. He drew up his oars and the boat thumped into the stones. When he threw them a mooring line, Gallen tied it off around one of the stone columns as Grainne reached out a hand to aid Cathal from the curragh.

Even the giant who formed this causeway would hardly dare step outside in such weather.

'Cáer's blessings,' she said, although her words were plucked from her lips on the wind.

Cathal embraced her, his wet beard scratching her cheek. 'Were you followed?'

'Who would follow us?'

Gallen clasped the old man's arm in greeting. 'I have not sensed anyone following us. Why the secrecy?'

Cathal pointed landward and they picked their way over the slick basalt rocks and descended into a gulley where the wind howled above them but did not penetrate the deep crevice they sought shelter in.

Grainne studied the old man's face. He had taught her at the northern druids' compound for many years before her graduation and, in the years since the Battle of Knockdhu, he visited her at Ailigh only once when he was on his way to the southern druids on routine business. His eyes, narrowed against the rain, were usually bright and cheerful, and the crease where his moustache met his beard was an eternal crack as he smiled.

But he was not smiling tonight.

'Cathal, you scare me with your silence.'

Cathal looked over his shoulder, then took from his pocket a small piece of fabric, a thumb's length square, and handed it to her.

'Cathal, what is this? Why do you not speak?' She rubbed the section of fabric between her thumb and fingers and recognised it at once. 'No. It cannot be.'

'What is it?' Gallen asked.

'Tell me this is not so.' She handed the cloth to Gallen.

'I do not understand.'

Cathal took Grainne's shoulders. 'I am sorry, dear one. The archdruid is dead.'

Grainne felt her knees buckle as he said it. The old man's arms wrapped around her body to support her, and she wept against his chest.

'How?' Gallen asked. 'When?'

Above them, the wind eased for a moment, and then it wailed over the wet rocks.

'I am sorry,' Cathal said again. 'I was not there to protect him. If I had been, I could have stopped it.'

Grainne pulled herself from his embrace and wiped rain and tears from her cheeks. 'Stopped what? Cathal, what happened?'

'He was murdered.'

Gallen made a fist around the small piece of fabric. 'Who killed him?'

'I cannot say. But he did not die alone.'

Grainne put a hand to Gallen's arm to still him. 'How many?'

'Too many,' Cathal said. 'Young, old—they were indiscriminate. Someone is killing our kind. The brehon are being slaughtered across the country.'

There was a pain in her heart. Her most gracious lady Cáer had not come to her to tell her of these evils. She had not sensed the passing of her master. A generous and kind man was gone, and no amount of fabric cut from his robes would comfort her. She closed her eyes and prayed that Cáer would guide the archdruid on his way to the Otherworld.

'Who would do such a thing?' she asked.

'Nobody knows. The assassins come in the dark and they leave no witnesses. Very few of those gathered at the northern compound escaped. Some into the mountains, some towards the east. They are too scared to gather in groups or to announce their presence in public.'

'I must tell my king,' Grainne said. 'He will gather his army and protect our kind.'

'There are too few left to protect. Go back to Ailigh. Lock yourselves away and do not venture abroad until you know it is safe to do so. Whoever these assassins are, they are well-trained, and they are vicious. They seek to annihilate us all.'

Gallen folded back the side of his robes to reveal the sword at his hip. 'Let them come. I will be ready for them.'

'You may not see them coming,' Cathal said. 'I must go.' He climbed the side of the rocks and they followed him.

Grainne said, 'Come with us. You will be safe behind Ailigh's walls.'

'I cannot rest. I have many more stops to make between here and the south.'

'You cannot venture across the land on your own. What if you are discovered and killed?'

'I skirt the land by boat. I am safe enough.'

The horses whinnied as the sky flashed white and the stone columns of the causeway glowed wet from the lightning.

'Get down,' Gallen shouted, and he drew his sword.

Two silhouettes rose above the highest stones, men with bows raised.

They ducked as an arrow sailed overhead. Gallen was quick to draw his slingshot with his free hand and seated a stone shot in its base. He whipped the sling and fired but the wind was strong and carried it away from its target.

Grainne pulled the short dagger from her robes. The assassins hopped with light feet from one stone column to the next as they came down the side of the causeway.

'Get to safety,' Cathal said. 'The boy and I will deal with these two.'

'I am not a boy,' Gallen said, pocketing his sling and taking the stone columns two at a time towards their assailants.

Grainne shook her head, her hood falling from her face. 'Get to your curragh, Cathal. Tell everyone. Be safe.'

The two men who bounded towards them were dressed in dark colours to blend with the night, and their faces were hidden with leather hide whose eyeholes and mouthpiece allowed them to see and breathe.

Grainne climbed the rocks behind her acolyte, the dagger clenched in her fist. 'Aid me, Cáer.'

The closest assassin swiped his sword at Gallen who ducked, weaved and parried. Their swords clashed but the ringing of the metals was dulled by the mournful wind and the sighing of the waves on the rocks beneath them. Gallen barrelled his shoulder into the man's chest and they tumbled together across the rocks.

The second attacker bore towards Grainne and she raised her dagger in defence, but she was whipped away by a hand from behind her, and as she fell to the greasy rocks, Cathal rose over her and threw his small blade at the man. It was a solid hit to the throat, penetrating the leather cover of his neck, and the man dropped to his knees before them. Cathal raised a foot and pushed him backwards.

Grainne scrabbled to the dead man, her robes snagging between the rocks, and she heard Cathal running towards

Gallen. She gripped the dagger's hilt, twisted to ensure the man was dead, and then she pulled it from his throat and tore the leather covering from his face. He was unremarkable of feature, a man just like any other.

Across the rocks, Gallen and his assailant had tumbled into the dark ocean. She could not tell one man from another as they fought together in the water, fists punching, hands gripping, heads butting. Cathal stood on the rocks above them and drew a second dagger from his robes. He tossed it into the air above the two men and Grainne saw both fighters clamber to reach for it. It was up to the gods if his action would help or hinder.

The blade dropped into the ocean beside them, sinking into the blackness below.

Grainne came to Cathal's side, glancing behind her to ensure there were no other attackers. When she turned her attention to the fighting men in the water, she saw Gallen's face, his nose bloodied, his red hair matted to his brow. He gripped the leather mask of the assassin, jabbing his fingers through the eyeholes, and then he punched his knuckles into the man's throat. The attacker went underwater, but came up with his arms flailing, scratching Gallen's cheek, and he punched his face until the acolyte was submerged.

He did not come back up.

Grainne gripped Cathal's sleeve when the attacker turned his attention to them. He swam towards them and they backed up the rocks. Cathal felt among his robes for a third dagger but produced none. Grainne looked back at the dead man as the sky flashed white; she had left Cathal's first dagger by his side.

The man reached the rocks and pulled himself ashore. He coughed water and drew himself to his knees. He was without his sword or bow, which meant they would be nearby and had fallen from him as he tumbled across the rocks with Gallen. Grainne scanned the flat-topped columns but, in the darkness, she could see no sword.

As the assassin rose to his feet, the water broke behind him and Gallen leapt forward, the glint of Cathal's dagger flashing as the sky lit the causeway in another burst of lightning.

He fell on their attacker and whipped the blade, penetrating the back of the man's neck. He raised his arm and stabbed him again, but the body beneath him did not move. His face had cracked against a column of stone as Gallen descended on him.

Gallen raised the dagger in both hands and brought it down. His eyes were wide, his lips stretched in a soundless scream of rage.

Grainne eased a hand towards him. 'Enough, Gallen. He is gone.'

He ignored her, plunging the blade into the man's back, gripping the attacker's hair and lifting his head from the rocks, and slicing the dagger across his neck.

'Gallen.'

At the sound of her voice, her acolyte stopped and closed his eyes. He nodded, dropped the dagger, and stood. Before turning away, he kicked the man's side.

'You fought well,' Cathal said.

'I am trained.'

'Who is your god?'

'Mogh Roith.'

Cathal offered his arm. 'You are a worthy champion for his name.'

'We should get somewhere safe,' Grainne said, 'before we are under a renewed attack.'

'Go home,' Cathal said. 'Do not stop. Take turns at the reins while the other sleeps, but do not stop until you are secured within your walls. I will send word when it is safe.'

'You cannot venture out to sea alone in such a storm, Cathal. It is too dangerous.'

'Manandán guides my curragh. I am not alone.'

Grainne collected Cathal's daggers for him and Gallen helped the older man over the slick rocks and down to his curragh. As the acolyte untied the mooring line, Grainne said, 'May all the gods journey at your side.'

'We will find out who these men belong to,' Gallen said, 'and we will have our vengeance.'

Cathal waved as his small boat cut over the seafoam. 'When it is safe, we will gather the brehon at the most sacred place. We will mourn our loss and then we will elect a new archdruid. We will rise from this; nobody has the power to stand against the gods.'

When he was out of sight and they stood alone on the high precipice of the towering causeway, Gallen touched Grainne's shoulder. 'We should bury them.'

Grainne wiped the rain from her cheeks. 'Bury one of them. We will take the other to Ailigh. King Rónán may recognise his colours or his face mask.'

Chapter 2

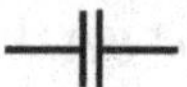

Rónán Ó Mordha cursed. Thick mud hugged the wheels of his carbad and churned under his horse's hooves. He whipped the reins and coaxed the gelding forward.

Cormac laughed, his eyes squinting against the rain. 'Remind me why you insisted on coming with us?'

'Get off your horse and help.'

When Cormac dismounted, he slapped Rónán's horse on the rump and the carbad jolted, the wheels slipping over the mud. The horse stomped and Cormac's tunic and face were splashed brown with flecks of dirt.

When the mud gave way to grass, Rónán looked back at his consort. 'What are you waiting for? We do not have all day.' Cormac muttered something that Rónán did not catch, but he laughed as Cormac leapt onto the back of his horse.

'Perhaps you should be on horseback and let the rest of us ride in the comfort of a carbad.'

'When you are king, you can ride on the back of a cloud pulled by seven swans. Until then, wipe the mud from your face and stop complaining.' Rónán pulled his cloak around his shoulders and flicked the reins. They were less than half a day from the mines and, if the weather continued to dampen everybody's spirits, there would be murder before they arrived.

He looked at the column of men behind him, some on horse-back, some on foot, leading packhorses and carts filled with trade goods. The wheat sheaves—what little he had to trade with—were covered by leather hides to keep out the rain, and behind the horses, sixty head of cattle were driven by their cowherds over the muddy ground. Their trade was lean. But times were hard.

They heard the mining activity before they saw the mines, hammering and clanking, the shouts of brusque voices and the creak of ropes and wheels.

From the top of the valley, Rónán called a halt to his men.

Cormac reined his horse in beside him. 'What is your name?'

'Bradán Ó Mordha,' Rónán said. 'I do not need reminding.' A king would not concern himself with trade journeys and, if the tribes he was trading with knew he was Overking of Ailigh, they would fleece him for all he had. He invented Bradán the year before when the boredom of a king's life made him weary. If he was not officiating royal duties, fighting border disputes, or overseeing the training of his boys, he had little to do but drink sweet wine and worry about his crops and his people.

'I could have handled this trade alone,' Cormac said.

'I trust that you could. You have the lead. Just indulge me while I am here.'

They slipped down the muddy valley towards the only salt mine north of Teamhair, the iron-dark clouds threatening to rupture and soak an already saturated land.

When they greeted the chieftain who retained the mines, too far from Ailigh to identify the overking, Rónán allowed Cormac to control the exchange.

Cormac clasped arms with the tall man whose braided moustache reached below his chin. 'The gods see you well, Garbhán.'

'I lost a son to childbirth this year,' Garbhán said. 'The gods do not see me well enough.'

Cormac made a sign of sorrow with his hand. 'The gods have plans we are not equipped to understand.'

Garbhán nodded and indicated the trail of men behind Cormac. 'What do you bring me this time, young man?'

'Twenty grouse, plucked and ready for cooking; sixty cattle; four wagons of emmer wheat.'

'Only four?'

'We have been blighted by the rust for the second year in a row.'

Garbhán pulled at the loose skin of his throat. 'Every field has been scarred by it. You did not bring wine?'

'Would I dare stand before you without the finest northern berry-wine you've ever tasted?'

'Bring a barrel to my brú and I'll have a place set for you. We will drink before doing business. Your men can huddle against the quarry-side from the rain. I haven't the space for them all in the mouth of the mines.'

Rónán nodded to his companions, and they arranged themselves against the quarry wall as the clouds unleashed their deluge, and then he followed Cormac into the chieftain's hut. He stood by the entrance while Cormac cracked open a barrel of berry-wine and Garbhán dipped two cups into it. The two men sat while Rónán stayed at the door, looking like the tradesman's guard he posed as.

Garbhán drank and smacked his lips. 'I do not know how you make the sweetest wine I have ever tasted, but I am grateful for it. My wives will hate you when I stumble home drunk.'

'Give half the wine to your wives and they will not care.'

Garbhán laughed and settled to business. 'I can give you forty-one sacks for your trade.'

'Forty-one? You gave me twice that last time,' Cormac said.

'What can I say? My men are working themselves to the bone before the season changes and they must stop for the winter. We all have mouths to feed, and slaves eat more than you'd think.'

Rónán saw Cormac's shoulders slump. 'What if I throw in twenty-five of the finest iron swords, complete with bronze scabbards?'

'I run a mine, Cormac, not a training camp like your king.'

'You can smelt them.'

Garbhán shook his head. 'I have all the iron I need.'

Before the bartering could continue, a shout came from outside. Rónán turned to the door. Men were running from the mouths of the mines and, above them, the land was collapsing down the hillside.

'Mudslide,' Rónán said. He did not wait for the others. He ran into the quarry field and stomped through the thick mud. At the entrance of the tunnel under the caving sludge, whose opening was growing smaller as the earth fell into its darkness, he gripped one of the slave workers by the arms. 'How many are inside?'

The slave pushed away from him and ran.

When Cormac and Garbhán caught up, Rónán said, 'Are all the tunnels connected? Can the men get out from the far side?'

'No,' Garbhán said, pushing up his sleeves and clawing mud back from the entrance as though he could stop the mudslide by himself.

'How many are down there?'

'I have two hundred men spread across the tunnels. In this one? Maybe twenty, twenty-five.'

'Twelve have come out. Where are the others?'

The mud churned and the tunnel entrance shrank. If the men did not come to the surface soon, they would suffocate when the tunnel was sealed, or drown in thick mud.

The tunnel walls were wet and leaking.

Rónán unclipped his fur cloak and kicked his boots off. To Cormac, he said, 'Clear the other tunnels before they, too, are affected.' He did not wait for a response.

As he turned into the mouth of the mine, Garbhán shouted after him. 'Keep turning right. Follow the smell.'

He descended.

The tallow candles that lit the tunnel blanched yellow against the rocky walls. His feet slipped in the flowing mud. The further he went, the higher the river of brown sludge rose, and when he followed the tunnel to the right, it was above his ankles.

He sniffed but could smell only wet earth.

Rónán called out and listened for a response. None came.

As the mud churned, he slipped and fell. Struggling to his feet, he continued. Behind him, the tunnel was in darkness as the dampness of the air extinguished the candles nearest the entrance.

He choked on salt dust. He was close.

'Hello? Can you hear me?'

The mud river rose. When he turned right at a cross-section, he was wading up to his thighs. And still the tunnel descended. The lower he walked, the higher the river.

When the tunnel opened into a cavern, the air was thick with salt dust and the pungent smell of stale sweat. Torches ringed the upper walls, but as he looked down, the steps that were carved into the rock salt disappeared into a lake of brown filth. The level continued to rise.

'Hello?'

A body floated face down in the mud. Rónán dived towards him, with no idea how close the bottom of the cave was. His palms smacked the ground, but he righted himself and swam through the thick pool. He turned the body over, but it was too late.

He wiped mud from his face and blinked. The cave grew dark. Of the four steps that were visible when he entered, only two could be seen above the slurry.

A shout came from the far corner. When he looked, it took some time before his eyes adjusted to the wet blackness.

'We're over here.'

Rónán swam towards the sound. As he approached, he saw seven men clinging to an outcropping in the salt wall.

'Are there others?'

One of the men pointed at the floating body. 'Just him in this section. Four or five others in the next cave.'

'How do I get to the next cave?'

'You can't. It's beneath us.'

The mud level rose.

Rónán mouthed a prayer to the gods. 'We have to hurry. We must swim back to the stairs.' He looked, but the stairs were concealed, and the entrance was growing smaller. 'Hurry,' he said.

Four of the men slipped down into the mud.

Rónán directed them. 'If you go under, hold your breath. This is not like water. If you get submerged, push harder. Use the far wall to grapple your way up again.' He looked at the men who remained on the ledge and realised they were not men at all. To the youngest, he said, 'How old are you?'

'Fourteen winters,' the boy said, his eyes wide, his clothes brown with caked mud.

Rónán offered him a hand. 'Trust me. We will all get out of here.'

The boy shook his head. 'I cannot swim.'

'The mud is thick. You will not be swimming. It will be like walking. Trust me. Take my hand. One at a time. Form a chain. You must not let go.'

'We will drown.'

'What's your name?'

'Tiarnán.'

'Take my hand, Tiarnán. I am Rónán Ó Mordha. Do you recognise my name?' When the boy nodded, Rónán said, 'I will not lie to you. And I will not let go. But we must leave now. Do you understand?'

Tiarnán took his hand and shuffled off the ledge. As he fell under the mud, Rónán lifted him and pushed his hair back from his eyes.

'Breathe. We are still alive. See?'

The remaining boys held hands and slipped into the muddy lough. The men who had made it to the far side were shouting their names, but the entrance was getting smaller.

'Go,' Rónán called to them. 'Get out of here. We are right behind you.' He kicked his legs, holding Tiarnán's hand. 'Keep your heads up. If you feel the boy behind you pulling you down, lift him up with all your strength.'

Rónán used his free arm and his legs to propel himself through the mud.

'Stop,' one of the boys called. 'Where is Ros?'

When Rónán looked, the boy at the back was missing. 'Pull him up.'

'He's gone.' The boy lifted his hand to show that it was empty. 'He let go.'

Rónán cursed.

'We're all going to drown,' one of them said.

Rónán kicked. When he reached the far wall, he hauled Tiarnán towards the entrance. 'Climb up. But don't let go of your friends.'

He turned, diving into the darkness, and felt his way through the mud. When he struggled up for air, he could see nothing. His ears were clogged with wet earth and he could feel himself getting sucked down.

He breathed, twisted, and dived into the roiling blackness. When at last his fingers clasped around something solid, he pulled, beat his legs, and pushed through the thick mud to the surface. The earth did not want to let its victim go. His lungs burned and he gasped. He dragged the boy up out of the sludge, smeared mud from his face, and slapped his cheek to wake him.

'Come on.'

He slapped him again.

The boy coughed and gulped air. Thick mud spewed from his lips.

Rónán hauled him towards the far entrance, though he could see little. He followed the sound of the boys' voices as they shouted at him.

Hands gripped his tunic and his arms. When they were above

the level of the rising mud, Rónán sat on the ground, submerged up to his chest, and he pushed the last boy ahead of him. 'Stay on your feet,' he said. 'Fight your way through it.'

He rose, weak, lungs still labouring, and he told them to clasp hands again. They battled through the mire towards the upper ground.

The tunnel was endless. The candles were extinguished, and they used the walls to guide them. Tiarnán slipped and fell under the river of mud, but Rónán gripped him before he disappeared. 'This is not a day for dying.'

They waded, leg muscles straining, clothes heavy against their skin, and as they veered left, they could hear the shouts and cries of men outside.

The mouth of the tunnel had collapsed.

'We're trapped,' Tiarnán said.

The mud beneath them was receding as it slipped down the throat of the passage.

Rónán felt the wall beside him, moved his hand along the side to the roof. Support beams were in place, and the roof was solid. 'The walls will hold. We must dig our way out.'

They clawed at the earth.

When shards of light penetrated the tunnel, Rónán blinked and scrabbled harder at the thick soil.

Outside, shovels were cutting through the wall of mud. Hands entered and Rónán pushed Tiarnán through the gap. When everybody was out, he crawled through the hole, gulping at the air with fervour.

Cormac knelt beside him and wiped mud from his face with his fingers. Rónán's vision was blurred. When he sat up, he blinked, his eyes watering, grit falling away from him.

'There were others,' he said. 'I could not get to them.'

'You did what you could.'

'It was not enough. Their cave was flooded. They had no way out.'

Cormac helped him to his feet. The rain washed his clothes. He looked back at the entrance. 'I could not save them.'

Garbhán clasped his arm. 'You saved more than I could have. I owe you my gratitude, my lord.'

'Do you have a druid?' Rónán asked. 'Those boys may have swallowed too much mud.' When he looked at the boys on the ground, Tiarnán smiled at him. And then he lay down in the rain and let it wash over him.

'I have sent for the local druid,' Garbhán said. 'My lord, I am in your debt.'

'Why do you call me Lord?'

'Even covered in mud, I would recognise the Overking of Ailigh. I was at the Tailteann games last year.'

'Why did you not say so when we arrived?'

'It seemed your man, Cormac, was doing all the talking. Who am I to disrespect you? Come. The druid will see to the boys; you should bathe.'

When he was cleaned and donned a fresh tunic from his pack, Rónán settled with Garbhán and Cormac in the chieftain's hut. 'The slave boys—are they well?'

'Thanks to you, my lord, they live. That tunnel will be out of action for some time, but I will have it dredged for the bodies of the deceased. They will be buried each with a sack of salt for the gods.'

They shared a drink to honour the dead.

'To business, then,' Garbhán said.

Cormac smiled at Rónán. 'Shall I take the lead again, my lord?'

And Garbhán laughed.

Chapter 3

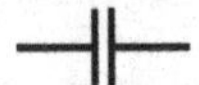

She was known as the warrior's wife, though she was without a husband. She came among them more than four years ago with her son while he was still a baby, and she begged the chieftain for a home. As a guest to his tribe lands, he complied.

'There is grief in your eyes,' he said. 'I can see it as clear as the pigs in the field.'

He offered her a brú on the outer reaches of his lands, and the smoke from her hearth seeped through her thatching day and night. Twelve nights later, when no one had seen her since her arrival, the chieftain called to her and entered.

The baby suckled at her and she whispered a song against his brow.

'The tribeswomen thought you had passed into the Otherworld. Are you well?'

She did not have the energy to cover herself from his gaze. The warrior's wife nodded.

'When was the last time you ate? Come to the great hall. We will feast to the honour of your arrival, even if it is twelve nights too late.'

'You do not need to honour me, Lord.' Her voice wisped over the yellow flames of her hearth. 'I am no lady.'

The chieftain, Banan MacColm, crouched beside her stool and placed his hand upon her shoulder. 'You are a woman in need of food. You would disrespect me if you do not eat. Your boy would not suffer the world without a mother, and I will not have your death sully my name. Come; eat with me.'

The warrior's wife closed her eyes.

'What is his name?'

'It is too painful to say, Lord.'

'A nickname, then.' He studied the baby's face. 'Breasal.'

Red stain. She smiled.

She ate with him in the hall but did not engage with the tribeswomen who questioned her. She cradled Breasal in her arms and when discussions became too loud, she lowered her face to his cheek and closed her eyes until the dizziness of conversation subsided. She had been alone for long months since leaving the north that her hearing was enhanced from the perpetual silence of the empty forests.

That night, she thanked Banan for his hospitality, and she offered to work for him to repay his kindness.

'Sleep first. Return your strength. We do not get many travellers and those that come never stay. You are welcome here.'

She did not expect to stay more than a few more nights, but here she was, standing in a field of cut grass, surrounded by the tribeswomen, each holding a blunted sword.

'Again,' she said. 'Parry, dodge, parry.'

The chieftain did not mind, and the husbands came to watch and laughed at first. But when one of the men offered to spar with her, she thwacked him to the ground and towered over him, the tip of her sword pressed against the flesh of his neck.

He stood and clasped her arm. 'I am big enough to know when

I am beaten. But do me a favour—lock your weapons away at night; I do not need my wife cutting my throat while I sleep.'

His wife laughed. 'It would not be the first time I tried.'

When Breasal was old enough to pay attention, the warrior's wife told him to sit by the rowan tree and watch. He studied her with intent, and in time he would fall asleep to the sounds of metal against metal. The half of his face that was stained red from his birth glowed bright in the afternoon sunlight or darkened his complexion when it rained.

'Orlaith,' one of the tribeswomen said.

So few people called her by name that she often forgot its existence. Even Breasal, nicknamed by the chieftain four years ago, no longer carried the weight of her husband's name.

The woman pointed to the rowan tree. 'Is he all right?'

Breasal lay on his back under the shadow of the tree whose bouquets of white flowers had given way to clusters of red berries, and they could see even from this distance that he looked rain-soaked despite a cloudless sky.

Orlaith ran to him. When she touched his skin, he was burning and feverish. She picked him up and carried him home. 'Get the druid.'

Banan's tribe did not have a druid of their own. One of the men mounted a horse and charged south while the women brought water for a bath. Breasal's thin eyelids, blue veins visible like forks of lightning across them, quivered as his eyes rolled, and he mumbled incomprehensible sounds.

'Plunge him in a bath of icy water,' someone said. 'We should cool him.'

The women of the tribe gathered in Orlaith's brú and fussed, but there was no clear consensus among them. Some said to cool him with water, others said to wrap him in thick furs and let him sweat the fever out.

Orlaith soaked a cloth and patted it on the boy's brow and cheeks. She filled a cup for him, but he would not drink, his sweat-dampened lips chapped underneath, and his gums were a pale pink.

He moaned and, as his head twisted, he vomited on the floor. His eyes continued to jerk beneath his lids.

And then he lay still.

By nightfall, when the druid arrived, Breasal had not stirred, but his breathing was no longer laboured. The wizened man gave the boy a foul-smelling liquid infusion, and he told Orlaith to make him drink it again in the morning. 'I will return in two nights. When his fever has broken, he will be well.'

Alone, she sat on a stool by his pallet bed and stroked his damp hair. His cheeks were red—not just from his birthmark. The sound of distant wolves howled beyond the borderline of the tribe. Five winters old and he had not so much as sprained an ankle or bloodied his nose. When he was born, she worried about his health. The red stain that marked his face and neck had panicked her and she watched the stain daily, assured that it would fade with time. But Grainne, the druid who birthed him, said it was of no concern. The boy was healthy and, although he would never rise through the ranks of men, he would not suffer from the mark.

He had been nameless, then. A boy with no name and no father.

His real father, the man who planted him inside her, was of less consequence than the man who would—albeit with brief fortitude—marry Orlaith and take the child as his own.

The warrior.

She closed her eyes. To think of Fionn was to peel back the scabs of her wounds. She had been in love. Was still in love.

The tribeswomen knew it. This was why they named her the warrior's wife even though he had journeyed to the Otherworld before they came to know her.

When Breasal, the child who had been known once by her husband's name, cried out in his sleep, she placed her hand on his chest and soothed him. She took the cloth and dampened his skin with it. 'Hush, son.'

His first illness in five years. Orlaith cried.

Sometime in the night, she woke, her head on the straw-filled mattress by his arm. When she raised her eyes, Breasal was staring at her.

'You are awake.'

He did not respond.

She traced the outline of his birthmark over his nose and across his cheek. 'Are you thirsty?' She dipped a cup into a bowl of water and returned to his side, but as she raised his head and brought the cup to his lips, he did not drink from it. The water spilled on his chin.

He blinked.

She pressed the back of her hand to his forehead and felt the heat that emanated from him. She pulled the furs away from him to let his body cool. 'Breasal, speak to me. Are you well?'

The boy closed his eyes. Orlaith lowered his head to the mattress.

She did not fall asleep again. When the dawn's rays crept over the hillside, she threw open her door and dragged his small bed towards the entrance so that he could watch the morning brighten. She had sat with him in the mornings on her journey south from Ailigh, watching the sky turn orange and then pink before settling on the blue of day. She would not break camp until the sun was visible and young Fionn gurgled his delight.

She knelt on the floor beside him now, stroking his hair, and she told him all the things she could see from the doorway as the colours that the moon had stolen from the land returned to their rightful owners.

She knew the colours of morning better than most. At first, the sky would wash grey, and the landscape was black against it. Then the distant mountains would flood with blue, turning green as the colour swept closer. Trees would turn from black to brown and the red heather was the last to skin itself in colour. When she could see the colour of the heather, she knew the morning was complete.

When a soft rain cooled the entrance of her brú, she did not mind. She fanned Breasal's skin with a damp cloth and sang to him as he slept.

Later, one of the tribeswomen, Etain, came to her with a bowl of curds. 'Has the fever broken?'

Orlaith shook her head. She ate without tasting the food. 'We should be training.'

'Breasal is more important than sword fighting,' Etain said.

Orlaith gave her son some of the druid's concoction, and she wrapped him tight in his furs.

'We will train again when he is better.'

Etain left her and Orlaith stoked the hearth. A fire was only ever put out during a fire festival, and it would do no good to the residence of a home if it were left to die untended.

Breasal moaned in his sleep.

When she came to his side, his eyes were open, but his stare was vacant.

She soaked the cloth and wrung it damp. As she raised it to his forehead, Breasal gripped her arm. He looked at her.

'The fields are burning.' His voice was hoarse, as though he had been screaming for days.

Orlaith filled a cup and let him drink from it. 'It is just the hearth, son. You are safe.'

He lowered his head and turned away from her.

'The fields are burning.'

'What fields?'

He did not speak. Orlaith touched her hands to his cheeks and she kissed the tip of his nose. She felt his body shiver. She considered sending for the druid; her son's fever was not breaking and now he was delirious.

She stood, but he gripped the hem of her dress and would not let go until she knelt by him.

She put a hand on his reddened chest. 'You are going to be well. I will make sure of it.'

Breasal took a deep breath, held it, and then released.

'All the fields are burning,' he said. 'And the souls are screaming.'

Chapter 4

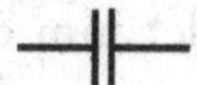

Rónán and Cormac returned to Ailigh with sixty-seven sacks of salt. They were road-weary and soaked, and they shared a heated bath as a cumal girl topped up their wine cups. Later, as a fierce northerly wind battered the hilltop, Rónán slopped through the wet embankment, his fur cloak pulled over his head, and stopped at a brú in the middle rampart. When he knocked, Achall called that he should enter.

He stamped his feet at the doorway and felt the heat of the hearth within.

Achall weaved a shuttle through her vertical loom and battened the yarn into the fell. Without looking at him, she said, 'Boots off. I do not need mud on my floor.'

Obliging her, Rónán stood by the fire to warm his feet. At the far side, visible through the flickering flames, young Áed chipped at the skin of a root vegetable, curls of white peel slipping to the floor around him.

'If you wish to eat with us, it is not prepared yet.'

'I will eat with Cormac.'

Achall grunted. Her shuttle whipped from one hand to the other.

Since their divorce five years ago, when she had made an

attempt on Fionn's life, she lived in this small home with her son. The pink scar on her cheek was a constant reminder of her wrongdoing, and it was a scar she shared with her aunt, Muirgel, who had also wronged Rónán in times gone by. Muirgel and her husband, Donal, were responsible for the deaths of many, most notably Rónán's childhood friend and bed mate, Áed.

Rónán consulted with his druid on his son's wellbeing at his mother's side, and Grainne assured him that the boy's place was at his mother's side, not languishing in the king's quarters, alone and without the warmth of his mother's arms.

'I made a promise to raise him as my own. I will not break my word,' he told Grainne.

'You will raise him well, but he needs his mother until he is of age to train with the sword.'

At seven winters old, Áed would enlist in the Ó Mordha army next year. Despite not being Rónán's child, and although his parents were no longer wed, the boy was still a king's son. Áed Ó Mordha, named for a fallen warrior, would command respect by his very presence of being; Rónán would make sure of it.

He crouched beside the child. 'We should take a walk.'

'It is raining,' Achall said.

'It is always raining. It is good for his growth.' He was a small child and, when he stood without a tunic, you could count the ridges of his spine or hang your weapons in the pockets between his ribs.

Achall had not yet looked at her former husband. Her hands flicked as the shuttle drove between them, the loom clacking and groaning in overuse. She had taken to weaving dresses for the women of Ailigh with such fervour that nobody was ever without a choice of linens.

'You will run out of threads by morning if you continue to weave so swiftly.'

'You would rather I occupied my time with chin-wagging and gossip? Or would you have me in the fields with the slaves, spitting in the dirt and tilling soil from dawn to dusk?'

Rónán curled his lip in distaste, though she could not see, and Áed flattened his lips to keep from smiling.

'Come, lad. A little rain hurts nobody.'

Rónán pulled his boots on, careful not to spark mud on Achall's floor—she annoyed him, but he did not seek her wrath—and he waited as the boy pinned a cloak to his shoulders and slipped his own soft-leather boots on.

'Keep him inside the walls, Rónán.'

Rónán bowed but said nothing.

Outside, the rain cut across the hillside, and the sky was an iron grey. The distant horizon was masked in the fog of a heavy downpour.

Áed huddled under his fur cloak.

As they approached the outer gates, Rónán signalled to the guard who swung the gate wide. As they crossed the threshold, Áed looked back over his shoulder as though Achall was behind him.

'Our secret,' Rónán said.

He led the boy down to the lough, mud sucking at their boots as they walked. When they stood on the sandy shore, Rónán bowed to the standing stone. It was two-heads taller than him, and into its side had been carved the likeness of a sword.

'Into the West the battle ends,' young Áed said.

Rónán had told him the stories of Áed the Executioner, of the great battles he fought and won for the honour of their people.

'You have his name,' he told the boy often. 'It will serve you well.'

He traced the outline of the sword with his fingers. 'Into the West. Where all warriors must journey.' He pressed his forehead to the wet stone, then he picked the boy up and heaved him to the top.

Áed scrambled into a seated position, his knees drawn up to his chin, and he watched the frothy waves grip the shoreline with white fingers.

'Stand up,' Rónán said.

Áed shook his head.

'Stand up.'

The boy squinted into the rain. 'I will fall.'

'If you do, I will catch you.'

'I am not a warrior, father.'

'You do not need to be a warrior to stand in the rain.'

Áed shifted his legs. The flat top of the stone, wide enough for the boy to sit on with ease, had been levelled with a stoneworker's tools, and Rónán would often climb atop it to consider his lot. He had erected the monolith on his return from Knockdhu seven years before, following Áed the Executioner's death and Rónán's coronation as Overking of Ailigh. He no longer visited the memorial as often as he ought to.

Young Áed rose and swayed in the wind, one hand out before his face to protect himself from the heavy rain. His cloak whipped behind him.

'Spread your arms.'

'The wind will carry me away.'

'Trust me, son. Spread your arms.'

Áed opened his arms with caution. 'I will fall.'

'Wider.' When he did so, his palms upturned, Rónán said, 'Now scream into the wind.'

'I will fall.'

Rónán faced the lough, closed his eyes against the stinging rain, and he spread his arms. He screamed.

The boy joined him.

Rónán said, 'Louder. The gods cannot hear you.'

Together, they screamed, their voices caught by the wind and carried on the air within the fat droplets of rain.

Áed's scream broke to laughter. Rónán motioned for him to jump and, with some coaxing, the young boy dropped into his arms.

'Did the gods hear me, *Daidí*?'

'The gods and all the ancestors. Tonight, when the sun is gone, if you are awake, you might hear them answer you.'

'What will they say?'

'They will probably say you should be asleep at such a time.' Rónán lowered the boy to the ground and then tightened his cloak at the neck.

Áed said, 'When the gods walk along the sand, why do they not leave footprints?'

'That is a question only the druids can answer, child. Have you seen the gods walk along the sand?'

Áed shrugged. 'At Imbolc, when I have eight winters behind me, what will happen to *Mamaí* when I move down with the other boys to start my training?'

Rónán crouched, his hand on the boy's shoulder. 'Why would something happen to her?'

'She will be all alone.'

Rónán knocked his son's chin with a gentle knuckle. 'No one

is ever alone unless they make it so themselves.'

Áed kissed his father's cheek. 'Some people are forced to be alone even when surrounded by others.'

They did not speak again as they were carried up the hillside by the driving wind.

The rain dogged the afternoon and, when he and Cormac had shared a meal in their private quarters, Rónán called a meeting with his tanist in the great hall. Diarmuid, who had assumed the role of king's heir when Cormac refused it, had been overseeing the preparations for harvest. The wheat rust plagued the northern tribes for its second year, and harvest would be light again.

Rónán stopped asking Cormac to fill the role that Fionn had left behind with his death at the Ó Nallon Pass. For months, Cormac declined the offer, stating that he would rather spend his days at Rónán's side—something he could not do as tanist. A king's heir had duties and responsibilities that divided their attentions except in battle. 'I am content to be your consort. I need nothing more.'

'As tanist,' Rónán told him, 'you would have the respect of all the people.'

'I need the respect of only one man,' Cormac would reply.

Diarmuid, a tall and fearless warrior who could cut a man down with his stare as easily as with his sword, had been the only other choice now that Fionn was gone and Cormac was unwilling to accept the position. He came to Ailigh with his wife and son, a young boy Rónán saw much of himself in. Darragh had been the smallest child in that year's intake and now, five years later, he was almost as tall as his father and just as broad.

Diarmuid's wife, Aoibhinn, had long served as one of the Ó Mordha tribe's cooks, and her stare, when she was angered, was more cutting than her husband's sword.

Rónán had watched all three family members grow in authority. If Aoibhinn asked a boy to do something for her, he would do so without question or suffer her wrath. And Diarmuid spoke of agricultural practices with as much intensity as he did battle tactics. He did not ask to be tanist following Fionn's death. But he did not refuse when Rónán willed it.

'I wish you would reconsider the position of tanist,' Rónán once whispered to his consort as they lay in bed. Cormac had turned from him, the sigh heavy on his pillow. It was the last time Rónán asked him. Diarmuid, when offered, took a knee, bowed his head, and promised he would not let his king down.

As the three men discussed the gathering of the crops and alternative solutions for the hungry mouths of winter, the door of the great hall opened.

'I would knock,' Gallen said, 'but my hands are full.'

He dropped a body at his feet without ceremony. 'We killed a couple of assassins, Lord. The archdruid is dead.'

'Dead? What happened?'

'Lady Grainne and I journeyed to the north-eastern causeway to meet with her mentor, Cathal. We were set upon as he told us of the Master's passing. I do not know much, but the archdruid was killed along with others.' He kicked the body at his feet. 'This bastard attempted to do the same to us.'

'Where is Grainne? Is she well?'

'She is well of body, my lord, but her heart is pained. She has gone to the northern compound in search of answers.'

Rónán was incensed, but he knew Grainne was strong of will. Gallen, her acolyte, would have no sway over her decisions. 'May the gods stand at her side.'

The young druid pulled the leather hide mask from the assassin's face. 'They each wore one of these. They fought with determination, even after injury. Grainne suggested you might recognise their colours.'

The man's clothing was drab and dark, lacking any distinguishing flair or tribal pattern. His hair, a muddy brown and shoulder-length, was plaited at the rear, and his moustache was trimmed short. The mask was sewn with attention to detail but was inornate in appearance. Black stitching circled the eyeholes and mouth section, indistinguishable from the black leather.

'It is cowhide,' Cormac said, turning it over in his hands. 'The leather has been dyed black, but it is unmistakable. The craftsmanship is elegant but raw. This mask was made in a hurry by hands that knew what they were doing.'

'Does that help us identify him?' Gallen asked.

'There is little to distinguish one head of cattle from another. It is cowhide, but beyond that, it could have come from Rónán's cattle, or from southern stock. There is no way to say.'

Rónán asked, 'Without the archdruid, who commands the brehon?'

'Until a new master is elected, my brethren are leaderless.'

'It cannot be safe for Grainne alone.'

'My lord, she has trained with the sword and she has her dagger. I do not sense any immediate danger for her.'

They sat to discuss their options. Grainne would return from the northern compound when she had gleaned as much information as possible from any druid who remained there. Gallen assured them he made her promise only to travel by day and to keep off the roads and trackways as much as possible. 'I would have stayed with her, but she ordered me to return to Ailigh to seek your counsel.'

Rónán said, 'She continues to journey alone despite my protestations. When she walks through that gate, I will chain a
guard to her so that she cannot do so again.'

'She can take care of herself,' Cormac said.

As they talked, Diarmuid poked at the body on the floor.
'What is this? There is some yellow grit beneath his fingernails.'

Gallen drew his dagger and scraped the nail clean. He brought
the blade to the light of a candle to inspect the grit at its tip.
'Emmer wheat.'

'He is northern, then?' Diarmuid asked.

'Just because emmer wheat is only grown in the north, does
not mean he is a northern man. It could be from the last meal
he ate.'

'We have little else to go on,' Rónán said. 'This mentor of
Grainne's—Cathal—will he be safe?'

'The gods will watch him. Soon, the druids will amass at
the most sacred place for the elections. Until then, we should
remain vigilant.'

'I can send men across the lands to warn your fellow brehon,'
Rónán said.

'Druids have a way of studying the warnings that no warrior
could compete with. Cathal has ignited a network of emissaries
that crisscross the hills faster than your horses could travel.'

Rónán clasped his arm. 'In Grainne's absence, I respect your
word. Study the body. See if there is anything more you can
learn from it.'

When he picked up the body and left, Diarmuid said, 'If
somebody is killing the druids, I am ready to hand off the role
of tanist to your consort, my lord. I'd sooner dance barefoot in

shite than face a group of god-killers.'

'My consort does not want my torc, Diarmuid.'

Cormac said, 'Can we stop talking about me as though I am not present?'

'He disrespects you, Lord.'

'We should discuss the need for his flogging.'

'I can arrange to have him hanged from the gateposts, Lord.'

Cormac stood. 'Enough.' When they laughed, he said, 'Grainne is out there alone. We should go after her.'

'I trust she knows what she is doing,' Rónán said. 'Gallen would not have left her if he did not believe her to be safe.'

'Somebody wanting the archdruid dead is one thing, but if they aim to kill all of the brehon, we will have much bigger problems than angry gods.'

'We will know more when Grainne returns. Until then, inform the perimeter guards to remain alert.'

When Diarmuid nodded and left them alone, Cormac said, 'You continue to make light of my decision not to become your tanist. You know why I said no.'

Rónán took his hands. 'I do. And I respect that. But as my consort, it is your duty to do as I ask.'

'A duty, is it?' Cormac stepped into his embrace. 'Lie down and I will show you another duty.'

They lay together on the warm furs by the hearth, their tunics discarded beside them. Cormac's kiss was voracious, his three-day stubble burning Rónán's lips, his tongue seeking solace between Rónán's teeth.

Rónán turned his lover onto his stomach as the fire crackled and popped. When he spat on his hand and moistened himself, he entered Cormac with force, and his consort took a sharp intake of breath. Rónán's hand gripped Cormac's hair as Cormac writhed beneath him.

It did not take him long to finish and, when he did, he rolled off Cormac's sweaty back and invited him on top. Their insatiable lovemaking was not something that waned with the years.

Their passion—five years since they first fell into each other's arms at the Ó Nallon Pass—was still ravenous. Unlike a married couple, whose decree was to sleep together for the purposes of procreation, their activities in bed did not grow stale. Without fail, their nightly embrace, when the day was done and their limbs where exhausted from training, became a coupling of bodies as much as of minds. Cormac could not slip under the furs of their pallet without Rónán becoming aroused, regardless of how tired he was, and initiating the desires of his flesh.

When they were spent, Cormac's snores were loud.

In his afterglow, Rónán closed his eyes. Five years they had slept by each other's side. Five years with only minor skirmishes at their borders and fewer conflicts between them.

But now the druids were being slaughtered.

Somebody, somewhere, had a reason to hate the gods. And no life could ever remain unaffected. Even if they wanted it to.

Chapter 5

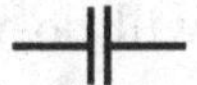

Grainne rode the horse bareback, his hooves kicking up dirt in their wake. She had unhitched him from the carbad and ordered Gallen to continue west towards Ailigh with only one horse leading the chariot. It would take her a night to reach the druid's compound in the northern peninsula where the archdruid divided his time between it and Emain Macha, the most sacred place, in the southern reaches of Ulaid.

The road, a simple track between a line of trees on the east and a bank of hills on the west that steeped down towards the mouth of the lough, was churned with recent rainfall and her legs were splashed with mud. She coaxed the horse on harder when he began to slow, hooves miring in the dirt. The rain had ceased, but her hair was washed to her cheeks with perspiration. A single blackbird cut the sky above her and she knew it to be a bad omen.

'You cannot go alone,' Gallen had told her. She doubted now whether her steadfast resolve had been warranted.

'I must see who remains,' she told him. 'Go to Rónán. Warn him. I will return in a day or two.'

'If we both go, I can protect you.'

'I can protect myself, Gallen. You said yourself, we have not been followed since leaving Cathal at the causeway.'

'But there may be more assassins at the northern compound.'

'I have my dagger. And I know how to travel with care.'

'A dagger will do little against an army of assassins.'

'Do you propose to tell me how to fight? I have been trained by Rónán Ó Mordha himself.'

'Their ranged weapons will do you in before you see them coming. Let me ride with you. We are stronger together.'

'Rónán must hear of this. Take the body to him and let me do what I must.'

In that moment, as now, on the road, she remembered her first meeting with the archdruid when she was just a child, taken from her family to train under his guidance. The sleeves of his robes were tattered and the creases of skin above his cheeks swallowed his eyes when he laughed.

'For our master, I must do what I can,' she told Gallen.

He agreed, with reluctance, to let her journey alone. He gave her instructions to stick to the trackways in daylight and find discreet corners to curl up in at night. 'Sleep in the trees if you have to. No one seeking to kill a druid will think to search the trees.'

She made assurances that she would be safe, and then she watched Gallen ride away from her before she stroked her horse's neck. 'Without a saddle, you must be careful with me.' She struggled onto his back and set off on the northern route. Her loose robes caught in the powerful wind behind her and her leather boots squeezed the horse's flanks.

Now, as nightfall approached, she drove her horse onwards, letting her eyes adjust to the darkness as they went. She would sleep in short spurts only when it became impossible to stay awake.

When she did have to stop and close her eyes, she encouraged her horse in between the trees a short distance from the track-way, and she curled up in the underbrush. She knew that if she pushed the horse any harder, she would exhaust him.

She had not intended to sleep so long, so that when dawn came and she woke, she cursed herself, made swift ablutions, and led the horse back to the track.

When she reached the compound later that morning, the unfortified gate was open and there was nobody stationed there to turn her away. The druids were a private people with many secrets; it would never be so easy to enter their realm unhindered.

Inside the entrance, it would still be another fifty or sixty rods before she reached the first outhouses, but there was no track-way to speak of, so she tethered the horse to the gatepost and continued on foot. She could feel the heavy weight of the dagger within the folds of her cloak as she walked.

At this time of year, these entrance fields would have been filled with blackberry pickers, children taking a break from their studies, teachers overseeing a production line of baskets. Today, they were swept only by the winds, ripe berries shivering on their stalks. She could hear no birdsong, as though they, too, mourned the loss of their master.

When she reached the first squat buildings, she called out and received no answer. Their doors were closed, but when she tried them, she found them unlocked, the rooms empty of life. Tables stood where they should, objects of divination scattered around them as always, and various medicinal tools lined their walls. Everything was as it should be, except for the presence of people.

She ventured further into the compound, a twisted feeling of dread knotting her stomach. 'Hello?' she called.

The chaotic placement of the buildings meant that it would be difficult for her to search them all, but she knocked and entered several dwellings as she moved, finding each one as vacant as the last.

She walked towards the great hall where, as the sun was lowering in the west, it should be filled with music and song. Cruits and drums should be colouring the evening air, and a multitude of voices singing their good spirits should be heard for leagues. She entered, the door scraping the ground and jamming where it often did—it was forever slipping on its hinges and no one, for all their skills, had seen fit to fix it.

Once, many years ago, she had asked the archdruid about it. 'Why does no one refit the hinges, or shave the door so that it does not stick?'

He had laughed, his eyes disappearing in happy creases. 'Every time one of you children open the door and it smacks your face when it sticks, you call out to your personal god in disgust. Regardless why you say their name, saying it is powerful. Calling your personal god puts you in their thoughts and they in yours. This is a good thing. Think often of your god and they will be there to help you when you need them.'

She stepped inside the darkness, the sun out of reach of its doorway, none of the sconces lit, and she smelled a faint, sour odour.

She found a flint set and lit the central hearth, then carried a taper to the sconces around the walls. The floor, illuminated by the yellow glow, had four dark blemishes splashed across it. The archdruid's seat, at the head of the hall, was likewise covered in a black stain. When she inspected it, carrying with her the taper that had yet to burn out, she understood the smell that had assaulted her when she entered—blood.

Grainne wept. He had died here, in the great hall, during evening song. The four other stains on the ground—messy, dried, black with sorrow—formed a visible line between the archdruid's chair and the entrance to the hall, as though whoever had come for him had fought his way through a throng, cutting down druids, acolytes, perhaps even children, in their bid to get to the archdruid.

She could picture him smiling as he always was, right before the door was thrown open.

She pressed her forehead to the arm of the chair where the dried stain was darkest, and she said aloud the name of every god she knew. 'Cáer, help me. Ethal Anbuail, help me. Danú, help me.' Several minutes later, when she had exhausted them all, she composed herself and stood.

Outside, the sun had formed a halo over the western hills. She did not realise how long she had knelt by the archdruid's chair. She shouted the names of her old teachers, of the children she had grown up with, but the silence that came to her was emptier than a wordless echo.

Frantic, she banged on every door, ran through every store hut and passageway and stable. The animals, cattle in the main, some sheep and boar, were in their pens, their food troughs empty. She clucked at them and promised to return with food, and she continued her search for her fellow brehon, those people of druidship who guided their tribes spiritually and emotionally.

In the eastern woods, she tripped over the gnarled root of an ancient tree and called Cáer's name. And in the distance, she saw a flickering light, faint, undetectable when she tried to focus on it. She stumbled over the scrub, moving swiftly from one tree to the next, trying not to make any noise but failing. Her breath was laboured as she tugged her cloak free from a patch of brambles. The sky was growing dark and the naked boughs that crowded above her were as plentiful as the sins of the people.

She pressed on, careening from one bole to another, and she was unsure how far she had run, or how long the moon had been present above her, glimpsed between the tall trees in the wake of the sunlight that faded against reason. When she fell to her knees, she covered her face with her hands, but then, in the silence that followed, she knew where she was. And she smelled golden samphire blossom on the air.

Grainne looked up and saw a solitary building, small, short, windowless.

She got to her feet. On the day of her arrival, barely seven winters old and terrified that she may never see her dear *mamaí* again, the archdruid had brought her here and locked her inside, in complete isolation.

'How long will I be inside?' she had asked him.

'Until you see sunlight in dimmest night.'

It was here that she had first encountered the goddess, Cáer, her most revered of mothers. Delusional, or so she at first assumed, weak of hunger and deprived of light, starved of all conversation for days or weeks or months, the lady Cáer appeared to her and called her Child.

Grainne pushed the door of the isolation hut open. It had been destroyed during the Great Invasion, but the walls still stood even if the door hung askew and the roof was gone. The darkness was at once familiar to her. She would wedge the door closed were it not already black within.

She knelt among the rubble of the collapsed ceiling and pressed her forehead to the damp, mossy ground. 'My most beloved lady Cáer, you have brought me here for reasons that escape my limited knowledge. Guide me, for I am far from worthy of your greatness.'

Beyond the walls, she heard a scuffle.

'Reveal yourself to me, my lady Cáer, that we might talk a while.'

Another scuffle, a quiet word.

Grainne stood and exited the isolation hut. It was not her lady Cáer.

'Do not kill us,' a small voice said.

She looked at the boy. He was seven or eight years old, dressed in his formal robes of training. Behind him, a girl some years younger.

When the boy saw the manner of her dress, identifiable as a druid, he fell towards her and hugged her.

'Where is everybody?' Grainne asked.

'He's dead,' the girl wept. 'The Master is dead.'

Grainne beckoned her into her arms along with the boy. 'I know,' she said. 'Still your tears. It is going to be fine.' When they were both quiet in her arms, she said, 'Tell me what happened. Where are the others?'

'We got lost,' the girl said. 'We were trying to make our way back to the compound. After the—after the awful deaths, everyone fled in all directions.'

'Someone mentioned going to the most sacred place,' the boy said. 'We tried to follow them, but we lost them among the trees. We do not know where the most sacred place is.'

She brushed hair from their faces and touched their cheeks. 'The most sacred place is not within this compound. It would take seven or eight nights to reach from here.'

'Are we going to die?' the girl asked.

'No. No one else need suffer. You are safe now.'

When they asked her name, she gave it. 'This is Anú,' the boy said. 'And I am Dérc.'

From behind them, the cracking underbrush announced another person. Grainne pushed the children behind her for protection.

'There you are,' a voice said. 'I have been looking for you since—who are you?'

Grainne stood erect and stated her name. The other woman stepped out of the shadows. 'I am Marí,' she said, 'mother-figure for these two.' They ran to her side. 'I have heard of you,' Marí added. 'You cast runes for a king and bring forth babies from dead mothers.'

'I do what I must,' Grainne said. 'Are you alone?'

'Many of us have journeyed south for the most sacred place. We gather in the woods a short distance away. Come, I will show you.'

When she met with the druids who numbered less than twenty, they were scared and hungry. 'Why do you hide here?' Grainne asked them. 'Your food and your beds await you.'

'Our brethren are being slaughtered,' one man said. 'We are protecting ourselves.'

'The Ó Mordha stronghold is two nights south of here. If you come with me, you will be protected.'

'If we go with you,' the man said, 'we will be slaughtered on the road.'

Someone else said, 'Maybe it was the Ó Mordha king who killed the Master.'

Grainne raised her hands for quiet. The hooded light of the fire was enough to illuminate the clearing but not enough to give their location away. 'I have lived with Rónán Ó Mordha for seven years; he is trustworthy. Come with me for protection.'

'It is dark, and bandits are widespread,' a woman said. 'Stay for the night. Nobody should go anywhere in the dark.'

Anú came to Grainne's side and took her hand.

Grainne nodded. The collection of druids shared their food with her, knowing her to be one of them, and she asked the question she longed to know.

'What happened?'

'We were at supper,' a man said. 'Everyone was happy, as is always the case at the end of day. The music was playing and each of us were singing. No one heard the door open. No one even knew what was happening until the second of us fell to the blade. At that point there was a lot of screaming, people trying to leave, or to flee.

'The archdruid, clapping to the music, was no wiser than we were. When some children screamed, he stood, raised his hands to hush the room, and then a hooded figure stabbed him in the chest. He fell back into his chair and—' The man stopped talking. He bowed his head.

'Was the assassin captured? Questioned? Killed?'

'No,' someone said. 'We have no murder in our hearts.'

Grainne stood. 'A man kills our master and you let him walk out of the great hall and go about his murderous day?'

'We had not the chance. Five assassins came in a cluster and killed our master. Then they raised their blades and stuck themselves in the neck. They must have been ordered to sacrifice themselves rather than murder their way out of a room full of terrified druids with not a blade between them.'

'It was horrifying,' young Dérc said.

His younger sister took his hand. 'But we are safe now. Am I right, Lady Grainne?'

Grainne smiled. But she had no words.

Chapter 6

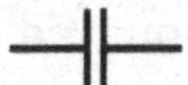

Her two cumal girls, her personal slaves, helped her into the sunken bath of heated water and, while she held her thick red hair above her head, they scrubbed her back. Her skin—white, age-blemished—was wrinkled and loose. In the years since she first came to the island of Thúr Rí, she had lost some weight, enough that it concerned her druid, who recommended more of this food and less of that.

The slave girls poured water over her hair and used scented soaps to make a rich lather, running their fingers through the strands to untangle it from a day of harsh winds and rain. The central fire crackled and spat. Beside her, untouched, was a cup of medicine for her aches. She would take it before sleep, as if sleep would ever come.

When they completed their process, she gripped the stone sides of the bath and lowered her head beneath the water. One of the cumal kept a hand beneath her head—tradition, so that no assassin could attempt to drown her while she was submerged. When she straightened up, she dismissed the two girls. She could finish alone.

When they closed the door behind them, she leaned back in the bath and listened to the sounds of the rain outside, blown against the thatching by a furious wind. The rain had been incessant since before dawn and now, with the sun long since sunken to slumber, there were no signs of its end. Samhain came always with winter at its heels. Three years ago, winter had even preceded the harvest celebrations and had lasted for three times nine days after Imbolc before the rivers thawed. Her druid had predicted as much, but announced thereafter, with good spirits, that such a winter would not be seen again in the queen's lifetime. Samhain, still a week away, was an affair she could do without.

She loathed the frozen months. Her knuckles would stiffen, and her knees would ache. She plunged her fists under the hot water for comfort and closed her eyes. Outside, a lone bird cawed its curse at the winter gods. She smiled.

This late in the evening was the only luxury of solitude that she had. For years, her people came to her with their problems, seeking solutions. Her chief warrior would demand her time, deliberating over matters of security. Her druid was the only person who never sought her attention; always, she had to seek out the druid.

She breathed the thick aromas from the soaps as she lathered her arms and her neck. When she finished, and the water was cooling, she called out to the empty room. The door opened and her two cumal entered. They helped her out of the bath, and she let them dry her body as she held her arms aloft. She did not speak to them and they would not look directly at her.

They clothed her in a dark green dress with a rose-gold cloak that they pinned in front of her throat with a golden brooch, and they placed a silver torc around her neck. She waved them away. She could still smell the flowered soaps that exuded from her skin.

She clenched and unclenched her fists, watching as her swollen knuckles whitened and popped. At night, the druid had her wearing splints to keep her fingers straight, but it would not be long before they were as twisted and gnarled as ancient trees.

She lifted the herbal drink that had been left for her and she placed it beside her bed. It was foul in both smell and taste, but it eased the pains in her hands and aided her sleep.

She opened her door and entered the great hall where her cumal hid in the shadows and her druid was hunched over a table. Her seat was lit by three wall-sconces behind it, positioned above a tapestry of her excellence.

She waited for the druid to finish studying whatever intrigued her. A cumal brought her a cup of wine, then bowed and retreated to the shadows. Even her queen seat ached her bones.

At length, the old druid straightened her back and twisted a creak from her neck. When she turned around, she said, 'Oh.'

'What intrigues you so?'

The druid approached. 'I cast the bones a thousand times, but I am faced always with a different answer.'

'To what question?'

The druid flattened her lips. 'How are your pains, my lady?'

'They bother me less than your avoidance.'

'The bones—they are undecided on the outcome of our endeavours.'

'Make them decide.'

'Fate is a wily thing, always changing.'

'You can take fate by the balls, druid, and ensure that it listens to our pleas.'

The druid bowed. 'My queen.' Before she turned away, she

said, 'Have you taken your tincture, my lady?'

The queen balled her fists again and studied her knuckles. 'I will take it soon.'

'And,' the druid said, her voice low, leaning forward, 'the nightmares?'

'They plague me still. I shall need something stronger.'

'I will have something with you in a moment.' The druid bowed and left.

From outside, she could hear the wind and rain. The gods, if they tried, could blow her island into the middle of the ocean.

When she first arrived, over six years ago, she had been lost and destitute. She carried in her pack a cloak of such finery as could only be purchased by a chieftain's wife, and the gold brooch that now adorned it. She had pulled her curragh against the shore and climbed the rocks to dry land, thankful to be on steady ground, and then she donned the cloak before anyone had seen her.

In the sight of some fishermen, she fainted, and they carried her to the king; a woman with such a fine cloak and brooch must belong to a king or a *flaith*. The king welcomed her into his house and, later, long after she had become his wife, she killed him and took control of the rich island. At only nine hundred rods in length, Thúr Rí was known across Éirinn as being the richest land. The king had amassed his wealth and hidden it in a cavern beneath his stronghold. He took great pride in showing her his riches not long after she first took to his bed, citing a widow's loneliness as her constant companion. The king had been an easy mark.

She finished her wine and rose from her seat. Her cumal hurried to her attention, retrieving the cup and opening her private door. Inside, alone again, she undressed and slipped under the furs on her bed. She lay for a moment, listening to the weeping of the rain, and drank the foul concoction that her druid had prepared. It would ease her into sleep but would do nothing for the nightmares that ghosted her nights.

She kept her eyes open until at last they closed against her will, and soon she was standing on a hill, watching as her first husband was slaughtered like a sacrificial goat. She clung to her son—in the dream, just a child—and wept when he was ripped from her arms and beheaded before her.

And then, as was always the case, their assassin turned his blade upon her and stuck her through the chest. She could feel the sword pierce the skin between her breasts and sink through to her back where it would protrude with agonising cruelty. She could feel, also, the assassin's laughter on her forehead, his breath sweeping over her lashes. Then he took a second blade and sliced her face.

Had she not taken the druid's sleep aid, here she would wake, drenched in sweat and screaming. But because of the medicine, she did not stir. As she died, she opened her eyes and her son was once again in her arms. The assassin slit her husband's throat and tore the child away from her. She suffered the nightmare over again until dawn.

When she woke, the rain had ceased. Birds crooned their morning songs.

She crouched behind a curtain to perform her morning egestion, and then she dressed and stepped outside. Her day would be filled with meetings and plans, but until she had broken her fast, she would always be left alone. Even her cumal did not attend to her until the morning meal.

She breathed in the crisp scent of storm-cleaned air and then walked around her compound. The guards, stationed at various points along the way, bowed when she approached but did not speak to her.

She laced her fingers together and squeezed them to ease the tension in their joints. She could feel her left knee clicking as she walked. She would need stronger medication very soon.

At the outskirts of her compound, she climbed the watch-tower steps and looked across the island. Morning traders were setting up and farmers were already tending their fields. A small flotilla of curragh were approaching the eastern shore. She could not identify their occupants, but she knew who they were.

She waited.

At length, fourteen warriors came through the main gate and their leader climbed the steps behind her. He cleared his throat when she did not turn to face him.

'Dásan,' she said.

Without looking, she knew he would bow. 'My queen.'

She cupped her hands inside the sleeves of her dress to hide them. 'What news?'

'Our plans are under way, my lady. Our men, and those we have purchased from mainland chieftains, have dispersed themselves throughout Éirinn and are lying in wait.'

'Is he dead?' she asked.

'Yes, my queen,' Dásan said. 'The archdruid and several of his followers have been slaughtered.'

'How soon before we have eradicated them all?'

Dásan hesitated before saying, 'With your pardon, my lady, there is no way of knowing how many druids follow the path. With the archdruid's murder, they have scattered like rats in a storm.'

'They may hide now, but they will assemble soon. They will seek a new leader and, when they do, make your move.'

'Yes, Lady.'

She turned to him. 'What of the one they call Grainne Ní Airic? And her keeper, Rónán of the Ó Mordha.'

He averted his eyes from the white scar on her cheek that stretched from ear to lip. 'They are alive still, but our plans are strong. We can move on them soon.'

She nodded. 'Tell your men to be swift with the druids. Pay them double if you must. The ground should be black with their blood by the Yule.'

'Yes, Queen Muirgel,' he said. 'It will be done.'

Chapter 7

For two days, Breasal drifted in and out of consciousness. The druid came as promised, and he stayed with the boy for a night, tending him, cooling him. He dripped his medicines into the boy's mouth and rubbed his throat to sooth the liquids down, and he listened to the murmuring of his heart as it quickened beneath his chest. He prayed to his gods and then made a cross-cut on the backs of Breasal's hands to let the pain out.

Banan MacColm, the chieftain, offered the druid a goat for sacrifice. When the blood had seeped into the earth and the druid's hands were red with its essence, he said, 'I have done what I can. He is in the hands of the gods, now.'

'Will he live?' Orlaith asked.

'I cannot say.'

'Why does he not wake? What is wrong with him?'

The druid had no answers.

When the morning light came, he packed his vials and bowls into his bags and said he was to travel to the most sacred place.

'Is it true?' Orlaith asked. 'Someone is killing our druids?' She stood beside him at the door, staring into the morning colours while Breasal continued to sleep.

'I wish it were not so.'

'I have a druid friend in the north. The Ó Mordha druid.'

'The north has been hardest hit, I am informed. If your friend lives, they will be in hiding or making their way to the most sacred place.'

'I pray that she lives,' Orlaith said.

She watched the druid ride away, west towards his most sacred place. With the archdruid and many of their kind dead, the druids and all the land were in fear. This was not the Fir Bolgs' doing. The foreign bastards had come seven years ago and were defeated. Two years later, those who were captured and enslaved rose in rebellion. The fighting that ensued across the country saw their violent end. As far as Orlaith had gleaned, not one Fir Bolg man was left among their hills or forests. Anyone coming into the docks that dotted the shorelines were vetted now in stringent adherence to procedure.

Besides, the Fir Bolg had no interest in the slaughter of druids. It was kings and hillforts they wanted.

Orlaith returned to Breasal's side. He mumbled in his sleep, but his words were not coherent. In her panic at his condition, she had failed to mention to the druid that her son had spoken of burning fields. She was not sure if it was the prophetic musings of a druid, or the ramblings of insanity.

By nightfall, his skin splotched and damp with sweat, glistening in the hollow of his collarbone and at his upper lip, Orlaith studied the rise and fall of his chest and the occasional movement of his throat as he swallowed. He had not spoken again.

Etain and the other women of the tribe attended her and brought food, hot from the central cooking fire, and water fresh from the spring with which she could drink and bathe. They touched Breasal's feet and whispered prayers to the gods.

'He will be well in the morning,' Etain said.

Orlaith nodded, though she did not believe it.

She spread furs on the floor beside his pallet bed and lay at his side, the door of her brú ajar to let in the early autumn chill, as though the cool winds could breathe on him and calm his fevered skin.

She woke in the dark of night—or thought she did—and sat up as a pair of eyes gleamed through the open doorway. She could not move. A wolf, shaggy and tall, watched her and Breasal. He did not snarl. With tentative steps, the wolf nudged the door wider and stepped in.

Orlaith held her breath and could not scream even if she had wanted to.

She watched the wolf sniff Breasal's exposed feet, then turn and leave with a quietness that felt unnatural.

It was a dream, she was sure. A waking dream. But in the stillness that followed, she closed the door and barred it. Her breath came in broken drags, and she wept against Breasal's feet.

She did not return to sleep.

The women of the tribe returned to Orlaith's brú with dawn's first light. When they asked of his wellness, she told them, 'There is no change.'

They had come in their training garments, with swords at their hips.

Etain said, 'We will stand guard over him while you sleep.'

'I have no desire to sleep.'

'Then we will sit with him while you bathe and eat.'

Etain had been the first of the women to come to Orlaith's side when she and her son arrived among them. Following the chieftain's feast in her honour, Orlaith returned to her home and closed the door against the night. It had pained her to speak or socialise when the grief at the loss of her husband was an open sore. She clung to her son, not yet a year old, and she wept against the red birthmark on his cheek.

The fire was a smouldering cinder by the morning, and she watched the pale smoke dance above the embers as though it held memories. She had not the energy to call out when someone knocked on her door. She was on the floor, her back propped against the foot of her small bed, the child in her arms, when the door opened. The tall woman with broad hips and shoulders knelt at her side. They did not speak.

Etain had touched her cheek and her forehead, and then wrapped her arms around her. And she waited.

She waited until Orlaith's shoulders sagged and her sobs came in waves of agony.

When her tears had ceased, Etain filled a cup of water for her, and then she helped her off the floor and took the child from her arms. She sat with her as a damp mist hugged the hills outside and, for a time, no words were necessary.

When Orlaith spoke, her throat was raw, but her words came fast and the spill of her troubles flooded the small home until Etain swept the entrance, brushing Orlaith's worries outside, and closing the door against them.

Orlaith nodded now as the women of the tribe gathered around Breasal, shoulder to shoulder, and they placed their hands on him in prayer.

She bathed and ate with efficiency. When her skin was scrubbed clean, she felt better for it, and she said to Etain, 'Help me carry his bed to the training field. The cool air may help him, and our training can resume.'

Four women picked up his bed with ease and they carried him to the field, placing him under the awning of rowan branches. Orlaith knelt in the wet grass at his side, and she kissed his cheek. 'Breathe the clean air, my sweet. The sacred rowan will strengthen and protect you.'

The early morning rainclouds had dispersed but the sky was as dull as iron ore. Orlaith watched the horizon, expecting a tall wolf to scowl at her from among the trees. She shook her head and drew her sword.

She had talked them through her drills and techniques enough that the women paired off and simulated attack and defensive manoeuvres without conversation. Orlaith walked among them.

'Hold the hilt firm, Caoimhe, but not in a death-grip. Remember, if someone whips the blade from your hands, you do not want to break your wrists as they twist.'

She took the woman's hands, prised her fingers loose, and readjusted her grip. When Caoimhe understood and Orlaith watched her parry and block, she returned to the head of the field to face them. 'I have no name for this move,' she said, 'but it is effective against any man who tries to swing at you. Etain, come for me.'

Etain moved forward in a fighter's stance, raised her arms and swung from the right.

Orlaith countered, knocking Etain's blade away as it came towards her, and with a fluid movement, she whipped her sword back in the opposite direction, smacking off the padded tunic that the women wore as protection. 'Two strokes, one move. Nudge your opponent's blade and flick back with your wrists to attack. If you are quick, he will not know what you have done until he lays at your feet with his blood spurting from his torn neck. Try it; but be careful.'

The swords they used were dulled but were not blunt. Orlaith and the women had fashioned the padded tunics from old clothing and stuffed them full of sheep's wool. They would not offer protection from a real blow, but for training purposes they were enough. Stiff collars protected their necks, and the cuffs were thicker than the sleeves to better safeguard their wrists from injury. The tunics were knee-length, and their bootstraps were wrapped up their shins.

The women took turns with the new manoeuvre and Orlaith watched them, offering pointers where necessary.

They were good girls, each of them. Her youngest student was fifteen winters old; her eldest, the young girl's grandmother, was fifty-five. When she first offered to teach Etain on a spring morning not long after her arrival, she expected the woman to react with buoyant cheer, much the way Aoibhinn—one of the cooks at Ailigh—had done, treating the exercises as nothing more than games. But Etain took to it with enthusiasm and her arm was strong.

Soon, all the women of the sept were involved.

Orlaith looked over her shoulder at Breasal. He slept under the shadow of the rowan tree. The furs were wrapped tight across his chest to keep off the chill.

She studied the women's form. 'Switch. Attack.'

They were quick to learn—quicker, perhaps, than Rónán's boys, or any man who joins the ranks of an army. Women were of sharper mind, she knew.

She sheathed her sword and let them practise, walking back to the rowan tree. When she knelt by Breasal and caressed his cheek with the back of her hand, he opened his eyes. 'Do you wake, or do you stare blindly again?'

He did not look at her. 'There is danger.'

'No, child.' She used the cuff of her sleeve to mop his brow. 'You are delirious, and your words do not make sense.'

'She has shown me the danger. The fields will burn, and no one can stop it. Not yet.'

She shook her head, kissed his warm skin. 'Tell me where the fields are, and I will stamp the fire out myself. Maybe then you will wake and return to me.'

Breasal closed his eyes and sighed, his throat rattling with phlegm.

'You cannot give me prophecies,' she said. 'You are five winters old. I will not allow it. Open your eyes, son. Open your eyes and come back to me.'

She wiped the rheum from the corners of his eyes.

'The fields are not burning, son. You are burning and I do not know how to cool you.' She leaned close to his ear and whispered, 'Hear my voice. Come from your sleep and wake. As your mother, I command it. Wake up.'

A light rain dotted his forehead and she let it fall on him. Let the gods cool him down with their tears if she or the druids cannot.

Etain and the women came to her side.

'The druid is away,' someone said. 'What can we do?'

'If he does not wake by morning,' Orlaith said, 'I will take him north to Ailigh. If their druid is still there, she will heal him.'

Etain put a hand on Orlaith's shoulder. 'The Ó Mordha druid will have gone to the most sacred place along with the others.'

'Then I will go there.'

'They will not let you enter.'

Orlaith stood, one hand on the hilt of her sword in its scabbard. 'They will have a hard time stopping me.'

Chapter 8

Diarmuid pointed and Rónán nodded in response. He crouched, nocked an arrow in his bow, and stepped over the brambles. He glanced at Cormac before taking another careful stride.

They had camped in the forest for the night in the hopes of snagging a few red deer at their early morning grazing. They came with six other men and a handful of boys—Darragh, Diarmuid's son; young Áed; some others who were capable with the bow or spear.

Rónán took another step and dropped his hand to signal that his son should stop. Áed was not adept with the bow, not like Rónán—the son of a fletcher—had been at his age, and it infuriated Achall that Rónán insisted the boy come along. His formal training would not begin before next Imbolc, but Rónán disregarded her wishes and made attempts at coaching him where he could.

With the harvest complete—only two fields salvaged from the wheat rust disease—it was clear to Rónán that provisions should be made for alternative sources of food. The winter, when it came, would be lengthy and harsh.

'Could we trade a few sacks of emmer wheat from Mac Fachtna's tribe in the east?' Cormac had asked.

'Or the Ó Neill's in the north?' Diarmuid suggested.

Rónán declined both proposals. Seanach Mac Fachtna and Torin Ó Neill, both worthy friends, would offer their wheat with ready willingness, but they, too, had been hit hard by the rust disease.

'Gather a dozen men. We will take to the forests on a hunt. The deer will be fat for rutting season.'

He beckoned Áed closer and when his son crept across the underbrush, carrying a small, lightweight bow designed just for his young hands, Rónán tapped his temple. 'Listen,' he whispered. 'Do you hear?'

Áed narrowed his eyes, then shook his head.

'Exactly. When there is no sound in a forest, there is a meal nearby. The prey is alert. They know we are here.'

Áed pulled the string of his bow taut. The thin arrow would do little damage. The purpose of his being here was not to make a kill but to learn the subtleties of hunting.

Rónán put a finger to his lips to remind the boy to be quiet, and then he nodded at Cormac and Diarmuid.

They advanced.

Deft feet, barefoot and free of boots, folded over the top of autumn-dried leaves and twigs. They stepped forward, glancing from the ground that they were treading on to the bushes before them.

Rónán raised his hand and they stopped. They had sighted, late last night, a small herd of deer—three or four hinds and half a dozen young. The larger stags, if they were close, would be calling out in search of the females, though they had not heard any roars or grunts. Approaching the bilberry-ringed clearing ahead of them would be enduring as they moved with quiet caution.

A couple of steps and they stopped for a moment, hoping not to startle the herd.

He nodded and they progressed.

At Diarmuid's side, his son, Darragh, flexed his shoulder and lifted his spear. The boy's aim was good. Rónán had coached him not long after his arrival at Ailigh and Darragh had taken to it well.

They stopped. The breeze stirring from among the boughs was moving in their favour, blowing against them so the herd would not be alerted by their scent.

The underbrush was thinning out; the clearing was ahead.

Rónán saw a hint of russet fur between the bushes.

He raised his bow. Young Áed did likewise.

He waited.

When they were motionless long enough, he drew his bowstring tighter. Without a word, the collection of men and boys dashed forward, arrows and spears sailing through the shrubbery.

The hinds barked their alarm. In a flurry, those deer that were not pinioned took off in a swell of kicked-up leaves and moss.

Two calves and three adult females lay on the ground.

Darragh cheered. Rónán strung his bow over a shoulder and withdrew his dagger, a serrated hunting blade. He knelt by one of the hinds and motioned for Áed to join him.

'Never let a deer bleed out from her wounds. We want to preserve as much of her as possible.' He handed the blade to his son. 'Take her throat.'

Áed gripped the blade but did not move to cut her. Her eyes were wide, but her body was motionless. An arrow protruded from her neck. The protracted bark she struggled to give was piercing in its agony.

'Puncture her throat, son.'

'I cannot.' Áed stroked the deer's head.

'I will not force you, Áed, but the kill is as much a part of this as the hunt. We are not here to seek thrills. She gives her life so that we may have ours.'

Áed nodded. He adjusted his grip on the hilt of the dagger and placed the serrated edge against the hind's throat for an elongated cut.

'No. This way—up and in; through the soft flesh and into her brain from below. You want to go through the mouth.' Rónán wrapped his hand around Áed's. 'I will do it with you. Push.'

The hind's dying gurgle made Áed close his eyes.

Taking his lead from Cormac, who always offered thanks to his kill, Rónán placed his hands on the deer's neck and lowered his head to her fur. 'We thank you for your sustenance.'

'How many will she feed?' Áed asked.

'Not enough.'

When they had gathered all the kill into carts and returned to their camp, Rónán instructed the men to urinate in a wide circle around their clearing. The fresh scent of deer blood would attract wolves, and the urine—coupled with a small fire—would keep them at bay.

'Are we going back for the others?' Darragh asked.

His father slapped the back of his head. 'They'll be long gone,' Diarmuid said. 'But he is right, my lord. If we want to feed the hungry all winter, a few deer will not be enough.'

'We should camp another night; chase their trail at dawn. The day is still early; take the boys and you may hunt for hare.'

'My lord.'

Rónán and Cormac stepped away from camp, treading down

the steep banking where the trees thinned to reveal a small stream. They knelt, cupped their hands in the icy water, and drank from it.

'Young Áed is fair with the bow,' Cormac said, 'but I saw his hesitation at the kill.'

'He still thinks with his heart. He will learn.'

Cormac stripped off his tunic and sat down in the shallow water that frothed around him. He splashed his armpits and his face. 'He is young. He has plenty of time to mature.'

Rónán knelt behind his consort and picked up a fistful of silt to scrub Cormac's back. 'He may never make a warrior.'

'He has willingness, Rónán, even if he does not know it. Give him time. And you are not my cumal; I can wash my own back.'

'No cumal knows where your tension lies better than I do,' Rónán said, twisting his knuckles into the skin below Cormac's right shoulder blade. He felt the knotted muscle pop.

Cormac sighed and moved his arm. In training the boys with the bow, his shoulder was often tight and tense by end of day. Rónán had taken to kneading his muscles at night with scented oils that Grainne had provided for tension and knots.

That evening, when Diarmuid and the boys returned from their hunt—three hare and four grouse that had been killed by slingshot beyond the forest reaches at the bog—Rónán's tanist admitted it was not a lot, but enough to feed the hunters for the night without resorting to filleting one of the deer.

Áed took a place between his father and the king's consort and they wrapped him in a fur for warmth as the sky above them dulled to deep evening black.

'I almost killed a grouse, *Daidí*.'

'Next time you will kill two.'

Áed yawned and folded a strip of dark rabbit meat into his mouth.

'Darragh,' Diarmuid said. 'Give us a song that scares the wolves away.'

Darragh grinned. 'Mother says I have a voice that pleases the gods.'

'Your mother says a lot of things, boy. Open that mouth and let us hear it.'

The boy stood up. At thirteen winters old, his voice had already broken, and his gruff tones made the men laugh. He sang the song of Ciabhan of the Curling Locks who took his goddess-lover, Cliodhna, from the Land of Promise and into Éirinn. But the great god Manandán mac Lir, who disproved of her love for a mortal man, sent a tidal wave—one of the three great waves of Éirinn—to sweep her back to his realm, and Ciabhan was desolate and alone.

The songs of old did not have happy endings. Just like life.

They applauded him when he was done, and Cormac nudged Rónán's knee. Between them, young Áed had fallen asleep, slumped against Cormac's shoulder.

The swirling smoke of the fire lifted Darragh's voice into the night air as he commenced another song.

By the first light of morning, when they rose and bathed in the nearby stream, they set out in search of the remaining deer. They would have scattered when they were attacked, but in time they would regroup and those mothers who had lost a young would be calling for their child. If they were lucky, the hunting party would come across a couple of stags who would be bigger than the females by half.

They crept through the underbrush with less care than

yesterday, and Diarmuid led the way, skilled at tracking. Rónán took the rear, ensuring that no boy lagged behind. Tracking deer was a tedious process, but once their trail had been found, the pressures of the kill would rise.

They journeyed half a day before Diarmuid was convinced that he had found their tracks, and the sun was low in the western sky, orange and flaming through the evergreens, when he lost the trail and had to backtrack.

'Here,' he said at last, while the others milled around a small clearing. 'This way.'

Rónán turned to follow his tanist, but he stopped when Áed called to him. When he looked, Áed was pointing in the opposite direction.

'It is this way, son.'

'*Daidí*. Over here.'

'The tracks lead this way,' Rónán said, returning to his son's side.

'Look, *Daidí*.'

Rónán cursed. 'Cormac. Diarmuid. Over here.'

When the others came to his side, no one spoke. At the edge of the clearing, dumped among the trees, a pile of corpses was tangled among each other.

Rónán drew his sword. 'Quiet.'

There was no sound, no fleeing assailant, no birdcall. The king stepped forward. He could not tell how many bodies there were, but he could see they each wore the ceremonial white robes of the druids.

'Are they dead?' Áed asked.

'Stay behind me, son. Men, protect the boys.' Rónán sheathed his sword and touched the skin of the nearest corpse. It was cold.

'Fan out. Search the area. They have been dead for some time, but their murderer may be close.'

Diarmuid and the others moved through the trees.

Cormac came to Rónán's side. 'If they were killed by an assassin, he will be long gone, Lord.'

'If they were killed by an assassin, what does that mean for Grainne? For Gallen?'

'Grainne will be well. She knows how to handle herself. And Gallen is safe within your walls, Rónán.'

When the men had returned without sight or sound of an assailant, they laid the bodies in a row and buried them. Eleven adults and three young acolytes.

Diarmuid said, 'I am surprised the skies have not opened with the gods' tears.'

'The gods,' Rónán said, 'will be too shocked to cry.'

Cormac pulled the king and his tanist away from the others. 'I was foolish to think that killing the archdruid was the end of it. These men and women, these children, there is no decomposition—they are not long dead. Whoever is running through our lands, killing druids, means to slaughter them all.'

'We will go back to camp and pack up,' Rónán said. 'If Grainne has not yet returned from the north, we should strike out after her.'

On the way to their camp, Áed took his father's hand. 'I felt their pain, *Daidí*. I felt their wounds.'

Rónán gave his hand a squeeze. 'Do not think on it, son. We will find who did this, and we will crush them.'

Chapter 9

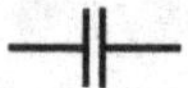

Grainne rose with first light and rolled a crick out of her neck from sleeping on a bed of dried leaves and stony ground. The fire had dwindled to warm embers and the clouds were high and white. She found Anú and Dérc playing a game with sticks in the dirt and, nearby, Marí was stripping herbs into a clay pot. The sounds of the forest were as they ought to be this morning, birds chirping, small mammals scurrying in the underbrush. She sensed no danger.

'You are the first to rise?' she asked Marí.

The woman nodded. 'After these two. If I do not put food in their bellies before the sun clears the mountains, they will turn into vicious beasts.'

Grainne studied the children at play. Yesterday's fear that came with her arrival had been replaced by a sense of calm between the siblings. Dérc balanced a twig on top of a stone and then flipped it with another stick. When he caught the twig in his hand, he grinned. 'I am unbeatable.'

'My turn,' Anú said.

'I left my horse at the compound,' Grainne said to Marí. 'I should go and feed him. And the rest of the animals that are housed there. Would you care to accompany me?'

'I would not look upon the master's property lest I cry.'

Grainne nodded her understanding. She made the journey alone.

She did not anticipate a return of the masked assassins, but she ensured the dagger was at her hip as she went. When she had fed and watered her horse and brushed him down, she filled the troughs with pre-soaked grains for the boar and the sheep. 'You will not be left alone for long. The others will return soon enough, I promise you.'

She returned to the clearing, picking up as many twigs and small branches as she could find, so that they had enough for the fire. When she stood by Marí, many of the others had woken and they helped her stoke the fire and raise a small cauldron of water above it for boiling.

After breakfast, contemplating the sadness that surrounded her, Grainne went to Marí and said, 'The isolation hut—I was placed in it when I first arrived here as a child, but I could never find it again. How is it so close to the compound that I could stumble to it in the dark last night?'

'Perhaps the archdruid's death has removed the mystery that encompassed the area. The hut has been out of use for some years. Dérc and Anú were the last to join us and that was two years ago. Many of us had all but forgotten about the place. You were the only one to escape it, I believe.'

'Excuse me?'

'On your graduation, so the story goes, you were taken from your bed and placed in the hut for a second time. In the morning when they opened the door, you were not inside. The archdruid found you here in this clearing.'

Grainne looked around. She did not recognise the area. There was a fallen tree that the archdruid had been sitting on when she woke, she could recall that much. But there was no such tree here now.

'I cannot say if it was this clearing but, yes. I am not sure how I got outside the hut when the door was locked.'

'It is true? They tell it as a legend around the fires in the evenings.'

She did not like that she was the subject of regular discussion. 'All stories are true to some degree.' She studied Marí's face for a moment. 'I must return to my king and tell him the news. If someone is killing brehon, he will do all he can to aid us. My acolyte has journeyed on to Ailigh. You and the others should join me.'

'They will never listen. They are too frightened to venture beyond the trees.'

'But the assassins killed themselves when their deed was done.'

'The archdruid wasn't the only target. There have been reports of murders in the east and south. We are all at risk. You may have a king to protect you, but for us, these trees form our only protection.'

'You must pass Ailigh on your way to the most sacred place. All of you could stay there for a night or two and journey south-east with the protection of the Ó Mordha.'

'I am not sure any of us will make the journey. None of us feel worthy to be the new archdruid, so let them gather and elect another.'

Grainne nodded. 'No one is worthy to replace the master. That is my fear. But without a replacement, our Order is reduced to nothing.'

Marí patted her arm and then walked away, signifying an end to their talk. But Grainne turned to the gathering and raised her voice for everyone to hear.

'Come with me to Ailigh, I beg you. There are twenty of you; how strong is that against a few assassins?'

'I'd rather keep my life intact,' someone called.

'By hiding in the forest? You are mere footsteps away from the compound. Would you rather hunt and hide the rest of your days than ever return to your beds? Where is the spirit of life that the master must have instilled in you? What joy is hiding when you can take back what is yours?'

'Do you even mourn our losses?' a man shouted. He had removed his druid robes to disguise his heritage.

'I mourn the loss of a great man more than you can know. When I came here, I was an innocent child, scared and lonely. But he gave me love. We can mourn him just as well from Ailigh as from the dark recesses of a choking forest. We should journey south to the most sacred place together. We have the strength of twenty behind us and my king will provide protection.'

'Protect yourself,' the man said. 'We are staying here until we know the threat is gone.'

'Marí, please. At least you and the children. This is no place for little ones to hide in fear. Come with me to Ailigh, I beg you.'

The woman put a hand on a shoulder of the two children. For a moment, she did not speak. Then she said, 'I understand your desire to return to the safety and comfort of your king. Lo that we all had a bare-arsed warrior to protect us. But this is our home, the only one any of us have known for many years. If you make it to the most sacred place, tell them I propose you as archdruid. Otherwise, please, let us be at peace.'

Grainne looked at the children. Her sad smile was reflected on their faces. She nodded and gathered her things.

She fetched a saddle from the compound's stores and coaxed her horse back through the gate, mounted and flicked the reins. She was saddened to be leaving behind her fellow druids, especially the children, and she prayed to Cáer to protect them. If a group of assassins were killing druids indiscriminately, they would all need protection.

As she rode along the track, a crisp wind stirred the autumn leaves, and her horse flared his nostrils. The late morning sun was shrouded in a scattering of grey clouds. She needed to hurry. Rónán should know the archdruid was not the only target. If he accompanied her south to Emain Macha, the druids could proceed with the election rituals surrounded by a wall of his warriors.

She whipped the reins harder; storm clouds gathered in the northern skies behind her.

When an arrow pierced the hide of her pack that hung from the side of her saddle, she drew the rein back and crouched behind the horse's neck. As the horse came to a stop, she threw herself from him and rolled away towards the trees. Her shoulder ached from the fall. She reached for the blade at her hip. A second arrow tore through the edge of her cloak but did not pierce her skin. She got to her feet behind a tree.

She could not tell how many assailants were on her tail.

The horse stomped its hooves.

Some distance away, she heard the crackle of the underbrush. She looked around, but she had nowhere to run.

The horse screamed and when she looked, an arrow had pierced his side. He pranced before his forelegs gave way beneath him.

There were no further arrows. She suspected whoever had shot the horse was too close to use the bow. That was her advantage.

Grainne lifted the hem of her robe off the ground to cause less noise, and she picked her way towards a tree further back from the dying horse. Although the branches above her were almost bare, she was shadowed mostly from the sun's light.

She gripped the hilt of her short blade and steadied her breathing. She could hear nothing over the noise of fear in her head.

She was too far from the compound to go back, and over a day away from Ailigh. Her only choice was to stand and fight—and die. She, a druid, even with some fight training from the great Rónán Ó Mordha, would have no chance against a man intent on her death. She prayed only that it would act as sacrifice to protect the others.

She stepped from between the trees, her short dagger gripped in both hands. At least when she died, she would see her beloved brother and sister again in the afterlife.

A man, dressed entirely in dark grey, ran towards her, swinging his sword over his shoulder. His face was masked in leather.

She hesitated. The blade in her hands now felt useless.

As she dropped it, the man fell to the ground at her feet, an axe in the back of his head. Grainne had to jump aside to avoid the sword that tumbled with him.

She crouched and looked for her saviour.

Sitting horseback on the trackway, she saw Gallen. Bounding beside him was his *Cú Faol*—a tall wolfhound that had been gifted to him by Rónán Ó Mordha after the Ó Nallon slaughter. The dog leapt forward and fell upon the assassin, tearing at his flesh with sharp teeth.

Gallen jumped from his horse and drew his sword. Before approaching her, he scouted the immediate area to ensure the assailant was working alone.

Grainne turned the man onto his back. Gallen's axe had split his head. He was young, the locks of his hair shorn at the sides, his brown moustache still too short to be braided. But he was indistinguishable from any other young man. His clothes were plain and unadorned, and he bore no jewellery with tribal markings. Had Gallen not arrived, she would surely have been killed by this assassin's hand.

She touched the rune over her heart and whispered thanks to the lady Cáer.

Gallen came to her, sheathing his sword. 'Are you injured?'

'No. Why are you here?'

'I had a dream.'

'Always, with you, it is a dream. I would be dead had you not arrived.'

'I saw you with your blade. You were hesitant, but your resolve would have come to you. Like any warrior, your life is more important than his. You would have done what needed to be done to protect yourself.'

'I have the gods to thank that I did not find out how strong my resolve really is.'

She retrieved her blade and went to the horse. He lay on his side, his dark eyes wide, nostrils flaring. A spasm twitched his forelegs. Grainne crouched and stroked his side.

'Allow me,' Gallen said. He gave the horse his death.

'We should bury him,' Grainne said. She did not mean the assassin.

'We do not have the time. No doubt your friend over there isn't alone in these hills.'

'Then can we at least move the horse off the road? I do not wish to give others a reason to suspect something happened here.'

'Even with the two of us, there is no way we could shift him. I am sorry, Lady.'

Sweating even in the cool wind that barrelled down the trackway, they covered the horse's body as best they could with dead leaves, and Grainne vaulted onto the back of Gallen's horse to ride pillion.

She told him what she had learned from the small collection of northern druids that were hidden among the forests. 'I expect there are many other murderers throughout the land, intent on killing every one of us.'

'Should we go back? Convince them to join us at Ailigh?'

Grainne gripped the horse's withers with her legs for balance as Gallen kicked the gelding forward. 'They do not listen to reason. I pray they remain safe.'

'I will make them listen to reason.'

'Leave it, Gallen. I wasted my time trying to persuade them. Had I not, I would not have faced death on the road. I begged them to come to Ailigh for Rónán's protection, but they stood fast and would not be moved. What have you told Rónán?'

'The king left for a hunt two days ago. He is annoyed with you for coming here alone.'

She pressed her cheek against his back as he forced the horse on harder. 'It was foolish of me to do so. But I am glad that I did. I have seen the devastation. Gallen, I am worried for the future of our kin.'

Gallen's hound sprinted beside them, his long tongue curling over his jaw. 'If my lady is worried,' he said, 'then I am also fearful.'

Chapter 10

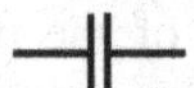

Orlaith opened her eyes when she felt something touch her face. She blinked, focused, and rolled out of bed, pulling her son into her arms.

'You are awake.'

'So are you,' he mumbled against her shoulder. 'Did I die?'

She slackened her embrace so that she could look at him. His fever was gone, his right cheek no longer rose-red like the left one, and there were no rivulets of sweat beneath his eyes. She kissed his face until he pulled away from her.

'*Mamaí*, I do not need to bathe in your saliva.'

'I do not care. You are well and I am happy.'

'I'm hungry.'

She looked around the room. She had eaten little in the preceding days and only now felt hungry, too. Etain had brought her a wrap of drained curds the night before that hung from a hook to dry. Orlaith took the fist-sized parcel and untied the knot in the fabric wrap. The curds were compacted into a ball and Breasal picked at it, tearing a chunk from its side.

She let him eat his fill before she attacked what was left.

She threw open the door of her brú and danced outside. 'He's awake,' she cried, the night still thick around her, the sept at rest, with doorways closed and gardens empty. She returned to her hearth where he sat, the crumbs of dried curds in his lap.

'Did I die?' he asked her again.

'I would never let you die.'

When dawn's light flooded their open doorway, Breasal sat cross-legged on the floor, elbows on knees, chin in his hands, and he watched the flames of the fire as though it was new to him.

'How much do you remember of the last three days?'

'Do you see how the flames dance like little people?'

She stroked the back of his hair, running her fingers through the knots that tangled there from days of sleep. Although he did not pull away from her, he did not lean into her touch. 'You mentioned burning fields in your fever. Do you remember?'

Breasal was silent.

'Son, do you remember?'

'No.'

'And the screaming souls?'

He looked at her.

'Never mind,' she said, a smile twisting the corners of her lips. 'You have come back to me. Nothing else matters.'

Etain and the other women came to them when they had risen. There was laughter and singing, and Etain picked the boy up in her arms and swung him around. 'The next time you decide to scare us like that, I will march you up the crag and push you over the edge.'

Even the men of the sept, and the chieftain himself, came and patted the boy's head. He shied away from the attention and Orlaith found him hiding behind their brú while the noise of cheerful people coloured the air.

'Why do you hide?'

Breasal made a swirled pattern in the dirt with his finger. 'I am not hiding.'

She crouched beside him and studied the design he had etched—three lines curling into spirals. A triskelion. A short distance on the left, there was another pattern, a symbol of two squares inside a circle. She did not know its meaning. Orlaith stood when she saw a third symbol further away. She followed the line, walking around her brú, smiling at the gathered people, but maintaining her path around the home. Breasal had etched a different rune at double-pace intervals, some she recognised, others so obscure that a panic swelled in her throat. Her son would have seen some of the runes carved into the sides of standing stones or monoliths, but he would not be able to comprehend their meaning.

When she walked back to his side at the rear of their small home, he had moved on to draw a new pattern, the last one to complete the circle.

'What are your etchings, son?'

'Just patterns.'

'And what do they mean?'

Breasal shrugged and did not answer. He completed the final spiral of his design and wiped his soil-stained fingers on his tunic. He looked at his work. 'It is done.'

'What does it mean?'

Again, he shrugged. He walked away from her.

Orlaith closed her eyes. She was relieved that he had come back to her from his delirium, but his actions were not that of a child at five winters old.

When the chieftain cleared his throat behind her, she was

grateful for the distraction.

'It is well that he is well,' Banan MacColm said. He was a tall man, but far from slender. The crow's feet at his eyes belied the youthful exuberance that was his usual demeanour. His hair, that was knotted behind his head, and his chin-length moustache, were tinged with flecks of silver. When she spoke to him, she tried not to stare at the chunk of skin missing from his left ear-lobe. Etain had told her it was a battle wound.

'I am indebted to you for your concern,' Orlaith said. 'You offered a goat for sacrifice when you had no cause.'

'Is he not a member of my tribe? That was my cause.'

Orlaith's smile was meant as thanks, but when he reached out and touched her shoulder, she knew he had other intentions. That his two daughters no longer had a mother was of grave concern for the tribesmen. She had passed from disease three years ago.

'To celebrate his return to us, would you join me for a drink this glorious evening?'

'My lord,' she said, but could not think of a reason to say no.

'You sound like you wish to refuse me.'

'No, Lord. My only concern right now is for my son. I would not wish to impose upon you.'

'He is welcome, too. I have long wished to have a son but have never been fortunate. He is a good lad.'

Orlaith could not muster the strength to reject his offer.

'A small cup,' she said. 'I will not let you get me drunk, Banan.'

'I am sure greater men than I have tried.' He bowed to her and left.

She was convinced he meant to propose to her, though she knew she had never given him reason to look upon her as a

potential bride. That afternoon, she led Breasal to the training
field so that she could watch over him, and as she trained the
women in combat, she could not shake the sense of dread that
fell over her. She may no longer be wed, but she was still the
warrior's wife. The women called her so when they thought she
could not hear them. It was an endearment.

When the sun took up residence in the western skies and settled to a warm but autumnal orange, she combed Breasal's hair
and made him wash his face and hands, and then she walked him
to the chieftain's hall. A cumal girl opened the door and showed
them in.

Banan MacColm sat at a table laden with food and he stood
when they entered. 'The food is hot, and the wine is warm.
Please, sit.'

'My lord, I was not expecting such a feast.' Orlaith sat across
the table from him and Breasal took the chair beside her.

'If I cannot feed the commander of my woman's army, I would
not be a man worthy of stewardship.'

'I do not lead an army, Lord, I merely train the girls in
defence.'

'And I am thankful for it. As are the men, though they would
not tell you.'

They ate as Banan regaled them about stories of war and the
history of his tribe. Before his rise to power, the tribe was led
by a young upstart called Miach who charged his men into battle
against the neighbouring tribe and lost. 'He did not die,' Banan
told them. 'Nobody did. The Ó Broin clan took one look at the
young bonehead and laughed him off their fields. They marched
him back to our borders and watched as his own brother slit
Miach's throat for his foolish audacity. But his brother had lost

an eye in some great war or other and could not lead the tribe with such a blemish. Other men wanted the position—some men crave power—and they fought for it day and night. For six months our tribe was without a chieftain.' He paused to chew his food and sip from his wine.

'What happened?' Orlaith asked. She put her hand on Breasal's arm to stop him from playing with his food.

Banan smiled. 'The final two contenders pitted themselves against each other with swords. The battle waged for three nights and——I swear it is true——they stabbed each other and died, side by side.'

'And you took control?'

'I would like to say I stepped in with dominance and asserted my authority, but in truth, I was the strongest warrior left among our people. The position fell to me, even as I had not wanted it.'

'But you have done well, Lord,' Orlaith said.

'It is true, I have. I made peace with the Ó Broins and now we share their druid. And my men respect me. But it is a lonely job, especially for a man without a wife.'

Orlaith busied her hands with some food so that she would not thump the table. 'Sadhbh was a remarkable woman. I wish I had known her longer.'

'A hard woman to replace,' Banan said.

Orlaith smiled at him and turned her attention to Breasal. He had lowered his head to the table, his hair masking half of his face, black bilberry juice staining his lips and chin, and his eyes were closed. His nostrils flared in sleep.

'I should take him to bed.'

Banan wiped his hands on a linen cloth and rose. 'Allow me, my lady.' He scooped Breasal into his arms with a grunt. 'He's going to have heavy bones when he's older.'

A cumal girl opened the door for them and Orlaith followed the chieftain into the crisp night air.

'This time of day, when the land is blackest and the rift between our world and the Otherworld is thinnest, I am reminded always of Sadhbh. Our daughters miss her dearly.' The two girls were not often seen in public; Banan MacColm protected them from the world, more so since his wife's death.

Orlaith did not have the words to deflect the conversation. She had stood among the tribesmen and women when the chieftain's wife passed into the Otherworld. She was not cremated, and her remains were buried beneath the floor of Banan's private quarters where he could sleep in her presence and she in his.

Sadhbh had joined Orlaith on the training field on multiple occasions, but she was not a fighter. Though her husband encouraged it, she was much more suited to darning and singing, which she performed with equal passion for both. As Banan had been welcoming of Orlaith when she arrived, so too did Sadhbh greet her with a pleasant smile each time they crossed paths, and she would take Breasal into her arms and twirl him until he giggled.

She was missed by the tribesmen with profound grief.

Orlaith looked at Banan as he cradled the sleeping boy outside the door of her home. 'Your grief is greatest.'

'You have grief, too, I see.'

'My lord,' she said, pausing to formulate the correct words. 'I have had a husband for the briefest of moments. And he is gone. I could not torture my heart a second time.'

Banan passed the child to Orlaith. 'You understand the nature of my invitation.'

'Mine is a lonely life, Lord, and is destined to remain so.'

'I appreciate your candour.'

So that they would not have to stare at each other in awkwardness, they looked at Breasal's sleeping face. The boy's brow was furrowed.

'It will burn under your feet,' he mumbled.

Orlaith kissed her son's head as Banan pushed open the door for her.

'He has the ways of a druid in him.' He followed her into her small home.

'No,' Orlaith said. 'He cannot.'

'It is good that he does. He could become a great healer.'

'It is not a life I want for him. Someone travels the land, murdering the brehon. Druids now live in fear.'

'All man lives in fear. But fear, like happiness, passes swiftly.'

'You have the ways of a druid, yourself, it seems,' Orlaith said.

'I have the experience of a long life. Nothing more.'

When he left her, she tucked Breasal under his furs and she stoked the fire. She stood in her doorway, staring at the concentric patterns her son had drawn in the earth, and she begged the gods to stop conversing with him, if that was indeed what they were doing.

She had seen much in her life, had felt powerful emotions and carried in her spirit the strength of ten men. But the thought of Breasal leaving her side to study the ways of the druids sapped all power and energy from her. She would not lose him.

Chapter 11

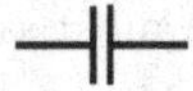

Grainne sat with Rónán and his council members. She had returned to Ailigh with Gallen as the autumn sun retired for the day and Rónán was quick to gather his men.

'It was a foolish thing, travelling alone in such times,' he said. 'If you had been murdered at the hands of a masked assassin, I would have journeyed to the Otherworld to bring you back and kill you myself. What were you thinking?'

'I did what I must, my lord.'

'You did only what you desired, with no thought for the consequences of your actions. Do you have no concept of your personal safety? You could have been slaughtered. You could have been found weeks from now, dead among the trees—or never found at all. You have been reckless in your actions. What *sidhe* spirit possessed you that you would do such an irresponsible thing?'

Grainne knelt before him, contrite. 'Allow me to beg for your forgiveness, Lord. My deeds may have been rash, but I acted on instinct, and I would do so again.'

'Stand up and embrace me, woman. You do not need my forgiveness. But in future, I will not have you venturing outside these walls without an escort. Is that clear?'

They settled at the table with the others and, though she knew she hurt his feelings, she was aware that his anger was garnered from love. That she could not look him in the eye was testament to her own penitence. 'I have learned a great many things,' she told them. When a cumal girl poured warmed wine for them and returned to the recess behind Rónán's chair, Grainne said, 'Many druids journey to the most sacred place. There is to be a period of mourning, followed by an election for a new archdruid. Whomever takes the position will then return to the northern compound only when it is safe to do so. He will gather those of us who are left, and we will be assigned duties in restoration of our Order. So many of my brothers and sisters have been taken from us. The archdruid—may Manandán lead him safely to the Otherworld—was not an isolated target.'

'We can attest to the truth in your words,' Rónán said. 'While on a deer hunt, we discovered a vast number of slaughtered druids in the forest.'

Grainne bowed her head and offered a prayer for their souls. 'Some druids gather in the woods near the northern compound. They are scared and unwilling to relocate. I expect many will retreat into hiding instead of making the journey to the most sacred place.'

'How long is the journey to your sacred place?' Cormac asked.

She acknowledged his question but addressed her answer to Rónán. 'Emain Macha is eight, maybe ten nights from here.'

'You cannot go alone,' Rónán said. 'It is three nights until Samhain. Attend to the celebrations, and then we will talk. I would much prefer you waited until after the Yule.'

'I understand your reticence, Lord. And I promise I will not leave Ailigh unaccompanied. But if I wait until the Yule, I may miss casting a vote in the election and my chance at helping to gather together the remaining brehon and aiding our recovery.'

'We still have no idea who is behind these attacks?' Diarmuid asked.

Grainne shook her head at the tanist. To Rónán, she said, 'Whoever is responsible, they make no demands other than the annihilation of my kin.'

'Who could have been wronged by the druids such that they seek to destroy you all?'

'I cannot say, Lord. But I fear for my brethren more than you can know.'

'We will find who did this, and you will have justice.'

'Justice is of less consequence than a new appointee to the role of archdruid. That is my utmost concern. I will attend to the preparations for Samhain, though I do so with a weighted spirit.'

In the morning, when she had measured the field and laid her markers for the Samhain fires, Grainne lay prostrate among the dying grasses and spoke to her most gracious lady Cáer. 'I do not deserve nor desire your protection, Lady. I ask only that you protect those of my brethren who are unsupported by the arm of a king. You have been my guide for years. It is my wish that you embrace your people in these bleak moments. Encircle my new friends, young Dérc and Anú, in your armoured support. I pray you see them safe.' Before she rose, she added, 'And award Marí the fortitude of mind to convince her companions to journey to the most sacred place.'

As she returned to the gates of Ailigh, she found Gallen outside, training with the sword in solo combat. Beside him, her niece, Bec, mimicked his movements with a short branch in her hands.

The girl, eight winters old, with large brown eyes that gave away her heritage, the product of rape from a Fir Bolg invader, was stronger of will than any child should be, and she was quick to anger when she did not get her own way. Perhaps that was why she sought solace in Gallen's company, for he, too, had once been a sullen adolescent whose frustration often drove him to anger. The calmness with which he now conducted himself would rub off on the girl, with any luck.

Curled in the grass against the palisade wall, Gallen's hound rested his muzzle on his paws and watched his master's movements. His eyes followed the man where he turned, twisted or lunged. The wolfhound, a shaggy beast who would ordinarily remain nameless but due to the bond he shared with Gallen, the acolyte had bestowed upon him the name *Cara*, which meant friend.

Gallen's actions were graceful and deliberate. With slow calculation, he adjusted his stance, widening his feet, twisted his hips, and raised his sword in an arc above his head. Beside him, young Bec copied his movements. Gallen's lips moved as he recited the names of taproots and their uses in medicine. Not content with advancing his swordsmanship, he used his training time to memorise his druidic studies also.

Grainne watched them for a time, entranced by his elegance—the only warrior she knew who could make battle look like a dance. Though he sweated under the cool autumn sun, there was no effort in his routine. He pushed his sword forward, turned his head, raised his free hand, and drew the sword underneath his other arm, rolling on his heels as his body twisted to face a new direction. Bec turned beside him, a child-warrior in the making.

Gallen's recitations were complete, and he recounted the names of the gods and goddesses, starting with his personal god, Mogh Roith. For each name, his body moved, his sword turning and feet sliding over the grasses.

When he noticed Grainne watching them, he nodded to her but did not cease his training.

'Look, Grainne,' Bec said, thin lips cracked in a smile under her curved nose. She gripped her branch in both hands and spun with a grace not too far removed from Gallen's.

'I see, child. You seek to improve your skills beyond that of Rónán's boys.'

'I am better than most, already.'

Grainne laughed. 'There is no contest.'

Gallen turned, his sword held aloft before him, and when Bec faced him in a mirror image, she said, 'Now?'

Gallen smiled. 'Now.'

As one, their movements quickened, the same actions they had been practicing, but with a speed Grainne could not follow. The sword and the branch turned, weaved, limbs following, feet kicking, and backs arching. In unison, they twisted, weapons flashing between them, too far apart to connect with one another, and Grainne could see how those slow and deliberate motions had become a violent dance of weaponry. They had not been practicing a calming meditation, but a powerful exhibition of battle. Little Bec grunted as she kicked a leg out behind her, the branch thrusting forward. The display was energising and entrancing.

When they stopped, Bec bounced on her feet. She dropped her stick and ran to Grainne, embracing her robes. 'Did you see?'

'I saw. That was remarkable.'

When Bec pranced through the gate, Gallen stooped by his hound and stroked his head. He bowed to Grainne as she approached. 'My lady. You still have your head on your shoulders, I see. King Rónán's wrath must not have been as violent as I feared.'

'Trust me, if he thought he would not upset the gods, my head would be floating in the lough without my body.'

'Respectfully, I agree with him.' Gallen lifted a linen cloth from beside the hound and he wiped the sweat from his forehead and neck. 'In these difficult times, no druid should walk the roads alone. It is too dangerous.'

Grainne bowed to him. 'I will take your considerations under advisement.'

'You tease me.'

'I do. But not without merit, Gallen. I am perfectly aware of the dangers of travelling alone, more so now than before. But I am wilful, am I not?'

'Indeed, you are, my lady.' He flipped his sword so that he held the blade and pointed the hilt towards her. 'You should train with me.'

'I do not have the need.'

The hound leapt to his feet and darted across the grass after a wasp. 'Cara, not too far.' Cara stopped in his tracks and returned to Gallen's side. 'What will become of our Order, Lady?'

Grainne turned from him. She did not have an answer. She had considered the question with constant thought since she learned of her master's passing. 'In time, we will recover. Éirinn has overcome great odds before; we will do so again.'

'Who shall be elected archdruid?'

'I expect it will be one of the senior brehon. A great many must still remain, even if they are in hiding. I trust Cathal makes it to Emain Macha before long.'

'How many druids are there throughout the land?'

'At one time, we were too numerous to count. Lately, our Order has been in decline. Since the Great Invasion, fewer people join our ranks, preferring to train with the sword instead.'

'They can do both.'

'Many can try,' Grainne said. 'But few are capable of mastering both the spirit of the mind and the force of battle. You, my child, are an exception.'

'I accept your compliment, my lady, but at eighteen winters I take offence at being called a child.'

Grainne smiled and touched his forearm. 'I have watched you grow into a powerful advocate for both Rónán's army and for your studies. But, to me, you will always be that angry boy I met five years ago. The boy whose cheeks coloured every time he failed to grasp a difficult concept. It is with fondness that I remember you so.'

As they turned to walk through the gates, Cara weaving between them, Gallen said, 'I will accompany you to the most sacred place. You may look at me as a child, but I will defend you in times of need.'

'It is clear that you would, Gallen, but Rónán has promised some warriors to escort me, though he wishes I wait until after the Yule. I will be well.'

'I am one of his best,' Gallen said. 'And as an acolyte, do I not have a say in who becomes our new leader?'

'As an acolyte, your studies are incomplete. Yours is not a position of authority, yet. Your skill will be needed here at Ailigh while I am gone.'

'As your personal acolyte, is my place not at your side?'

'Your place is wherever it is most needed, Gallen. Here you can continue your studies and assist our king in his deliberations. Do not fear for me. Rónán's men will be my protection and no harm will befall me. This is your opportunity. This is your chance to prove to me that you are a worthy brehon. Perhaps, one day, it will be you who takes the mantle of archdruid and at such times, you can instruct me in any way you see fit. But until then, this is your place. Everybody has a path, even if they do not have a plan.'

He bowed to her with restraint, and he whistled so that his hound would follow him. She watched him walk away, the soil under his feet compacted and hardened, prepared for the coming winter. He was upset, but in time he would come to realise that she was right—his place was here at Ailigh where he could be of use to Rónán.

When she returned to her quarters, Grainne could not shake the sense of dread that plagued her and snapped at her ankles with vicious teeth. She cast the bones from her pouch and did not like what she divined. Her people—the people of Éirinn— had been through great hardships for centuries untold. Invasions, battles, and plagues. The gods give with one hand and take with the other. And still, her lady Cáer remained silent, heedless of her prayers.

She swept the bones back into her pouch, and she returned to the Samhain field to oversee the building of the fires. She could not stand idle. If an assassin's arrow would come for her, let it come.

Chapter 12

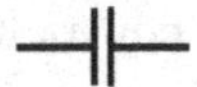

The Samhain fires burned.

At the top of the ceremonial hill, dancing around the central balefire, Ailigh's men, women and children wore clothes of dark colours to blend in with the evening dusk, and their faces were painted blue or green or red to disguise themselves from the *sidhe* who would soon step from the Otherworld to besiege the living.

Ailigh's gates were sealed, a sprig of rare white heather pinned to the gatepost to ward off angry spirits at the time of crossing, when the sun slid from the sky in hiding. Kneeling on the grasses outside, Rónán Ó Mordha followed his druid's lead. Grainne bowed to the earth, and they poured a milk offering to the gods. When it had seeped into the soil, she lifted a painted stone the size of her palm and handed it to the king.

'Are you ready?'

He studied the swirled pattern on the surface of the stone before following her away from the gates and up towards the blazing fires. Grainne beat her alder staff on the ground with every step. It was a deliberate procession, timed to coincide with the sky's celestial activity.

Rónán walked a slow pace behind her. Eight years he had been

Overking of Ailigh, and still these rituals, his participation in royal affairs, was as alien to him as was a woman's body. He had grown up within the walls that were now a jagged silhouette against the dark sky behind him. Raised without parents, he was the product of a community. He did not remember a time in which his fingers were not curled around the hilt of a sword. The heavy torc at his neck was a constant reminder not just of those kings who had gone before him, but a realisation that he was one spoke in a large wheel; other kings would succeed him, other men—better men—would rule the north when the blood of his body had wept into the roots of the heather that ringed his lands.

Grainne bowed her head before the central fire, and her voice raised in song. Gallen came to her side with a flaming torch and the crowd were silent. She spoke in the god-tongue of the druids as her acolyte interpreted her words for the gathered kinspeople, invoking her most precious Lady Cáer to nourish them through the winter months, inviting the dead to walk among them as the doorway between their lands and the Otherworld was thrown wide. She begged the *sidhe* to pass them by and she twisted her limbs in a dance to appease the gods, the folds of her ceremonial robes lifting in the breeze.

On this first day of the new year, and in honour of their deceased, twenty willow fires burned in a circle around the central fire, and the field was lit golden like the dawn. At each fire, a boy wearing the purest of blue linen tunics held a sword, representative of the many warriors who had fallen since Rónán took the kingseat eight years ago. When Grainne ended her song and bowed, the boys plunged the weapons into the fires so that their handles stood erect, a sentinel for the dead.

Rónán smoothed his thumb over the pattern on the stone in

his hand. Grainne had explained the meaning of those swirls and lines that afternoon, but he could not recall what she said. He cast the stone into the central fire. In the morning, the ash that coated it would be studied for omens.

'We remember our friends who have journeyed to the Otherworld and who walk inaudibly among us tonight,' he said aloud. The gathered people were silent. 'All those who have entered Tír na nÓg at the beckoning of the gods. Fathers, mothers, sons, daughters—not one among us is untouched by death. We shall speak of them this night that they are remembered in the dawn, and for all the dawns that we are lucky to see. We shall name them aloud that they might hear us and know that they have not been forgotten, for it is because of them that we exist. We light our fires and make our sacrifices to the gods in memory of them. From their sacrifice, we live on in their honour.'

The hush that fell upon them was dampened by the slough of the smoke that encased the field in a grey silence.

Rónán took a ceremonial sword, forged by an old friend's hand, and held it aloft. 'Áed Ó Mordha, Overking of the North. Died at the Battle of Knockdhu. And Fionn Ó Mordha, who died at the Ó Nallon Pass.' He drove the sword into the flames, the hilt angled upwards, and he bowed his head and closed his eyes. The hilt of his own sword gleamed in its scabbard.

A voice said, 'Dáíre. Died in battle.'

They fell silent again until someone said, 'Lorcan. Died on the battlefield.'

'Áine. Died of a sickness.'

Names were given from across the field and a silence draped over the grasses so that even the wind did not stir.

When all the names had been recited, Grainne, accompanied

by Gallen, sang a song of the Second Battle of Mag Tuired, the defeat of the Fomorians by the Tuatha Dé Danann. Their voices carried across the hillside to the reverent smiles of all who gathered there.

She touched Rónán's shoulder and then turned to the crowd. 'The new year has begun. May peace find you always and may the *sidhe* forget you and the gods remember your name.'

The people cheered, and the musicians played a high-tempo tune that had feet tapping and hips swaying.

Barrels of beer had been rolled up the hill and were cracked open. Cups were dipped, and bellies were filled with a feast of foods. Bowls were left among the grasses for the spirits of the dead to attend them and eat with their kin. The bright fires were a stark contrast to the night, the moon sheathed in violet clouds as the sun fell into slumber. Even the lough, far below, could not be seen by the light from the multitude of flames.

The cattle and sheep were brought in from summer pastures two nights ago and the smell of them ripened the air around the hillside. Before dawn, some of them would be slaughtered in sacrifice. Grainne knew those that were worthy, and her day was spent in preparation for the rituals.

Rónán filled his cup and, in a quiet moment in which nobody sought his counsel, he looked around at the throng of people, Ó Mordha boys given to him from the tribes over which he ruled, neighbouring clans who brought gifts to him as their king, and visiting messengers from local chieftains. Families from other tribes came for the Ó Mordha celebrations of Samhain because their own druids had journeyed to Emain Macha or had been killed by unknown hands. The hillside was thriving with revelry.

Rónán looked across the field for Cormac. His consort would

stand beside him later, when the animals were sacrificed, but for now he had no part in the ceremonies. Rónán caught his eye as he danced among the fires with some of the younger girls who adored him, and they waved to each other.

Lit by the flickering orange glow of one of the furthest fires, Rónán saw his son sitting alone. His training would begin in earnest at Imbolc, but Rónán could tell he did not desire to feel the weight of a sword in his hand. He was content with staring at the clouds that skimmed overhead or watching his mother weave her garments for the women of Ailigh. He would ask incessant questions that no child his age should have the capacity nor the desire to understand.

Rónán took a second cup, filled them both from a barrel, and joined young Áed by the fireside. He handed one to the boy. 'What do you see in the flames?'

Áed looked at his father, eyes blinking into focus, and he took the cup of beer. His feet, always bare, even when his mother insisted that he wear the leather shoes Cormac made him, were coated in dried earth and he scraped his heel over the toes of one foot to scratch them. He cupped the beer in both hands but did not drink. When he looked back at the flames, he said, 'I see the heads of wolves, but with the wings of a hawk.'

'You do?' Rónán leaned forward, staring at the fire.

'What do you see?'

'Nothing,' Rónán admitted. He drank. 'Why do you sit alone?'

Áed did not answer him.

When the boy sat his cup on the ground, untouched, Rónán said, 'Drink, before the flames warm it too much.'

'No thanks.'

Rónán looked beyond the fire for Áed's mother. He could not see her among the people as they danced or drank and ate.

'She has gone home,' Áed said. He did not look up.

Rónán watched him scratch his feet together. 'What else do you see in the flames?'

Áed shrugged. 'Only wolves with wings. Nothing else.'

'And when you look at the grass or the hills, what do you see?'

Áed turned his head, his eyebrows raised. 'I see grass and hills. What do you see?'

Rónán laughed. He would speak to Grainne tomorrow. For months he worried that the boy was growing distant from his peers, and now he had a hunch as to why that was. That the boy's real father had been little more than a bully, and his mother equally so, Rónán saw more of a druid's spirit in Áed than he saw a warrior.

'What are your wishes for the coming year?'

Áed was staring beyond the flames, but he did not appear to be looking at any one thing. 'The same thing I wish for every year—that my mother and father would reunite.'

Rónán drank from his cup. Some wishes were not meant to come true. When Cormac danced towards them, Rónán was thankful for the interruption.

'Dance with me, my lord.'

'Are you drunk?'

'It is Samhain. It would be remiss of me to remain sober. Dance with me.'

Rónán brushed his hand away with a laugh. Cormac turned his attention to the boy, pulling him to his feet. They danced a circle around the fire and when they returned to Rónán's side, Áed kissed his father and Cormac and then walked away, the churned soil sucking at his bare feet.

Cormac sat with a thick sigh, picking up Áed's cup of beer. 'You look troubled, Lord.'

'I am.'

'Tonight is not a night for worry, Rónán. The dead are near to us, and the *sidhe* have been tricked into leaving us alone. In the morning, we can worry about the druids and the crops and whatever else fills your dark thoughts. For now, you should be drunk like everyone else.'

'I do not think I should call Áed to join the boys at Imbolc,' Rónán said.

'He disappoints you with his lack of enthusiasm for the sword?'

'No. His curiosity lies elsewhere. But I am torn. I fear he means to become a druid. He is the same age Grainne was when she was sent to the druids' compound. But at this time of discord, all druids likely wish they were anything but.'

'Allay your fears, Lord. Once the animals have been sacrificed and the year has begun anew, we will push all of our efforts into finding and eliminating the druids' foe.' Cormac drank the beer in his hand and mopped his chin. He planted a wet kiss on Rónán's cheek.

'You are drunk,' Rónán said.

'As you should be.'

Rónán wrapped an arm around his consort's neck and pulled him tight. 'You are drunk enough for both of us. But you speak true. We should be acting, not reacting. Tomorrow, we will send scouts throughout the land. Someone must know who is responsible. No man can arrange the slaughter of so many druids without announcing it to somebody.'

Cormac looked around and then leaned in close to Rónán's

ear. 'We have time before the sacrifices. We should sneak away to the lough in the darkness.'

'Even drunk, you are insatiable.'

When Grainne and Gallen left and returned to the hill with an array of animals for the sacrifice, Rónán and Cormac took their seats to officiate. Áed sat between them, his eyes studying the chosen animals with great interest. Again, Rónán searched the crowd for Achall. Though Áed had no official duties during the ceremonies, he was still a member of the king's household, and his mother should be present to witness his glory.

In the years since their divorce, Rónán had observed Achall's reluctance to participate in tribal celebrations. She would weave her garments and speak kindly when spoken too, but her contribution to matters of importance had fled like the salmon in the lough. She and Rónán no longer argued. She held strong to her opinions on raising her son, and she made known her thoughts when it was deemed necessary but, with increasing frequency, she relented to Rónán's command with ease.

He was grateful for the quiet and heartened by Cormac's presence at his side, but he had lived with his former wife's incessant rants and disputes for so long that being without them was peculiar.

Grainne cleared her throat and bowed to the king. 'My lord, I have brought to you these offerings that together we might please the gods. Do you consent to their sacrifice in your name?'

Rónán stood to participate in the ritual. 'I do.'

'Take this ceremonial blade and hold it aloft so that the gods may see you and recognise you.'

Rónán took the blade from her and held it up for all to see. The musicians had stopped playing and the crowd drew closer to witness the sacrifice.

Grainne spoke in her god-tongue and Gallen echoed her words. She took the dagger from Rónán and, as Gallen held the first sacrifice in place, she cut the goat's throat and held his head back so that his blood would spill on the grass at Rónán's feet.

As the animal's legs buckled under him and Gallen struggled to maintain his grip, one of the other goats bleated a strangled cry. In the silence that followed, Rónán looked at the sacrificial animal and watched it vomit on the grass. Behind it, the third sacrifice, tied to a post, turned in agitated circles on unsteady legs. Its rear end was a mess of diarrhoea.

'Grainne,' he whispered.

She followed his gaze. She had no words. As one, both animals dropped to the ground in violent convulsions before death took them.

Gallen released the first sacrifice and it fell before him. He inspected his hands for blood spatter. 'An omen.'

Rónán approached the animals but Grainne stopped him. 'Not too close.'

'What dark power is this?'

'The gods torture us,' Diarmuid said as he came forward.

Young Áed was on his feet and clung to his father's side, and Cormac made a sign with his hand to ward off the *sidhe*.

Grainne looked at the ceremonial dagger in her hand. The reek of death fogged the hilltop. 'My lord, I cannot wait. The omens are against us. Surround me by your men—five hundred of them if you must—but let me journey to Emain Macha. My people need all the help they can get.'

Chapter 13

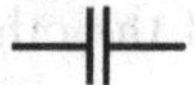

Queen Muirgel rose the morning after Samhain, and she knew the world was turning in her favour. Though the days would grow shorter and darker, her plans would bear fruit and her war against the mainland would flourish. At last count, fifty-seven druids had been relinquished of their lives, but reports had still not come in from the southern reaches of the country. The final tally would be far greater. She had no way of knowing how many people followed the ways of the archdruid; many hundreds, at least, she was certain. For years, their numbers had fallen as older druids succumbed to age, and fewer children were initiated into the Order. Her old clan had been without a dedicated druid for eight years before Grainne Ní Airic had come to them. She had cast a certain charmed spell over their foreign guest in those last days, and then she betrayed them in favour of the Ó Mordha tribesmen.

And Muirgel could not abide traitors.

In her bid to eradicate Éirinn of the brehon, Muirgel had used some of her late husband's enormous wealth to buy the allegiance of many members of the Fianna, independent warriors for hire. Dásan, her chief warrior, had made the arrangements and, when he reported back to her, he had told her that very few Fianna warriors refused her offer. Those that did—the ones who claimed to have druidic family members or higher morals— were slaughtered by Dásan's men.

Muirgel broke the night's fast with a plentiful bowl of wheat grain, ground and mixed with butter, and then she stood on the watchtower where her knuckles ached, and her knee hummed in pain. Her night had been plagued with nightmares again, and she grew weary of their attentions. Completing her plans would bring about their end, but until then, her druid had been testing new combinations of herbs and liquids, with no ready solution.

'Your troubles are seated deep within your gut,' the old woman had said. 'It is likely as not that any remedy would only be temporary until you cut the trouble from your soul.'

The dawn sky was heavy with grey clouds and the gulls black- ened her view. On the horizon, across the sea and shrouded in morning fog, she could make out the stain that was Éirinn. She had not stepped foot on the mainland in years, but soon she would stamp across its path and destroy those who would not follow her ways. The new ways.

She would raise a new druid army. No more would they sep- arate themselves from the world. When her triumph came, they would not turn their faces from war. Her druid army would fight—for her, yes, but also for the gods. If they spoke a word and it was disobeyed, they would draw swords and make demands. Druids were weak; her druid army would be a force of might, spreading the songs of the gods to all that would listen, and slaughtering those who would not. Not just Éirinn's gods, but those of the Fir Bolg, too. She had come to know their names during her time with the foreigner, Eorid, who had agreed not to slaughter her people in exchange for the Ó Mordha kingseat. She did not know whose gods were stronger but allying herself with both could be of great benefit.

She knew these gods were on her side. They had blown her curragh towards Thúr Rí and rescued her from hardship. They had touched her blade and guided her hand towards her king's throat. They had given to her a warrior chief, Dásan, whose loyalties were incalculable. And soon they would give her the heads of those she sought—Grainne Ní Airic for her treason, and Rónán of the Ó Mordha for the deaths of her husband and son.

She gripped her fur cloak and returned to her rooms where she sent for Dásan. When he arrived, she had already stripped herself of her clothes and positioned herself on the bed for him.

During their union, she asked him for the details of their campaign, and as he spoke, she pressed herself against him firmer, her nails leaving imprints in his back.

'The druids amass at their most sacred place. They will soon be drawing elections for a new leader.'

'Yes. We will slaughter them all.'

'We will fill their mouths with dirt so that they cannot speak in the Otherworld.'

'Is she among them?'

Dásan grunted. 'I cannot say. I have had no report of the Ó Mordha stronghold.'

'Faster,' she said. She held him tight. 'The Ó Mordha army will perish, and the king's stronghold will fall.'

Dásan gripped her shoulders and bucked. 'It will be over soon.'

'Yes,' she said.

When he was spent, he stretched beside her, wiping sweat from his eyes with his forearm. His silver chest hair glistened. It was convenient for him to desire her. She needed no husband—refused to entertain the idea—but Dásan's desire was what fuelled his need to oblige her.

She rose and called her cumal. The two girls entered and turned their backs as Dásan stood and dressed. When he bowed and made his leave, they brought a heated bowl of water and bathed their queen. They poured scented oils in her hair and wrapped her hands in cloths soaked in a brooklime solution before they dressed her. Over the cloths, they put on a pair of loose-fitting leather gloves to keep the cloths in place and to hide them from her people.

She exited her compound and walked among the market traders. Taxes were due, and each hawker was ingratiating in her presence. She admired their pottery and their willow-bast creels and panniers, and her eye was drawn to more than one bronze trinket. The people adored their queen for her interest in their labours, and they allowed her to haggle beyond what was customary.

Her cumal carried her purchases some distance behind her and they followed wherever she walked.

When she was done, she visited the farmlands and enquired as to the health of the animals and the wealth of the winter stores. With an island of such small size, she could reach all its inhabitants within a day. Her army was small, but well trained. What she lacked in numbers, she more than made up for in tactics. She had spent the last two years reaching out to many mainland chieftains who had voiced their concerns over the Ó Mordha stronghold and its ruler. She granted them gifts and invited them to attend her island for fire festivals. She whispered words of contention in their ears until they bowed to her and pledged their small armies to her will, in combination with the Fianna warriors she had also bought. She bedded those that were open to it and offered slaves to those that needed something younger. In time, those chieftains' armies would march under her orders. And that time was now.

As the day dulled into night and a light rain fell, she smiled that her plans were on target. Soon, her men would be able to report on the mass killing of hundreds of assembled druids. Then she would phase in her new warriors.

In her chamber, she called for her druid.

'How are the omens, old woman?'

The druid bowed. 'The rain falls fat, but a wind comes to cleanse us. The gulls circle east in favour of us.'

'And the bones?'

'As yet inconclusive, my queen.'

'What do they say?'

'A war is rife, but fate favours neither side. I invoke the gods to turn their eyes upon us. In the days to come, we can count on their generosities.'

'You have made appeasements?' Muirgel asked.

'Nightly since our endeavours commenced.'

Before retiring for sleep, Muirgel paced her room. To the druid who awaited her instruction, she said, 'Tell me, when was the last time the cursing stones were used?'

'It has been many years, my lady. The cursing stone is not a thing to be used lightly.'

'But you know the ritual?'

'To be used for fortune or misfortune?'

'The latter.' When the old druid did not respond, Muirgel turned to her. 'Well?'

'My lady. It is a thing of great power, and it comes with warnings.'

'I have heard the warnings before. Prepare for the ritual.'

'My lady.'

Muirgel dismissed her, drank her foul concoction, and slept. She did not suffer greatly from nightmares that night, save for a solitary voice calling her name. She could not say whose voice, or whether it was male or female, only that it cried for her with harsh intensity.

By morning, she was sick of her own name.

In the light of day, she told her cumal to fetch the ironsmith. When he arrived, he knelt on the steps before her seat, and bowed his head.

'I need a kennel,' she said.

He looked at her for a moment, then lowered his face. 'A kennel of iron, my queen?'

'If I had wanted a kennel of wood, I would have sent for a wood smith.'

'My lady. For how many dogs should it be constructed?'

Muirgel stood. 'I do not intend to fill it with dogs.' She pointed to the far corner. 'Floor to ceiling, it should fill the corner of my hall. How quickly can it be done?'

'I will start immediately, Lady. How far apart should I space the kennel bars?'

'Close enough that a person could not escape it.'

He lowered his head further. 'A human person?'

'You may go,' she said.

The smith bowed and backed out of the hall.

Muirgel walked to the corner that she had indicated. She appraised the area, turning to face her seat, ensuring that, even in a crowded room, her raised seat could be seen from this position.

She was satisfied. The world was turning in her favour and fate would follow suit.

Chapter 14

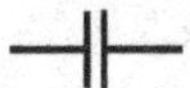

Rónán stood on the outer palisade wall and watched as Grainne rode south-east towards Emain Macha, her most sacred place. Though she was escorted by thirty of his finest warriors, he was not convinced of her safety. A hundred men—though he could not spare them—would still not suffice. Gallen, who stood beside him, folded his arms across his chest and sighed.

'Do not look so forlorn, boy,' Rónán said. 'She will be well.'

'Your words belie the fear in your eyes, Lord.'

'It is hope in my words, even if it is not in my heart.'

Gallen punched the wood of the palisade. 'I should be out there with her.'

'She knows what she is doing, Gallen. Do not question her.'

'She is my master. It is my duty to protect her.'

'It is your duty to do what you have been told.'

As a dust cloud carried the druid over the horizon, Rónán came down the ladder and waited for Gallen to join him on the ground. 'The older I get, the shorter the years become. It will not be long before the Yule. Will you be able to make the preparations without your master?'

'The Lady Grainne has taught me well, Lord. But I pray she returns to us before then.'

'As do I. But we should be prepared for her lengthy absence.'

Young Darragh, Diarmuid's son, jogged towards them, his cheeks puffed and reddened. 'My lord,' he called.

'This one,' Rónán said to Gallen, 'brings nothing but trouble with him wherever he goes.'

Before Gallen could respond, the boy said, 'The sheep, Lord. And the goats. They are sick.'

Gallen took Darragh by the shoulder. 'Sick like the sacrifices from last night?'

Darragh shrugged himself from Gallen's grip and addressed the king. 'Lord, my father says they are dying.'

'How many?' Rónán asked, but he did not wait for a response.

He heard the warbling bleats of distress before circling the outer rampart to view the winter pasture fields, and he realised the noise of it had been ringing in his head even as Grainne embraced him and said her goodbyes that morning. He had noted with an absence of mind that his livestock was unusually vocal, and the thought had left him as quick as it came.

Gallen caught up with him at the edge of the hill by the well, and they looked down at the carnage below. Three ringed fields of sheep and two of goats were awash with the stench of faeces and vomit. With a glance, he could see at least twenty sheep lying on their sides, still and rigid in death.

As they approached the nearest field, Diarmuid, Cormac and the shepherds were attempting to corral the infected sheep together.

'My lord,' Diarmuid said. He prodded a sheep who had been trembling before him and, rather than dart away from the blow, it collapsed on the grass. Its limbs shuddered and its eyes span in maddening circles. Its rump was bathed in a sticky mess of diarrhoea and a fat tongue flicked between its jaws as it gagged.

'What happened?'

'The shepherds alerted me this morning, Lord. They tremble and wander without coordination. They vomit and defecate, and then they convulse and die.'

'The goats, too?'

'It is with luck that the cattle are not affected.'

Gallen crouched to inspect one of the fallen animals, a lamb from last year's breeding, young and fleshy. With a branch that had been lying in the grass, he moved the head, opened the jaws, and lifted the docked tail. He turned his head from the stench.

'A tick infestation would not spread so rapidly,' he said. 'Besides, there would be bleeding, and I can see no signs of it.'

'Do the gods truly hate us?' Diarmuid said.

'This is not the gods' doing. See, here?' Gallen pointed the tip of his branch at the lamb's mouth. 'Vomit. Mixed with the lining of her insides. And here, she expelled faeces without spasm. An involuntary action.' He looked around the field at the other sheep. 'They tremble, but not in fear.'

'The sheep do not need to fear the gods for the gods to slaughter them,' Diarmuid said.

Gallen stood. 'If the gods hated us, they would click their fingers and the animals would drop dead without spasm or sickness.'

'Then what is the cause?' Rónán asked.

'I cannot say without further inspection. If the Lady Grainne was still here, she may have a better understanding.'

'But she is not. Do what you must, Gallen. These animals, the Ó Mordha tribe—we are in your hands now.'

Gallen bowed. 'Separate the sick from the healthy; keep an

empty field between them. If this sickness is airborne, we do not want it spreading.' He turned and pointed at two boys. 'Sétanta, Láeg—cover your mouths and noses and carry this lamb to the druid's quarters. Quickly, now.'

The boys set to work and, at the top of the hill, Gallen's hound, Cara, barked and yapped but would come no closer.

Rónán watched as the acolyte strode up the hillside behind the boys, then he covered his mouth with the edge of his cloak. 'Do not breathe the sickness,' he said. 'You, men, carry the dead to the side of the field for burning. The rest of you, isolate the lame from the healthy. Let's get those that are unaffected down to the lower pastures.'

They whooped and hollered and clapped their hands. Another sheep fell to its side in front of Rónán and he jumped away from it as it expelled the contents of its stomach from both ends. The cry it issued was weak and stilted. Within seconds, its legs stopped twitching and its body was lifeless.

He calculated his losses. Because of the wheat rust, his live-stock were already undernourished. The cattle, though they still produced milk for churning, were drying up. And the goats' milk was tarter than usual this summer. The sheep, bred for their meat almost as much as for their wool, had been stunted in growth and their coats lacked the sheen of previous seasons. The wool had been yellowing on their backs since last winter. Already, in one field alone, he counted more than thirty dead. He could not assume that their pelts were salvageable until Gallen had found the cause of their sickness.

He clapped his hands to encourage the sheep before him to move across the field. A short distance from him, Cormac held the loose sleeve of his tunic against his nose and mouth, and he stamped his feet and waved his free arm to shift the animals. They worked in tandem to clear the field.

When they crossed into the second field, shooing the healthy animals further down the hillside and the infected ones behind them into the previous field, Rónán slipped in excrement and caught Cormac's sleeve to stop himself from falling.

'I am normally the one getting covered in muck and shite,' Cormac said. 'If the gods are not on my side today, they never will be.'

'If you haven't fallen face first into this filth before the end of day, I will push you into it myself.'

'You know it will happen. You should not look forward to sharing a bath with me this evening.'

Rónán clapped his hands again. 'Even wading through shite, you still make me laugh.'

They pushed forward as three more sheep fell to the grass, bleating and crying in death. He did not mean to joke——the situation was dire——but Cormac continued to bring out the roguish child in him. He was a *rí tuath*, an overking, and yet he was little more than a boy of twenty-four winters. The absurdity of youth strikes an adult's heart in times of difficulty.

With a lack of coordination, the sheep limped around the field. They bleated and griped, and their song was a lamentation. Heads and tails quivered, and legs buckled like tallow candles burned in the middle. A healthy lamb, one of this year's breeding, stood by his mother who retched and convulsed on the ground. The lamb pranced, but it did not appear infected. Rónán scooped him into his arms, though he was too big to remain their comfortably. 'Come on, young man. Let's get you to safety.' He carried the lamb into the third field and released it.

They were forced to mix the sheep with the goats and, when they had separated the healthy from the dead or dying, Rónán stood on the low stone wall and counted. Cormac and Diarmuid came to his side.

'Lord?'

'Seventy-three sheep and fifty-one goats,' Rónán said. The field was crowded, but this was now the extent of his livestock, save for the cattle that were housed on the far side of the hill. He came down off the wall. 'Tell the shepherds to count the rams and the ewe. If these are not infected, we will have to rebuild our stock one lamb at a time. Same for the goats. Has Gallen returned?'

'No, Lord,' Diarmuid said.

'I have never seen the like before,' Rónán told them. 'Anyone who has been near the animals in the last day should bathe at once. We do not know what contagion this is, or how it spreads.'

Rónán and Cormac retreated to their home to wash. When the cumal girl came with heated water for them, they dismissed her and used the scented soaps to lather each other's skin. Their usual arousal at being naked together was not present today as Rónán agonised too much over the hardships that had befallen his tribe. Even as Cormac scrubbed his lower back, Rónán closed his eyes and saw only dying sheep.

Later, when they had shared a cup of wine and made attempts at intimacy that was awkward and pained and unfocused, they dressed and walked around the outside of their home towards Grainne's quarters.

When they entered, Gallen was hunched over a table, a cloth wrapped around his face and tied at the back of the neck, and the guts of the lamb were spilled out before him as he cut and poked through them.

'I am not sure what I am looking for, my lord,' Gallen said. 'There is no necrosis, but its blood is thin, and its stomach was swollen. I was about to cut it open to inspect its diet.'

The stench was intolerable. Rónán and Cormac remained by the open door and allowed Gallen to continue his dissection.

There was a puff of gas as the acolyte sliced the stomach lining and the bloated belly collapsed on itself. He prised the flesh apart and rooted through the contents.

'I will never forget this smell,' Cormac said. 'All the days of my life, the insides of a sheep will smell worse than the fetid stink of war.'

'My lord,' Gallen said. 'This is—I cannot explain it.'

'Explain what?'

With a pair of bronze tweezers, Gallen extracted something from the sheep's stomach and held it up to the light. 'It is unmistakable.'

'What is it?'

'These are the needles of a yew tree, Lord. Sacred, yes, but also toxic when ingested.'

'How is this possible?' Rónán stepped closer to peer at the needles clipped to the end of Gallen's tweezers. 'The nearest yew tree is four hundred rods from here. A shepherd would not have done this. What good is a shepherd with no sheep to herd?'

'I do not know how it is possible, Lord, but the needles are distinctively yew. Shorter and flatter than the pine. They are singular instead of clustered. I did not recognise it at first, but the sickness—the nausea, the disorientation, followed by death—it is a deliberate poisoning, for sure.'

'Who could have done this?' Cormac asked.

'*Why* is my immediate question,' Rónán said.

'Forget who and why,' Gallen said. 'The toxicity of yew needles means that from ingestion to death, it must have been consumed this morning—or late last night. Whoever did this may still be close.'

'I'll kill her,' Rónán said.

'Who?'

He left Grainne's quarters and tramped through the inner rampart towards the archway that led to the middle level. Cormac followed him.

'Who will you kill? Rónán, speak to me.'

'Who was missing from last night's celebrations?'

'I do not know. Orlaith? Achall?' Rónán could hear the realisation in his voice without looking at him. 'Rónán, no. Wait. You cannot accuse her.'

Rónán strode to Achall's door and hammered his fist against it. He did not wait for an answer before pushing the door wide.

'Not content with killing my tanist, now you attack my livestock?'

'Rónán, stop,' Cormac called.

Achall, standing at her loom, jumped in fear from the intrusion. 'What do you accuse me of this time?' She faced him with her hands on her hips, the spindle still gripped in her fist, a cotton thread trailing from its end. Áed rose from the floor by the fire where he had been sitting and stood at his mother's side.

'Why would you vex me with your poisonous ways?' Rónán said. Five years ago, in a bid to instil her son as Rónán's tanist and rightful heir, she had tried to murder Fionn with a pouch of toxic herbs that her aunt, Muirgel, had instructed her in. It had been a failed endeavour, but an endeavour, nonetheless. It was this incident that led to the scar on her cheek, from eye to lip, when she had wilfully begged Rónán to cut her like he had Muirgel.

'What nonsense do you spout from shameful lips?' she asked him.

'No one knows the intricacies of poison better than you,' Rónán said. 'What glee do you find in murdering my livestock?'

'Rónán, please,' Cormac said. He gripped Rónán's hand but Rónán whipped his arm away.

'Get out of my home or make sense in your words, Lord.'

'Rónán, please.'

'*Daidí?*'

'You may be king of these hills but, in this home, you will treat your former wife with respect in front of your child.'

'*Daidí?*'

'Why would you poison my livestock? What good does it do you?'

'Rónán, come on. Step back from your words.'

'Answer me, woman.'

'I have no idea what you are talking about.'

'*Daidí?*'

Rónán took the three paces to Achall with a swiftness that was unexpected. He gripped her cheeks in his hand. 'You live on my land a free woman. What have I done that would deserve your wrath?'

Her words were muffled. 'I do not know what madness overcomes you.'

'*Daidí*, why do you hurt *mamaí*?' Áed asked.

Rónán released her. He looked at his child. 'Women are vexatious, son. You will learn this in time.'

'I have done nothing to wrong you.'

'You deny poisoning my livestock?'

'I take your wool and I turn it into clothing. Why would I poison them?'

Cormac stepped forward and took Rónán's arm. 'Rónán, please. Calm yourself.'

Rónán took a deep breath before speaking again. He looked from Achall to his son and then to Cormac. 'She tried it with Fionn. You know she is capable.'

'That was a long time ago,' Cormac said.

'I have repented for my crimes.'

Rónán slumped onto a stool. 'If not you, then who?'

Achall pushed the loom's spindle into the weave and crouched before her former husband. 'I do not know what you speak of. If someone is killing your sheep, it has nothing to do with me.'

'You poisoned Fionn.'

'I had my reasons for that, misguided as they may be. I have no gripe with you, Lord. You know it.'

'No one else would have done such a vile thing. This is your specialty.'

'You accuse me still?' Achall stood, turned from him, and pushed the spindle through the weave to the far side. 'Get out of my home.'

'If not you, then who?' Rónán repeated.

'I may not be your queen any longer, Rónán, but in this home, my rules are law. Remove yourself from my walls. You are forbidden from seeing your son.'

'You do not have the right.'

'Watch me.'

'I will take him from your arms and remove your head.'

'Get out.'

Rónán lunged for her, but Cormac jumped between them and pushed Rónán back against the loom. It collapsed to the floor at their feet, a mess of tangled thread. 'Enough, Rónán.'

Áed yelped and Achall stumbled back.

'Lord, come. We should leave.'

'I'll kill the whore. You dare threaten me, *bitseach*?'

Achall said, 'If you refuse to trust me, you cannot trust your son, either. He is my flesh, not yours. If you seek a culprit, look to those who are slaughtering the druids, but it is not I. Turn your eyes from me. I will not see you again.'

Rónán reached for the sword at his hip. 'You have no right to keep me from my son. I am *rí tuath*.'

'Rónán, that is enough. She is the boy's mother. She has every right to control his fortunes.'

'*Daidí*?' Áed questioned, his eyes wide and hands useless at his sides.

Rónán looked at the boy as though he only now recognised him. 'Son,' he said. He felt his anger ebb from his tightened muscles. He would have strangled her had Áed not been present.

'Take your personal war elsewhere, Rónán. You are no longer welcome in my home.'

Rónán clenched his fist, but when Cormac's fingers encircled his, he relaxed. She had no part in poisoning his animals; he knew it and was glad of it. Men jump to conclusions faster than salmon jump up stream. But she threatened his relationship with his only child. She had gone too far. 'This is not over, woman. You will not keep me from my son. To try it will be your death.'

He marched outside, the cool autumn air soothing his threadbare nerves.

As he walked away from Achall's home, he said, 'My own

son.'

'She will not keep you from him. No druid in the land would deny her the right to do so—overking or not—but she is softer than she sounds. I will talk to her.'

Rónán filled his lungs with early evening air. 'How many times must I threaten to kill her before I act on it?'

'I do not know. Six? Seven?'

When Rónán looked at his consort, he could not help but laugh. 'Tell me when I've reached six. If she did not poison the animals, then who?'

'What if she is right? Whoever killed the druids, could they truly be the cause of this?'

'No army—assassins or otherwise—would slaughter the brehon and then turn their attention to lowly sheep. I cannot fathom it.'

Cormac took Rónán's hand as they continued home. 'We should call a meeting of the chieftains. Someone is attempting to destroy our world. It is time we fought back.'

Chapter 15

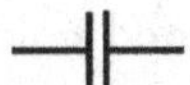

As the daylight waned, Grainne knew they would reach the mountain pass beyond the Ó Mordha borders before the sun crept to its nightly death. They had journeyed for most of the day, stopping only once to water the horses and allow them to rest. She would have been happy with only a handful of Rónán's men at her side, but he insisted that thirty of his warriors should accompany her.

'Four of five men can keep apace,' she told the king that morning. 'With so many, I feel like I command an army.'

'I will not have you taking chances,' he had said. 'The men will follow your lead but listen to them if they sense any danger. These men are trained scouts. If you fall under attack, you must do as they tell you.'

He demanded that they keep off the roads as much as possible and to travel only by daylight. When the sun slipped towards the horizon behind them, Dáithí, the lead warrior who accompanied her, pulled his horse alongside hers. 'My lady, we should make camp.'

'We should push on, Dáithí. We still have four nights' travel ahead of us.'

'Do not make me pull the horse from under you, Lady. King

Rónán begged you to listen to us.'

'We must make haste.'

'The horses are tired, Lady. We cannot push them any harder.'

Grainne shook her head, but she knew that he was right. They made camp in a nearby clearing and, given its proximity to the road, they lit no fire. The men huddled together under furs for warmth and Dáithí distributed cold meats and cheeses among them. Grainne sat apart, praying to her most gracious lady Cáer. When the moon cast a grey hue across the clearing and the muted colours of night took hold, one of the men whispered a song of valour, his voice little more than a murmur, and several others joined him. Grainne had heard the song many times before, but never with such soft, desolate vocals. She was chilled by more than the night air.

At first light, they broke camp and Dáithí led the way back to the road.

They passed a three-night journey without incident, setting a cold, fireless camp when the moon was visible through the clouds, tethering the horses to trees deep off the trackway, burying themselves in furs and fallen leaves. Grainne slept little, but when she did, her dreams were dark and swirling, like black smoke under a molten sky. With the constant cloud cover, she could see nothing in the night and was consoled only by the soft sounds of the men stirring beside her and the horses grazing nearby. Neither insect nor wolf came near her.

On the fourth morning, they drove the horses harder than was sensible, but time was precious. She pleaded with Dáithí to quicken their pace. By nightfall, she judged she was too close to her destination to stop now. 'It is not much further,' she told the men.

They broke long enough to rest the horses, brushing them down with dead leaves, and then they mounted and kicked their flanks to spur them forward.

The moon, through a break in the clouds, gave them scant light to travel by, but it was enough.

When they reached the valley on the east of Emain Macha, the hilltop before them was a hive of activity. Fires burned, and the sky was thick with smoke. Their climb up the hill was encumbered with the smell of burning meats.

A guard had been stationed there, spear in hand, but he looked young and afraid, his black robes evidence of the Order to which he belonged.

'Brother,' she greeted him.

Recognising her as one of his kind from her clothing, he said, 'They've already started. You should hurry. You have not brought a sacrifice? Only brehon are permitted to enter, Lady.'

To Dáithí, she said, 'I suspected as much. I am grateful for your companionship on the road.'

'We will set camp at the vantage point a hundred rods back, my lady. We have been instructed not to return to Ailigh without you.'

'Do you have enough provisions?' she asked.

Dáithí said they did.

Grainne hurried up the hill and into the outer enclosure. By the light of the fires, she guessed there were two hundred or more druids and acolytes present. She had never seen so many in one gathering before. She looked around for an apparent leader but could see none. Without the archdruid's direction, they appeared to be as lost as she felt.

She pushed through the crowd towards the fires. On her

right, druids were filing into a small brú.

'Grainne,' a voice called to her. When she turned, she saw Anú, the young girl she had met in the northern compound. The girl threw her arms around Grainne's waist.

'Are you alone?' Grainne asked. 'Where is your brother and Marí?'

'They are around. After you left, some of us decided to travel here. We were scared but we made it.'

'I am glad that you did,' Grainne said. 'Can you show me where Marí is?'

The girl led her through the people and then pointed to the fires. Marí was standing over a sheep, ritual blade in hand. Grainne could not hear her words from here, but she knew the prayers she would be uttering. She waited until the older woman had slit the sheep's throat, and then it was taken from her by two men and suspended over a pit into which its blood drained.

'Marí,' Grainne said when she stepped towards her. 'I am glad that you made the journey.'

Marí wiped her brow and nodded.

The fires were stacked high with the corpses of animals. 'How many have been sacrificed?'

'Not enough,' Marí said. 'And we will continue until we know we are safe.'

'Who takes charge here?'

Another sheep was brought before the woman. 'A committee of men,' she said, nodding towards the brú.

Grainne went to the building and when she entered, she found three men sitting at a table. The hearth had not been lit.

'Affiliations?' one of the men said.

'North. I serve the gods for the Ó Mordha tribesmen.'

'And what is your sacrifice?'

'I did not bring one. I was not made aware of your plans here, Lord.' She looked around. Only then did she notice, in the dark recess of the room, a cage in which an odd animal crouched.

'We are making appeasements,' the man said. 'If the gods are angry, we must assuage them.'

Grainne lifted a candle from the table beside her and walked to the cage. The beast was small, its fur a golden-brown colour, its face pink. The forearms appeared twice the length of its hind legs and it looked at her with wide eyes. 'What is this strange being?'

The man, with a sigh that indicated he was tired of answering the same question, said, 'They tell me it is called a *moncaí*. It was a gift from a foreign traveller some fifteen summers ago to the archdruid. It remained here even after the master returned north.'

'It looks like a child with an abundance of hair.' In the candlelight, the beast's eyes were as yellow as its fur, sad eyes that studied her just as she studied it.

'She will be sacrificed in the morning.'

'Sacrificed? But it should be analysed. The way it looks at me—as if it knows what I am saying.'

'It has not the gift of speech,' the man said. 'I am told the archdruid kept it as a pet, but I find the idea preposterous. It is as though the gods, envious of our status, tried to make us anew and ended up with that hairy thing. Now,' he said. 'We are all praying for the speedy recovery of our days and an end to our troubles. May the gods protect your shoulders. Sleeping arrangements are such: find a patch of grass that is unoccupied. We will take numbers again in the morning and then we can discuss matters as a group. The cooking fires are at the north if you are hungry.'

'Do we know who is behind the assassinations yet?'

'We come closer every day to the discovery of our assailant.'

She was dismissed.

Outside, she found Anú and Dérc eating what appeared to be undercooked breads, but they were not complaining. Marí and several of the other older druids were still engaged in the rites of sacrifice.

Grainne sat with the children. 'How long ago did you arrive?' she asked them.

'Two days,' Anú said.

'Have you seen the beast?' Dérc asked.

'I have,' she said. 'Isn't it wonderful? How long have they been performing the sacrifices?'

'Since we got here.'

'I'm surprised there are any animals left,' Dérc said. 'But people keep arriving and bringing more. Are you staying for the elections?'

'It is my honour in helping to name the man who should lead us,' Grainne said.

'The gods don't know who it will be yet,' Anú said.

Grainne stroked her cheek. 'You speak to them?'

'Don't you?'

'Yes, we all do. But mostly they do not answer.'

The young girl sighed and tore bread with her fingers. 'They cannot tell me who will lead us, but they sing to me.'

'More than one?' Grainne asked.

Dérc said, 'Marí has been testing her but has been unable to determine the root of her dreams. But they come almost nightly to her.'

'What do they sing to you?'

The girl thought about it. 'Mostly about the ancients. I do not understand much of it.'

Grainne brushed the girl's hair back from her face. 'You will understand them one day. Just keep listening to them.'

Later, when the children had fallen asleep where they lay, Grainne looked for Marí and found her sitting with her back to the palisade fence. Her apron was stained with blood.

'Where is your king?' the old woman asked.

Grainne sat beside her. 'He awaits my return at Ailigh.'

'There used to be a certain air of mystery in our daily lives,' Marí said. 'The uninitiated would fear our kind as being all powerful. They would worship us as the mouthpiece of the gods and praise us wherever we travelled. But now we are being slaughtered. We are living in a dark and terrible age. If I wake in the morning and the sky has turned green, I will not be surprised.'

'I do not know what has become of us,' Grainne agreed. 'The archdruid is dead and tomorrow we sacrifice his strange animal from foreign shores. We are no closer to understanding who wishes the end of us—or why.'

'Nor why the gods have abandoned us.'

'Anú,' Grainne said. 'The gods speak to her?'

Marí dusted her hands on her apron and struggled to stand. 'I cannot be certain. There is no logic in their words to her, no clues to their meanings. At least none that I can discern.'

Grainne eased herself up off the ground. In sitting, she had only then realised that her body was stiff from riding for so long. The adrenalin of reaching her destination had powered her muscles and her mind, but now her body was begging for sleep. Her knees creaked when she rose.

'Good night,' Marí said. 'I will find the children and settle down; there is lots to do tomorrow. We have extra furs if you need them.'

Grainne thanked her but said she had some of her own. She went to check on her horse, tethered inside the outer gates, and she looked across the dark distance for signs of Dáithí and his men. She could see none. When she returned to the enclosure with her pack, she found a patch of grass and lay down for sleep. The intense darkness took hold of her within minutes.

In the morning, the congregation of druids gathered to witness the renewed appeasement sacrifices.

Marí had been replaced at the sacrificial pit by another of the druids, the man Grainne had spoken to in the brú the night before, and when the *moncaí* was brought into the enclosure, a silence choked the crowd.

She had heard of the beast in her studies, but Grainne had never seen one and the archdruid himself had not mentioned owning one, at least not to her. She wondered what type of foreign merchant would carry such a creature with him for trade—and what the archdruid had offered him in exchange.

The animal walked upright at the end of its chain. It was inquisitive, its eyes searching the faces of those around her. One of its forepaws—hands, not paws, Grainne thought—curled around the chain at its neck, and it waddled a little when it ambled through the people.

The druid chanted, but all eyes remained on the golden beast. He sang louder.

The assembly bowed and responded to his chants, raising their voices as one.

At the head of the gathering, the *moncaí* raised its arms towards the druid as if for comfort, but he did not pick her up. He knelt, and she walked to him.

Grainne understood the need for appeasement, but this strange creature should be studied for its humanlike qualities, its lifespan, its understanding of the world around it. It looked like a child, like a small, fur-covered human. They had sacrificed enough, she thought. But it was not her place to say so. 'Cáer's blessings,' she said, soft enough that nobody would hear.

The druid renewed his chanting, calling upon the gods of grace and of war. In song, he repented for their misdeeds, and for the straying of their kind from the work of the ancients. Through this atonement, he pleaded, the gods would turn their loving arms towards their people and put an end to their sufferings.

The collected druids called upon the name of their favoured god and pressed their foreheads to the earth.

Grainne closed her eyes, whispered Cáer's name again, and lowered her head to the flattened grass. She could not watch. She knew the animal's spirit would march to the Otherworld, and if its offering were accepted, the gods would welcome it into their world. The sacrifice of so many animals had never been warranted before, but they would all be brought in from the cold harsh autumn and into the warming embrace of the gods.

She wondered if the creature would struggle. In its fur-cloaked mockery of humanity, perhaps it would cry like a man, or call out in its dying gasp. Grainne kept her forehead against the cold earth. The sounds of the chanting druids filled her with remorse. This was a part of life—even Anú and Dérc will have to make appeasements in their time—but she hoped the children were not looking now to witness the death of such a magnificent creature.

She kept her eyes closed and whispered Cáer's name in repetition until it numbed her lips.

The chanting rose in volume. She could hear the beast's chain rattle. She knew the druid's ceremonial blade would be in the air, coming in a downward arc. The *moncaí* would be held down, lying on its back, staring at her assailant. Her long arms would be splayed and held down for ease of access.

The chanting became a drone.

Grainne clenched her eyes tighter.

'Cáer's blessings,' she whispered. 'Cáer's blessings.'

When the chanting stopped and a silence suffused the hilltop, Grainne felt warm tears on her cheeks.

It was done.

She kissed the ground on which her most gracious lady Cáer must once have walked, and she felt a hand on her back. She raised her eyes.

'Do not cry,' Anú said.

Grainne held the girl until the smell of burning flesh faded from her and black smoke clouded the sky.

Chapter 16

Muirgel wretched but could expel nothing. For nine days she had fasted, consuming only one small morning meal and drinking one cup of water. She stopped taking her tincture for the duration, and when her druid visited her each evening, the old woman sang to her the tales of the ancestors so that her soothing voice would lull her to sleep. But sleep came and went with such swiftness that Muirgel could have closed her eyes for longer by blinking in the wind. She would dismiss the druid at night with venom on her tongue and an emptiness in her stomach caused by more than fasting.

She was preparing for a ritual of such graveness that it must be carried out with absolute precision or it would not work—or worse, work in reverse.

Tonight, her fasting would be done, and the ritual would be complete. When she dressed, she fitted a gold torc around her neck and she wore her finest cloak and brooch over a wool dress dyed green like the lands on which she stood. But autumn had at last arrived on the island of Thúr Rí, and the hillsides were swaddled in a blanket of wet leaves. The druid had foreseen its arrival only yesterday, but Muirgel did not mind; the fallen leaves covered the stains of man with a pristine redness so that even unhealed scars could not be perceived.

The cold brought with it a renewed ache in her knuckles, and her right knee cracked with every step. Bending to pull on a pair of soft leather boots revealed a stiffness in her lower back, but she tightened her lips and straightened, allowing herself a moment for the pain to dissipate before venturing outside.

She pulled her cloak around her and stepped into the night. The bitterness of the bile in her throat left an undesired taste, but any taste was better than nothing.

The gates of her compound had been thrown open, and a guard stood at either side. They bowed as she approached. By now, the islanders would have heard about the coming ritual and, rain or not, they would be standing on the hillside to watch. She wished, for a moment, that Dásan had been there to walk with her, but he was on the mainland attending to another ritual. She would make the walk towards the northern reach of the island alone and, in doing so, would show to her people that she was strong and noble and dependable.

She allowed herself the use of her regal staff, cut and shaped from the belly of a yew tree—the same tree that Dásan had taken clippings of needles from to take to Éirinn. She leaned upon it now as she approached the base of the hill. Her knee was crying, but she ignored it. Later, when the ritual was complete, she would allow her cumal to bathe her in heated water and would let the old druid lather her leg in her foul-smelling pastes. She would drink her tincture this evening and hoped that sleep would come swift and deep, cutting the dreams from her head with its sharpened edge. After this ritual, she may sleep until Yule without a care.

Fat raindrops jostled in the air around her as the clouds

drummed overhead. She lifted her face as she climbed the hill-side, allowing the rain to cool her burning cheeks.

The islanders had gathered the length of the hill in two rows. She walked between them, her stride slow, nodding to them as though this was a part of the ritual, when in truth her knee would not allow her to move any faster. They crossed their arms over their chests and bowed their heads in respect of their queen as she went, and then they crowded in behind her, huddling close to each other for warmth.

The old druid stood at the top of the hill in her white robes, visible against the blackened sky only when the rainfall eased its dance. She opened her arms to her queen as Muirgel moved closer.

At the crest of the hill, Muirgel looked at the bullán stone beside which the druid waited. She stared at the three cursing stones that rested in the larger stone's depression, and then looked out towards the ocean that was dark and persuasive in its undulations. If the ritual did not bring about the desired outcome, she would throw the druid from the steep cliffs before her.

The druid cleared her throat and faced the queen. 'You would use the cursing stones against a man,' she intoned. 'If you have been wronged, the man named will be cursed and his life will drain from him within the year. If you have not been wronged by this man, the curse will reverse upon you. Do you understand the words that I have spoken?'

'I do,' Muirgel said. She wished again that Dásan stood beside her. It was not desire or comfort that she sought, but his dependable strength.

'And what do you say of it?' the druid asked. 'Have you been wronged?'

'I have been wronged,' Muirgel answered.

The druid made preparations. For the nine nights of Muirgel's fasting, the old woman had studied the omens and watched the skies for the passing and alignment of the stars. If conditions were not favourable, she would have refused the ritual to continue. But with this evening's cloud cover and heavy rains, the old woman looked pleased.

She knelt in the sodden grass beside the bullán stone and faced east, indicating that her queen should kneel beside her. With the aid of her staff, Muirgel sank to her knees and faced the same direction. A pain snaked the length of her thigh. The druid mouthed her words of prayer, and then she turned to face west. When Muirgel had shuffled beside her, she mouthed more words in a silent incantation to the dead who dwelt across the waters in the Otherworld.

Then they faced one another, and the druid helped her queen to stand. The gathered crowd remained in silent awe of the spectacle.

'Have you fasted and fasted true?' the druid asked.

Muirgel closed her eyes against the renewed protestations of her knee, and said, 'I have fasted true for nine nights.'

'With your fasting and your declaration of wrongdoing, is it your intention to curse the man who will be named here this night?'

'It is.'

'Then the ritual may commence.' She stepped back from the bullán and indicated it. 'Walk three times in reverse of the sun, pausing upon each pass so that you can rotate the cursing stones—also against the sun. In so doing, you must speak aloud the offender's name—his name and nothing more. Do you understand the words which I have spoken?'

Muirgel gripped her staff with impatience. 'I understand.'

The druid bowed to her queen. She took from her acolyte a crackling torch and she waved it in the face of the gods, then she cast the torch over the cliff where it sputtered in the ocean before extinguishing. 'You may proceed.'

Muirgel filled her chest with icy air, and she walked around the bullán stone in the direction her druid had indicated. As she walked, she brought to her mind the image of her son—not grown as he was when he was murdered, but young and innocent and full of mischief. Faolán had been her only child, son of a chieftain, and he grew to be strong and forceful of nature.

He was a brute of a man but had been a pleasing child. She called to mind the colour of his eyes, the length of his hair, the width of his shoulders. She remembered the songs she sang to him even when he was in her belly, songs that she did not often recall for the pain that they caused her.

In due course, he had been set to replace his father as chieftain for their tribe. He would be uncontested, his reign deemed apropos by their people for fear of the swiftness of his blade. As his mother and chief advisor, Muirgel would have succeeded where her husband had failed, towing their tribe into larger reaches of land, growing in strength as their neighbours bowed to them. With Faolán as chieftain, Muirgel would have her dead husband's other wives and children slaughtered for their slothful ways.

She completed her first pass of the bullán, stood before it, and reached out for the leftmost stone. It was spherical in shape and blemished on its underside from years of inertia. She twisted the stone circular to the left, then she did likewise with the second and the third.

'Rónán of Clan Ó Mordha,' she said. 'Overking of Ailigh.'

The druid made a movement with her hands, a fluttering of the fingers that matched the twirling descent of the rain that eased as the evening progressed. Already, Muirgel's footprints in the soft earth were filling with puddles of water. The old woman nodded, and the queen started around the bullán a second time.

With the base of her staff cutting through the sludge as she moved, she recalled the life of her husband. Donal, son of Ultan, had been an ignorant man, foolhardy and drunk. He sipped beer at breakfast and drank wine in the afternoons, and he was hardly a match for her under their furs at night. She was his first wife, the chief wife, but when he took a second and a third wife, she was thankful for the respite. The man was quick to temper, and she negotiated with him often to calm him. He had been as wily as a stoat in a hot summer, but by her words she had controlled him.

He was pathetic, but he stood tall and fat and his blade was always sharp. Their people paid taxes on time, and she had watched their wealth grow over the years—before their surrogate son had driven his sword through her husband's chest at Knockdhu.

She stood before the cursing stones, leaning against her staff for support, her knee threatening to skew from under her, and she reached for the first stone, turning it away from the sun. When she had twisted all three stones, she said, 'Rónán of Clan Ó Mordha. Overking of Ailigh.'

She turned to face the druid, watched her perform her finger dance in the air, and then she made her third and final pass around the bullán stone.

The hush that fell over the islanders was muffled further by the autumn fog that came in off the sea to shroud them.

Muirgel turned her mind to her offender, Rónán of the Ó Mordha. The boy's father had been killed and Rónán became their surrogate, as was the tradition among Éirinn's tribesmen. When a child is left unloved, his chieftain and all the sept assume his care. He had been no more than ten or eleven winters when he was blood-bound to her husband, thick locks of wheat-coloured hair falling around his shoulders, eyes wide, back strong. Already he had been training as a warrior under the Ó Mordha clansmen and she was told he was good with the bow.

Years later, when war came, he had excelled, and upon the death of his king, he assumed the responsibility of all his people.

And then, in a fit of rage, he had murdered her husband and her son, a callous display of undeserved treatment.

She touched the faint scar at her cheek. He had bestowed the wound upon her and told her that she would remember him forever.

And she did. But here it would end.

She finished her final pass of the bullán. She breathed deep, reached out, and turned the cursing stones.

'Rónán,' she said, 'of Clan Ó Mordha. Overking of Ailigh.'

The silence was expectant, the people shuffling a step closer.

The old druid took Muirgel's hands and raised them up before her face. She touched each of the queen's palms, and then she bowed. She twisted her fingers and turned in a circle.

And the rain stopped falling.

The sky above them was black and vacant.

Muirgel leaned against her staff and waited, her breath held tight.

The druid bowed and bowed again. She turned to the people and raised her arms, shaking rainwater from her sleeves. 'It is done.'

And the islanders cheered for their queen.

When Muirgel returned to her quarters, passing the kennel that was being erected in her great hall, she slipped into her bed. Her fasting was over, but she felt no desire for food. She closed her eyes, intent on remaining so for only a moment before reaching for the druid's tincture, but sleep took her at once.

And her sleep was empty and void of dreams.

Chapter 17

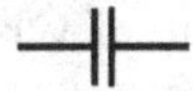

The sun had not yet risen when Orlaith wrapped Breasal in a gargantuan fur cloak that went around his small body three times.

'I cannot move,' he complained.

'You can walk, and that is all you need.'

He made a display of walking from one side of their home to the other in a tight-legged waddle. 'What if the rain comes and the valley floods and I cannot swim to safety? I will drown.'

Orlaith used a finger to draw a pattern on the boy's forehead. 'There. Now you are protected.'

'From drowning?'

'From drowning and dying and sneezing.'

'I do not believe you.'

Outside their home, Etain waited for them. She had a deer-fur shawl over her shoulders and carried an empty basket made from willow bast. She laughed when she saw Breasal. 'It is the first days of autumn, not the deep winter. Why do you wrap him so tightly?'

'I am taking no chances. If he so much as sneezes, I will march him home again.'

'I am protected from sneezing,' Breasal said.

They set off across the hillside and down the steep slope of the crag into the rich valley that was thick with blueberry bushes. By the time they reached the depths of the dell, the sun had cracked a hole in the black sky and stretched its rays towards them. Breasal had shrugged his cloak loose enough so that he could walk unhindered, but Orlaith checked it throughout the morning to ensure he was still covered from neck to calf.

Blueberry picking was one of Orlaith's favoured pastimes in this early autumn season. That sweet scent of fresh berries—something close to the smell of cut wood—that sailed across the valley in waves of olfactory pleasure reminded her of her childhood. She would pick the berries and strip the blueberry leaves from their stalks to give to her mother who would infuse them in warmed water to drink. 'It will give you a long life,' she would say.

As they set to work picking blueberries in the early morning sunlight, and Breasal marched up and down the manmade path between rows of wild bushes, Etain sang a work song to aid their progress. They had set off in advance of the dawn to avoid the coming rain that the winds foretold, and to acquire as many berries as they could before the morning birds took their share.

'Banan hinted again at a proposal last night,' Orlaith told her friend. 'Third time this week.'

Etain dropped two blueberries into her basket and flipped another into her mouth. 'I know you mourn The Warrior, but you could do worse.'

'I have not the patience for another man.'

'He would seek to bed you for a son to call his own.'

'He is a great man, a fair leader, but he has more chance of siring a son from one of his sheep than he does of getting me into bed. I am running out of ways to tell him that I have no desire left in me for anyone.'

'Banan MacColm will wear you down. I saw him do it with Sadhbh. She was always homely and quiet. For months she would not look at him or give an ear to his voice, and still he won her heart.'

'I would sooner lie with another woman than break my heart for a man again.'

'I do not see that inclination in you,' Etain said.

'No. But it would cause less sorrow, would it not?'

'And much less strife.'

They worked through the morning, cloaks wrapped tight around their shoulders, swords ever-present at their hips; for months now, Orlaith had insisted the women keep their blades, blunted as they were, with them always. Now that Breasal was no longer delirious, she had increased the tribeswomen's daily training. They would complete their chores in the morning and then train until mid-afternoon before retiring to their homes to see to their husbands and their families. Orlaith would cook for her son and ensure he ate as wholesome a diet as possible for a child of five winters, then she would instruct him in personal combat training with the sawn-off pole of a broom. She had attached a wooden cross-guard in order to mimic the feel of a sword. His strokes were wild and carefree, and she noted little passion in him for weaponry. But she trained him daily regardless.

She plucked a bush free from the last of its blueberries and then pocketed several leaves. She would make a tea with them later and insist Breasal drink every drop. 'Don't wander too far,' she called after the boy as he ducked between two rows of bushes.

'*Mamaí*,' he whispered.

'I see you. Stay close.'

'*Mamaí*.' Breasal crept to her side, small feet flicking from under the cloak. When he stood beside her, she held a blueberry to his lips, and he swallowed it without chewing. He leaned towards her as though for a kiss, but instead he whispered, 'There is a man.'

'There is always a man,' Etain said from the opposite side of the bush. 'It is the way of the world.'

'He is close,' Breasal murmured.

Orlaith straightened up and looked across the valley. 'Where did you see him?'

'I felt him.'

'One of the tribesmen?'

Breasal shook his head.

When he did so, Orlaith saw a blur of movement across the row. She dropped her basket, pushed Breasal behind her, and drew her sword. 'Etain.'

Etain had seen it too. She pushed through the blueberry bush and withdrew her own sword. 'Who is he?'

'Breasal?' Orlaith asked.

'A bad man.'

Etain strode forward. 'That's good enough for me.'

Orlaith crouched and told Breasal to stay behind her. 'Is the man alone?'

Breasal closed his eyes for the answer and then nodded. He pointed.

The two women edged forward with care not to create too much noise. A wind stirred the leaves of the bushes and silver clouds scudded overhead. The storm that had been promised was still hugging the distant mountains.

There was no movement beyond them and, for a moment, Orlaith wondered if her son had seen only a deer or a wild boar instead of a man. But a flash of silver in the morning sunlight caught her attention. 'Show yourself,' she commanded.

Etain crouched lower and indicated that she would circle around the back of the row. She ducked under a swarm of midges and hacked at the bushes before her with her sword.

The man was fast. He leapt from the shrubbery and flashed his sword. The blade glanced off Etain's and the stocky woman fell back from him.

Orlaith pounced, her sword raised. Though his attention was divided, the man saw Orlaith's shadow come towards him and sidestepped her.

'Back off, *bitseach*. I have no quarrel with either of you.'

'Who are you?'

'Just passing through.'

Orlaith swung her blade and he blocked it. The clash of metal rang in her arms. The man kicked out and connected the sole of his foot with her stomach. As she fell, she gripped the man's tunic, pulling him down with her. He rolled arse over head into the brambles and as Orlaith turned, she saw Etain descend on him blade first.

'*Mamaí*,' Breasal shouted. When she turned to him, the man's dagger flew over her shoulder. Etain had missed her mark and tumbled on the ground with him.

Orlaith flicked her sword so that the blade was pointed downward, and she kicked Etain out of her way, bringing the sword down on the man's shoulder.

She drove it home.

The man screamed as she pinned him down.

'Who are you?'

'Get off me, you whore.'

She twisted the blade, and his scream ran an octave higher. 'Who are you?'

The man's hands gripped the blade and tried to push it from his shoulder, but Orlaith leaned upon it with all her strength.

'Check his pack,' she told Etain.

The man struggled against Orlaith's sword so that she had to kick his face to still him. He was strong.

Her friend ripped the bag from the man's free shoulder and rooted through it, emptying the contents on the ground. There was nothing of note. She came to her knees and searched the pockets of his tunic. She pulled out a black leather bag and turned it over. There were holes in the front of it.

'It is not a bag,' Etain said. 'It is a mask.'

Orlaith pressed against her sword and twisted it further. 'Who are you?'

The man released his bloodied grip on the blade and closed his eyes. His hands reached inside the neck of his tunic and when he withdrew a second dagger, he was too quick for Orlaith to stop him.

He flicked the small blade across his own neck. For a moment, he looked at her, his eyes hard, his throat attempting to swallow but managing only to spew thick blood across his chest.

And then he was gone.

Etain rose. She kicked the man's sword away from him as though he could use it still in death.

Orlaith let go of her sword and turned to Breasal. She came to her knees and hugged him. 'Are you all right?' He nodded against her hair.

'We should go,' Etain said. 'There may be others.'

'Who the gods was he?' Orlaith asked. She turned back to Breasal. 'Quick. Give me your cloak.' She unwrapped him from the huge fur and spread it on the ground. 'Help me roll him onto it. We will drag him up the hill and take him to Banan.'

'We should piss on him and leave him here,' Etain said. 'He is dead. Banan cannot make him talk any more than we could.'

'We should take him all the same. Banan may recognise him or that mask.'

They spent an age dragging him out of the bushes and rolling him onto the fur.

Now that he was bereft of his cloak, Breasal said, 'I am freezing.' Etain gave him her much smaller fur shawl and then they dragged the man up the hillside.

Breasal ran ahead several rods before stopping to allow them to catch up, then running further to repeat the process.

When they were near the top of the hill and in sight of the sept's walls, Etain said, 'Damn it. We left the blueberries.'

As they entered the gates, Banan MacColm approached with his advisors. He looked down at the dead man and then at Orlaith. 'I hope he is not a friend of yours.'

Orlaith handed him the mask. 'He attacked us in the blueberry dell. He had this in his pocket.'

Banan inspected the mask and handed it to one of his advisors. 'I do not recognise it. Did he speak before you kicked his arse into the Otherworld?'

'He was a bad man,' Breasal said.

'I am sure he was, little man.'

'He had nothing to say with a sword in his shoulder. He slit his own throat before we could force him to talk.'

'We should send for the druid in the next tribe,' Banan said.

'The druid is away to his sacred place,' Orlaith told him.

'Then his acolyte. Someone must recognise him or this mask.'

'I fear he is one of the men intent on killing the brehon.'

'Then it is bad luck to have him inside our walls.' Banan pointed to two of his advisors. 'Carry the body outside and bury him in an unmarked grave. If he offends the gods, he should not be allowed to carry a name with him into the Otherworld. Did he injure you?'

'We held our own,' Etain said. 'And it is thanks to the boy for alerting us.'

Banan took a knee before Breasal and offered him his arm. 'You are a true hero, young man. When the druid returns, I will have him devise a song in your honour.'

Breasal scrunched his nose. 'I am tired,' he said.

Orlaith took his shoulder. 'My lord. With your leave, I will get him to sleep.'

She curtsied and turned for her home before Banan could invite her to another meal, another evening of drinks and proposals. When she closed the door behind her, Breasal was already stripping off for bed.

'It is early still,' Orlaith said. 'Do you wish to eat first?'

With a yawn, Breasal said, 'You eat for me.' He slipped under the furs of his bed and when she knelt beside him and touched his forehead, his breathing had already slowed.

His skin was warm but not hot. His fever, she was certain, was not returning. She doubted Banan would send for the druid's acolyte as he had suggested, but in the morning, if her son still complained of fatigue, she may carry him to the next tribe for the acolyte's advice. With all the druids congregating at their most sacred place, it would be up to their trainees to offer guidance and medicine.

As the afternoon wore into evening and Breasal continued to sleep, Orlaith unstitched his tunic and added a fabric section to either side, widening it for future use. In the past, when she had items to trade, she would acquire new dresses and discard her old ones. It was only in recent years that she had learned—with Sadhbh's and Etain's help—how to unpick and sew a garment to lengthen it or extend its width. And Breasal had grown so much in his years that she could not trade her worth to keep up with the demands of his growing limbs. Etain and the other women had given her many lengths of dyed linen in payment for her weapons instruction.

She was grateful for their training. Had she been alone in the blueberry dell, or if Etain had been with her but was untrained with the sword, their battle might not have turned in their favour. Breasal might now be motherless.

In her wooden chair by the hearth, she made the final stitches on Breasal's tunic and allowed her eyes to close in slow deliberation of thoughtfulness. This stranger was not the first man she had drawn swords with and, as the sun dies and is reborn daily, so too did she know he would not be the last. Wherever she journeyed, men—or women—always had a mind to kill her, but to date she was loath to let them. This is what life is—an unwillingness to die.

She sat upright in her chair when Breasal's scream woke her. She rushed to his side, conscious that the fire had dwindled to hot embers and the room had grown dark while she blinked.

She touched his chest and soothed him with hushing sounds,

her lips pressed against his ear. His scream continued, an agonising cry that caught in his throat and made him choke. She scooped water from the barrel into a cup and made him drink. When he was calm, she said, 'I am here, son. I am always here.'

He did not look at her. 'They are going to die. They are all going to die.'

'Who?' she asked.

He did not respond at once.

When he closed his eyes again, she thought he had returned to sleep, but he reached up and scratched his neck and she could see that he had made his palm bleed by digging his fingernails into it during his nightmare.

'Everyone,' he said at last.

'Who is everyone, son?'

'*Mamaí*. They will all die.'

'Who will?'

'Only a king who loses everything can end it.'

Chapter 18

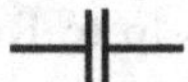

Three of his pasture fields were now worthless. The flames from the deceased livestock conquered the grasses with angry claws, spreading with uncontrolled abandon to reach each opposing stone wall. The ditches that ringed the fields stopped the fire from licking over the stones and invading additional pastures, and Rónán could hear the bleating and screaming of the lambs in the nearby field over the sound of the crackling flesh of their dead kin.

'It is a waste of wool and meat and bone,' he said.

Cormac nodded. Across the field, the shepherds fanned the flames back on themselves to contain them at the gates, and above them, carrion birds beat their wings on the black smoke. The northern horizon held a storm along the ridges and later, when it arrived, it would douse the flames and put them out. But for now, the smell of seared flesh was all too thick.

'We're being watched,' Cormac said, his voice low.

When Rónán looked up the hill behind him, he saw Achall and Áed standing by the outer palisade. The boy held his mother's hand, but they did not move. They stared down the hillside towards him.

'If I have hurt her feelings, it is her own fault,' Rónán said.

He dismissed the image of her and returned his attention to the fields. 'Have any of the chieftains arrived yet?'

'Fergal Ó Fuinseog is in the barrel hut. How he managed to get here from Knockdhu before any of the others, I have no clue. He either rides on the back of a giant goose, or he set off for Ailigh over a week ago.'

Fergal had been a great help to Rónán over the years. He had been responsible for helping to take Knockdhu back from the foreign bastards at the time of the Great Invasion, and he had aided Rónán's victory at the Ó Nallon Pass some years ago. It was there that he had lost the lower half of his left arm, rendering him ineligible to serve as chieftain. He had handed Knockdhu over to his tanist and he lived there in relative comfort. Though he was no longer a lord, Rónán appreciated his counsel all the same. He would make the journey to Ailigh once or twice a year, for no other reason than to visit friends and drink ample amounts of beer or wine, and when he came it was always with a smile and a humble word of advice.

Rónán tore his eyes from the burning massacre before him and sought out the position of the sun. 'I think I'll join him for a drink. Are you coming?'

'I'll help the shepherds fan the flames and join you soon. Don't drink the hut dry before the other chieftains arrive.'

When he turned to mount the hill, Achall and Áed had disappeared.

Fergal greeted him as soon as he entered the barrel hut. He rose from his stool and wrapped his one and a half arms around the smaller king. 'You get more handsome every time I see you,' he said.

'Then you must be getting more drunk as the years pass, old

friend.'

'Less of the old, more of the friend.' He sat at the table and kicked a stool out for Rónán to sit with him. 'Boy, two beers. On the double.'

'Does it pain you still?' he asked, nodding at the shorn arm.

'You ask me that every time, lad.'

'And every time, you have a different answer.'

Fergal laughed and drank half a cup of sweet beer in one swallow. 'When I wake in the mornings, my missing fingers feel like they have returned. I reach up to scratch my head and prod myself in the eye with an elbow.'

Rónán smiled at the visual image. 'I have had my iron smith fashion a metal arm for you after your previous visit. I had intended to bring it to you when I next visited Knockdhu. I will have it sent for.'

'You make me whole again,' Fergal said. He drummed his knuckles on the table and his face grew serious. 'What whoreson bastard has you looking so glum, Rónán? I saw the burning fields as I arrived. What is going on? More wheat rust?'

'It is not the fields we are burning but the livestock that once grazed upon them.' Rónán lowered his voice. 'They were poisoned, Fergal. And I have no idea who is responsible.'

'How many survived?'

'Not enough to get us through the winter, that's for sure.'

'When I was your age, the world was a much simpler place. Nobody dealt with poisons or subterfuge. Your enemy would kill your king, you'd retaliate, and then everybody would get drunk and do the same thing the next day.'

'If only things were still so simple. I will spare you the details until we meet with the others. How is that new wife of yours?

Have you sired her a litter yet?'

Fergal waved his hand for two more beers. 'Our druid—may he now walk with the gods—told us she was barren. But that does not stop us from trying. I am too old for weans now, anyway. They do nothing but get under your feet until you accidentally crush their skulls with your boot, and then their mothers blame you for their lack of wellbeing.' He raised the stump of his forearm that protruded from his elbow, and said, 'I can count on my fingers how many children I would like.'

When Rónán told him of Achall's threat to stop him from seeing his son, Fergal said, 'Never piss off a woman, even if she is no longer your wife. In fact, former wives are the worst kind of wives. You get all of the nagging and none of the sex. Let her have her moment of stubborn idiocy. When she calms her soul, she will relent. Give it time.'

When Cormac entered, Fergal greeted him as warmly as he had Rónán.

'The chieftains are here, Lord,' Cormac said. 'I have gathered them in the hall.'

As the three men walked up towards the great hall, Fergal said, 'The good thing about you two is that you'll never get pregnant.' He slapped Rónán on the back. 'Some things come as blessings, lad.'

They assembled with the chieftains—Torin Ó Neill from the north, Seanach Mac Fachtna from the east, both of whom aided their battle at the Ó Nallon Pass, along with Ainmire Úi Balon who led the tribe to Rónán's immediate south. Ainmire had brought his son to the meeting, citing his desire to show the boy the ropes. The lad, Ardál, was in his twentieth winter and his father was long over fifty. He was a head taller than Ainmire and it would take you an age to trace the width of his shoulders.

As was tradition, each man made a display of removing his sword belt and leaving his weapons outside the hall. When tempers flare during council meetings, as tempers are wont to do, it is best to minimise the risk to personal safety. A punch to the nose would not kill you—even if Cormac considered otherwise. 'I have seen many men die from a swift jab to the face,' he once told Rónán.

Diarmuid was the last to arrive. He bowed to the king and greeted the others with warmth. 'The storm is drawing close, but the livestock have been dealt with.'

Drinks were poured and then Rónán dismissed the cumal girls so that the men could speak in private. He did not sit at his kingseat, but joined the table with the others; here, in a sealed room, they were equals. A tallow candle was lit and placed in the centre of the table. When it was burned out, the meeting would be done, and he would resume his status as overking.

'I call you here for many reasons, not least the murder of the druids. I know Fergal's druid has been taken from us; who else has lost their guidance?'

Torin Ó Neill said, 'I am still waiting for that acolyte of yours to complete his training. My men have had no guidance for many years.'

'We acquired a druid three years ago,' Seanach Mac Fachtna said. 'He has travelled to Emain Macha to be with his kin. I have had no word of his progress.'

'Ainmire?' Rónán asked.

The old man shook his head. 'He was slaughtered in his sleep twelve nights ago. His acolyte, too. The assassins came and went in the night, and we were none the wiser.'

'I am sorry for your loss,' Rónán said. 'I had hoped one of you might know who targets the brehon.'

'He is not a northerner, that is for sure,' Fergal said. 'Whoever does this, they have no spine.'

'We have stepped up our night watches,' Seanach said. 'Even with our druid at Emain Macha, we take no chances.'

'We should employ runners daily,' Rónán said. 'A network of dialogue between our allied tribes. Sooner or later, one of us is going to learn something, and when one does, we all will.'

'I'll have my son oversee our men,' Ainmire said. 'They will leave at dawn and be here by nightfall each day.'

The chieftains agreed. Once a day they would send a runner towards Ailigh and Rónán would send men out in each direction. They would be fed and given a bed before returning. It was their hope that an assassin would be captured and questioned. As Fergal said, 'No man, trained or not, can hold out long enough if you suspend him by the balls from the gatepost.'

'What if we set a trap?' Torin asked. 'Dress Fergal up as a druid and send him out into the road.'

'I'd make a fine druid,' Fergal laughed, waving his stump in the air.

'If you *were* a druid,' Seanach said, 'that missing limb would have grown back by now.'

'I will make it grow back just so I can punch you in the face with it, young buck.'

Rónán checked the length of the candle. 'My other concern is the winter months. We have all been affected by the rust disease. And now my animals have been poisoned. I fear your livestock might also be at risk. It makes no sense, but we cannot rule out this tribe of dark assassins killing both druids and livestock alike.

If it is complete confusion they are after, they are succeeding.'

They discussed the possibilities of who might be behind the poisoning until Seanach said, 'I can spare you twenty ewes and five rams, Rónán.'

'And goats I have plenty,' Torin said.

Rónán shook his head. 'I am not looking for handouts. I mention it only in fear for your own livestock. But I will happily trade for them if you consent to it.'

As they discussed options for trade—cattle in the main, some iron ore and bronze ingots, and a small number of cumal girls—the candle on the table sputtered and dimmed. Their meeting was over, though their discussions had not completed.

'We will convene again in the morning,' Rónán said. 'For now, Diarmuid will show you to your rooms and then we can dine together.'

'Forget the fine food,' Fergal said. 'Bring on the beer.'

Rónán assembled his elite warriors and some of the younger boys who were adept with the cruit or fipple flutes, and a banquet of meats and cheese and flatbreads were dished out for his guests. Gold bowls filled with dipping oils were placed by each honoured chieftain and, though the breads were flat and crisp thanks to the shortage of wheat, they were softened in the oils and were tasty regardless. Rolls of butter were served on bronze plates and no finger was left without grease by nightfall.

The boys played their instruments while the men dined and, later, when the dishes were cleared away, the younger men danced. Fergal caught the eye of a cumal girl and slapped her on the rump as she passed.

Rónán shook his head in mock dismay. 'Your wife may be barren, Lord, but I can assure you she is not. She has been pregnant more times than you have had cups of beer.'

Fergal picked up his empty cup, inspected it, and discarded it on the floor. He reached for Rónán's cup, drank it in one pull, and smacked the wooden cup back on the table. 'By my reckoning,' he said, 'that means she's due another pup.' He stood and followed the girl outside.

Cormac slumped into Fergal's vacant seat beside Rónán. 'I am too old for dancing.'

'You are too young to complain about it,' Rónán laughed.

'I have spoken with Seanach. He continues to refuse a trade. He wants to give us his sheep and says if we offer him a trade for them, he will slit the sheep's throats and let them bleed out on the road before they get here.'

'I will not take his charity.'

'He does not see it as charity, Rónán. You saved his life at the Ó Nallon Pass. He is indebted to you.'

'He owes me no debt.'

'I told him as much. But you know what he is like.'

'He is more stubborn than you,' Rónán said.

'I am glad you can still smile in such dark times.'

'If I did not, I would throw myself over the palisade walls and be done with my life.'

Cormac touched his arm. 'You know I would not let you. Now, while everyone is busy dancing, let us sneak through the underground tunnel and down to the lough like we used to. I'll grab a wineskin.'

The tunnel entrance, at the back of the inner wall, weaved down in darkness through the hillside and out at the mouth of the lough. Twice a day, with the tide, the base of the tunnel was waterlogged, but now, with the sun down and the tide on its way out, the stretch of sand before it was the perfect place for clandestine relations. Cormac insisted on it, though they had an adequate home and a bed in which to enjoy themselves. To Cormac, it was an adventure. Rónán, on the other hand, had enough adventure in his life without the need for being seen rutting in the sand by one of Ailigh's boys; he was their king, not a spectacle. But he smiled and kissed Cormac's cheek.

'Go and warm the sand. I'll be there in a moment.'

When he excused himself from the chieftains and bid them goodnight, he slipped through the door and up to the inner wall, crouching as he entered the mouth of the concealed tunnel. At the edge of the lough, Cormac was already naked and awaiting him. They kissed. The afternoon's storm had passed, and the sunless evening air was fresh. The smell of smoke lingered like an unwanted gift. They were slow to climax. In the years since they shared a bed, their lovemaking had become less frequent, but still passionate. As his consort, they were unable to marry, and the thought of it—though Rónán joked about it often—was preposterous. There were no issues with a man taking another man, but marriage was between a man and a woman. Cormac's position as Rónán's consort was acceptable, though his neighbours would appreciate him taking a new wife. What you did in the confines of your bedroom—or the edge of your lough—to the people of Éirinn was of no concern. But a man should have a son to carry his name. Rónán, though he had no son by flesh, still had Áed, the fatherless child he had raised as his own and considered him as such. He was Áed Ó Mordha—named for the tribe—son of Rónán, Overking of Ailigh. No one could take that from him, least of all the spoiled woman who was once his queen.

'Where is your head?' Cormac asked, his skin warm against Rónán's. His fingers travelled down the hollow indentation between Rónán's abdominal muscles to the thin trail of blond hairs that started below his navel. He sat astride him.

'Sorry,' Rónán said, reaching up to touch Cormac's cheek. 'I am here. I am always here.'

They returned through the tunnel when the moon was shrouded in silver clouds and the lough was a black mirror, broken only by the puckered mouths of salmon and the occasional frog. Those frogs would return to the lough's murky edge at Imbolc to spawn their sticky eggs. Man does not make the seasons. Animals do.

When morning came, Rónán and Cormac awoke, a tangle of limbs in their fur-covered bed. They bathed and broke their fast, and Cormac balked at the idea of cooked meats, preferring instead to drink a cup of water.

'You started the evening on beer, and ended it on wine,' Rónán said. 'It is your own fault you suffer now.'

With his head in his hands, Cormac said, 'I will thank you to keep your opinions to yourself while I die quietly.'

The slow walk to the great hall, under a morning sun free of cloud that shone bright white upon their searing eyes, was marred by the rains from the night before that made their boots mire in the softened ground.

'I can still hear fipple flutes,' Cormac said. 'Are they still dancing?'

'It is in your addled mind,' Rónán told him.

They slumped into their seats in the hall and one of the cumal girls approached with a tallow candle. Cumal girls did not often speak to their masters without first being asked a question, but before she lit the candle, she said, 'One is missing, my lord. Should I light it regardless?'

Rónán looked around the room. Heads drooped with alcoholic shame and eyes were squinted. Torin was there, leaning against the table as though he was about to vomit on it. Diarmuid licked his desiccated lips to moisten them and the thyroid cartilage in his throat bobbed as he swallowed.

Beside him, Ainmire's son, Ardál, scratched his stubbled neck with sharp fingernails, leaving red tracks from chin to breastbone.

'Where is your father?' Rónán asked him.

Ardál nodded, indicating the floor beneath the table.

When he looked, Rónán saw the old man curled up under a stool. 'Leave me here to die, Lord,' Ainmire mumbled. 'I am no longer worthy to be in the presence of anyone who can drink without death.'

At his immediate right, Fergal drank a fresh cup of wine as though the alcohol had little effect on him. 'Some men can hold their wits like they hold their cock—with great ease. Others,' Fergal said, pointing a finger at the collected men, 'should still be supping at their mother's tit.'

Rónán scanned the faces again. 'Where is Seanach? Did he drink too much that he has forgotten to rise with the sun?'

'I will check his brú,' Cormac said, struggling to stand from the table.

Rónán laughed. 'You need some berry-water. I will go.'

He trudged through the middle rampart to Seanach's door. The chieftains were all housed in the middle level, indicative of their status and for its proximity to the barrel hut. When he knocked, he received no answer. He knocked again and called,

'Seanach, your wife is here. She wants to know why you snore like a boar.'

When still no answer came, he tried the door and found it unlocked. Inside, his eyes needed a moment to adjust to the gloom. The hearth was a burning ember, and thin tendrils of smoke rose towards the thatching. The shape of Seanach in bed under his furs was one of peaceful slumber.

'Seanach. Did you drink so much it killed you?'

Rónán nudged the furs and Seanach did not stir. When he pulled the covers back, Seanach Mac Fachtna was staring at him, his eyes sightless.

A dagger protruded from his breast. And blood had dried across the bristles of his chest hair.

Chapter 19

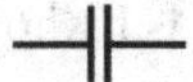

Grainne opened her eyes and was standing in a small clearing drenched white with flowers. A strange summer sun shone bright above her, and dandelion seeds danced in the air around her head. She turned. Behind her, a white-haired boy with eyes of purple smiled. He wore a long white *léine* tunic that reached his calves, and a gold circlet encased his upper arm. He pointed east and when she looked, she saw her master, the archdruid, dressed in brilliant white robes.

'Master,' she said, her voice a gentle echo.

The archdruid smiled, his eyes disappearing in happy wrinkles.

She went to him, but as she reached to embrace him, he was gone. She smelled samphire and when she turned again, the boy, Ethal Anbuail in his boyish guise, was kneeling beside a swan so white as to be glowing.

Grainne cried and pressed her fingers to her eyelids. She lay prostrate on the ground before the elegant swan and kissed the earth. 'My most precious lady Cáer,' she said. 'How is it that you come to me after so many years?'

The swan stretched her neck and preened. 'Fate curls rivers with its wicked charms, child.'

She dared not look at the swan or the boy. 'I was convinced

that we would never meet again until the next life. I have longed to hold you one more time.'

A hand touched her head, and she felt the warmth of kindness. When she looked, the swan was gone and, in its place, the goddess Cáer knelt before her. Her eyes were wide and full of compassion.

'Rise, child,' she said. 'It is I who should bow before you.'

Grainne rose to her knees and, with tentative movements, embraced her goddess. Cáer kissed the tears that journeyed a thousand acres on her cheeks.

'Many dark paths lie ahead. No one can choose which you will take.'

In the distance Grainne heard the trumpeting of a war-horn, the unmistakable call of a carnyx, and she heard the marching of a thousand feet.

'Do the Fir Bolg return?'

Cáer shook her head. 'This war is not yet your concern. But another threatens your ways.'

Grainne blinked, and they stood in the old isolation hut, the room in which she had first seen her most gracious goddess. The door was thrown open and hung from its hinges, and the walls were cracked and crumbling. A large section of the roof had caved in around them and weeds and flowers sprouted from the earth among the rocks. Dust floated through the dry air like an army of flies.

Cáer took her hands and smiled. Her face was lit from within, her eyes bright with worlds. 'What is the sunlight in dimmest night?'

'I am,' Grainne said.

'Now is your time to show it.'

'What must I do?'

The earth under her feet trembled and the building collapsed around them. They remained unharmed, and when the dust thinned, she could see beyond the line of trees a multitude of druids, black robes and brown, their hoods drawn up over their faces so that she could not say if she recognised them. They stared at her, expectant of an answer to a question she was not aware of.

'I cannot say what must be done,' Cáer said. 'My words are a guide. Your people need a leader. They need to be encouraged to hold their elections today. Their sacrifices are appreciated, and my kin dine on their resolve. But without a strong hand to lead them, all will be lost. Time runs frozen on a stream of coming blood.'

One by one, the druids that congregated around them disappeared, vacant spots of vague memory.

'Where do they go?' Grainne asked.

'They go the way of all things.'

Less than half remained and still they were fading from view.

'I will convince them to hold their elections as soon as possible.'

'Child,' Cáer said, 'shining light of wisdom. You are revered among all peoples. Act swift. Guide your people to do right. I journey with you wherever you go. I am but a whisper away.'

'I have felt your presence,' Grainne said. Often, in times of grievous decision-making, she understood with an innate sense that her most gracious lady Cáer had been at her side.

Only a few druids remained beyond the treeline.

When she looked back at Cáer, Ethal Anbuial stood beside her, no longer a boy but an aged man. He took his daughter's hand.

With her other hand, Cáer touched Grainne's cheek with delicate tenderness, and she smiled.

The last of the druids faded from her vision. And then so too did her most gracious lady Cáer and her father.

Grainne fell to the broken earth and wept.

When she woke, she rose and sought the eldest druids who had assumed charge of the appeasements. A new dawn brought further sacrifices and the air was dense with the ripeness of the dead.

When she found the men making sacrifice by the firepit, she bowed to them and begged their attention. The grasses under her feet, browned with the autumn death, had been heated by the nearby fires. Behind her, a line of morning dew was circular around the outer reaches of the flames' heat.

'The lady Cáer has come to me in a vision,' she said.

The eldest man cut the throat of a sheep and passed the blade to his fellow druid. He stepped before Grainne. 'A good vision has a fair warning,' he said. 'How does your lady appear?'

'As a swan-lady,' a small voice behind Grainne uttered with excitement.

Grainne turned. Anú stood there, carrying a twig around which she had fashioned a dress of linen. 'A swan-lady, yes,' Grainne said. She crouched to Anú's level. 'Have you seen her?'

'I saw you in a dream.'

'And the swan-lady?'

Anú nodded. 'You were crying. Why were you crying?'

Grainne touched her cheek. 'Tears of compassion for all that has been and all that will come.'

The old man folded his arms. 'Two visitations in one morning. What compels her?'

Grainne turned to him. 'We must begin elections at once. Without an archdruid, I fear what lies before us.'

'We must continue our appeasements until we know that we are safe.'

'Elect a new leader and he can ensure our safety. The Lady Cáer commands it.'

'How could that be so?'

Grainne looked around at her fellowship, the two hundred or more druids that made camp at Emain Macha. 'We require a head,' she said. 'Right now, we are a body without direction. Our limbs spread across the lands—how many of our Order survive in the fields and forests, unable or unwilling to attend us here? Many appeasements have been made in the days since you came here. How many more before the gods turn to you and shake you in their anger that we do not have a head for thought and fairness?'

The man slapped her face and Anú inhaled with sharp fright.

'You dishonour me.'

Grainne bowed, refusing to touch her reddened cheek. 'My intent was not to do so but to reveal to you a purpose given to us from the most gracious lady Cáer who watches our every motion and cares deeply for our people and the lands to which the gods have granted us.'

The old man folded his hands inside his sleeves as though putting them out of sight would deny the thing that they had done. 'Your lady is most gracious indeed, and we are less deserving of her light than we often believe.' He turned to the young girl. 'Tell me, child. Did the swan-lady speak to you in your dream?'

Anú glanced at Grainne before shaking her head. She put her hand to her cheek in expectation of a blow. 'The swan was crying as well.'

The man's features softened. 'When a god cries, we are all but doomed.' He straightened up and turned to Grainne. 'My words have been harsh. Your vision is kind and fair. I will assemble a council and we will begin preparations for immediate elections.'

That evening, Grainne sought out the children and sat with them while Marí was engaged in further appeasements. She could not believe there were any animals left in the world. Anú hugged her and nestled into her side as she ate a bowl of mashed vegetables.

'Are you well?'

'I wanted to kick him when he slapped you,' the girl said.

Grainne shook her head and wrapped an arm around her. 'I spoke improperly to a master. I was at fault.'

'If I were there,' Dérc said, 'I'd have gutted him for you.'

Grainne smiled. 'I appreciate your kindness. But it is done. I wronged him with my words and my penance was swift. Think no more of it. Tomorrow, they will commence elections and soon we will have a new head.'

When the young girl had her fill of food and dozed into Grainne's warm breast, Grainne tapped Dérc on the leg and said, 'Marí is not your mother, am I correct?'

The boy nodded.

'May I ask your story?'

'My story?'

'Your birth and your childhood,' Grainne said. 'We are all the story of our past.'

'Our mother was a cumal, a chieftain's slave. I do not know the story of my birth, but that she was able to keep both of us says a lot about the chieftain. Whatever anger his wives felt that he bedded his slave girl, he was within his right to maintain us. But as bastard children we had no inheritance. At his death, all the property he owned would be divided among his legitimate children, of which there were many. When we were old enough, we were to serve him in the ways that our mother did, bathing him, sweeping his floors, fetching his wine. We would be subject to the life of a cumal until his death.'

'What happened?' Grainne prompted when the boy fell silent.

'Two years ago, when I had six winters, our father was killed by the Fir Bolg south of the Ó Nallon Pass where your king brought victory. In the aftermath of war, two of the chieftain's sons were in contest to rule. The fight was bloody and violent. I cannot say who won or who now rules the clan, for our mother, in the disturbance, carried us from the sept and kept us in the forests.'

Grainne stroked Anú's hair and waited for Dérc to continue.

'We bathed in the big lough—I do not know its name; perhaps the biggest lough in all of Éirinn—and we slept high in the branches of trees at night, for the forests were filled with wolves and boar and all sorts of wild beasts. In the days, we foraged for berries, and mother was good at snaring the smaller mammals so that we could eat. She would set traps and lie in wait, because the smell of an animal would draw the bigger beasts who would eat our food before us if they could.

'That sunless season was the worst; worse than sleeping here on the grasses. We did not have furs and so we clung to each other at night in the cold branches of naked trees. Even now, Anú comes to my bed at night so that I can hold her, but I do not think it is for warmth. I think it is just habit of memory.'

Grainne held the sleeping girl tighter, and she mourned for

their childhood.

Dérc continued. 'It must have been the Yule, or close to it, for the day was extremely short. Mother left us in the trees so that she could hunt and by dark she had not returned. We waited, holding each other for warmth, terrified by every sound of hooting bird or crunching twig below.

'By morning she had still not returned. We came down the tree and I left a mark on its bark in case our mother would return, and we went in search of her.'

He stopped talking then. He lay down and turned away from her, but he shuffled closer so that he could feel the warmth of her leg on his back. Grainne pulled the fur blanket over his shoulders and stroked his arm.

At length, he said, 'I found her before Anú saw, and I told her to turn away. She was too young to see such things. Mother had been mauled—I cannot say by what; a wolf, no doubt.'

Grainne closed her eyes against the tears that she knew would come. She turned and lay Anú down against Dérc's back, and then lay behind them and adjusted the furs so that they were covered in their warmth. In the distance, she could hear the chanting of the appeasements that Marí was still engaged with. Many of the other druids were asleep.

She had thought that Dérc had fallen into slumber, but in the darkness, she saw his head turn, distant firelight glinting in his eyes.

'I had no tools to burn or bury her,' he said. 'But I clawed at the earth with my hands until they bled. The hole was not deep, but I had hoped it would be enough to cover her and give her protection from the beasts that stalked us. And then I carried Anú back to the tree in which we had made home, and we slept there for a further three nights.'

Grainne's tears had come, and she did not try to hold them back. But she wept in silence, for any sob she uttered would interrupt the boy from speaking.

'Every morning since the passing of our mother, Anú told me of her dreams the night before. I was unconvinced that a robed woman had come to her in her sleep and told her which way to journey, but we had no choice. We had picked the area clean of berries and, in the thick winter, even the small mammals were not to be found; I had not mastered mother's use of the traps, even if we could find a hare or two.

'I obliged Anú. I told her I believed that her dreams were real and that we could journey the way she instructed, but in truth I did not know which direction to travel and hers was as good as any.'

She heard him sniffle, but it was not a tearful sound. Grainne reached out and pulled the furs closer to his face to protect him from the cold.

'We journeyed for four nights, maybe five. We continued to sleep in the trees, and we only walked by daylight. She had little legs, so we could not go far each day. We ate what we could, chewing dried sap from the trees just so that we would have something in our stomachs. It made both of us ill, but there was nothing else to eat.

'One day, at the height of the sun, we came across a trackway through the trees. Anú stopped and would go no further. "Why have you stopped?" I asked her. "We are here," she said. We were in the middle of a forest, standing on an overgrown trackway, and she sat on the ground and smiled at me.' Dérc laughed, his voice muffled by the furs and by sleep. 'I asked her what she was doing, and she said, "Now we must wait." And we did. Before sundown, we heard a cart rolling towards us and I tried to lift Anú from the track so that she would not get trampled by the horse, but she would not move. When the cart came into view, Anú stood and waved. The woman in the cart dismounted and asked us what we were doing, alone in the forest. Anú walked to her and embraced her and said, "We were waiting for you."'

Grainne wiped the tears from her eyes, and she smiled. 'Marí,' she said.

'Yes.'

Grainne patted the furs over his shoulder, and he adjusted his position for sleep. Then she kissed Anú's small head, and she curled herself close to them.

'You are both blessed by the gods,' she said. And when she slept, Anú danced in spirals through her dreams.

Chapter 20

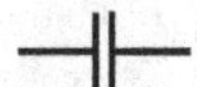

'You cannot go alone,' Etain said.

'What choice do I have? I will not ask you to leave your husband or your children. Continue the training in my absence. Do not let the girls fall fallow.'

Orlaith packed enough supplies for three days, though she did not know how long she would be gone. She dressed Breasal in his finest tunic and wrapped him with a fur cloak. She ensured the leather straps of his winter boots were fastened and then turned back to Etain who stood in her doorway.

'We will be no sooner gone than we are back.'

'What use will an acolyte be to you, Orlaith? He has not completed his studies, and Breasal's dreams do not make him delirious or feverish.'

'The acolyte will know more than you or I.'

'I will not let you go alone.'

Orlaith approached her friend, leading Breasal by the hand. 'I understand your desire to protect me but, woman, I am warning you. Stand aside or I will cut you in two.'

'What lengths will you go to in order to get yourself murdered on the road?'

'Those brigands are not a patch on me, Etain. Let twenty of

them come and I will slaughter them all. Now, please, step aside.'

'At the very least, wear your finest dress as you travel. You could be mistaken for a poor druid in that garb.'

Orlaith smoothed the front of her dress. It was pleated with two colours and the bodice was frilled, but it was otherwise unadorned. 'I am fine. Can I go before I lose the daylight?'

'Have you got your sword?'

'Plain as day at my hip.'

'And your daggers?'

Orlaith touched her right side where one was hidden, and then the pocket that she had sown under her left arm. 'Yes, mother.'

'If you are not back by tomorrow evening, I will come after you.'

'I would expect nothing less.'

Etain backed out of the door and let Orlaith and the child pass. They mounted a carbad that Banan MacColm loaned her— far too wise to ask her not to go—and then Etain handed her the reins. As they set off, she heard Etain shout, 'Be back tomorrow, or I will kill you myself.'

'Such death,' Breasal said, his features set in a cryptic expression.

As they passed through the low stone wall that bordered Banan MacColm's land and turned east to follow the trackway, a solitary holly-blue butterfly danced before them. Though they had been in abundance during the warmer season, it was not unusual to see one in the infancy of autumn, floating free on the breeze as though it had forgotten to journey south or lay its eggs and die.

The morning was unseasonably warm, and the sun was clear and bright. Orlaith shielded her eyes from the glare with a hand as she steered the horses. She knew the neighbouring tribe's druid was not there—he had told her so—and would no doubt have reached his most sacred place by now, somewhere out in the distant east. But it was her hope that the man's acolyte would have some words of wisdom for her, some tincture that Breasal could drink at night to put an end to his nightmares. She would not allow him to become a druid; it was not the life he needed. She had expected to grow old with him, watching him as he tilled a farm and married a wife and gave her grandchildren. That was the life she had ordained for him. He would be a fine farmer and he would raise a sword when he needed to. If he could not rise through the ranks of man because of the birthmark that washed half of his face in red failure, he could at least own a farm and a wife.

In the sunlight, the left half of his face glowed with a visceral heat.

She nudged him as the horses carried them along the narrow track. 'You can count the butterflies as we go. It will do you good to learn your numbers.'

'There is one,' he said. 'There will be only one.'

When the sun was high overhead, she reined in the horses and pulled the carbad to a stop by a shallow ditch. There had been no further butterfly sightings, and no attack by murderous brigands.

She worked with silent efficiency, unfurling her pack and spreading a fur rug on the cool ground. She took out two small leather wraps, undid the knots at their strings, and handed one to Breasal, who had settled on the fur at her side. He picked at the hardened bread with disinterest and, as he chewed, she watched him. His eyes never stopped taking in his surroundings, as though he was studying the landscape, taking note of the trees at their back, or the shapes and patterns on the stones and rocks at their feet.

A hedgehog, not often seen by human eyes, scurried through the scrub and Breasal laughed. When it was gone, he returned his attention to the ground. He picked up two flat stones of equal size, rubbed them between his thumb and fingers, and then raised them one at a time to blot the sun from his eyes. He pocketed the silver-grey stones in the pouch at the front of his tunic.

It had been years since they were alone in the forest together, and Orlaith was reminded of her journey from Ailigh after the loss of her husband. She had embraced the overking and then her brother, and she walked away without focused intent, leading a horse into the forest at the south of Ailigh's hills, in the direction Rónán had returned from the Ó Nallon Pass with Fionn's body in tow. Her baby, who, at the time, had taken Fionn's name, was swaddled tight in her arms and their nights were spent in quiet solitude, the evening air disturbed only by the sounds of distant wolf packs and the scurrying of rodents among the trees.

She had been lost——emotionally as well as physically——and her only anchor to sanity had been her child. He was the one that forced her to wake in the mornings instead of slipping into the tearless void of lunacy. She would bathe in icy streams and dampen a cloth to clean her son, holding him tight always, unwilling to feel the remove of that contact, and then they would watch the morning blossom into life and they would continue their aimless journey.

She studied him now, the length of his thick eyelashes, the curve of his chin. She would not let him become a druid, not so long as someone was out there killing them with indiscriminate blows. It was no life to have, gods be damned.

When they had finished their meagre meal, she packed their things away and uncorked a waterskin, letting Breasal drink as much as he desired before she swallowed the remaining water with greed. There would be a stream nearby to refill it, and they would be at the neighbouring tribe lands before nightfall.

When they mounted the carbad and returned to the road, Orlaith sang a song that she had often heard Etain sing as she worked, but after a few lines she forgot the words and the rest of their journey was passed in silence.

They rolled among the tribe's dwellings as an orange sun turned the sky a golden red in the west, and a line of clansmen and women filed towards one of the small homes at the outskirts of the village.

Orlaith tethered the horses and took Breasal's hand. 'We have come to see the druid's acolyte,' she told one of the men.

He flattened his lips. 'You are too late. You may join the queue if you seek to pay your respects.'

There was no justice, Orlaith thought, if even young acolytes were being slaughtered. She squeezed Breasal's hand, but he pulled free from her grip and stood behind the man in line. He lowered his head and waited.

Orlaith put her hand on his shoulder and stood with him. 'How did it happen?' she asked the man.

He spoke over his shoulder, shuffling forward as the line moved. 'He had been picking herbs in the druid's garden when seven arrows pierced him. Those of us who were nearby to witness it ran in the direction the arrows had come from, but there was no sign of anyone. The world is dying.'

'And all the fields are burning,' Orlaith said, remembering

Breasal's prophetic ramblings.

The man grunted. 'There is the truth of it, all right. It will not be long before the sun drops from the sky and never returns. Mark my words.'

They stepped forward with the line. From inside the druid's home, Orlaith could hear the weeping and keening of women. Death was lamented, though a druid would assure you the spirit journeys to the Otherworld. A wake is not for the dead but for the living; a chance to mourn your losses before returning to daily life.

'He will be buried in the morning,' the man told her. 'My wife has a bed that my son no longer uses. You are welcome to it. Not that anyone will sleep tonight.'

'You do me a great kindness, Lord.'

He flapped his hand in a dismissive gesture. 'They call me Cian. My wife, Fionnuala, is one of the mourners you can hear wailing.'

Wailing women were a staple of funerals and they would raise their voices in mourning for the seven days of a man's wake before he is buried. After the funeral, the women would retire to their beds and sleep for days.

When they got to the head of the queue, Cian ducked under the frame of the open door and entered the darkness.

Orlaith said, 'You do not have to enter if you do not wish to.'

Breasal said nothing. At his sides, he clenched and unclenched his fists as though with a nervous energy.

At length, Cian came out of the druid's home where the acolyte was laid in wake, and he told Orlaith to find him by the central fire when she seeks a bed.

She did not have to nudge Breasal forward into the darkness.

When they entered, candles burned in every corner and the petals of flowers were strewn on the floor for the acolyte's spirit to scent his feet before journeying to the gods.

Four women were cross-legged on the floor, crying and wailing and reaching out to touch the frame of the bed while their other hands worried at their beads of eternity.

Orlaith ruffled Breasal's hair and then knelt at the foot of the bed. She touched the young man's shrouded feet, as was custom, and then she bowed her head to the ground in honour of the life that he had lived. She knew Manandán would come for the man's spirit to lead him to the Otherworld, and she wondered, as people often do at wakes, if the gods knew the way to this man's side or, indeed, if they were too busy welcoming other druids into their arms to notice a lowly acolyte. She worried this young man might wander the earth for years without a beckoning from the gods.

When the wailing stopped, Orlaith looked up. The four women pointed with fear and disgust. Breasal had climbed upon the bed and knelt beside the deceased acolyte. From his tunic, he took the two flat stones he had found in the forest and he placed them over the acolyte's eyes before kissing the man's forehead.

She called to him. 'Breasal, do not be disrespectful. What are you doing?'

'The lady told me to.'

'Who did?'

'The dream lady.'

'Come down from there, son.'

Orlaith apologised to the wailing women, but they regarded the boy with squinted eyes and curious smiles. Perhaps recognising something in him that Orlaith hoped to deny, the women rose and embraced Breasal before returning to their stations on the floor and resuming their mournful cries.

She took his hand and led him from the home.

'Did I do wrong, *Mamai*?'

'No, son. I do not believe you did.'

It seemed to Orlaith that the further she tried to hide his druid ways, the brighter they shone.

She shared a drink with Cian and his wife that evening as Breasal slept on the floor with his head in her lap. And when the morning came with a wash of mournful rain, the people of the tribe followed a procession towards the grave site at the edge of the sept. Orlaith clung to Breasal's hand and refused to let go in case he threw himself upon the body before the tumulus was laid.

The chieftain addressed his people and spoke at length of the perils of dark times they faced. Though his druid was at Emain Macha, and the acolyte was departed, he imposed a curfew on his tribesmen. Everyone must be inside the walls that ringed their borders when the sun touched the western ridges.

Orlaith expected Banan MacColm would do the same when she told him what had transpired.

After the funeral, when she was preparing to leave, Cian and his wife came to her and offered her a small pack of cheese and curds for the journey. The woman, short and sturdy, leaned down and hugged Breasal. She stared into his eyes and said, 'When it is your time to pass from us, many years from now, the wailing will be twice as loud as ever heard throughout the land.'

Breasal kissed the woman's wrinkled cheek. 'The dream lady is pleased with you,' he said. 'She will wait by your bed until you are ready to go.'

There was nothing he could say now, Orlaith thought, that would ever make him sound like a five-year-old boy.

Chapter 21

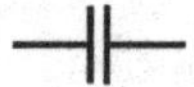

Rónán's men spread out across the ramparts, searching every brú and store hut. He was certain they would find nothing, but it was his duty to try. Seanach had been a great friend over the years since the man took control of the Mac Fachtna tribe on Ailigh's eastern reaches. His death—within his own walls, no less—was Rónán Ó Mordha's responsibility.

He humbled himself before Seanach's men when he informed them of his passing. 'I will not stop until his murderer has been brought before me and beheaded,' he told them.

The four men huddled together in deliberations before one of them approached him. 'Seanach Mac Fachtna was a true chieftain, and a friend to the Ó Mordha tribesmen. I will personally return to our lands to inform Seanach's tanist of his death. I will take his body with me and there will be a period of great mourning. After this time, if you have not presented us with our chieftain's murderer, relations between our tribes will be demolished and we will be forced to invade your borders in retribution. You have seven nights.'

He paid the men a tribute before they left in honour of his fallen friend. The man was right. Though he did not drive the dagger through Seanach's heart himself, he was responsible.

While his men searched the hillside and the surrounding forests for signs of hasty retreat, Rónán gathered his guards and questioned them. They had seen nothing through the night, they said, save for the drunken revellers who weaved through the ramparts with merry abandon, as was always the case.

Diarmuid came to him with news that he had spotted some broken and flattened shrubbery in the southern forest that was indicative of a careless hideaway, some small evidence of discarded food, but that he could not be certain how long ago the camp spot had been used.

When the remaining chieftains reconvened, their hangovers forgotten but heads sore with concern, Fergal said, 'It is not your fault, Lord.'

'When you walk through my gates, I am responsible for your security. This is my burden.'

'I cannot fathom why anyone would do such a thing,' Torin Ó Neill said. 'If you are going to sneak into a king's fortified sept, why kill one of the visiting chieftains and not the overking himself?'

'Perhaps Seanach was the target,' Ainmire Úi Balon said, and his son nodded in agreement. 'Does he have enemies?'

'He is a tribal chieftain,' Rónán said. 'Who among you does not have an enemy?'

From his position at Rónán's left, Cormac said, 'I cannot help but think this is connected to the assassination of druids.'

'Druids, livestock and now chieftains?' Rónán asked. 'If this is their game, I do not understand the rules.'

Fergal nursed his shorn limb as though it pained him. He had buckled his new metal arm on and was clearly unused to the feeling of its weight. 'The thought did cross my mind, also, Rónán.

This is not a war in the traditional sense. Why has no one stood on a battlefield and declared their intentions? I would feel happier if they outright attacked rather than dicking about in the shadows.'

'Spineless bastards,' Ardál agreed. 'If they seek to pit us against one another, it will not work.'

'It is already working,' Rónán said. 'With Seanach's death, the Mac Fachtna tribe has every right to exact revenge upon my borders. Is this their endgame? Distract us while they— what?—charge in from behind and take our seats? But why us? Why the north? If you seek to govern, you would strike at the heart of Éirinn's leadership; you would take the Ard Rí's seat at Teamhair.'

Fergal slapped his metal fist on the table. 'I am not doing that bastard journey to Teamhair again. I am running out of arms to lose. But how do you fight an enemy that you cannot see?'

'We have seven nights to find out.'

Their journey towards Teamhair five years ago, when the southern king, Rían Ó Hargon, had stamped his way north in his campaign to free the Fir Bolg slaves and rule all of Éirinn, had been an arduous expedition. They fought the foreign army at the Ó Nallon Pass and, though they were successful, they had lost many great men. And Fergal's left arm.

The chieftains looked at each other around the table but none of them had an answer. If their enemy was cloaked in shadow and hidden from view, without demand or staged attack, there was no way of knowing who targeted them or what their goal was.

'It is confusion they seek, and they are winning,' Diarmuid said.

Fergal stood. 'I need a drink. But I assure you, Lord, I stand at your side. Whether it is to fight a nameless enemy, or Mac Fachtna's men, you can count on me.'

Torin and Ainmire agreed. Torin said, 'Seanach's tanist will know you are faultless when we stand beside you against him. This is not a war he will win.'

To Cormac, when the others had returned to the barrel hut, Rónán said, 'I am at fault. They each know it. As do you.'

'You cannot blame yourself.'

'Who else is to blame?' Rónán said, his voice raised, his cheeks flushed in anger. 'He was murdered within my walls. I am as good as guilty of murdering him with my own hand.'

'Rónán, nobody blames you.'

'Everyone blames me.'

'This was not your fault. The assassins are——'

'Enough. I am to blame, and I will face the retribution that is owed to me.'

'It could have happened to anyone.'

'It happened to me. I will not argue with you. Leave my side.'

Cormac cleared his throat. He bowed and left.

In a rage, Rónán swept his arm across the table, flipping cups of water and plates of fruit onto the floor. The tallow candle blinked and stuttered.

He returned to the inner wall from the great hall and checked the gate of the concealed tunnel that led down to the lough. It was barred and had not been tampered with. He unlocked it and journeyed down through the hillside, rich with the smell of wet earth, and wondered if they had left the tunnel gate open the night before. But he was certain they had barred and locked it on their return. At the time, he may have been outside the walls, rutting in the sand with Cormac, when the assassination of his good friend took place, or he could have been asleep in bed. Regardless, he had not been able to stop it.

Not since Mordha the Terrible had his tribe faced such hard times. Mordha, father of his tribesmen, who could slay five hundred men with one stroke of his sword, was said to be a giant of a man with a moustache that stretched as far as his nipples and fists the size of boulders from Mac Cumall's Causeway. It was said he was a son of the son of Lugh, and as a lad, when he rejected the Morrígan's advances, she wept for seven years.

Mordha took only one wife, a golden-haired daughter of Aengus. Her father was the illicit son of the Dagda and the very comely Boann and, in his bid to hide their affair, the Dagda made the sun stand still in the heights of the sky for nine full months. Boann fell pregnant, grew with child, and gave birth to Aengus within one day so that no one was any the wiser. The annals of time do not say how many children Mordha and his wife produced, but it was more than enough boys to fill an army.

At the time of his pre-eminence, when all the land adored him for his skill in combat, it is told that the Dagda came to him and said, 'Mordha, you who are skilful with the sword and mighty of mind. My son Aedh has been killed and I am to build a rath to house his remains. And the rath shall be called Grianán Ailigh. Will you honour your people by residing in this rath to protect my son's remains?'

Mordha the Terrible, who loved the king, agreed that he would remain at Grianán Ailigh until his dying day and he would defend the hill on which the Dagda's son was buried. What followed was fifty years of torment for Mordha, who battled armies on all sides as rival clans devised plans to topple Grianán Ailigh and claim the hillside and the kingship as their own. From the top of Grianán Ailigh's walls, Mordha the Terrible threw stones that blinded the armies who attacked him, and he spat a venom from his lips that burned the flesh of his enemies.

The remains of the Dagda's son, Aedh, were never disturbed, even after the Dagda's passing into the Otherworld, and though Mordha the Terrible did not know another day of peace, he fought each opposing army with an almighty vigour that made fear grow in the hearts of man. For fifty years, the sword was a permanent fixture in his hand, and he would strike a man to kill him, and blink his eyes for a moment of sleep, so that he was rested even on the battlefield. He fought this way for the seven years of his war with Ulhail from the south, and when he finally slaughtered Ulhail on the field outside Grianán Ailigh, on the shortest day of the year when the sun stood still, the Morrígan came to him in the guise of a crow, and she perched upon his thatching and watched over his home for seven days while he slept.

Rónán could not imagine warring for fifty years. When he was eight years old, he came to Ailigh to train under the rule of King Déaglán and his tanist, Oisín, and he took the tribal name of Mordha the Terrible. He and Áed, his first love, had been in awe of Déaglán, and they longed to live up to Mordha's good name.

Now his neighbouring chieftain was dead within his walls and his livestock were poisoned. The druids were being slaughtered and the wheat was withering with rust. He felt as though it was his fault. Every sting that itched him was a betrayal of the Mordha name. Though Mordha the Terrible was the father of his tribe, Rónán was now its leader. In taking the oath of kingship, he had the honour of protecting the remains of the Dagda's son who was buried beneath Rónán's brú in the centre of the hill. He did not think often of those remains, buried under so many rods of earth beneath him, but every time he passed through the secret tunnel that led from his inner walls to the lough, when he reached the small section on a downward turn where the soil was not so much black as it was red, he wondered—is Aedh's body nearby? With an absence of mind, he would touch that rich red soil as he crept along the tunnel, and he did so now before he came into the afternoon sun by the lough's edge.

He was king of the sons of Mordha, overking of the north. When he died and passed from this world to the next, Mordha the Terrible would stand before him and block his way. Not in the history of all that has been told has there been a murder within Ailigh's walls. He could not consider himself a failure, for even a failure has attempted to succeed.

He walked across the shore of the lough from the tunnel's exit and came to the standing stone that was erected in Áed's honour. He touched the sword carved into its side and pressed his forehead against the rough stone.

Though Cormac was his consort, and he loved him true, he could not—would not—forget the boy who made him feel love for the first time. He had grown alongside Áed, fought beside him, and held him as he died in his arms. Rónán closed his eyes. 'What has become of us?' he asked. 'You journey among the gods and recite your truths to their ears, and I am here, alive, struggling to succeed where you left off. The world is a dark place, Áed. It is so dark that I forget about you sometimes and your name is furthest from my mind. I am sorry. Though I have found new love, you are always in my heart. It cannot be any other way.'

When a hand touched his shoulder, he closed his eyes. He knew it was Cormac—he did not need to look—and he knew that Áed sent his consort here to comfort him.

'I am sorry, Cormac,' Rónán said without turning to him.

Cormac slipped his arms around Rónán, pressing his chest to Rónán's back. 'If you were not angry with me, I would not have felt the need to seek you out and hold you. Your words do not hurt me, Lord, because I see in your eyes that you do not mean them.'

'I meant them when I said them.'

'And now?'

Rónán leaned his head back against Cormac's cheek. 'Now, I do not want to say another word.'

They made love on the sand as the sun crept high in the sky, with Áed's standing stone beside them and the Dagda's son buried deep within the hillside. And when he climaxed, Rónán held Cormac tight and wept against his hair. Seanach was dead. And his livestock were poisoned. And Grainne was half a country away—alive or dead, he did not know. And all the world was against him.

They returned to the inner walls of Ailigh, and when Rónán bathed from a heated bowl of water, he kissed his consort and dressed, journeying down to Achall's home on the second rampart.

'I will ask to see my son,' he told Cormac.

'When she is ready, she will let you,' Cormac said.

'I will ask her every day until I see him.'

When he knocked on Achall's door, he got no response. He knocked a second time and found the door barred.

He heard young Áed's voice call, 'Who is it?'

'It is your father, son. Open the door that I may see you.'

'*Mamaí* is asleep. She sleeps most of the day. I cannot open the door. Why does she keep me from you, *Daidí*?'

Rónán sighed and pressed his hand flat against the pocked wood of the door. He did not say it aloud, but he thought it was for the best. He was no role model.

He was no son of Mordha.

Chapter 22

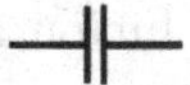

Muirgel stood upon the watchtower that overlooked the rough sea. The froth of heavy waves smacked against her island. Above her, a siege of herons rushed towards the distant cliffs of Éirinn as the eastern sun birthed from the horizon's loins. The cold season had invaded her shores and her bones, and she held with tight fingers the fur-lined cloak that adorned her shoulders.

It was the Day of Pardons, an annual opportunity for her people, the farmers and the landowners, to come to her with their concerns and she would offer her wisdoms and verdicts. The King of Thúr Rí was the instigator of this delight, and Muirgel, against her better judgement, had agreed to keep up the ritual when her druid implored her. She was kind and fair to her people lest they turn on her.

She suffered the tribulations of her islanders—their land disputes and cattle thievery, their adultery and property destruction—with a tight-lipped quietude that belied her desire to lock herself away in a prison of her own making.

This was her penance for slaughtering the island's king in his bed after he had taken her with a yearning that outlasted his prowess. He may have been a better lover than Donal, her first husband, but he was always quick to climax and quicker to sleep.

She did not love him, but it was an act of kindness that clutched her fist around the hilt of a dagger and sliced it across his neck as his drunken snores echoed through the room and clung to the walls as a memory. She did the island a kindness by dispatching him. He was a weak leader, a man too fond of drink and sex to be any good to his people.

She looked east towards Éirinn and waited in the morning chill. A small convoy of ten-man curragh boats were approaching, their small sails unfurled in the wind. Dásan would be among them.

When they docked, she watched as her bed-mate climbed the hillside and crossed under the gates. He slapped the back of one of his warriors and laughed with him before turning towards the watchtower and mounting the stairs to stand behind her on the platform. She did not look at him.

'My queen.'

'What news?'

'The northern territories are in disrepair, my lady. They squabble among themselves, and their food sources are low. Their animals are dying at an alarming rate.'

'It is not enough.'

'It is just the beginning, my lady,' Dásan said. He came to her side to look across the ocean. 'While my men instigated the phases of your plan, I received word from our distant cousins.'

'Are they well?'

'They flourish, Lady. I had paid them substantial tribute. They will act according to your will.'

'I am glad to hear it.' Muirgel turned from the wall and Dásan took her hand as he helped her down the narrow, rain-soaked steps. 'It is the Day of Pardons.'

'I will bathe and be at your side, my queen.'

Muirgel returned to her great hall and sat alone as her islanders gathered outside. She adjusted the fur across her knees and fingered the elaborate torc at her neck with three filigreed balusters that slanted to her breast. It was decorated with intricate carvings of the giant elk that once roamed Éirinn, whose bones, when pieced together, were as tall as three men.

Dásan, bathed and dressed in his finery, entered from a side door, and took the stool at her left. The druid, once she had opened the main door to allow the people to enter, would take her place at Muirgel's right. Their purpose during the Pardons was to advise or inform their queen when she did not have all the facts of a case brought before her.

The hall filled with her people and, in the corner, the iron-smith stopped his work to watch. His kennel was almost complete, the large iron door prepared and ready for hanging.

The druid stood. 'Great people of Thúr Rí. Your queen bids you all vigour and longevity. The winter months are upon us and, as the days darken, now is the time for penance. Speak your crimes before the sun is reborn and let the darkness swallow your misdeeds. Free yourself of the burden of your sins. Step forward, all who wish to speak.'

Seven men came forward from the crowd and knelt before the raised dais. The youngest was no older than fifteen or sixteen winters, the eldest long into his fifth decade.

The druid sat and pointed at the boy. 'Free yourself of the burden of your sins.'

The boy blushed, his head low, and mumbled his crime.

'Speak louder,' Dásan commanded. 'Your queen does not hear the whispers of cowards.'

'I took relations with my cousin,' the boy said. A ripple of laughter washed through the crowd as though his crime had been known by all in advance of today's trials.

'Bring forth this boy's cousin and her parents,' Dásan said.

When they stood before the dais, the druid asked, 'Is she with child?'

'She has not had the sickness yet,' the girl's mother said.

'We will watch her in the coming weeks. I will prepare an elixir so that she does not produce a child. Do you wish that they be wed?'

'I do not,' the girl's father said.

'My queen?'

Muirgel nodded with thoughtfulness. It was an expression she had practiced often. 'You will do your uncle's bidding until the sun is reborn. This is the end of the matter. No further retribution will be sought.'

The boy bowed, placing his forehead on the ground, and then he rose from his knees and left, his cousin and her parents trailing behind him. Muirgel saw the look in the girl's eyes—yearning mixed with shame. It would not be the last time the boy had his way with her.

'Free yourself of the burden of your sins,' the druid said.

The second man bowed. 'I took three of my brother's sheep when my own ewes gave me still-born lambs. I offered him penance, but he would not accept.'

Muirgel was already bored. That the Day of Pardons coincided with her plans across the ocean was a great pain to her. She would spend the morning listening to the petty sins of man, absolving them of their wrongs, and then presiding over trials that were not freely given. Those who come forward to confess were given leniency for their honesty. Those who underwent the trial of their transgressions would, if found guilty, suffer significant costs.

Muirgel pardoned the man of his sheep theft on the condition that he returned the stolen lambs, and said, 'This is the end of the matter. No further retribution will be sought.'

She listened to the remaining confessors with abject disinterest. She had asked her druid some years ago why the people needed to speak aloud their crimes before she could absolve them. No crime, during the Day of Pardons, was too shocking for absolution. A man could admit to murdering his family and Muirgel would honour the tradition of pardoning him. It had been her intention to shorten the lengthy procedure by offering an all-encompassing forgiveness of offences.

'A crime needs to be spoken aloud before it can be absolved,' the old druid said. 'Even when we confess to the gods, we do so with ready lips.'

It made little sense, but Muirgel did not press the matter.

When the morning had given way to afternoon and the confessions became trials, Muirgel sat upright in her chair and worked the knuckles of her left hand with her thumb. When she pressed against the pain, it lessened.

By early evening, if she had to listen to another accusation of inappropriate sexual relations, she would slice the throats of every man and woman on the island, climb into a curragh, and set sail for some other distant shore.

The final trial of the day saw two men stand before her. She looked around for an adulterous wife but saw none. 'This man stole my field,' the accuser said.

Muirgel smiled. 'And where did he take it?'

The defendant said, 'The field was rightfully mine and always has been. It belongs to my father's property.'

'The field has been in my possession for generations.'

'Your family stole it from mine.'

'Enough,' Dásan said. 'Address your queen with respect.'

Muirgel stood and heard her ankles pop. She had forgone food while the trials continued—as had everyone else—and now her stomach screamed. To the accuser, she asked, 'How far back can you claim the field as yours?'

'My father's father's father weaned his lambs on that field, my queen.'

'And you—how old is your claim to this field?'

The accused said, 'My grandfather's grandfather was born among those grasses when his mother could not make the journey to the druid. Ask anybody—the field is rightfully mine.'

Muirgel looked at her druid.

'Not me,' she said. 'I may be old, but not old enough to birth a man's grandfather's grandfather. It will have been my predecessor.'

Muirgel studied the two men, then turned to the gathered crowd. 'Who can lay credence to either man's claim?'

The islanders were silent.

'Very well. I have considered it, and this is your forfeit.'

'Mine or his?' the accuser asked.

Muirgel returned to the dais and sat before speaking. The hush that draped over the crowd was thick with expectation. 'As none among you can prove ownership of this field, it now belongs to me. You cannot squabble over something that is not owned by either of you. This is the end of the matter. No further retribution will be sought.'

Both men tried to argue their case, but Dásan stood and silenced them. 'Your queen has spoken. The matter is concluded.'

He cleared the hall and when he stood alone with Muirgel, she said, 'Post a guard at the gate of this field. I am not convinced either man will not sleep in it this night to stake their claim.'

When she returned to the watchtower to stare across the waters that separated her island from Éirinn, the sky was dark, and the winds were strong. She gripped the wall and searched the blackness for the hint of rocky formations on the horizon. Nothing was visible beyond the stretch of her own hills and the foam that nestled there in rockpools that, when she was a child, she would have plundered for toad spawn if she had lived so near the coastline.

She heard the hooting of nightbirds and, as the wind took the breath from her lungs, she realised her chest burned. She sought out her druid.

'Your joints are stiffening, and your bones are weakening, my queen. It comes with age.'

Muirgel raised her chin. 'If my bones are soft, yours must be liquid.'

'You need to exercise your body as you do your mind. A brisk walk every morning and evening is in order. I will double your nightly tincture so that you are invigorated by morning's light.'

Before retiring to her quarters, Muirgel said, 'When Éirinn is mine, I will walk daily the length and breadth of it. But for now, do something about my pains or it will be you who takes a walk—off the cliffs.'

The nightmares came to her again that night. She could not wait a year to know that her curse on Rónán Ó Mordha would work. When she had turned the bullán stones against the sun and spoke aloud his name, she knew the gods understood her pain. He had wronged her and would succumb to the gods' wrath within the year. But a year was a long time to wait. By her actions, she would hurry along his fall from the stones upon which he stood.

And her pains would subside as his increased.

Chapter 23

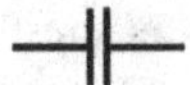

Orlaith refused to cry as she drove the carbad home after the acolyte's funeral. In the drizzle of rain that beaded on their hair in the early afternoon gloom, she glanced at Breasal with a regularity that told her she was obsessing. But the boy stared at the narrow track ahead and turned to look at some flower, bird or tree when her eyes came to him.

He was too young to understand, she assured herself. He would not know that the words he spoke, or the dreams he suffered, were given to him by the gods. She had asked him, as they rolled out of the sept, to describe the dream lady that he mentioned, the one who told him to place his flat stones upon the acolyte's sightless eyes. He had shrugged and said, 'Bright.'

'How do you mean, bright? Was she smiling and happy?'

Breasal pursed his lips and pointed at the sky. 'Bright like the sun.'

'Was she tall? Short? Fat? Beautiful or ugly?'

'She was bright,' he insisted.

They did not speak again until they broke in the late afternoon to eat at the same spot they had eaten the day before, when their journey had been ahead of them and she was not yet convinced that her son was destined to be a druid. Breasal walked in circles looking for the hedgehog they had seen yesterday, and Orlaith spread a fur on the wet ground. The rain had ceased but the clouds were leaden and pregnant.

She unfurled the wrap of cheese and dried curds that Cian's wife had given her, and she split them into equal portions. The cheese had a hardening shell, but the centre was soft and moist, and it flaked against her lips as she tore from it with her teeth.

She did not want him to become a druid—but she could not stop it. If she refused to allow him to attend any of the druids' compounds for training, the gods would speak to him still and his dreams would intensify. She knew how it went for others. There were whispers in the dark from unnatural voices, vivid dreams of untold realities, and soon the apparition of a god or, in Breasal's case, a goddess—his dream lady—who would tell him her name and then he would no longer belong to Orlaith but to his goddess. And though she wished the gods had never laid eyes on him or heard his name, she could not curse them, for gods were above the curses of man.

She could no longer hope that his dreams would diminish and his eyes would stop shining with wet enthusiasm when he spoke the words he had heard in his dreams. There was no denying his nature. Soon, her child would no longer be hers. Whether of his own volition, or at the behest of a druid, he would be taken from her arms and, when he visited her again, he would be a man, an unrecognisable adult who would not seek the comfort of her embrace.

'Sit with me, Breasal,' she said, nudging his portion of cheese to indicate it. He sat and scrunched his nose with disappointment that the hedgehog had not come to visit him. Orlaith tousled his hair and she noticed a narrow scratch on his left temple, a dark red line masked by the redness of his birthmark. When she leaned close to inspect his wound, she saw the broken line of dried blood that curled beside his thin eyebrow and rose into his hairline. 'What is this?'

Breasal ate his cheese with delicate bites.

'Who did this?'

She parted his hair to see the extent of the damage, tracing the thin line with her fingertip. He did not flinch. The dried crack in his scalp curled again and twisted in a new direction, one line that continued from his temple, through the side of his head and over the top of his crown before turning and cracking back on itself.

'Who did this?' she repeated.

She brushed his hair from the twisting scratch and saw, with a sickening realisation, that the pattern it made was identical to one of the runes Breasal had drawn in the soil around their home. She reached for his hand and inspected his fingers. The nail on his forefinger was splintered and there were particles of dried blood embedded beneath it.

She pulled him tight against her. 'Why, son? What does it mean?'

With his face buried in her cloak, he turned his head and said, 'Tears are not for now. Tears are for other times.'

'What other times?'

'Many other times.'

She sobbed against his hair.

When she stilled herself, she wrapped the remaining cheese and curds back into her pack and nudged her son onto the carbad. 'If we hurry, we will be home before dark.'

'Tighten your cloak,' Breasal said. 'It will rain.'

'Did the dream lady tell you that?'

He looked at her with narrow eyes. 'The clouds told me that,' he said, and before she had whipped the reins, the black clouds were torn open and their contents saturated the land.

They wheeled into their sept as the diffuse light of evening softened towards darkness, and Etain sat on a stool in front of Orlaith's door with a cloak held above her head against the rain. She came to them and slapped the horses' necks as Orlaith and Breasal dismounted.

'Well? Is he cured?'

'How long have you sat here?'

'Since the moment you left.'

'Etain, you'll catch a fever. Come inside.'

'Is he cured?'

When they gathered by the fire in Orlaith's brú and Orlaith helped Breasal into a clean, dry tunic, she wrung her thick hair by the flames and the rainwater sizzled as it splashed the burning logs.

'The acolyte is dead. Killed some days before we got there. Whoever targets the druids, they are also killing the innocent trainees.'

'So, he is not cured.'

'Etain,' Orlaith said, the shock thick in her voice. 'A young man is dead. Have respect.'

'What will you do now?'

'How can you cure such a thing?' Orlaith added another log to the fire and draped Breasal's wet clothes over a stool to dry. Outside, a violent wind rattled her door. 'If he is called, we cannot stop him from answering.'

'When the gods knock,' Etain agreed, 'you let them in, or

they will blow through your house as though it were made of reeds.'

Orlaith poured a cup of sweet wine for her and Etain, and then she settled on the floor beside Breasal's bed. He had climbed into it without a word and now his breathing was slow and deep. His eyes twitched in his sleep.

'He is dreaming,' Etain said. 'When his eyes wander in his sleep, he is searching for something in his dreams.'

'He will wake with more words of godly wisdom, then. A puzzle we cannot fathom.'

'What will you do?'

Orlaith drank from her cup before responding. She had been considering her options all day—for many days, she realised— and could only now come to a decision. 'I will go north to Ailigh. The druid, Grainne, may be able to guide me.'

'I told you, she will not be there. All druids congregate in the east at their special place.'

'Sacred place,' Orlaith corrected. 'That may be so, but my brother is there, and the overking, Rónán Ó Mordha. If Grainne has journeyed east, they will know the way. They will help me.'

'What help is mortal man against an army of assassins intent on killing our druids?'

'What help are the gods?' Orlaith asked.

Etain slumped on the floor beside Orlaith. 'Please. It will do no good. It is better to harbour here in safety. Shield him from the world and no one may ever know the dreams he endures or the words he speaks.'

'I can hide him from man, but I cannot hide him from the truth, Etain. I will journey north tomorrow.'

'Then at least leave the boy here. Go to Ailigh, see your

brother and his king, bring them back so that they can help protect him. But do not take him on the road with you.'

'I will not let him out of my sight.'

'It is too dangerous.'

'Have I not trained you with a sword? You know what I am capable of. Do not argue with me, Etain.'

'Were you never taught to respect your elders?'

'Piss off, you are barely a winter older than me. I have made my mind up.'

'Twelve winters if a day,' Etain said. 'Now change your mind before I break your bones and you cannot go anywhere.'

'Break them and I will crawl to Ailigh. Is that what you want? I will crawl there with Breasal on my back if I have to.'

'It is too dangerous.'

'You said that already.'

Etain stood. She tipped the remains of her wine into the fire and sat the cup on the small table against the far wall. 'I know you want an answer to his woes, but if he is truly blessed, you cannot stop it. Let him converse with the gods in the comfort of his own home. As soon as you reveal his ways to anyone outside our tribe, you expose him to the assassins who will seek his ruin. You will be his death.'

Orlaith turned from her to watch her son sleep. 'I know you have love in your heart, but your words cut deeper than a sword. It is late and I am tired. Good night, Etain.'

'Orlaith.'

'Good night.'

Etain left and closed the door behind her with a quietness that revealed her care for the child's sleep even in her anger.

Alone with Breasal's nasal breathing, Orlaith pressed her back against the wattle wall and closed her eyes. She listened to the crack of the flames that licked over the blackening logs and, when the wind eased outside, she opened her door and circled her brú, searching the wet earth for signs of her son's runes. There was the occasional faint indent in the ground, but the runes had long since vanished. She wondered if they were still protected even if the runes had disappeared. But, more to the point, protected from what? If her son had carved a safeguard spell that hid him from the assassins, she was not convinced that taking him to Ailigh would be a good idea. But if the runes were nothing more than a god's blessing, he could be discovered with readiness no matter where he lay his head.

She circled her brú twice before returning to the warmth within and closing the door. She nudged Breasal's small body deeper into his bed and she lay down beside him. If the gods spoke to him in his dreams, she would hold her breath and listen. In the quiet of night, perhaps she would hear them.

She would not implore them to leave him alone; it was too late for that. When the gods speak to you, you answer them. There was no other choice.

He would listen. And he would speak the words of the gods to anyone who could hear him. The only way to stop it was by removing his heart from his chest. But if anyone tried, she would kill them all. She would stand before him for the rest of his days, even as he preached his godly words, and she would protect him as any mother can—with violence in the face of fear.

She understood Etain's warning but, just as her son had no choice, so too was she bound by her duty to his care. She would take him to Ailigh in the hope that Grainne had not yet journeyed east. Orlaith had not returned to the northern tribal lands in which her brother resided since her husband's funeral. She was not sure she was strong enough to face her own fears, never mind Breasal's. But she would make the journey and, in doing so, she would alleviate Breasal's confusion as she lessened her own anxiety.

She curled her arm around his chest and pressed her lips against the back of his head. They would lie together until the day of her death. No man or god will ever come between them.

In the morning, when the birds shouted their orders to the dew-coated insects, and the wet crack under her door was bathed in early sunlight, she rose and pulled the furs over Breasal's shoulders. She would wake him as late as possible, for the days ahead would be long and arduous. She gathered two packs and filled them with what she felt was necessary—food and cloth-ing, a brush for their hair, the only clasp she owned that held her wiry strands out of her eyes, and their wooden toothpicks for their morning rituals. She found a small flat stone outside their home, and she dusted the dried earth from it and dropped it into Breasal's pack in case he needed to place it on someone else's eye.

She had not returned Banal MacColm's carbad or his horses the night before, and she watered them and brushed them down as the sun crept skyward from the eastern horizon. If she were quick, they could leave before anyone noticed their absence.

When she returned to her home and stirred Breasal from his slumber, he sat up and blinked against the glare of a fresh morn-ing, the door wide and the woodlice scurrying in the doorway.

'Are you not hungry?' he asked. She would, on any other morning, have already prepared breakfast for him.

'We will eat later. Where are your boots?'

'Where are we going?'

'North,' was all she said.

'North to the king?'

She looked at him, held his face between her hands and kissed his forehead. 'Yes, son. North to the king.'

He climbed from his bed and donned his boots.

When they left their brú and turned to walk the short distance to the carbad, Orlaith saw Etain approach. The woman wore her training garb, her sword secured at her hip.

'This is not the time, Etain. Train the others in my absence. But you will not stop me from leaving. I have a duty to my son.'

'And I have a duty to you,' Etain told her. 'We all do.'

From among the huts, Orlaith's trainee female warriors stepped forward. They each wore their padded tunics and their swords hung at their left hips.

'I am sorry,' Orlaith said. 'I do not have time for this.'

'We will not let you go alone,' Etain said.

'I have Breasal and all the gods at my back.'

'That is not what I meant.'

Orlaith mounted the carbad and motioned for Breasal to join her. 'Ladies, please, this is not the time for foolery. You have your lives, your husbands and fathers. Go back to your homes. I will be well on the road.'

'It is not you we worry for,' Etain said. 'We have met with our husbands and our fathers. We have told them the way of it. If Breasal journeys north, so too do we.'

Orlaith shook her head. She stepped down from the carbad and stood before her friend. 'I cannot ask you to do this.'

'You are not asking; we are commanding it. Orlaith, if you go, we go. It is all arranged. We have our swords and our provisions.

Are you ready?'

'Etain,' Orlaith said. She had no more words.

'I know. You are sorry for what you said last night. Say no more of it. You were right to worry, right to seek answers in the north. But I—we—will not let you worry alone.'

Orlaith embraced her. She looked at each of the women and smiled.

'Hush now,' Etain said. 'If you spill tears, I will gouge your eyes out with a rusted blade.'

Orlaith laughed. She hugged Etain again and she mounted the carbad with her son. 'Are you ready?' she asked him.

He looked behind him at the assembly of women, and then he pointed to the road. 'The path is this way,' he said.

'The path is always that way,' Orlaith said, ruffling his hair. She whipped the reins, and the horses cantered forward. Behind her, forty girls and women in thick, padded tunics and winter boots, formed two lines and marched in unison. Etain sang a hero's song. And soon, the others sang along with her.

Chapter 24

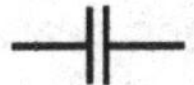

Emain Macha was steeped in silence. As the sun rose to cast its rays upon the grass, the assembly of druids took to their knees and pressed their foreheads to the damp earth, facing westward, as was tradition. With closed eyes, they prayed to their gods for guidance.

Grainne called upon her most gracious lady Cáer, and in the emptiness of her mind, she was greeted only with quiet. A hand-drum beat a solitary thump and its note echoed inside her head. Silence settled around her. She could hear, beside her, Anú's shallow breath. And then a voice cried out from across the enclosure.

'Ashton, son of Pol.'

Without looking, Grainne knew that the druid who had been named would stand and face the sun.

The drum beat again.

Somewhere outside, the horses whinnied.

'Gilleán, son of Osán,' another voice spoke.

Grainne tightened her eyes. Two names called; two remaining. She pleaded to Cáer that the goddess would speak to her, but still nothing came.

Another name was called. 'Caoimhe, of Clan Ranait.' The

female druid would now stand with the other two.

Beside her, Anú pressed her hand on top of Grainne's. When Grainne looked at her, the girl whispered, 'She tells me your name.'

Grainne shook her head, and before Anú could speak aloud, a fourth name was uttered into the silence. 'Rannal, son of Tuile.'

The drum rattled a longer beat. The four nominees stood while the assembly took to their haunches. The nominees raised their hands to the sky and praised the sun god, and then they knelt. The remaining druids rose and came forward, placing their hands on the heads of the four nominees in turn, gifting them the love and wisdom of their gods.

A sacrifice would be made and, in the morning, a new archdruid would be elected.

In times of history, when it was necessary to elect a new leader, the process would have begun on the nearest fire festival with feasting and moments of godly solitude. Visions would be invoked around the fires, and discussions of merit would be had. Bones would be cast, and omens studied. But although the archdruid died before Samhain, they did not have the luxury of attending his bedside and coming together in time for a festival. With his murder—the only known murder of an archdruid in all their memorised history—the rules and regulations had been swept aside; the election must take place now or their Order would suffer for it. There were no senior members of the brehon left, and those that gathered at Emain Macha amounted to little more than two hundred. Two hundred druids to serve a nation, to oversee births and deaths, marriage and separation, illness and disease. Two hundred druids to uphold the laws of man and the laws of the ancients. There was not an island small enough to warrant the need for so few druids.

When the naming ceremony had ended and a goat was brought forward for the sacrifice, Grainne found Anú sitting on the grass in the sunlight, her cloak drawn over her head for extra warmth, her dress pulled tight around her legs.

'Where is your brother?' Grainne asked as she knelt beside the girl.

Anú did not respond. Her eyes were glazed.

'Anú?'

Grainne reached out a hand to touch the young girl's shoulder.

'She said you would not want it,' the girl said.

'Would not want what, dear child?'

'The swan-lady said your name to me, but she said you would not want it.'

'Why would she say my name?'

'Why do they say anything?'

'I am not the required calibre, Anú. I feel more like an acolyte, always learning and studying.'

'Does the archdruid not study most of all, child?' Anú said, though her voice was strange. Grainne touched her chin, tilted the girl's head, and could see that her eyes were still murky and distant.

'Who says these words to me?'

Anú took her arm, her grip tighter than was necessary. 'There will be a union of druids. It will help. Until then, there is only hope.'

With quiet reverence, Grainne said, 'Cáer?'

Anú blinked, the colour of her eyes returning to normal, her grip on Grainne's arm loosening.

'What does that mean?' Grainne asked her.

The girl said nothing.

Grainne stood and took her hand to help her up. 'There are storm clouds coming from the west. Looks like early snow. We should seek shelter. Where is your brother?'

Outside the compound, the horses cried again, their whinny-ing calls echoing around the enclosure. The squat buildings that surrounded her were darkened from last night's rain, and the druids, though they were pleased the nominations were com-plete, shuffled across the hillside with a slow determination.

A dull patter followed, and Grainne assumed it to be fat drops of rain, but she felt none of them. She looked up.

The sky was black with arrows.

'Run!' she shouted. She lifted Anú in her arms and sprinted behind a nearby hut. They had no warning. Rapt in their own worries, any guard stationed outside the walls will have already fallen. She worried for Rónán's men—Dáithí and the others who had accompanied her on her journey east. They said they would wait for her across the hillside.

Grainne crouched and shielded the girl in her arms. She peered around the hut to witness the deaths of many of her peo-ple. The arrows rained down thick and hard, piercing bodies as they had pierced the sky. She could not recognise anyone in the panic. Scanning the bodies and those who were still scrambling, she did not see Dérc or Marí. She could not identify the four nominees, or the elders whom she had first spoken to upon her arrival.

The goat, not yet sacrificed by ritual blade, was now pinned to the earth by arrows.

At the east of the enclosure, the walls were shaking as their enemy forced themselves against it. Soon it would topple.

A second hail of arrows rained over them, their tips doused and lit with fire. Even as she saw them, the thatching of the hut beside her was ablaze.

She lifted Anú again. Inside the larger hut on the other end of the complex, a tunnel led down into the foothills on the west. She pointed to the hut and said, 'We need to go there. It's our only way out.'

'No,' Anú cried. 'We will die.'

'I won't let that happen.'

Grainne shifted the girl's weight so that she carried her with one arm, and she lifted her robe to release her dagger. She had hesitated once before, when her life hung before her, but this time she would protect Anú, child of her goddess. She would kill a hundred men to save the girl if she needed to.

She studied the distance, the obstacles that she would have to overcome, and watched the sky for another rain of arrows. In the east, the palisade wall was about to collapse.

'I want Dérc,' Anú said, her eyes and her voice wet with tears.

Druids, for the most part, had some training with weapons as a defensive art, but most never expected to have to use one. Grainne gripped her dagger tight, and as the eastern wall came down and an army of masked warriors forced their way over it, she made a run for the far brú. There would be no more arrows unless the army did not care about losing their own men.

The wall at the north was collapsing, too. Soon they would be surrounded. Her only hope was that the intruders had no knowledge of the escape tunnel. The hut she was running towards was bright with flames. If she did not get inside soon, its thatching would fall, and their escape would be blocked.

Many other druids, those who were not dead or wounded,

were making their way towards the same hut. Grainne prayed that all of them would get out unharmed.

'Anú!' a voice called. 'Anú, where are you?'

Grainne stopped running. She turned towards the voice and saw Marí holding a young acolyte in her arms—Dérc. His body was limp and lifeless.

'Marí!' Anú cried.

A warrior, tall and stocky, rose behind Marí and stuck her with his sword. Both the woman and the boy fell to the ground.

Grainne buried Anú's head against her robes. She turned. Another warrior from the northern end of the complex had come around the hut and was fast approaching her, his sword raised behind his head for a swing. She ducked, holding the girl tight, curled her shoulder, and rolled out of the man's way. As she came to her knees, she jabbed out and caught him in the thigh with her dagger. The cut was deep, and his leg slipped from under him.

The man twisted as his knee buckled, his sword arm skewing wide. Grainne dropped the girl, reached for his arm, and jabbed him again in the chest. She pushed him away from her, not waiting to see if he was alive or dead, crouching over the girl to protect her, and then reaching out to take the man's sword.

She was better with a dagger, could move its weight with more ease, but a dagger required a close quarry, and she did not want another man to get too close.

She screamed as the warrior's blade cut her hand, but she pulled it towards her, turned it, took the hilt, and reached for Anú who scrambled to get to her brother.

The girl slipped in the mud, tumbled, and then pushed forward on her knees. Grainne chased her. Marí and Dérc, their bodies a tangle of limbs on the ground, were unmoving. The woman's blood seeped across her robes and dripped to Dérc's lifeless face.

On her feet, Grainne turned, still screaming. She swung the sword with wild carelessness, nicking the neck of another warrior. He turned to her, but as he did, dark blood spurted from his wound. He clasped his hand over it but hiding a wound does not heal it. He dropped to his knees.

Grainne looked around to find her bearings. The hut was to her left. All around her was fire and death. The door had been thrown open, druids crowding its entrance. But she was close.

She raised the sword for protection, and she doubled back for Anú. 'Come, child. I am sorry, they are gone.'

People were screaming. Anú jostled beside her. Grainne stepped over a fallen druid, stumbled, and as she approached the entrance to the hut, she forced Anú down onto the ground, pushed her forward. 'Go,' she said. 'Through their legs. Get inside.'

'It's on fire,' Anú cried.

'Get inside. There is a hatch in the floor. Go through it. Get outside the compound and wait for me.'

'Don't leave me.'

'I'll be right behind you. Go.'

Anú crawled along the ground towards the entrance and forced her way in between the druids' legs.

Grainne turned, the only line of defence between the doorway and the warriors.

A tall man swung towards her. Grainne held her breath. She did not close her eyes; blind sight is no sight. She took the sword's hilt in both hands, and she calculated the timing of her swing. Druids spend their lives calculating the movement of the stars, tracking the motion of the waves and the rise and fall of the tides.

And just like casting the bones, she cast the sword wide, planting her feet and swinging her hips. The blade sliced through the man's face and stuck there. She could feel the vibrations rattling the length of her arms. She let go of the hilt and it stayed in his head.

Grainne turned, pushed into the crowd of druids clambering to get inside the hut. She forced the bottleneck inside. She could not think of how many were left alive behind her. She could only think to get Anú to safety, the girl who spoke to her with her goddess' voice and prophesied a future union. The one whose mother was buried in a winter forest, and now suffered for her dead brother and guardian.

Inside the hut, Grainne pushed the others towards the floor hatch. She had not been inside the escape tunnel before, but she expected a short drop before a downward slope leading to the outside. 'Go,' she insisted. 'Hurry.'

She looked around. The central pillar stood as it should, but the thatching above her was smoking on the inside, a sure sign that the flames were making their way through the outer layers. As the terrified druids dropped into the tunnel, she flipped a table on its end, kicked one of its legs until it tore free from its housing, and she lifted the wooden leg. She turned to the entranceway and looked into the brightness beyond.

Outside, the raiding assassins were closing in on them. They would understand where they were congregating.

Grainne raised the table leg and poked the low thatching on the inside of the entranceway. Smoke billowed. She poked again, pushing the wood into the thatched layer, twisting it and tearing at it until it fell around her.

She prodded again, loosening the reeds, and a large section collapsed in front of her, blocking the doorway with flames.

The last of the druids were escaping through the tunnel entrance and she ran to it. But as she did, a cry issued from behind her. A warrior jumped through the flames, his hair and clothes alight, but his sword was raised, his scream piercing, eyes wide.

He came upon her, but she jumped back, tripping over the empty space of the escape hole, falling backwards, landing on the ground with a thump. Her back sang in hot pain. But she swung the table leg in the air, hammered his body with it, and he leapt to the side, the flames engulfing him.

He fell.

Grainne cried out in agony as she twisted towards the tunnel, her back tight with a searing ache. And as she allowed her body to crumple and fold inside the tunnel, the roof of the hut came down above her.

When she landed in the darkness, a pair of hands reached out, pulling her further inside the tunnel, and she watched a section of burning thatch falling. It lit the area enough that she could see the man who grabbed her.

'Come,' he said. 'We need to flee. No one else is getting through this tunnel.'

She crawled, the pain in her back biting her flesh, and the darkness was endless.

They moved through the tunnel until she thought it was veering downward, deep into the earth. She had no sense of direction; she just kept moving, hand over hand, knee before knee, and the smarting in her lower back was hot and wet and white with blazing spasms.

When she fell into the dull afternoon sunlight at the farthest reaches of Emain Macha's foothills, she gulped fresh air in ragged breaths, and she lay on her stomach among the autumn leaves.

'She's hurt,' someone said. 'Help me lift her.'

She did not have the energy to reach for the pain in her back, but she could feel it radiating along her spine. 'Anú,' she said, her voice weak. 'Anú.'

The young girl came at a crawl in front of her, curled herself into a ball, and cradled against Grainne's shoulder.

And together they cried for Dérc and Marí, and for all the fallen.

Chapter 25

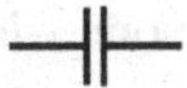

The road forked and they took the northern path. They had journeyed for two days, stopping as the sun dipped its toes in the horizon, and once a day to eat. The women had carried with them an ample supply of food and, on the first day when they stopped, Orlaith asked, 'Who among you has a mouth the size of a lough? This is far too much food for a few days' travel.'

'We will need to give tribute to your brother's king when we arrive,' Etain told her.

When they stopped in the daylight, they ate with quick efficiency, and then formed pairs among themselves to practice their swordsmanship. At night, when they made camp amid the trees that bordered the road, they polished their blades, performed ablutions, and sat around the small fire as Etain or one of the other women took turns at reciting the tales of Éirinn's heroes.

Orlaith closed her eyes when Eimear, whose voice had a quiet excitement as she told her stories, recited the Battle of Knockdhu as it had been retold by the travelling bards.

'And the king, Déaglán, perished from his wounds, and as he died, his tanist, Oisín became the next king. But his reign was swift and the Fir Bolg bastards shot him full of arrows—a hundred arrows or more, it is said. And it is then that his tanist, Áed the Executioner, took control of the northern territories. The Executioner was a giant of a man, forty rods tall, and he tore through the ranks of foreign scum with a blade that was twice his length and just as broad. But the Fir Bolg bastards made sacrifice to the wrong gods, and they bested Áed the Executioner on the fields outside Knockdhu. Three kings in quick succession perished, but the fourth, the one who is now overking of Ailigh, Rónán Ó Mordha, stripped himself of his clothes and frightened the foreign bastards by the size of his rod. He slaughtered them all, and those that were left were locked in captivity. And the Mighty King Rónán, whose name is revered across our lands, rebuilt the north with his own bare hands.'

The women applauded her recitation, but Breasal poked his mother in the ribs. 'How could there be some left in captivity if he slaughtered them all?'

'The foreigners were wily bastards that spawned out of the ground,' Eimear told him. She leapt forward and grabbed his feet. 'Watch yourself, now, or they'll get you in your sleep.'

He pulled his feet from the ground and looked at Orlaith.

'They are all gone now, son. Do not fear.'

He leaned close to her, so that the others would not hear, and cupped his hand around her ear. 'I was not really afraid.'

'I know you were not, my love.' She wrapped her arm around him and poked the fire with a short branch.

They retired for the night under fur-lined blankets, huddled together for warmth. And in the morning, as a sodden sky plundered the horizon, Orlaith and the girls packed up their things. They ensured nothing had been discarded, no wraps from their food, or clay jars or waterskins, no leather tie-string or fur bedding. When they moved on, the only visible remains of their stay would be the fire scar that they doused and covered with dead leaves. They were not hiding their tracks as much as paying respects to the forest that harboured them through the night. To irritate the forest gods would be to hamper their journey.

The further north they travelled, the more desolate the landscape. Though they did not cross through septs, they marched along borderlands and could see stubbled wheat fields burned black to ward off the wheat rust that had decimated the crops. The rust disease had returned for its second year and few fields this far north had been spared. Before leaving Banan MacColm's tribe lands, Orlaith realised she should have asked him to gift her some sheaves of wheat for the northern overking. But she could not journey back now.

She drove the carbad horses at a slow gait so as not to outrun the girls who marched behind her, and Etain walked often at the side of the carbad, questioning Breasal with mindless puzzles. 'Who decided that a tree would grow skyward, and its roots would grow down?' she would ask him.

'A tree would look silly with its roots in the air and its leaves in the ground,' he told her.

'It would not if all trees did it.' She kicked a stone from her path and said, 'If the earth is made of soil, where do stones come from?'

Orlaith stroked Breasal's hair when he said, 'The earth is made of both.' He was humouring Etain just as she was indulging him.

The day passed without incident, and when they stopped to eat, Orlaith climbed a tree to search the northern horizon. It had been so long since she came this far north that she was convinced they had taken a wrong turn at one of the forks in the road. But the track of the sun told her they were on the right path.

When she hopped back to the autumn-hardened ground, she said, 'There is a sept up ahead. I see fires burning an invitation.'

'Good,' Etain said. 'Can we stop there for the night? I am thoroughly sick of the cold ground and the snores of the women mingled with the wicked laughter of wolves.'

'You are not scared of a few stray pups, are you, Etain?'

'I am afraid I will not catch enough of them to make a meal.'

They journeyed to the sept before early evening and when they arrived, the travellers were greeted with excitement; it was not often a band of female warriors in padded tunics passed through a tribal sept.

'You are welcome here,' the female chieftain said. She explained that her husband had perished at the Ó Nallon Pass five years before and no man spoke against her. They gave her tributes and begged that she lead them.

All around, her fields were barren and blackened with soot. 'You were hit hard from the rust disease?'

'We did not do enough to deflect the gods' anger. I am afraid my people are poor, and we have little to offer you. I have not the beds for you all, but our granary is almost empty. Most of you will fit there for the night. It is all I can give.'

Orlaith reached for one of their packs and opened it to reveal a selection of foods wrapped in linen. 'We have come with plenty, and we are willing to share, in honour of your hospitality and perhaps a song or two from your good storytellers.'

'Storytellers, I have plenty. The gods have brought you to us.'

'Perhaps you did not anger them as greatly as you thought.'

Orlaith studied the small sept as her women unloaded their packs and arranged the food on a table that was brought from the chieftain's hall to the central field near the fire. She counted no more than twelve brú huts for the chieftain's people, and the goats were thinner than twigs. The wool on the sheep was tinged yellow on their chests and rumps. The people looked as feeble as their animals, and they gathered with greed at the table.

'There is enough for everyone,' Orlaith told them, and she stroked the cheek of a young girl who watched her with eager eyes from her mother's arms.

Breasal took a small wrap of wheat-bread from the table and Orlaith watched as he carried it across the field to a boy no older than seven winters. He stood in a tattered tunic and his left leg was missing from the knee. He was supported by a sturdy tree branch that was propped under his arm and dug a sharp point into the earth.

Breasal held the package out and the boy took it from him with tentative fingers. Breasal pointed at the wrap and then indicated his mouth as if the boy had no notion what the cloth contained.

One of the tribe women came to Orlaith, her eyes on the exchange between the boys. 'Eoin lost his leg at birth and his mother died bringing him into the world. He has neither hearing nor speech. How is it that your boy understands this?'

'He understands much more than he should at his age.'

'He is gifted,' the woman said. She touched Orlaith's arm and then lifted a small section of cheese from the table.

'I wish we had brought more food,' Orlaith said.

'You have given us plenty and the gods will see you kindly,' the woman said. 'I am Ealga.'

They shook hands in the way of men.

Later, when the tribespeople had enjoyed their fill of food, musicians struck up their instruments and the ladies danced. Etain lifted Breasal into her arms and twirled him around the field.

Ealga returned to Orlaith's side by the fire and said, 'How is it that you each carry a sword and there is not a man among you?'

Orlaith wiped the grease of food from her fingertips and took a drink from a cup of water before speaking. 'It is unusual, I grant you, but these women have been training with the sword for years. We need no men to bow to, though most have husbands and sons back home.'

'Are you Fianna?' Ealga asked, referring to the band of landless warriors who roamed Éirinn.

'The Fianna would be lucky to have us. We are just tribeswomen, same as you. We journey north to see the Ó Mordha king.'

'For what reason?'

'We are friends, he and I.'

Ealga laughed. 'Then you are hardly just a tribeswoman like the rest of us. Did he train you along with his army of boys?'

'A little.' Orlaith touched the hilt at her hip. 'But mostly, I trained myself.'

'You have that look about you.'

When Etain danced her way towards them, she spun Breasal in a circle and then eased him to the grass. 'If I let him, he would dance the feet right off me.'

Breasal curled into Orlaith's lap and she smoothed his hair and kissed his temple where the scar of his self-inflicted rune was turning pink as the dried blood cracked and peeled. The field was alive with singing and laughter and some of her younger girls were flirting with the boys of the tribe. Hands would wander tonight, outside the reaches of the flames.

Ealga reached out and touched the boy's reddened skin. 'Was

he born with it?'

'It is a mark of his birth.'

'You should bathe him in a bath of goat's blood mixed with the ash of a rowan tree. That will wash the stain from his skin.'

Breasal looked at the woman. 'It runs deeper than the skin. It is me. Why should I wash it away?'

Orlaith drew him tighter into her embrace. 'It is not a stain, is it, son?'

'It is me.'

Ealga nodded. 'I meant no disrespect, Lady. Goat's blood and rowan ash are used for many cures. You have my apologies.'

With a smile, for she knew the woman did not mean to upset them, Orlaith said, 'I am not the one who can grant you forgiveness.'

'It is well,' Breasal said.

Ealga took the boy's hand and kissed it. 'You are blessed, young man. If only my son was half the man you are.'

'The pale half or the red half?' Breasal asked. When Ealga stared at him with wide eyes, he laughed and then buried his face in the folds of Orlaith's cloak.

She had not known her son to be so humorous, though he was indeed wise beyond his age, the words of his dreams always thick with foreboding, and she realised now that it had been a long time since she heard him laugh with a keen openness.

Ealga smirked and winked at Orlaith. She finished her cup of water and tousled Breasal's hair before walking away.

'I made a joke,' Breasal whispered to Etain who was sitting nearby.

'I know you did, my boy. I am glad to hear it.'

That night, Orlaith, Breasal and the women huddled together

in the warmth of the chieftain's granary, using the few sacks of grain for pillows, and soon the hut was sweltering, and the winds howled over the thatching outside. Orlaith held her son tight and listened to the sounds of his breathing, and she wondered why, the further north they journeyed, the less disturbed Breasal's sleep had become. She was convinced she had made the right decision, taking him to Ailigh.

Her brother will have changed, no doubt. And Rónán, too. And, despite their history, she came to the realisation that she even missed Achall. Everything changes. People, places, attitudes. She lived in a world where boys become druids overnight, and where kings no longer fought one another but banded together against a common threat.

She fell asleep with an image of Rónán and Cormac in her mind, standing at each other's side, beckoning her into their arms.

By morning's light, the chieftain came to them, and she took Orlaith's hands and held them to her breast. 'You have been a most welcome interlude to the chore of our lives. I can see that you are a powerful woman with a strong mind. Take these girls as my gift to you. They are willing and they are tough. Let them carry your packs on the road and train them with the sword.'

Orlaith looked at the three girls who stood beside their chieftain. They were youthful and smiled with exuberance. 'We are not an army,' she said. 'We are just friends.'

'Do friends not make the best armies? You have provisions and plans, and I see that you are a strong leader of your women. You may not feel like an army, but you look and act as one. Here, these unwed girls wallow with the rest of us in dire times of need. With your warriors, they will have purpose.'

Orlaith glanced at Etain and saw her smiling. Until now, they were a collection of wives and daughters. When she took the chieftain's hand to seal the pact, she became a warrior, a chieftain to these women. The three girls would march with them and learn the ways of the sword and, in time, they would become as fearless as the MacColm tribeswomen.

'I will not forget your kindness, mighty friend,' the chieftain said. 'We had nothing, and you brought to us a feast. May the gods walk forever at your side.'

As they rolled out of the sept, with the new girls in the middle of the formation, Orlaith looked at her son and she knew—where Breasal goes, the gods will always follow.

Chapter 26

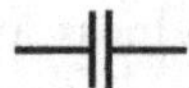

Rónán shielded his eyes from the glare of the low autumn sun and watched from the rampart walls as Torin Ó Neill rode north. The chieftain of the northern-most tribe under Ailigh's rule promised he would return with additional men, long before Seanach Mac Fachtna's replacement descended upon the Ó Mordha hills.

'Do we know who Seanach's tanist is?' Fergal asked.

'I met him once. A stoat of a lad called Anlon. Good with the sword. He seemed like a level-headed man, but under the circumstances, it is his right to blame me and seek revenge.'

'With any luck,' Diarmuid said from his place on the wall beside them, 'he will keep his calm when he approaches our hills. I will meet with him. Tanist to tanist. He cannot refuse a parlay. This need not come to war.'

Torin Ó Neill had disappeared among the northern trees and Rónán turned to descend the wall. 'The snows will come soon enough. If they siege against us, they will perish in the cold. I am not expecting a war.'

'You should always expect a war,' Fergal said, coming down the narrow steps that were cut from the same timber as the palisade wall. 'Expect everything, and when it happens it will not be a surprise.'

'I always appreciate your wisdoms, old man.'

'Such sarcasm. Did you hear that, Diarmuid? If I kill him, you can take his place, and then this Anlon weasel will not have an opponent to fight.'

Diarmuid drew his sword and held it out, hilt first, for Fergal's use.

'Enough,' Rónán said, though a smile softened the corners of his mouth. Diarmuid sheathed his sword with a laugh and Rónán said, 'I will meet you both in the barrel hut later. Warm a stool for me.'

He crossed the outer rampart and circled the middle, climbing the slope towards the inner wall. When he knocked on Grainne's door, Gallen called that he should enter.

The acolyte was stooped over a table, studying the bones he had cast before picking them up and casting them again.

'What do they say?'

'They say something different every time, my lord, and none of it promising.'

Rónán inspected the pattern of the blackened bones as though he could decipher them. 'Remind me—who is your personal god?'

'Mogh Roith, Lord.'

'And he does not speak to you?'

'Not the way Cáer speaks to Lady Grainne. I have dreams that need decoding. Some are clear, some are puzzles of such complexity I could spend years interpreting them.'

'And what do the bones say on this throw?'

Gallen looked at them. 'If I am correct, this coupling, adjacent to this cross, signifies a rise in—I cannot think of the word. Wisdom, perhaps. The bones have never been my strongest divination, Lord.'

'We could use a rise in wisdom,' Rónán said. He looked around the room. He could not recall how many days Grainne was gone, but it felt like years. 'Do you think they will have had the elections for archdruid, yet?'

'I cannot say. There will be sacrifices and prayers, but I am just an acolyte. The gods do not yet reveal to me the ways of power.'

'You will be graduating to druidship soon?'

'After the Yule, all being well.'

Rónán picked up a small vial with a linen stopper and sniffed it. He had expected a pungent smell, but a floral scent greeted him. He replaced the vial and watched Gallen cast the bones again.

'My lord, I may only be an acolyte, but I can see that something troubles you. I have keen ears for listening if you need to speak.'

'There have been no more signs of yew poisoning?'

'The livestock are well, Lord.'

'And this business with Seanach?'

'There has been no more evidence of intrusion and I gleaned nothing from his body or the room he was housed in before his men took him home,' Gallen said. 'My lord, forgive me, is there something else on your mind?'

'It is Achall,' Rónán said, unsure of how to proceed with his words. 'I am told she sleeps most of the day and few people see her venture from her brú. The boy, Áed, has been locked with her for many days.'

'I will call on her to investigate. I understand she has anger towards you and, if you will forgive my forthright words, she was once your queen. Now, she is little more than a seamstress. Her position in life has changed over the years that it is possible she does not yet know how to act around you or, indeed, within the confines of your walls.'

'You do not think she suffers from an illness of the mind?'

'I cannot say until I speak with her. But, my lord, though I am soon to graduate, my studies are incomplete. Grainne may have a better understanding of worrisome minds than I.'

'Speak with her, please,' Rónán said. 'And perhaps have one of your dreams of divination.'

'I am afraid they do not work that way, Lord. The dreams come when they will. I cannot close my eyes and dream solutions to pertinent problems.'

One of Ailigh's trainee boys came to the open door, wet with sweat and shivering. He bowed in the presence of Rónán and said, 'My lord, I feel ill.'

Gallen beckoned the boy in, touching the back of his hand to his damp forehead. 'The winter months are truly upon us, it would seem. If you sneeze on me, I will ask the king to carve your nose from your face.' He ushered the boy towards a stool and readied a tincture. To Rónán, he said, 'I will pay her a visit when I am done here.'

Later, as the evening sun galloped towards the western clouds, Rónán joined the chieftains in the barrel hut. They sat around a long table, Cormac and Diarmuid at either side of him, Fergal, Ainmire and Ardál sitting opposite. Their cups were full and their conversations empty. They had five days before the Mac Fachtna clan would march to their foothills and demand Seanach's killer. When Rónán was unable to produce such a person, they would announce their plan for war. As was custom,

Rónán could request a three-night stay so that he can assemble his army. But his army lived within his walls and the stay would not be necessary. If he requested it, Anlon Mac Fachtna, Seanach's replacement, would know that Rónán was stalling for no reason.

Five days. If Seanach's killer was not one of his own men—and Rónán could not believe any of his warriors were capable of the cold-blooded murder of a chieftain and friend—then whoever had thrust the dagger into Seanach's sleeping body had escaped over the wall and into oblivion.

Fergal unhooked his metal arm and dipped the stump of his elbow into the wide neck of his cup, and when Diarmuid questioned him, he said, 'When the pain comes, alcohol numbs it.'

'It would numb it quicker in your belly, would it not?' Diarmuid said.

'A man's rituals are sacred, you mangey hare. Leave me be.'

Ainmire worried at the inside of his cheek with visible irritation. 'I should have come with more men. But my army is too far to reach us in time.'

'I beat Mac Fachtna's tribe once already,' Rónán said. 'Before Seanach took the seat. I can do so again if it comes to it.'

'It will not come to it,' Cormac reasoned. 'Everyone at this table vouches for you, Rónán.'

Rónán covered Cormac's hand with his own for a brief comfort. 'We can only hope Anlon sees sense.'

When Ainmire and Ardál retired to their quarters for the night, Fergal called for another round of drinks. 'When this business is over, I think I will build a barrel hut in the middle of nowhere and have people come from all corners of the earth to taste my sweet beers. I will trade the south for wines and the east for their ales.'

'Barrel huts are diminishing with the lack of wheat,' Rónán said. 'No one will come to an empty hut.'

Fergal nodded agreement and finished the dregs of his cup before the drinks were replaced by one of the boys who weaved among the tables with pitchers of beer or heated wine. The boy struggled with the half-empty jug and Rónán saw the patches of sweat under his arms.

He took the jug from him and said, 'Go to bed, boy. I do not need a winter flu circling my hills.'

Diarmuid said, 'If Darragh catches any sickness, his mother will smack it out of him. Every year it is the same. He is one of the first boys to drop with the annual flu.'

'But he is always quick to recover,' Cormac said. 'Last year, was he not the first boy back in the training fields, practicing his arm with the spear?'

Fergal rapped on the table with his knuckles. 'My Lord King, you surround yourself with old wives and wicker-women.' He placed his hand under his chin with effeminacy. 'Perhaps your women will succour me when I, too, fall ill.'

'If you snore worse with sickness than you do in health,' Diarmuid laughed, 'there will be no succouring, but a pillow held tightly over your face. I can hear you clean across the hilltop.'

Fergal grunted. 'Beer-snores is a profoundly serious condition. It is in my blood.'

'There is beer in your blood, for certain.'

They continued to talk and joke with avoidance of their woes. In five days, everything would change. If he lost the support of his eastern neighbour, it would not be long before Anlon Mac Fachtna spread word that Rónán's peace was fake, that his gates were not secure. Other tribes would turn on him.

Before retiring to bed, Fergal pulled him aside from the others and said, 'You beat them before—you said so yourself. I see the worry in your eyes. You stress too much, Lord. All will be well.'

Rónán clasped his arm. 'I appreciate your kindness and your friendship.'

When he and Cormac walked up the hillside to their inner wall, Rónán scanned the outer palisade. Six guards were stationed around the wall, watching the dark horizon in all directions. Anybody coming in or out would be seen.

They slept under the heat of their furs, Cormac's back nestled against Rónán's chest, and the morning came quick and bright. Outside their doorway, they heard a disturbance, and when Rónán dressed to investigate, he saw a line of boys outside Grainne's brú. All were drenched with sweat, and some were doubled over in pain. Two of the younger boys closer to the entrance were on their knees, retching in the flattened grasses and expelling the contents of their stomachs with violent force.

Cormac pulled his tunic on as he stood beside Rónán. 'This is not the winter flu.'

Gallen came from Grainne's brú and hurried another boy inside. Rónán followed. 'How many are sick?'

'More than I can count, Lord. Almost half the boys, from what I can tell.'

'A winter sickness would not spread so fast,' Rónán said.

'That is my fear.'

'Yew poisoning, like the livestock?'

'They have not the symptoms for yew poisoning. Can we have some beds set up? I do not have the space here and we must separate the sick from the healthy.'

Rónán nodded and left. He summoned some of the older boys who were yet unaffected, and they dragged pallet beds from communal brús to arrange in the great hall. The room had enough space for fifty beds when the tables and Rónán's kingseat had been removed, and when they were finished, no bed was unoccupied.

The smell of vomit was rife on the air, and the thick, cloying heat of sweat turned Rónán's stomach. The groans of the sick boys bore a cacophonous weight over the hillside.

Gallen moved from one bed to another, administering a cloudy yellow liquid, and he had gathered some of Ailigh's women who wrung linen cloths to daub at the children's foreheads and necks. Faces were splotched red with a heat rash as some of the women carried bowls of water into the hall and bowls of vomit out.

A second bay of sickbeds was set up in the granary, where Cormac and Diarmuid had shifted the sacks of grain into a nearby brú, and yet more beds were filled with sweating and vomiting boys in Grainne's quarters.

Gallen, sweating from the workload, took a moment to sacrifice a goat to the gods for their assistance.

Rónán and his men helped where they could, applying salves, rubbing backs as the boys leaned out of their beds to empty their stomachs into waiting bowls, but he realised they were treating symptoms before having the time to investigate the cause. As a child, he had ingested some wild mushrooms that caused sweating and vomiting, and the most lucid hallucinations he could imagine, but there were not enough mushrooms in the nearby forests to sicken so many boys.

As he patted the back of one of his young trainee warriors, he waited for him to cease his retching before asking, 'Did you eat or drink anything you shouldn't have?'

The boy shook his head and wiped his mouth with the back of his hand. He was unable to speak. A thick strand of mucus leaked from his nose and, as he lay back in the bed, he groaned. The smell of fresh faeces accosted Rónán's senses.

'Worry not,' he told the boy. 'All will be well.'

When all the boys had been administered to and Gallen slumped on a stool, exhaustion clouding his eyes, Rónán handed him a cup of water.

'Some years ago, my former wife used a pouch of herbs to sicken Fionn. She placed it under his bed. Could this be similar?'

Gallen shook his head. 'I was a child when Fionn was sick, but I remember it. We have shifted so many beds this morning that we would have seen any attempts at poison. Have you checked the cook's cauldron?'

'It had already been emptied and cleaned after the morning meal. I checked the drainage channels, but I am unsure what evidence I should be looking for. It was food—some meat and creams. Nothing more.'

'You do not suspect your former wife's involvement, this time?' Gallen asked.

'I do not. She has not ventured from her brú in so long that I cannot see how she would be capable.' Some of the boys hacked a loud and racking cough that interrupted Rónán's words. In the lull that followed, he said, 'I should call on her and see if young Áed is well.'

The coughing spread across the room and before Rónán reached the doorway, Gallen called him back. The acolyte stood by one of the boys who covered his mouth with his fists and choked on his own coughing fit. When Rónán approached, he saw spots of blood on the boy's fingers.

'It is getting worse,' Gallen said, 'and I do not yet have the knowledge to cure it.'

The boy looked up at them, his eyes wet and reddened, his cheeks flushed, lips dark with fresh blood, and when he tried to speak, his chin trembled and he fell back into a fit on the bed. Blood sparked his lips.

His limbs spasmed and his head jerked.

Gallen pulled his belt cord from his robes, doubled it and forced the thick strands between the boy's teeth to stop him from biting his tongue. He held his shoulders to lessen his violent movements.

And when the boy became still and unmoving, Gallen wrung a cloth and wiped his face. But the boy's eyes did not focus. Gallen felt for a pulse in the child's chest and in his neck, held the back of his hand above the boy's mouth for signs of breathing.

And he closed his eyes.

'I am sorry, Lord. He is dead.' Gallen motioned for Rónán to follow him to the doorway. 'My lord, you should quarantine yourself in your quarters until I know more. Whether this is a deliberate poisoning or a virulent sickness, we cannot have you succumbing to it.'

Rónán had no words. He looked around the room at the boys who had seen their friend, their brother, fall into a fit and die. He recognised the fear in their eyes, the thought that must have come to each of them—who will be next?

'These are my children, Gallen. I will not hide myself when they are sick. What can I do to help?'

Gallen handed him a fresh linen cloth. 'Then at least cover

your nose and mouth, Lord. You need to take precautions.'

'What can I do?' Rónán repeated.

They worked tirelessly for the remainder of the day. When Gallen's store of medicinal herbs ran empty, a dozen women took to the nearby forests to gather the flowers and leaves that he described for them. Others worked to clear the sickbed areas and sterilise the bowls for reuse. By nightfall, three more boys had died, but the sickness was not spreading. Boys were confined to their communal sleeping areas and Diarmuid marked the outer walls of each brú that housed the sick. No one was allowed in without first covering his face against the sickness and his hands and arms were to be scrubbed before leaving.

Rónán investigated the cause of the illness while Gallen worked to reverse its effects, but he could find no evidence of wilful poisoning and he knew nothing about the virulence of disease. He called at Achall's door and got no answer. 'Just tell me if Áed is sick or well,' he shouted.

'He is well,' Achall's angered voice came to him through the door. 'Leave us.'

'Let me see him.'

'We are healthy. Leave us alone.'

An early sleet stabbed the landscape when morning came. And the dawn brought with it four new deaths.

The bodies were stored in an empty brú, covered by coarse-woven linens yellowed with age, and Rónán knelt before them and pressed his forehead to the ground at their feet. Cormac knelt beside him.

'What have we done to offend the gods so much?' Rónán asked. 'Am I cursed? What king in all of history has suffered so greatly in so short a time?'

'You are not cursed, Rónán. We will fix this, and we will overcome.'

'Whatever this sickness is, it spreads too fast for us to contain it.'

'My lord?' a voice said from the doorway behind them.

When Rónán turned, he saw two women with a young boy between them. He knew Orlaith's voice before recognising her face, and he and Cormac rose to embrace her.

'You come at a terrible time,' Rónán said, 'but I am glad of your presence, Orlaith.'

'Why are you here?' Cormac asked his sister.

The young boy who held Orlaith's hand slipped from her grip and he knelt on the floor in front of the covered bodies. He lowered his head in respect for the dead.

'He is the reason I am here,' Orlaith said. 'But we can discuss that later. What ails your children? Put us to work. How can my women help you?'

Chapter 27

Grainne was unable to keep her eyes open. Her lower back was bruised black and purple from her fall inside the burning hut, but the skin was not broken. When they stumbled into the hillside, two of the druids picked her up and hurried her towards a copse of tall pine trees. The escape tunnel had brought them out no more than eighty rods from Emain Macha and in the distance they could see the black smoke of death rising into the sky like a beacon for the gods.

One of the men took off his outer robe and two branches were fitted through it to fashion a stretcher. They carried her the rest of the day, against her protestations that she could walk, and when they stopped at nightfall, they crushed dock leaves and hitched up her clothing. They applied the sticky salve from the leaves to a compress torn from the stretcher and wrapped it around her body.

Anú wept. At five winters old, she had lost her brother and her guardian, witnessed the deaths of many, and now her feet were sore from walking so long without rest.

For days—Grainne had lost count how many—they marched through the dense underbrush at the edge of the forest that bordered the rippling hills of the western lands. Her back ached with each step she took over the uneven ground and she would pause to stretch the knots that formed in her shoulders.

That first evening, when they doubled back to the spot Dáithí and Rónán's men had made camp, she found their bodies hacked and bloodied. It had been thirty of Rónán's men against hundreds. The assassins had come upon them before attacking Emain Macha and flies were thick above the ground. The few druids who had escaped with her worked to bury them, and Grainne prayed to her most gracious lady Cáer for their swift journey to the Otherworld. If they had journeyed home when she left them, they would be safe.

Twice since dawn this morning Anú's robe had been snagged on some wet underbrush and Grainne, brain-weary and sore, fought to free her before lifting the girl into her arms and carrying her a distance. She would not have been heavy under normal circumstances, but with days of marching through thick, undulant land, and a lack of sustenance from nutritious food, Grainne felt her strength leave her in great waves of broken heat.

They walked until the last of them were exhausted, and then they stopped to rest or eat what they could find, hidden among dense foliage in case they were being followed. They took turns walking at the fore and rear to scan the distance for movement.

Sleet arrived yesterday, and the naked branches of the trees were not enough cover to protect them. This morning, as they trudged over wet ground, a fine mist of rain shadowed Grainne's vision. The winter birds were silent as the druids passed under the trees.

'We should stop now,' someone said. 'Rest a little.'

They had foraged enough brambleberries in the previous days to last them a short journey, and so they found a clearing and built a fire for warmth with the few dry twigs and leaves they could gather. The berries were at the end of their autumn ripening season and their juices were a divine treat from the gods.

Grainne nursed Anú's head in her lap and looked around the fire. They amounted to seventeen, an almost equal number of druids and younger acolytes. They had gathered at Emain Macha for shelter and elections, under a pretence of safety—and not one of the survivors was a candidate for archdruid. Those four who had been nominated perished among the burning rubble at the top of Emain Macha. She wondered, again, how many druids remained across the land, those who were unwilling or unable to make the journey to their most sacred place.

In the first days of their escape, she hoped that others had managed to flee from their assassins, but she knew that it was doubtful. The escape tunnel had been blocked by burning thatch and the enclosure had been overrun with masked warriors; they were lucky, one of her companions told her, that they had managed to get out alive.

'What do we do now?' an acolyte asked. He was a young man of sixteen winters and his face was creased with worry.

'Ailigh,' Grainne said. 'We go to Ailigh and seek protection from my king. He is a good man. He can help us.' The Ó Mordha king was renowned among them for his hand in driving out the foreigners. She could think of no better man to defend them. 'Rónán Ó Mordha will help us defeat these assassins and restore order.'

The acolyte nodded as if it was the only viable course of action, and the others did not object. 'The gods are angry at us for not electing a new archdruid,' the young man said.

'The gods are not quick to anger. They gave us signs and we

ignored them. They will offer us more omens in the coming days,' Grainne said.

A blackbird cawed in the branches above them, and they took turns to keep a watch through the night.

Grainne used the stars, when they were visible through the grey clouds, to plot a course towards the Ó Mordha stronghold, and each night she studied them again to correct any misdirection they may have ventured upon. They kept off the roads as much as possible, taking slow steps among the bracken. She used the stars also to seek guidance from the gods but, with the dense cloud cover, she was given no sign. In the evenings, climbing high up into the branches of hibernating trees to keep away from the forest predators, Grainne closed her eyes and willed Cáer to come to her, to offer her advice, but her dreams had not been prophetic.

She felt abandoned.

The following morning, they waded through a shallow river, stopping to bathe in the icy water, and then they rested in the valley as the late autumn sun did little to warm them. 'The White Strath,' she said, naming the river they had just crossed, 'flows towards the northern ocean. If we follow its course, we will reach Ailigh in two nights.'

The small band of druids cheered their good fortune through the exhaustion that froze their limbs. 'I will be glad of a chance to eat more than berries,' one of them said.

As they set north again, Anú took Grainne's hand. 'We should have buried Dérc and Marí's bodies,' the girl said.

Grainne nodded and squeezed her fingers. 'When the world returns to normal, we will go back and bury the remains of all who fell. It is our duty to do so.'

Anú kicked her feet through the wet grasses. 'They are in the Lands of the Lost and cannot get to the Otherworld without our guidance.'

'The gods will find them. Do not fear. They will be beacons in the realms of death. Shall I carry you for a while?'

The girl held her arms aloft to be lifted. When Grainne picked her up, she wrapped her legs around the druid's waist and rested her head upon her shoulder. Grainne could not imagine how distraught Anú must be. She remembered Dérc's tale of their life before Marí came upon them in the forests—two young children bereft of their mother who perished before them, a brother and sister so indebted to each other's company that the little girl would often come to Dérc's bed at the northern compound and crawl in beside him for comfort and warmth. Anú had lost her world—father, tribe, mother, brother and guardian. And now she was displaced along with a small grove of druids who wandered through the autumn landscape in fear of their lives.

No innocent life could ever recover from such tragedy.

One of the female druids, fatigued to the point of sleep, slapped her face to cut the pain of tiredness from her eyes and sang the song of the goddess Macha, for whom their most sacred place was named. She came from the Otherworld and visited the farmer, Cruinniuc, whereupon she acted as his wife without a word, cooking, cleaning and mending his tunics. Cruinniuc, though confused at her presence, accepted it when she smiled upon him and that evening he bedded her, as was a husband's right. Macha fell pregnant at once. Later, when he left to attend a festival in the east of Ulaid, she told him she would only remain his wife if Cruinniuc did not utter a word about her presence. If he spoke of her to anyone, their deal would be done. The farmer promised, as all men make promises, but he bragged to the king that his beautiful wife could run faster than his horses. The king, when he heard this, forced Macha to race the king's geldings and, though she was swollen in her final term with child, she indeed ran faster. She won the contest and, on the finish line, she cried out in great pain and gave birth to two children—Fír and Fial. For her humiliation, she cursed the men to suffer weakness in their bones for nine generations.

'*And upon that hill where her children bore claim, stands now Emain Macha, the place of her name,*' the druid's song concluded.

Emain Macha—or Macha's Twins.

Grainne stroked Anú's hair as they walked, risen on the spirits of the druid's song. 'Have you had any visitations, my child?' she asked the girl.

'The swan-lady is quiet. Do the gods forget us?'

'No, child. They have more pressing matters for now, and they will be embracing your brother with all their strength. When we get to the Ó Mordha stronghold, we will gather our thoughts and make sacrifice. The gods will hear us and speak when they are ready.'

When Grainne felt the child stiffen in her arms, she stopped walking and asked her what was wrong.

'Wolf,' Anú whispered.

Grainne urged the others to halt, and she turned to locate the threat. High up on the hillside in the east, a lone grey wolf stalked them. The druids huddled together.

'It runs alone,' Grainne said after studying the area for some time. 'Abandoned by its pack or separated by injury. We are many, it is one.'

'It will be hungry,' someone said.

'Arm yourselves with stones from the riverbank. If it comes closer, we will scare it off.'

Anú clung to her. 'He wants a new *mamaí* and *daidí*.'

Grainne stroked the girl's hair. 'It will not find them in us. He will not attack if we stay together.' They walked with slow steps for a while, keeping the wolf in sight. It hunkered now and again, and at other times it paused to watch them, but it did not draw any closer. It sniffed the air and circled itself a few times, following their path, but by mid-afternoon the wolf grew weary of them and ran up the hillside and out of view.

'Be vigilant,' Grainne told them. 'It may not be gone for good.'

By dusk, they set camp on the riverside, lighting fires around them to keep predators at bay, and they sang with loud voices to show their strength and dominance over the creatures of the night. The dark smoke that swirled around them would scare the wolves enough to grant them peace for the evening. The sentries would be alert for the duration of darkness.

She had lost count of the days since the Emain Macha massacre and still their gods lingered in silence against their pleas. It was an omen, but she did not speak her thoughts aloud.

Surrounded by smoking fires on the north, south and east, and with the river at their backs, she was convinced of their safety from night stalkers. Once, when the moon was high, and the clouds parted enough to give the landscape a silver hue, she thought she heard the high-pitched howl of a solitary wolf, but it could have been the wind crying through the treetops.

'We are less than two nights from Ailigh,' she told the others. 'Be strong, we are almost there.'

'We have avoided the most pressing concern,' one of the men said. He was called Art and, though he was the eldest among them, he was an acolyte who came to the order late in life. He was, he had told her, still some years away from graduating to his druidship. 'We have no archdruid, no focus. Who will guide us?'

'The gods will guide us until we can gather any remaining druids from across Éirinn.'

'If there are any left.'

'There has to be,' Grainne said. 'I cannot believe that all those who did not make it to Emain Macha have been murdered. There is still the Southern Order, I am sure.'

'When less druids remain than there are gods,' someone said, 'the world's strife begins.'

Anú's eyes widened. 'If a god has no druid, does the god die?'

'No child,' Grainne told her. 'They will wait until a new druid comes to them.'

The gathered druids and acolytes nodded as though the words had been spoken in prophecy.

When at last Grainne slept, relieved of watch duty by Art, her dreams were plagued with violence. She watched Rónán Ó Mordha break the land with his sword, plunging it into the earth to create a chasm that etched its way around the hill of Ailigh. She saw the river turn to blood and witnessed the skeletons of the dead rise to fight against the living. She saw carrion swoop down to the earth to pluck the souls from those who fell, and she watched, with horror, an entire forest burn to ash within the blink of an eye. But then she stood among a wedding feast in brightest sunlight and watched the revellers dance and sing with joyous hearts. She could not see the faces of the man and woman who were to be wed, but she understood their great importance to a future of prosperity in a landscape blighted by rot.

A swan flew to her side, folding its great wings upon itself and preening its neck. But it did not speak.

When she woke, she huddled closer to Anú for the warmth that the girl provided, and she cried for the dead, and cried more for the living.

Chapter 28

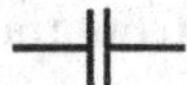

The sound of retching pain washed over Ailigh's hilltop, mixed with the tears of the women who mourned Ó Mordha's losses. Before the first full day of sickness was ended, nine children had died. Now, two days later, the bodies that were laid in wake numbered more than twenty.

Gallen worked with tireless efforts to find a cure for the boys and, though some of the men and women of Ailigh were also sick, the effects did not hit the adults so hard. The acolyte could not determine the cause of the illness that worked its way through the hillfort, but he was certain that it was not contagious. Those who did not fall sick on the first day were spared from the wrath of infection.

'It is becoming more likely,' he told Rónán, 'that this was a deliberate poisoning. Though without a sample of the food they consumed, I cannot say what was added to it.' He had infused dill leaves, a natural antiemetic, in heated water and forced the boys to drink it, but it did little to quell the vomiting or stem the bleeding that came when they coughed. 'I would investigate the stomach of one of the deceased, but I would not wish to anger the gods.'

'Keep working, Gallen. We cannot lose any more.'

Rónán stayed in the great hall where the beds had been removed and the deceased boys were lying in rows on the rush-covered floor. The acolyte climbed the ceremonial hill to give sacrifice. Gallen's hound, Cara, walked among the ranks of bodies, sniffing their shrouds and whining. He came to Rónán's side and nudged his hand, then settled on the floor beside him.

'My lord?' Diarmuid said from the doorway. 'Forgive me, I do not mean to interrupt your prayers.'

Rónán rose from his knees. 'I have few prayers left. Darragh—is he well?'

'Yes, Lord. He was spared the sickness, I am glad to say. But there are more deaths. Their bodies are being brought here now.'

'How many?'

'Three since the last one. I know under normal circumstances we would lay the boys in wake for seven nights.'

'No,' Rónán said, pre-empting Diarmuid's request.

'My lord?'

'I will not cut the wake period short. If we run out of space, I will house their bodies in my own quarters or I will lay them out on the hilltop for the gods to see. You cannot ask me to disobey the laws. They will lie here under watch until seven nights after the final death.'

'Yes, Lord.'

'Has anyone managed to get Achall to open her door yet?'

'The men take turns knocking and begging her to open, but she refuses, Lord.'

Rónán unbuckled his sword belt and held it out to Diarmuid. 'Hold this. If I take it with me, I may strike her through.'

For two days, since the sickness began, Rónán had implored Achall to open her door and let him see the child. She insisted he was well and refused to let him out in case he contracted the sickness. 'You have hundreds of boys,' she told him through the door. 'I have only one.'

He respected her right to protect her child, but his patience was growing thin. He had ensured that one of his men stood at her door and knocked with frequency, and when he walked around the hillside, he saw Cormac thumping on her door.

'She has stopped responding,' Cormac said. 'No one has heard her utter a word since dawn.'

Rónán steeled himself and knocked his fist against the wooden door. 'Achall, I have had enough. Open this door now.' He did not wait for a response but knocked again. 'Achall, I am warning you. Open the door or I will have your head.'

'Go away.' Her voice was tight and strained, muffled by the door between them.

Rónán shook his head. 'Stand back from the door, Achall. I am coming in.' He thrust his shoulder against the wood and heard a crack, but it did not give. He shoved again. When the frame splintered, he kicked the door wide.

'He is well,' Achall cried. 'It is just a winter flu.'

Áed lay on his pallet bed, swaddled in thick furs, and Rónán could see his grey pallor under the sheen of sweat. His arms twitched as he shivered.

'It is a flu. Nothing more.'

Rónán pulled the furs back and touched the boy's damp neck. 'He is on fire. How long has he been sick?'

'It's just a flu.'

As he picked Áed up, he said, 'By all the gods, if he dies, I will slaughter you and bury you upside down.'

'It is just a flu. I am treating him.'

'Get out of my way, woman.'

'Give me back my son.'

Rónán stomped over the claggy ground as he came around the hillside and through the inner rampart. Achall followed and shook herself free from Cormac's grip.

'Give him back. He is mine.'

Rónán carried the boy to Grainne's quarters where he saw Gallen swilling a bowl with fresh water.

'Give him to me.'

Rónán stepped through the doorway. 'Cure him, Gallen. Whatever it takes. Cure him.' There were no beds free, so he laid the boy on a table.

'Has he coughed blood yet?'

'I want my son back. He is mine.'

Rónán took her arm. 'Has he coughed blood?' he asked. She shook her head. Her hair was wild and loose, her eyes wide, and tears dripped from her lashes.

Gallen gathered some fresh dill leaves and poured water into a bowl from the cauldron above the fire. 'When was the last time he vomited?'

'It is just a winter flu,' Achall said, but her voice was now weakened and full of fear.

'Answer him,' Rónán demanded.

'He spewed this morning, but he has eaten nothing in two days.'

Gallen crushed the leaves into the water and stirred the anti-emetic. To the tincture, he added fennel to help soothe the boy's stomach, and chopped willow bark to combat his fever. When it was ready, he drained the particles from the liquid and held the boy's head to make him drink. Áed sipped and then choked, and Gallen helped him lean forward, rubbing his back to ease his pain.

'I can treat him,' Achall said. 'Give me the tincture and I will cure my son.'

'He needs constant care,' Gallen told her.

Achall came to her son's side and wrapped furs tight around him before lifting him into her arms. 'He should be at his mother's side.'

Rónán grabbed her arm and took the boy from her. When he laid him on the table again, against her protestations, he gripped her shoulders. 'Calm yourself. You are unfit to care for him.'

'He is my son. Mine.'

'He is mine, too,' Rónán said. He dragged her outside as she wailed. She scratched his face with her nails and spat on him. Rónán slapped her cheek, her scar pink and puckered.

She fell to her knees and cried, clutching at Rónán's boots. 'Give me back my son. I need him.'

'You need to calm yourself. Because of you, he has not been treated until now. He should have been here two nights ago.'

She howled, her fingers clawing at his legs. 'I need him. He is all I have.'

Rónán did not see Orlaith and her son approach, but when she stood at his side, he watched as the boy, named for Fionn but called Breasal—meaning red stain—reached out and touched Achall's face.

She looked at him, tears thick on her lashes, and then she drew him into an embrace. She rocked him in her arms and cried against his red hair, and Breasal hushed her with soothing sounds. He freed one arm from her tight clasp and smoothed the wild mess of hair that framed her pained features. He did not try to pull away from her until she was calm and released him.

'Do not cry,' he said, as Achall knelt in the mud, puffing air through numbed lips. She hugged herself and rocked her body in small motions, but her tears had dried.

'I still do not know what brought you here,' Rónán told Orlaith, 'but I am glad for it.' He went into Grainne's quarters and returned with a fur, which he draped over Achall's shoulders. 'Come. You need sleep.'

His former wife allowed him to help her stand, and he and Orlaith led her back to her home. Orlaith tucked the distraught woman into her bed, and Breasal swept the floor that, in the weeks since she had shut herself away, was thick with dust and strands of linen scrap. The broom pole was huge in his small hands. Rónán repaired the busted door as best he could, enough so that it would close and remain shut. He prised the lock from the inside so that she could not imprison herself again, and then he sat with Orlaith at her side while Achall slept.

Orlaith said, 'I see great changes in her since I was last here.' Breasal sat in her lap and stared with open eyes at Rónán.

'I do not know what has become of her. She was well until recent days. She took to weaving since our divorce. Perhaps five years of thread dust has driven her mad.'

'I have seen other women over the years become possessive of their children, but this is extreme. How long has she refused to come out of her home?'

'Too long,' Rónán said. 'It is great to see you, Orlaith. Cormac and I have missed you. We thought we would never see you again.'

'I thought so, too,' she said. She stroked Breasal's hair. The boy had not taken his eyes from Rónán since they settled at

Achall's bedside.

'This strong young man brings you here, but I am yet to understand why.'

'I will not bother you with it, now, Lord. You have enough to contend with.'

'Indulge me, please. Too many things swirl through my mind that I could do with something to focus on.'

Orlaith told him of Breasal's fever and the words he spoke in his delirium. She told him about the druid who treated him before journeying to Emain Macha, and of the young acolyte who had been murdered outside his home. 'I was hoping Grainne might be here that she could reassure me.'

'If he is to become a druid,' Rónán said, 'there is nothing either of us can do to stop it.' To Breasal, he said, 'Is this what you wish for your future?'

Breasal stared at him but said nothing.

'I have lost so much in recent times,' Rónán said, 'that if you have any words for me, I would be grateful for them.'

The boy reached forward and touched his fingertips to Rónán's forehead. 'The fields have burned, and children wander close to gods.' He kept his fingers there for a moment before tracing a rune against Rónán's skin.

'If they are close to gods, I can feel easy.'

Breasal leaned forward and crawled onto Rónán's lap. He cupped his hand against his ear and whispered, 'There will be no cease until all is gone.'

'That is what I am afraid of,' Rónán said.

Chapter 29

Orlaith wrung a cloth and sponged it against Áed's temples, cheeks and neck. Her warrior women were put to work throughout Ailigh, caring for the sick boys, helping at the cook's cauldrons, or sweeping floors and carrying news between Gallen and the king.

She walked among the beds and spoke to those boys who could answer her, but she dedicated much of her time at Áed's side. Achall confined herself to her home, though Rónán had removed the lock on her door, and when she was not busy aiding in the care of the boys, Orlaith would visit the woman and sit with her, just as Achall had sat at her side when Breasal was born.

Much had happened between them, though Orlaith cared little for reminiscing. There was a time when she would have whooped and hollered with joy at Achall's misfortune, but now, seeing the empty sadness in the woman's eyes, she felt sympathy towards her. If Breasal had fallen ill as Áed had, Orlaith would be inconsolable.

'He has not yet improved,' Orlaith told Achall this morning. 'But he has not worsened, either. He sweats and shivers, and he coughs, but there is no blood in his mucus. That is a good sign.'

Achall looked at her when she spoke, and nodded her head in

understanding, but she said nothing. When a mother is speech-less, she is enduring all the pain of the world. Orlaith touched Achall's arm as though her fingers could impart comfort, and Breasal, who would seldom leave his mother's side, sat on the rush-covered floor at Achall's feet and he brushed flower petals against her bare toes.

When Etain came to Achall's open doorway and cleared her throat, Orlaith beckoned her in.

'My lady. You have not eaten today. Shall I fetch you a bowl of curds?' She wore her sword at her left hip, as all Orlaith's women did, and the emblem of their tribe was stitched into the breast of her padded tunic. In the days since they left Banan MacColm's sept and marched north, though they had packed other clothing, Orlaith's warriors did not remove their branded tunics. It had become a uniform and, though no two tunics were coloured the same, they each bore the insignia of MacColm's heritage, and could be identified by it. Some months before, the women had sat together around the central fire and picked at the stitching to modify it. Under MacColm's wolf-head motif, they sewed a shield penetrated by a sword. Etain had joked that they should be known as the Wolves of Éirinn, and though the name had never been uttered again, their husbands soon referred to them as she-wolves.

Orlaith asked Achall if she wanted some food, and when the former queen did not answer, Orlaith shook her head to Etain who bowed and left.

'I will return to Áed's side, Lady. I will update you on his wellbeing later.'

She turned to leave but Achall's cold voice stopped her. 'You achieved your goal, it would seem.'

'My lady?'

'A bunch of women with sword and scabbard.'

'An army,' Orlaith said. 'At least one in the making. You have made your feelings clear on the matter, but I assure you these women are strong and mighty. And they are no less of a woman for the sword in their hands.'

'It is good that a woman can have an objective and achieve it. You are truly blessed, Orlaith.'

Achall's words came with such a sincerity that Orlaith blushed. 'You have changed in the last five years, my lady.'

Achall turned from her and stroked Breasal's hair. 'I am no more a lady than you. If we refuse to change, we will grow old in darkness.'

'You may no longer be Rónán's queen, Achall, but you will always be a lady.'

Achall brushed the comment away with a flick of her fingers. 'Tell me,' she said, 'are your warriors ready? A war is coming; Áed told me so.'

Orlaith took Breasal's hand. 'This one has hinted at similar. They are ready.'

On her return to Gallen's brú, she saw her women carrying pails of water between homes, and some were chopping wood for fires. One of the new girls—she did not yet have the time to memorise their names—clapped her hands as she herded three sheep through the rampart.

'They do not want to die,' Breasal said. Orlaith had picked him up so that his boots would not stick to the autumn mud that they walked on.

'Who does not want to die?'

'The sheep.'

Orlaith rapped his chin with a gentle knuckle. 'Not wanting to die is a good attitude to have.'

The smell of smoke and burned animal flesh hung on the air like a perpetual reminder that Rónán Ó Mordha had lost more than half of his livestock. It would have induced hunger had it not brought with it a sense of transience. The gods breathe life into careless limbs, and they take it as readily.

As the girl clapped her hands and yelped at the three sheep, she bowed to Orlaith and said, 'They leapt their wall in a blind panic and tore through the hilltop.'

'What startled them?'

The girl shrugged. 'They do not want to die,' she said.

Orlaith returned to Áed's side and helped him drink from a small cup, holding her hand under his chin to stop any spillage. 'Your mother says hello, dear one. She will come and visit you as soon as you are well.'

Breasal dragged a stool to Áed's bedside and climbed onto it. The two boys looked at each other with unblinking eyes. When at last Breasal reached out and touched Áed's burning forehead, he said, 'Dian Cécht. Father.'

Without hesitancy, Áed said, 'Airmed. Daughter.'

Orlaith listened, but the boys said no more. The exchange, as confusing to her as if they spoke a foreign language, settled with a chill in the pit of her stomach.

Her thoughts were interrupted when Gallen entered, looking harried and exhausted. His hound came at his side, a giant, panting blue-grey dog whose eyes were as gentle as his jaws were mean.

'When is the last time you slept?' she asked him, fetching a cup of water from the barrel in the corner of the room.

He drank with thirst. 'I have no time to sleep. How are the boys?'

'No change.'

'Right now, I will consider that a good thing,' he said. 'Help me strip these vines? I wish to try something new.'

'What are they?'

'Hops plant. I am hoping if I crush the seed cones and the leaves into a heated drink, it may act as a numbing agent to soothe throats against the coughing.'

Orlaith sat with him while others came and went, tending to the boys, and they stripped the vines of their cone flowers. The hound lay by Gallen's feet and shadowed him when he moved.

As they worked, Orlaith said, 'Breasal and Áed had an interesting exchange—almost as if they were referring to each other by different names.'

Gallen thumbed a seed cone from the vine and dropped it into a bowl. 'What sort of names?'

'Dian Cécht and Airmed.'

Gallen smiled. 'Father and daughter.'

'That is exactly what they said. Who are they?'

Gallen looked at the two boys, Áed stretched out on his bed, Breasal on a stool beside him. 'Dian Cécht is a god of healing. Airmed is his goddess-daughter.' He rose from his stool and approached the boys. 'Do you know me?' he asked them.

'Mogh Roith,' Breasal said.

To Orlaith's son, Gallen said, 'Father or daughter?'

'Daughter.'

'She has come to you?'

Breasal nodded. They clasped arms as men who had never met before.

Gallen said, 'I feel your anxiety, Orlaith. There is much to be fearful of in the days ahead. But there can be much light, too.' He returned to the table where they had been stripping vines. 'Do you know the story of Dian Cécht, his daughter Airmed and son Miach?' when Orlaith indicated that she did not, Gallen said, 'You will. In time.'

One of the boys coughed and when he sat up, they could see blood on his chin. 'I am next,' he cried, the panic constricting his throat so that his words were forced.

Gallen attended him and made him drink an antiemetic. When he was calmed and reassured that death would not find him, Gallen came back to his hops plants and crushed the few seed cones he had removed from the vine together with a handful of leaves. He stewed them in boiling water and set the bowl aside to cool.

They worked throughout the day and soon the boys were quietened by the hops. It was not a cure, Gallen told her, nor did it lessen their symptoms. But it would numb them to their pains.

When Rónán and Cormac visited them that evening, there was no coughing, no groaning or cries. 'If I did not see them breathing, I would think they were already gone to the Otherworld,' Rónán said.

Breasal came to him and took his hand.

'Young man, did you cast a sleeping spell upon them?'

'No,' Breasal said, a hint of the five-year-old that Orlaith missed. 'I am just a boy.'

Rónán leaned down to him. 'For your mother's sake, you should stay that way forever.'

'Is there anything we can do?' Cormac asked Gallen.

'If you have yet to pray to the gods, you should do so now.

Otherwise, I am still investigating the cause of this sickness. If you know the nature of plants, you can assist me.'

'I can just about identify a rowan tree from a dandelion. Does that help?'

'Immensely,' Gallen said. In dire times, humour went a long way to aiding moods.

With nothing more to do for the evening, Orlaith joined Rónán and Cormac in the great hall where the deceased were laid in wake. Though she had not witnessed any more death today, the bodies appeared to have doubled since she stood here that morning. She touched her hand to her heart. 'So much pain. Though the dead may be forty, there are eighty parents who have also died within their hearts.'

'And if Gallen cannot identify the cause and devise a cure, there will be many more,' Rónán said.

Breasal slept in Orlaith's arms, tired from a day of channelling godly words. She had no doubt that he was to become a druid, and at last she accepted that she could not stop it. So too, it seemed, was Áed, destined to listen to the voices of gods and recite truths to human ears.

They knelt on the ground before the bodies and the two men bowed their foreheads to the floor. Orlaith lowered her head in tribute and shifted Breasal's weight in her arms. She rubbed his back and hoped that her son's goddess was listening to her pleas. She begged for a cure, for relief. And she begged for an end to the druids' suffering.

When they stood, Cormac took Breasal from her arms. 'Your pain of grieving has made you avoid it since your arrival, Orlaith, but it is time that you visit Fionn. I will watch him until you return.'

She did not realise she had been reluctant to visit Fionn's grave until her brother told her so. His marker, at the foot of the hillside, was notched into the incline so that it offered some shelter. As she came down the slope, she steadied her breathing. When she stood before the stone slab that covered his remains, she closed her eyes against the hot tears that burned there. 'I hate you. You are the only man who will ever make me cry.' She ran the edge of her thumb under her eyes. 'Your son is to become a druid.' Although Breasal was not Fionn's biological child, the tanist had taken him on with his marriage to Orlaith and they had, for a brief time, been a unit, a family.

She knelt on the wet ground and touched the stone. 'If I were strong enough, I would pull this slab aside and crawl in beside you. But our son and my warrior girls need me.' She laughed. 'Yes, you did not mishear me. It seems I am the chieftain you were destined to be.' Upon Rónán's death, Fionn was to take over as Overking of Ailigh.

'I think about you every day. Most often on the days that I do not want to. I hope you remember me, and the souls of our departed retain their memories when they cross the mound to the Otherworld. Do you have your smiles and your laughter? Some days, I do not. Others, when you come to me in dreams, I wake with a smile and I cry. This is what you have made me. But I am stronger for it.'

She leaned down and kissed the stone slab. 'It feels no longer than a day since you held me. One day and a million years.'

She promised she would come back to his side with the dawn, and she entered Ailigh's gates and returned to the brú that Rónán had given to her and Etain. Her friend was asleep, the fire burning low, and Cormac sat in a chair with Breasal on his lap. Her son's soft snores had lulled her brother into a droop-eyed state of relaxation, but he stirred and blinked when she entered.

'You have a gentle nature,' she said. 'How is it that you became a warrior?'

'There is no room for gentle men in this world,' he told her. He handed Breasal back to his mother.

'There is always room for gentle men. Do not hide it.'

When Cormac left, she tucked Breasal into the bed beside her and closed her eyes for sleep. The stench of sickness had adhered to her nostrils so that she could not shake the smell. She buried her face in Breasal's hair and inhaled him. He was the smallest druid she had ever met. She vowed, in the presence of every god who would listen to her, and especially to Breasal's dream lady, whom she now knew to be Airmed, daughter of Dian Cécht, that no harm would befall her son. She would stand in the path of any man who dared to confront her.

She fell asleep with that thought in her mind and, in her dreams, she swung her sword and felled five hundred men. Their blood ran as a river beneath her feet while Breasal clung to her back, his arms tight around her neck, legs at her waist.

In the morning, just before dawn, when the birds had not yet stirred, she woke as Breasal prodded her shoulder. He had climbed from the bed and stood beside her, his eyes wide and something like a grin on his lips.

'What is it? What is the matter?' she asked.

'They are coming.'

She sat up. At the other side of the firepit, Etain snored.

'Who is coming?'

Breasal climbed onto the bed and cupped her face in his hands. His smile was open and wide. 'The druids are coming.'

Chapter 30

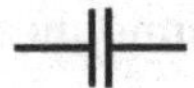

Grainne and her companions had journeyed through the night. They stopped once to rest sore feet and tired limbs, but when she told them they were close to Ailigh, they pressed on towards safety. They spoke little, preferring the solitude of their own thoughts, and Anú alternated between sleeping in Grainne's arms, or walking beside her. She held the pleats of her dress so that it didn't trail in the grass as she picked her way over the muddy ground.

In the darkness of night, they crept in short waves from treeline to shrub, conscious of the noises they made above the sounds of the night animals. Grainne had stopped worrying that they were being followed by their second day on the road, and now the attack on Emain Macha felt like an age-old memory. One of the male druids in her company, adept at the composition of song, was creating a detailed narrative of the archdruid's demise and the subsequent attack on their most sacred place. He had sung the first three verses not long after they crossed the White Strath, when the wolf had dogged their trail, and Grainne was moved by the sympathy of his words. In time, his song would resonate across Éirinn, and no man would be unaffected by her master's death.

They marched in single file through the dense forest at the southern reaches of Ailigh, holding hands in a chain so as not to lose a member of their band, and when they came from the trees, the dark hillside before them was silhouetted by a cloudless sky of ancestors twinkling down upon them. The moon was low in the western reaches.

'We are here,' Grainne announced, though she had no need. She pointed at the path that wound up the sloping hillside and as they climbed, a child ran towards them from Ailigh's open gate. When the small boy stood before her, Grainne crouched. Anú, asleep in her arms, stirred and brushed the hair from her eyes.

Though she had not seen him since his birth, Grainne recognised his blemished face, the red mark that covered his left cheek, and she smiled. 'Fionn. How is it that you are here?'

The boy's eyes widened but the smile on his face did not falter. 'You know me?'

'I helped birth you, dear one. Where is your mother?'

'I am here,' Orlaith said. She was a shadow on the hillside coming towards them, her red hair matching the shade of the boy's skin. They embraced and Anú, still in Grainne's arms, kissed Orlaith's cheek.

'I was certain you would never return to Ailigh, Orlaith. Have you just arrived? Why do you venture out in the dark?'

'You have missed so much,' Orlaith said, looking at the small collection of druids and acolytes. 'Ailigh is in trouble. We should hurry and wake the king.'

Confused, Grainne instructed her companions to follow, and as they entered Ailigh's compound, the guard on duty clanged the gate bell.

When Grainne eased Anú onto the ground at her side,

Orlaith's child came to her and took her hand. She accepted it with silent approval and Grainne narrowed a questioning eye at the boy's mother.

'His conversations with the gods are the least of our worries right now,' Orlaith said.

The gate bell rang clear and as the small company of druids mounted the inner ramparts, doors were opened, and warm smiles greeted them. 'We are saved,' a woman said. 'The gods have sent us many druids.'

As they approached the inner wall, Orlaith explained, 'Many of the boys are sick. Poison, Gallen says, but he does not know the nature of it. Too many have already died.'

Grainne quickened her step. When they came through the inner wall, Rónán had stepped from his threshold with Cormac at his heels. The gate bell stopped ringing.

'It is well that you are well,' Rónán said, taking Grainne into his arms. 'The boys are sick.'

'I am told. Where is Gallen?'

She entered her quarters and found herself surrounded by beds filled with coughing boys. Gallen, a linen cloth tied around his face, was mopping the brow of one boy while offering comforting words to another who was being sick. Grainne's fellow druids fanned out without instruction. Trained in medicine, the seventeen remaining druids of Éirinn made quick work among the boys, fetching water, emptying used bowls, and administering Gallen's antiemetic.

'I do not know the cause, Lady,' Gallen said. She could see the terror in his eyes. 'We have lost so many and I cannot stop it.'

'You are doing well. You suspect poison?' Grainne touched the back of her hand to one boy's forehead and pulled at the skin of his cheeks to inspect the whites of his eyes. She noticed some blistering around his lips and chin, which was likely caused by his vomit if his skin reacted to the poison on its way out of his body.

Gallen told her how long the boys had been sick and how many had already perished—though he could not know a precise figure as he struggled to work alone.

'You inspected their food?'

'There was none to inspect. The cooks had already cleaned the cauldrons when we discovered the sickness.'

'Have you checked their stools?'

Gallen straightened his back. 'Their stools? I was too busy to do so. Forgive me, Lady.'

Grainne touched his arm in comfort. Though he was close to the first ceremony of his druidship, he would kick himself for failing her and their king. She, too, would not have coped in his position.

Anú and Orlaith's son sat together on the floor in a corner. They still held hands and they watched the room with silence.

Grainne instructed one of the druids to go to the latrine behind her home where the boys' waste was dumped. When the woman returned with a bowl of excrement, Grainne wrapped her face to ward off the sickening smell and used a long pair of bronze tweezers to sift through the contents.

She plucked a seed and rinsed it in a bowl of water, and when she held it up, she said, 'I suspected as much.'

'A grain?' Gallen asked.

She shook her head. 'It is the seed of a whitethorn berry. The berries are edible, but the seeds are toxic.' She turned to her shelves, collecting vials of dried rose petals, coltsfoot, dandelion root, gorse, lavender and many other jars and bottles. She crushed them into a large bowl and hooked it above the fire. Smoke rose from the bowl before long.

'Fumigation?' Gallen asked.

'Charcoal. The blackened herbs should be ingested. It will soak up the poison if any remains in their bodies.'

When the dawn sky brightened to a dull grey, most of the boys had been administered the charcoal. It had been crushed and compacted into small pellets that they were made to swallow with the aid of water.

When Achall appeared in the doorway, Grainne removed the cover from her face and turned to greet her former queen, but she saw thick tears on the woman's lashes. 'Where is my son? Rónán stole my son from me.'

Grainne looked at Gallen for an explanation.

'He is here, in a bed. Somewhere,' her acolyte said.

She scanned the boys in rows of beds but did not see young Áed. Achall flitted from one child to another, and Grainne could see the tension in her temples.

'My son,' Achall cried. 'Where is my son?'

'Still yourself, Achall. We will look for him together.' Grainne took the woman's arm and they walked among the beds, calling Áed's name. He did not respond.

When they had searched all the beds in her quarters and had not found him, they moved to the granary where the remaining sickbeds were, and still he was not among them.

Achall was inconsolable. 'He is dead. By all the gods, my son is dead.'

Grainne left Achall in Orlaith's care and she hurried back to Gallen. 'He cannot have vanished,' she said. 'Are there any other sickbeds?'

Gallen, harried and exhausted, looked around the room. 'He was here, I am sure of it. Or the granary. There have been so many sick boys I cannot—he was here. I am sure.'

Grainne stepped close to him so that nobody else could hear her. 'Did he perish in the night?'

'No. I am sure he did not.'

'Do not fear, Gallen. We will find him.'

She stepped into the cold morning sunlight, calling his name. She received no answer. When she walked among the bodies in the great hall, she prayed to her most gracious lady Cáer that she would find him well. With every shroud she lifted, she dared not look upon the sallow faces of the dead children. Gallen was fatigued; in his current state of sleeplessness, one deceased child could look like any other.

The serene faces of lifeless boys brought tears to her eyes. There were seventy or more. Whomever had poisoned their food did so with a heartless spirit. The intention was not to weaken them but to destroy them.

Áed was not among the dead.

She called his name from the middle rampart, but he did not respond. Soon, many of the adults walked among the homes and store huts, shouting for him to answer them. Rónán, eyes wide with terror, checked Achall's home, and Cormac raced to Rónán's brú to look for him there.

Achall wept. She threw open doors and screamed his name.

She climbed the walls and shouted.

She slipped on the wet wooden steps of the palisade wall and when she landed on her rump, she sat there and cried into her hands.

Grainne crawled under the granary to search among the stilts that raised the dry room off the ground. If Áed was delirious in his sickness, he could be anywhere.

She found Rónán walking the length of the latrine, scanning the filth for signs of a body, but the boy was gone.

When the gate bell rang out across the cloudless morning sky, they hurried to the guard tower. 'Is it him?' Rónán called.

'No, Lord. It is an army.'

When Cormac caught up with them, Rónán said, 'Mac Fachtna's men. They have come for their reparations.'

'It cannot be,' Cormac said. 'Their seven days is not up.'

'An angry army does not keep track of the days,' Rónán said. They climbed the ladder to the tower and saw a small army, no more than one hundred men, amassed on his hillside.

'Send out your king that we might talk in parlay,' one of the men shouted.

'I do not have the time for this,' Rónán said to Cormac.

Grainne said, 'It is parlay. I will go.'

'Grainne, Seanach is dead. So much has happened that we have yet to speak about. Mac Fachtna's men want his murderer, but I cannot give them what they seek.'

'They are not Mac Fachtna's men,' Grainne told him.

'I will not ask again,' the voice called. 'Send out your king that we might talk in parlay.'

'What is the nature of your business here?' Cormac shouted.

'We will speak only with the king.'

Rónán touched Cormac's back. 'Round up the men. I want archers on the walls and fighters on the ground but keep them inside the gate. If they break parlay, I do not wish to be out there alone.' To Grainne, he said, 'Find my son. Please.'

He descended the steps and Grainne turned from the army outside. She watched Rónán's archers running into formation around the wall, and then she continued her search for the missing boy.

Orlaith comforted Achall on the steps where she sat, and below them, watching the women, Anú and Orlaith's son were still holding hands. From the moment they met, they had not left each other's side.

Grainne crouched before them. 'Have you seen the lady's son, Fionn?'

'I am Breasal,' he said. 'They do not call me Fionn now.'

'Do you know where he went?'

Anú said, 'He is not among the dead.'

Breasal said, 'He is not among the living.'

Behind them, the gate closed when Rónán stepped outside on his own.

Chapter 31

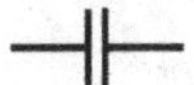

Rónán stepped out through the gate with his sword at his hip and a spear in his hand. Behind him, he heard the footfalls of his archers on the wall.

'I am Rónán Ó Mordha, Overking of Ailigh. What is your business?'

The army's spokesman came forward but remained out of firing range. In his hand, he held a section of linen. 'I trust the malady afflicting your boys has been devastating.'

'Who are you?'

'I am not your greatest concern. Your army is weakened, your stores are low. We may only be one hundred men, but we are well-provisioned. It is not a siege we want, but we are prepared for it. Open your gates that we may claim your hillfort in the name of my master.'

'Who is your master?'

'It is a name that you will hear soon enough. Open your gates. Ailigh is no longer yours.'

'You dare stand before me with a sorry excuse for an army and make demands of me? I will have your heads on pikes before your mother's tears can spill for the memory of her bastard child.'

'Mine is not the mother who will cry,' the man said. He

unfurled the linen in his hand. When he held it up, Rónán saw that it was Áed's tunic, sweat stained from his nights of fever.

'Where is my son?'

'The boy is well. He is on his way to my master. You are to come with us.'

Rónán hefted the spear. 'Bring my son back to me. I will not give you a warning.'

'He does not belong to you now. You will come willingly, or we will burn your hillfort to the ground.'

Rónán released the spear with a strong arm. Though the man was some distance from him, the spear sang through the air, and he was not fast enough to move from its path. It struck him in the chest, pinioning him to the ground at his back. Áed's tunic skittered from his fingers and caught in the grasses.

'Where is my son?' Rónán shouted.

Another member of the army stepped forward, his face covered by one of the masks the druid's assassins wore. He kicked the dead man's body so that it slid down the pole of the spear and he pulled it from the man's chest. He planted it in the ground. 'We do not wish to fight you, but we will if you force our hand. If you want your son, you will come with us.'

Behind him, Rónán's gates opened and Cormac, Fergal and Ainmire Úi Balon stepped out ahead of Rónán's warriors.

Ainmire came to Rónán's side. 'Ardal? What is the meaning of this?'

The masked man who had spoken laughed. He pulled the covering from his face to reveal himself. 'Father,' Ardal said. 'Perhaps now I can face you on the battlefield, eh?'

'What devious fuckery is this?' Ainmire said. 'Give the over-king back his son and kneel before me so that I can strike you for your insolence.'

Ardal flicked his wrist and one of his men nocked an arrow. It tore through Ainmire's neck. As the old man fell, Rónán leapt aside.

'That has got to sting,' Ardal said. 'Rónán Ó Mordha, I am supposed to bring you to my master, but I will happily bring her your head instead.'

Rónán's skin burned red with anger. He flicked his sword in an arc to loosen his wrist, and he ran towards the army. At his rear, his warriors flooded from the hillfort. The sky darkened with arrows.

The opposing army charged up the hillside as Rónán ran to meet them. He cut through one man and forced him back into another. When they fell, Rónán stepped on the living man's neck and raised his sword. 'Where is my son?'

The man twisted to free himself and Rónán brought the sword down, penetrating his chest.

He turned, pulling his blade loose, and swung. The man who stood before him raised his shield and Rónán's sword connected with it. But he drove forward with his shoulder, butting against him, and then he turned in the mud, flicking the blade up and under the shield. The man yelped as the sword struck his lower abdomen.

Rónán wrenched the shield from the man's arm, twisting and breaking the bones, and he threw it at another of the men who approached him.

Across the hillside, he saw Orlaith and her women fan out among the warriors. She used both hands on her sword to cleave a man's head from his neck and then twisted her body to attack another.

Cormac, beside his sister, let loose a javelin that connected with a man's side.

Rónán ducked under a warrior's swing and he came up with his shoulder braced for impact. He struck the man in the chest and they tumbled together on the wet grass. They rolled. Rónán pinned the man under his knees and gripped his throat with his free hand. He jammed the sword point under the man's armpit.

'Where is my son?'

'Bastard,' the man said. Blood coated his nostrils from his fall.

Rónán pushed the sword into him, from the armpit and up through his shoulder, into his neck. The grimace on the man's face faltered and his jaw slackened.

He rose, jumped over the fallen man, tearing at his flesh as he pulled his blade free, and he felt a new assailant come up behind him.

He swept his sword in an arc and Fergal jumped out of its reach. 'I sleep off a hangover and you start a war without me. We will have words when this is done. Who the fuck are they?'

'They have taken Áed.'

'Then start cleaving heads until we get him back,' Fergal said. He turned from Rónán to enter the fray.

Rónán's warriors were strong, but they were well matched by the intruders. With many of his boys sick or dead, and the men weak with hunger, a larger army might have torn through them quicker. He flipped his sword, bringing it down on a man who tried to barrel into him. It struck his arm and cut it from him before entering his fleshy side.

Rónán twisted the blade. 'Give me back my son.'

'You will never have him.'

The man fell to his knees. Rónán swung. His head rolled in

the churned earth.

His warriors were beating them down the hillside. The archers on the wall had come down to join the fight; they had no clear shot in the melee. Orlaith and her women frightened the men. In their padded tunics, they looked unhinged, long hair whipping in the breeze, swords loose but controlled in their hands. Female warriors were not unheard of, but nor were they common.

When it looked as though the intruding army was losing, they did not lay down their weapons. They fought on with a bitterness Rónán had not seen since bearing down on the Fir Bolg invaders.

He found Ardal on the field, ripping a short blade through the throat of one of Rónán's warriors. Rónán dived at him, and they tumbled.

'Where is my son?'

Ardal smiled. 'Too far for you to catch him.'

Rónán leapt at him. He whipped his sword and Ardal sliced to meet him. Iron clanged. Rónán flicked his wrist, butting the man's blade aside, and he stepped into his space with his free hand raised. He gripped Ardal's throat and elbowed his sword arm. When he flicked his own blade down, the man's hand was shorn from his wrist and it fell with his sword.

Rónán hooked his ankle behind Ardal's leg and pulled. Ainmire's son collapsed to his back and Rónán stepped on his wounded arm. He dug the point of his blade against his neck. 'I will stand here and watch you bleed out. Tell me where my son is.'

'Never.'

'Do not test me. Where is he?'

When Ardal did not respond, Rónán raised his sword and brought it down on his shield arm, tearing through the flesh and severing the limb.

'Where is he?'

A carnyx horn blew. The battle was done.

Rónán stepped back from the wounded warrior as Ardal screamed in pain. 'You are the last of your men,' he said. 'Tell me where my son is, and I will end your suffering.'

Ardal spat blood that dripped on his chin.

Rónán sheathed his sword and reached down to grip his wild hair. He dragged him up the hillside as he continued to scream and bleed. Rónán dumped him at the gate. 'Grainne,' he shouted. 'Somebody fetch the druid.' When she came, Rónán said, 'Cauterise his wounds. Do not let him bleed out.'

Grainne pointed, and two of Rónán's warriors picked the writhing man off the ground.

When Cormac and Orlaith approached Rónán, Cormac said, 'We will find him, Rónán. Do not fear it.'

Orlaith had picked up Áed's white tunic from the ground out-side. There was fresh blood on it, but Rónán was certain it was from the battle; he had not noticed bloodstains when the spokes-man had held it up for his inspection. 'My women will scout the hillside,' she said. 'If any man remains outside, he will be brought to your feet, Lord.'

Rónán nodded and marched through the rampart towards Grainne's quarters. When he got there, his druid had heated a thick blade and was searing the man's shorn arm. He sat on a stool, a bone comb in his mouth to bite on against the pain. The blackened stump of his right hand had already been charred.

Grainne stepped back as Rónán approached. He kicked Ardal Ó Ainmire square on the chest and sent him sprawling on the floor among the boys' beds.

'Get up.'

'I am armless,' Ardal spat.

Rónán stooped and gripped his hair. He pulled him upright and punched his face. Ardal fell again.

'Get up.'

The warrior spat blood.

'Get up.'

'You intend to punch me to death?'

'Get up.'

He pulled him by the hair again until he stood on weakened legs. The smell of burning flesh sent the nearby boys into coughing fits.

'Where is my son?'

'Ask your wife.'

'What has she to do with your offence?'

'More than she knows.'

Rónán jabbed his knuckles into Ardal's throat, and he fell to his knees, spluttering and blinking tears from his eyes. 'Bring Achall here at once.'

While he waited, Rónán forced the silent man back onto a stool. He lost consciousness from his wounds and Rónán slapped him awake.

'You cannot torture me,' he said. 'I have no hands for you to pull fingernails from.'

'You have toes,' Rónán said. 'I can make do. Where is my son?'

When Cormac brought Achall to Grainne's quarters, her eyes were wide, and her cheeks twitched. Her voice was weak. 'Where is my son?'

Rónán stood behind the wounded man, gripped his hair, and

yanked his head up. 'Do you know this man?'

'I want my son,' Achall pleaded.

Rónán took his sword and lay the sharp blade against Ardal's neck. 'What does my ex-wife have to do with my son's disappearance?'

'Her family is responsible.'

'What family? She has no family.'

'The woman with the scarred face.'

'Muirgel,' Achall said. The slackness had evaporated from her face and her voice was hardened. She stepped forward. 'Where is she?'

Ardal swallowed against the blade at his neck.

'Where is Muirgel?' Achall demanded. 'Where has she taken my son?'

Rónán said, 'Muirgel disappeared after Knockdhu. She is nothing.'

Ardal laughed. 'She is a rich and mighty queen. And she will be your downfall.'

Achall came closer. She gripped Rónán's blade and pressed it against the man's flesh so that it made an indentation but did not break the skin. 'Where is she?'

'You will find her on Thúr Rí. She anticipates her family's reunion.'

Achall pressed harder and she screamed. The blade cut into Ardal's neck and sliced deeper. As Achall continued to scream, her spittle washed his face just as his blood washed his chest.

When his features slackened in death, she stood back, releasing her grip on the sword, and she looked at her hands. They were carved open from her grasp on the iron blade.

She held her bloodied hands up to Rónán.

Rónán pulled his sword free from the dead man's neck and the head slumped forward.

'Gather the men,' he said. 'We go to Thúr Rí.'

Chapter 32

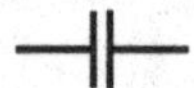

Orlaith held Achall's hands in a wash bowl to cleanse them and the water swirled red with her blood. Ardal Ó Ainmire's body had been tossed outside the gate to be burned with his fellow warriors.

She did not know who Muirgel was and, when she saw the vacant expression in Achall's eyes, she knew not to ask. She lifted Achall's hands out of the water and wrapped them in strips of linen. The cuts she sustained from pressing against Rónán's sword were deep, but Grainne said they would heal. The druid had sequestered herself in her quarters with the men and women who accompanied her that morning. It was too soon to tell if the herbal charcoal had counteracted the whitethorn berry poisoning, Grainne told them. They would know by morning.

Rónán was gathering his men together and they would leave for Thúr Rí before the afternoon was done.

When Orlaith knotted the fabric around Achall's hands, she held a cup of water to the woman's lips to drink. Achall raised her damaged hands as if to grip the cup, but she did not touch it and let Orlaith hold it for her as she sipped.

'Rónán will bring him back,' Orlaith said.

Achall nodded, but it seemed absent of understanding.

Orlaith did not know if Achall had killed a man before. If she had, she doubted it was with the force of a blade in her own hands.

'Do they pain you?'

Achall looked at her hands, fingers pink from the cold water, bandages damp and knotted, fraying ends tangling beside her thumbs, and then she looked at Orlaith. 'Where is my son?'

'Muirgel has taken him. But we will get him back. Do not fear.'

'Muirgel,' Achall said, her voice distant. She looked at her hands again. 'I am tired.'

Orlaith nodded, helped Achall to stand, and she walked her towards her bed. When she lay down, Orlaith draped a thick winter fur over her. 'You have had an ordeal. You should rest. Get some sleep.'

Achall inspected the knots on her bandages. 'I do not want to sleep. I want my son.' She yawned. 'I want my *mamaí*.'

Orlaith stroked the woman's cheek with the back of her finger. 'I cannot give you your mother, but I will help retrieve your son. Sleep now. When you wake, we will have news of him.'

Achall turned onto her side and curled into a ball. A thick tear dripped over the bridge of her nose. 'Where is my son?' she asked her heather-filled pillow.

Orlaith stepped outside and eased the door closed. Etain stood nearby with Breasal and the young druid girl called Anú. They were holding hands and had done so since the girl arrived with Grainne that morning.

'We will aid the men at Thúr Rí,' Etain said.

'We fought well outside the walls against a small army, but are they ready for war?'

'Your girls fought just as well as the men. You know they are ready.'

'And the new girls?'

'Train them as we march,' Etain said. 'Our only problem is these two.'

Orlaith looked at her son. His face was expressionless and matched the look on the girl who was a similar age and height to Breasal. She crouched before them. 'What is your name, little one?'

The girl's smile was sad and reflected the pain in her eyes. 'My brother has gone to the Otherworld.'

'I am sorry,' Orlaith said. 'If our brothers cannot be with us, the Otherworld is the best place for them, where they will be safe.'

'She is Anú,' Breasal said.

Orlaith touched her son's cheek. 'In your dreams—in your thoughts—do you know if the Lady Achall's son, Áed, is well?'

'He is not among the living,' Anú said.

Breasal said, 'He is not among the dead.'

'What does that mean?'

The children shrugged.

Etain said, 'If he is neither living nor dead, is he with the *sidhe*?'

'There are no fairy mounds here,' Breasal said. Fairy mounds were a passage to the lands of the *sidhe*. To enter would have time stand still for you while all the world aged.

'Breasal,' Orlaith said. 'I must join King Rónán and your uncle, Cormac, on the road to an island called Thúr Rí. There will be fighting.'

'I have seen you fight. You have trained for it.'

'I know, son. We have all trained hard. I do not want to take you with me into battle.'

Breasal stepped closer to Anú so that their shoulders touched, and the girl cupped her hand around his ear to whisper something to him. Breasal nodded.

Orlaith said, 'We cannot ask Anú to join us. She will be well here, with Grainne and the druids.'

'I will stay,' Breasal said. 'I can help protect her.'

Orlaith cocked her head. 'Did your dream-lady tell you to protect Anú?'

Breasal squinted into the distance in search of an answer. 'No.'

Orlaith stood. To Etain, she said, 'I will ask Grainne to mind him. It is best for him if he stays.'

She attended Cormac in Rónán's brú where he was cleaning his sword. He embraced her when she entered.

'You wear the sword like a man,' he said, 'but I did not expect you could use it so well.'

'A sword is not a man's game. It is for anyone if they have the training.'

'Your women are strong. They were a great help outside.'

'Who is this supposed queen of Thúr Rí?'

'Achall's aunt,' Cormac said. 'I am told Rónán scarred her face after the Battle of Knockdhu and then she disappeared. She has not been heard from since.'

'Is she dangerous?'

'If she is responsible for poisoning Rónán's boys, his livestock, and perhaps even the deaths of the druids, dangerous is an understatement.'

'My women will join you on the road. You will need as many swords as you can get.'

'It is not my need but Rónán's.'

'He will refuse my help in his pride. Speak with him, brother,' Orlaith said. 'My women may be few, but you know us to be mighty.'

'He will not refuse you if you ask.'

'Speak to him.'

Cormac sheathed his sword and picked up his shield. 'Prepare your warriors, sister. We ride out when everyone has gathered.'

She did not see Rónán or her brother for the rest of the afternoon. Around the hillside, Ailigh was alive with men as they readied themselves for the march, and women who ran after their husbands and their sons to ensure they had rations for the journey and hugs for memories.

She knocked on Grainne's closed door and when it opened, she saw some of the sick boys sitting up in bed. Though they were still weak with poison, their colour was returning to them. Grainne, Gallen and some of the other druids walked among the beds, distributing cups of water and small bowls of food—sweet autumn berries to nourish them.

When Grainne took a moment away from the sickbeds to greet her, Orlaith said, 'I will take my women to Thúr Rí with Rónán and his men.'

'You do not need to ask,' Grainne said. 'I will keep your son safe in your absence.'

'You scare me with your knowledgeable ways.'

'I scare myself, sometimes. When do you leave?'

'I wait to hear the bells sing. My women are gathering their things. I am heartened to see the boys are looking better.'

'It is still too soon to tell, but I see improvements in them. It is a good sign.'

'Lady,' one of the boys said. They turned to him. He coughed, but it was not a wracking choke. 'I am too weak to fight, Lady,' he said to Orlaith. 'Will you remember my name when you stab someone in the gut?'

'What is your name?'

'I am Conal.'

Orlaith patted his knee. 'I will sing your name aloud when I cut the first man down.'

'And the sun will glint off your blade and dazzle you with beauty,' Conal told her.

'Should I stab him just the once for you, or repeatedly?'

He smacked his fist into the palm of his other hand. 'Stab him until he is mush. But do not forget my name.'

'I will never forget your name, Stonal.'

'Conal.'

She winked and he laughed.

She returned to Achall's brú to check on the woman, and she found her still in bed. She was not asleep but stared at the flames of her hearth with darkened eyes.

Orlaith took the stool beside her bed. 'We will leave soon. We will not return until we have your son, this I promise you.'

'Do not make promises you cannot keep.'

'I do not make them lightly.'

Achall sat up in bed and adjusted the furs around her. 'The flames remind me of an army, marching ever unto death.'

'Do not be so morbid, Lady. In war, one army always returns the victor.'

'Bring me back my son, Orlaith. I order it.'

'You do not need to make demands when I offer it willingly. We will bring him back.'

'We have gone in opposite directions, you and I. You have risen to lead an army; I have fallen and become nothing.'

Orlaith touched Achall's shoulder. 'If you have a family, you are not nothing. All sons need their mothers. All mothers need their sons. He will be in your arms before the Yule.'

Achall's face drew vacant. 'I will pray to the . . . frogs that you succeed.'

'The gods. You are confused, Lady. Get some rest,' Orlaith said. 'You will need your strength when Áed is returned to you.'

When the gate bell tolled its call to arms, Orlaith adjusted the sword at her hip, and left to join her army.

They assembled on the hillside outside the gates. She joined the ranks among her women, and Etain waved her forward. 'Lead your women, Orlaith. You are no longer the warrior's wife, but a warrior. Your command will be our rule.'

She came to the head of her small regiment. She did not address them. She nodded and they bowed to her. She turned when Rónán stepped into his carbad and raised his hands for hush.

'We have been through trying times,' he said. 'It has seemed that the gods abandoned us when we needed them most. But the druids have returned, and they have healed our boys—your sons. We are few, but we are strong. Many of them lie in sickbeds, or they lie in wake, awaiting their graves. Their souls march west towards the Otherworld. I am grateful for their service. And for yours.'

The gathered army cheered. Orlaith could not count them but knew them to be four hundred strong.

Rónán raised his hands again. 'This is my fight, to return my son to my side. For many of you, your grief is strong. I will not object if you wish to stay here and grieve your losses. I know your pain. I will not beg you to fight at my side.'

'We are Ó Mordha,' one of the men among the army shouted. Those around him laughed. 'Where the king goes, we go.'

'I am indebted,' Rónán said. 'But I free each of you of any obligation to your king. I will turn my back if you do not wish to be seen. Go back to your sons if that is what you need. I will not think less of any man who walks away from a fight to retrieve one son when so many other sons have already perished.'

He turned his back.

There was silence.

No one moved.

At length, one man clanged his sword against his shield. Soon, others joined in. 'Rónán,' they chanted. 'Rónán.'

Orlaith saw Cormac touch Rónán's back and when he turned to face them, the assembled army cheered him.

He nodded, flicked the reins of his carbad, and the carnyx boy blew his marching notes.

Orlaith strode forward, her women behind her, Etain at her side. She could feel a knot of tension at her chest. She may only have forty warriors, but now she commanded her own army.

Only good things could come of it.

Chapter 33

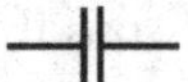

When they marched down Ailigh's hillside towards the lough, Rónán had no thought in his mind beyond retrieving his son. Muirgel, Achall's aunt, had been inconsequential in his life. The wife of Rónán's chieftain, the man who fostered him after his father's murder, was instrumental in bringing the foreigners to Knockdhu seven years before insofar as she had made the journey with her husband. He knew her to be cruel, to whisper viciousness in her husband's ear and watch as he carried out her bitter machinations, but he did not consider that she could instigate such a calculated strike—taking down the druids, eliminating his livestock, and poisoning his trainee warriors.

He had so little left. Looking behind him, he saw four hundred men and boys—older boys, those who were not affected by Muirgel's whitethorn berry poisoning. The bodies of those who had passed beyond the veil of death still lay in wake in the great hall. When their seven days of mourning had carried them towards Manandán's spectral ship, Grainne and her druids would cremate them and bury their remains with their swords. Their homes would lie empty, like the fields that no longer felt the weight of his livestock.

The men who followed him now, those who had lost their

sons, marched with him not out of devotion to their king but with heavy hearts and fury. If they could kill their child's murderer, it would ease their pain of loss. All death needs avenged. That is the law of war, and that is why war will never end.

Before leaving, when the men were preparing themselves for the march, Rónán called upon his former wife. Orlaith had bandaged her hands and put her to bed. Achall did not speak to him. It was as though her mind had escaped through her bleeding hands and seeped upon the floor to be forgotten. Her face was slack and without colour, and her eyes—normally so fiery with spite—were lacklustre and free from the sheen of life.

She lay on her side, facing the fire, but he was not certain she saw the flames that danced there.

'We are leaving now,' he said. When she did not acknowledge him, he added, 'Thúr Rí is not far. I will have him home in little more than ten days.'

Her breathing was shallow, hair spilling over her lips to hide her face.

'Do you hear me? I will bring him home. You have my word.'

Rónán turned and closed the door behind him. When he called for his able men to march at his side, he ensured enough of them would stay at Ailigh to defend its walls in his absence. Seanach Mac Fachtna's men would arrive soon, and they would be asked to await Rónán's return as a pact of peace. They would see that Ailigh was lacking in men and, if they had any morals, they would oblige.

One of Rónán's men stood outside Achall's door, not a guard but a sentry. Rónán nodded to him. He could feel the pains of war already in his gut.

Grainne met him at the gate before he stepped outside to

address his men. At her side, Breasal and Anú stood shoulder to shoulder. They could have been twins had her hair not been white and his flaming red.

'I wish I could attend your side on the road, Lord,' Grainne said, 'but I am needed here.'

'Cure the sick and bring them back to health, Grainne. We have not yet spoken about your most sacred place.'

'It would stick in my throat to speak the words aloud, Lord. I have deliberations to make with my fellow druids. May all the gods travel at your back and protect your fore. I will make sacrifice that you find Áed and bring him home safely.'

They embraced. Rónán knelt before the children and said, 'Any final words of wisdom, young man? Now is the time to speak them.'

Breasal said, 'I do not have words. Just an image. There is blood in the water.'

Rónán nodded as though it meant something.

At the edge of the lough, in view of the standing stone, Rónán's army fanned out. They gathered their curragh boats and, rather than waste time skirting the southern regions of the lough and the river that flowed into it, they rowed across the water, twenty men to a ten-man curragh. At the far side, the hide-skinned boats were picked up and carried over their heads. They would need them when they reached the shore before setting sail for the island of Thúr Rí.

Cormac remained at Rónán's side as they marched. Behind them, Fergal struck up a warrior's song in memory of Ainmire Úi Balon, and the few men around him sang along.

By sunset, still a four-night march from the coast, Rónán had hoped to press on into the dark, conscious of the head start Áed's kidnappers had gained, but they were hampered by a storm that tore in from the north and brought icy needles that stabbed them. They took shelter among the evergreens and set camp as best they could.

'In this weather, nobody is travelling. Áed's captors will not get any further ahead of us,' Cormac assured him.

They sat at the edge of the forest with a small, hooded fire that did little to warm them, and Orlaith, Fergal and Diarmuid joined them.

'If Torin Ó Neill returns to Ailigh with his army as he promised,' Diarmuid said, 'they will not be far behind us. A day at best.'

'I hope he reaches Ailigh before Mac Fachtna's men do,' Cormac said.

'The children are on the mend,' Orlaith told them. 'A few days and they will be well enough to fight, I am sure.'

'They were weakened too much to recover so soon.'

A silence fell upon them, and a wineskin was passed around. Beyond the treeline, the icy rain beat the ground with its anger.

When Rónán turned in for the night, huddled under thick winter furs beneath the cover of a thin tent canopy, he took Cormac in his arms and held him tight. They did not speak.

With the dawn, Rónán was fatigued. He had slept little, plagued by thoughts of his child, shackled and carried to a distant island, a dark place whose exports aided its wealth. How Muirgel had assumed control of the small territory without his knowledge, he could not say. The island had a king, last he knew.

They broke fast and cleared the area, protective of the lands on which they walked, and the curragh boats that had been propped among the trees were picked up and carried along the narrow trackway that wound its way towards the far-off coast.

The days passed with interminable end. His column of men snaked west across the northern reaches of Éirinn, a series of upturned boats and tramping feet. The curraghs protected them from the rain as they marched, and when they broke to eat, they hunched beside the boats to shield themselves from the bracing wind. Winter was gripping the forests and dales with her icy fists. The ocean, when they came to it, would be rough and enraged at their passage.

For two nights they walked under a leaden sky that sagged heavy with rain. Thunder cracked throughout the countryside with an aggressive roar, and sheet lightning lit the noon clouds that glinted in Rónán's eyes as he led the march.

On the second day, they approached the westernmost tribe before the dense forest that stretched towards the coast. The tribe had no affiliations with Ailigh and the chieftain, a man Rónán had met only once, ruled his people with a powerful grip. He governed his clansmen and bowed to no one.

Rónán offered him a dozen iron ingots on his return from Thúr Rí for his hospitality, and he asked if the chieftain had seen anyone travel beyond his borders in recent days.

Brín Ó Cairbre, silver-haired and stooped, who walked on bowlegs with the aid of a cane, ordered his cumal girls to serve Rónán and his noblemen a meagre meal of cold curds, but said his army must remain outside his border walls. 'Not one man or goat has passed this way that I cannot account for.'

'You are a great man, Brín Ó Cairbre, master of all that you own,' Rónán said. 'A man who rules his tribe for forty years is a man worthy of renown. Your people are lucky by your presence.'

'Do not goad me, child,' Brín said. 'Flattery eats at a man's soul the way wine eats at his willpower. These twisted legs have carried me upright since I was a boy, and no man makes fun of me lest he gets a kick in the backside.' The chieftain stood from his seat, his ornate cane acting as a third leg—the only straight one he had—and he hobbled down the three steps that led from his dais. 'I keep my business to myself, same as everyone should but no one does. Other man's war is not my business.'

'I do not seek war,' Rónán said.

'No. But war seeks you, or so the songs tell. Deny it and I will have your head. You breeze through a man's tribe lands with a whirlwind of passion and in your wake lies devastation and pregnant sheep, so as I hear it.'

'You have been listening to the wrong bards, my lord. I will not take up any more of your time. All I ask is that you allow us to camp outside your walls for the night. We will be gone by dawn.'

'If you ask a favour, I will grant it. If you make demands, I will set my dogs on your sorry arse. You have eaten the meal I had prepared for you. Step beyond my gates and camp where you may. When I wake with the yapping of the pups at dawn, I expect you will be gone. Do not return to my gates with war in your fists. I will have your head if you do.'

Rónán bowed with theatrics and turned from the chieftain. He told his men to step back two hundred paces from Brín Ó Cairbre's walls and when they lit their fires, Cormac said, 'Why did you not challenge him?'

'It would be no challenge.'

'But you could take his land and his people with little force. He insults you and you turn your back on him.'

Rónán smiled. 'He insults himself, not me. He has been a

thorn in the Ó Mordha tribe's side since he took power forty years ago. But he keeps to himself and if you did not hear the cries of his dogs and his wives, you would not know him to be alive. Let him have his small glory. It is all he has.'

In the morning, though neither chieftain nor overking sought war, war came to them regardless.

Five hundred warriors marched from the coast and set upon them with ferocity. They were dressed in similar garb as those men who faced Rónán outside Ailigh and their arms were strong.

Rónán's sentries raised the alarm before the opposing army came too close, and Brín Ó Cairbre, on the back of a horse and strapped to it by the waist, rode through Rónán's camp with a raised fist. 'You brought this to my border. When I slaughter these bastards, I will come for you.'

Brín's small army, less than fifty men, marched towards the open field where the Thúr Rí warriors amassed, and Rónán's men assembled beside them, swallowing Brín's tribe by their force.

Brín rode out into the field with a sword in one hand and the horse's reins in the other, his lank hair whipping behind his head, and he avoided a barrage of spears before gutting two men in quick succession.

'That,' Rónán told Cormac, 'is why I did not challenge him.'

They charged into the field. Orlaith and her women flanked left as Cormac and Diarmuid tore to the right with a contingent of warriors. Fergal and Rónán sliced through the middle of the field.

Rónán's shield was tight on his left arm. With no spears to hand, he scooped up a sizeable stone as he ran, and he hurled it into the onslaught. The small rock bounced from one warrior's head and grazed a second. The first man fell.

He sidestepped a swing from his opponent and crashed into another warrior. As they fell, Rónán flicked his blade with precision and cut through the man's throat. Blood splashed his mouth.

He wiped his face with the back of his arm and raised his shield as another man bore down on him. His sword whipped through the man's leg and, as he fell, Rónán sliced the blade through the warrior's face. His tongue slid from his lips as the head flipped through the air.

A short distance to his right, he saw Fergal swing his sword. The burly man had a custom-made shield that was strapped to his shoulder. The metal arm was not enough to support the weight of it in battle or it would tumble from him.

Fergal's mouth was open in song, though no sound could be heard above the din of war. Rónán realised that if Fergal's death did not occur on the battlefield, and he was set upon by a band of hungry wolves, Fergal would die an angry man. He lived for the fight. If he was not swinging his sword, he was raising his right arm to drink. Any death that did not come from the sword or from stomach rot would pain him more.

Brín Ó Cairbre's horse rode through Rónán's path and he jumped aside of it. Brín swept his sword downward to slice a man through the chest, and as he turned the horse, whose hooves pranced on the brown grasses, Brín said, 'You owe me one.' His laughter echoed as he rode towards the distant warriors.

Rónán spotted him, tracking his movement as he fought through the field. He ran. When Brín's horse was hacked in the leg by a short axe, Rónán leapt, gripped his arm around Brín's waist, and hauled him from the horse. He had forgotten the old man was tethered to the gelding's chest and, as they fell, the horse tumbled with them. Before the beast fell on him, Rónán pulled Brín's twisted legs free from under it.

'We are even,' he said. He jumped to his feet, twisting his blade so that it sliced through a warrior's forearm, and he ran forward, leaving Brín Ó Cairbre to undo his own ties.

Diarmuid fought alongside his son, Darragh, and the father and son whipped their swords in unison. They cut through two men with precision.

The field was a bloodied mess. Before the carnyx boy blew his final notes, Rónán kicked out at his nearest opponent, his heel connecting with the man's chest, and when he fell, Rónán twisted and kicked his toes into the man's throat. Wracked with coughing, the man did not see Rónán's sword descend on him.

Rónán turned to see Orlaith stab one man in the stomach before using her leg to butt another man to a stop. Her sword flicked backwards, and the second man's blood arced to join the first on the wet ground.

The battle was done.

Rónán breathed. He wiped the blood from his face and counted his losses. The sixty dead were cleared from the field.

Brín Ó Cairbre had not untied the rope that tethered him to his horse. Instead, he had hacked at it with his sword so that, when he approached Rónán on the field, the rope trailed behind him. His wide gait reminded Rónán of a spider.

'I do not care for war,' the old man said.

'That was not a war. It was a skirmish.'

'Regardless, I have lost sixteen men. How will you account for them?'

Rónán stepped into Brín's space. 'I have no desire to strike you down. For the loss of your sixteen men, I will give you sixteen years. If your old carcass can survive until then, that is how long you have before I return to your borders and claim your lands. You may hope that you die before you see my face again. Step aside, old man. I need to retrieve my son.'

Chapter 34

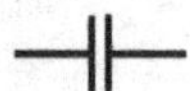

Grainne closed her eyes and bowed her head. The children's health was improving and, this morning, two days since she administered the charcoal antidote, one third of them were out of bed and walking on weak limbs. Aoibhinn and her cooks prepared a hot meal of stewed pork and root vegetables, and even those children who were still too weak to climb from their beds had mustered enough strength to eat.

She gave thanks to her most gracious lady Cáer and threw open the door of her home to alleviate the stench of sickly children. She crushed dried petals and scattered them under beds and in earthenware bowls that were heated above a flame to diffuse their floral scents through the stale air.

When her home and the granary no longer smelled of festering sickness, Grainne picked her way through the winter mud to visit Achall. The sentry outside her home bowed, knocked on her behalf, and pushed the door open.

Achall emerged from the darkness, her face streaked with tears, and she gripped Grainne's robes with tight fists. 'Have you seen Áed? He was here just a moment ago.'

'Rónán has gone to fetch him.'

'Where has he gone? I cannot find him anywhere.'

'He is well,' Grainne said. 'Rónán will bring him home soon.'

Achall released Grainne's robe. 'I wish that man would stop taking my son on hunts. He is too young.'

'Yes, Lady. Let's go inside; we can wait for them together.' She escorted the former queen into her home and, when Achall sat on a stool by the embers of her fire, Grainne poked the cinders and added another log. 'It is freezing in here. Did you not see that the fire was dying?'

'I was hot.'

Grainne touched her palm to Achall's forehead and cheeks. 'You do not have a fever. Have you eaten?'

Achall's eyes widened and she stood. 'I must find Áed. He is hungry.'

'Áed is with Rónán, remember?' Grainne helped the woman sit. She inspected her eyes and her tongue. 'I will get you a tincture. You should sleep.'

'There is nothing wrong with me, druid,' Achall said.

Grainne knelt before her. 'Achall, do you know who I am?'

'Of course, I do. You are a druid.'

'What is my name?'

'Where has my husband taken my son?'

Physically, there was nothing wrong with Achall. But Grainne worried for the state of her mind. That she had called Rónán her husband, when they had been divorced for five years, was troubling. The trauma of losing her son must have addled her brain.

'Rónán will bring Áed home very soon. A few days at most. Come. You should get some sleep. You need to be well rested for their return.'

'A few days?' Achall said as Grainne led her to the bed at the far side of the fire.

'Hunting,' Grainne confirmed. 'They won't be long.'

She stayed until Achall stopped talking, huddled under her furs, and then she returned to her home to prepare a tincture. She mixed rosemary with the juice of blueberries to aid Achall's memory, and to it she added lavender to soothe her mind and still her body. A few days' rest and she should return to health.

That evening, when she dined with Gallen and her niece, Bec, they spoke of things that bore no weight. The poisoning and its resultant sickness were pushed aside, Achall's confusion was not discussed, and the war that was sure to come in the wake of Áed's kidnap was the farthest thing from their lips. They talked, instead, of the coming winter, of the wheat rust disease that blighted them and their lack of grain, of the Yule celebrations that—despite their disinterest in rejoicing—would light up the festive hillside regardless.

When she lay in bed later, listening to the soft snores of those children in the annex who were still too weak to leave, she slipped into a darkness that was swift in coming and gripped her with a tightness that comforted her chest.

In time, her bare feet felt the sticky dew of spring and, when she turned her head, she knew she was in the presence of her most gracious lady Cáer.

The hillside—an unfamiliar field of bright buttercups—extended skyward into pink clouds. The honking call of a skein of geese broke the otherwise silent incline, and a swan—solitary in its brilliance—settled on a rock that was carved in the swirled patterns of an ancient people, and she folded her wings.

Grainne knelt and pressed her forehead to the warm ground. 'My lady. Do not look upon me, for you will see the face of failure.'

A hand touched her hair and, when she raised her eyes, Cáer's wide smile greeted her with warmth. Her eyes, a swirl of unidentifiable colour—every colour—were moist and sad.

'Child,' the goddess said, her lips unmoving. 'You are so few, and yet you radiate the light of our times.'

'Many have died, my lady. I do not know if my brethren walk beyond the walls of Ailigh or if those within are all that remain.'

'The time is now, child. You cannot win against the darkness if a firm hand does not guide the way.'

'The archdruid nominees have perished, Lady. We have no one fit to lead.'

'The time is now,' Cáer repeated.

'We are so few.'

'And yet you radiate the light of our times.'

When she opened her eyes, swallowed in the darkness of her quarters, she wiped the tears that dampened her cheeks. One among her kin would lead the druids through these dark times. There was no other option.

As the dawn broke cold and wet across the hillside, Grainne called her fellow druids to her side. The seventeen druids and acolytes who accompanied her from Emain Macha, together with Gallen and young Breasal who refused to leave Anú's side, gathered with her in the great hall, standing among those bodies who lay in wake. The wailing women were relieved of their duties and the door was barred and locked.

'The most gracious lady Cáer has come to me in the night,' Grainne said. The orange glow of the torches that were ensconced in the walls brightened the shrouds of the dead and the faces of the living. 'We are without a head. We cannot continue with no direction.'

In the silence that followed her words, she could hear the rain as it attacked the thatching above her. A damp stain spread across the daub-wall in the far corner behind the kingseat.

'None of us are qualified to lead,' one of the druids said. 'We are provincial druids and acolytes not yet learned in the ways of the earth.'

'Betha,' Grainne said, indicating the oldest woman among them. She was not yet forty winters old, but their numbers were so few. 'You are most senior. Will you honour the gods with your leadership?'

Betha shook her head. When she spoke, her voice was soft but grating, a harsh sound that hinted at a lifelong chronic cough. 'I do not have the qualities nor the stomach to lead. Look to another.'

The male druid who had composed the song of their master as they journeyed west cleared his throat. Grainne could not recall his name. 'The child wishes to speak.'

Anú, who had been walking among the bodies of the dead, stooping to adjust their shrouds so that no part of their flesh was visible, turned and came to Grainne. She raised her arms to be lifted, and when Grainne held her, the girl said, 'It should be you.'

Grainne stroked Anú's cheek. 'No, child. There are others more worthy.'

'The swan-lady told me. It should be you.'

'I agree,' Betha said, and the others nodded in accord.

'I cannot.'

'You are no less qualified than the rest of us,' one of the others said.

Gallen stepped forward. Beside him, Breasal took his hand.

'My lady, if the goddess Cáer spoke your name to the girl, you cannot go against their demands. It seems you have been chosen.'

'I am not the one,' Grainne said.

'You are the only one.' Gallen released Breasal's hand, and he knelt before Grainne. 'Your people beg you.'

'Rise from your knees, Gallen. I am not qualified to lead.'

'If the child says you are named, you have no choice,' Gallen said. He lay prostrate before her, his forehead on the rushes that covered the floor.

'Gallen, please. Stand.'

His voice was muffled. 'I will not rise until you accept our leadership.'

'I cannot.'

Betha said, 'You must.'

She lay face down on the floor beside Gallen.

And the others joined them.

When only Breasal stood before Grainne, he raised his hand towards Anú, who slipped from Grainne's arms. Together, they faced her, and then lowered themselves to the ground to lie with the druids among the dead.

The rain had passed. The lonely song of a solitary bird filtered through the cracks in the door.

'I cannot,' Grainne said again. 'Please, stand.'

Her druids did not move.

'We are so few. We do not know if other druids remain alive. Someone beyond these walls will be a more suitable candidate.'

From the floor, Gallen said, 'Mogh Roith commands you.'

'Boann commands you,' Betha said.

'Maeve commands you.'

'Bríg commands you.'

'Lugh commands you.'

When all the druids had named their gods, Anú raised her head. Her eyes, wide with wonder and bright with otherworldly light, blinked twice before she spoke. 'Cáer commands you,' she said.

Grainne knelt before them and bowed her forehead to the ground. 'I accept.' When they rose and congratulated her, she said, 'I will do so only as a temporary measure. Your words have been kind, but I am still a child in the eyes of the gods.'

'We all are,' Betha said.

'When these troubled times are done, when we can gather together with all those druids who could not make it to Emain Macha, another will be chosen in the mandatory ways of our people. I am just an interim.'

An archdruid had not been elected in so long that those who gathered around Grainne did not know the rituals that should be made to honour the occasion. Grainne returned to her private quarters to prepare herself, and when she stripped to bathe, she immersed her face in a bowl of heated water and she cried.

When her body was cleansed, she donned a simple green dress with two pleats in the front, and a fabric belt that tied at the rear. She cinched her hair back with a thin green ribbon, and she removed the leather strap that had been wrapped three times around her wrist on the day of her graduation. It would be retied during her inauguration as archdruid.

In a bronze hand-mirror, she stared at her own eyes. They were not the eyes of an archdruid. She felt like a fraud.

'My most gracious lady Cáer. I do not know why you have given me this grief, but I need your help. I cannot make decisions for these people when I can hardly speak my own mind. I will honour your wisdoms if you honour me by your presence. Walk beside me that I may learn from you.'

That evening, with the setting of the sun, the druids and acolytes, along with Breasal, gathered in an oak grove four hundred rods from the eastern base of Ailigh's hills. Seven torches were lit, and seven sentries stood with their backs to the circle. This was not a ritual for public eye.

Grainne, accompanied by her personal acolyte, stepped from the shadows among the trees.

'I do not have the head for this,' Grainne whispered.

'Hush,' Gallen said. 'You are the mouthpiece for the gods.'

When he walked her to the centre of the grove, he bowed to her and took his place among the others.

Seven gifts were bestowed upon her. A robe that she should always be warm; a staff—cut that afternoon from a living yew tree—that she might always touch the earth; a torc of gold to adorn her neck; a circlet for her arm; a bouquet of white heather to ward her; a chalice carved of oak and filled with spring water that she may never thirst; and a wrap of wheat-bread still warm from the stones that she may never hunger.

She was made to sit on a stool that had been placed there, and her bare feet were bathed and dried by her people. A goat, bright with youth, was sacrificed, and the songs of the gods were sung.

Betha, whose voice did not lend itself to music, carried the low notes of her god-song as she walked three times around the grove. In her hands, she held a section of white linen, and when she passed her fellow druids and acolytes, they kissed the fabric and pressed their foreheads against it.

When the linen was presented to Grainne, she kissed it, sealing a pact with those assembled, and she lowered her head to it.

Betha unfurled the fabric and draped it over Grainne's shoulders.

Her leather strap was wrapped three times around her wrist, once for her goddess, second for the earth, and third for her people.

She was stripped of her clothes that she should stand naked before the gods, accepting of their words and selfless in the faces of her people. The new robe—a simple brown fabric that, in the custom of her master, was unadorned—was placed upon her shoulders and when she slipped her arms through the sleeves, it was buttoned by Gallen who, until his graduation, would remain at her side as her acolyte.

When the rituals were complete, Breasal approached Grainne and knelt before her. He beckoned her ear so that he could whisper to her.

Grainne knelt in front of him and touched his cheek. 'Sweet child, what words do you have?'

The boy leaned towards her, his voice low. 'The gods are pleased,' he said. 'But death is near.'

Chapter 35

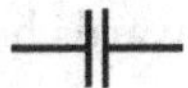

Orlaith opened her eyes and the dawn had not yet broached the cover of naked tree limbs above her. They took shelter for the night among the trees that stood sentinel in the valley between two mountain ranges on the north and south. They were a day from the coastline and the dream that danced at the corners of her memory was of endless journeys and Fionn at her side.

She adjusted the furs around her arms and sat up. Etain's rhythmic breathing twitched the mossy grasses beside her. Her women were huddled together in twos and threes under thick winter furs and the snores of Rónán's men amassed nearby was enough to wake the dead.

The campfire glinted in the clearing and, above the sound of the sleeping men, Orlaith heard whispered voices and recognised her brother among them.

She rose and picked her way over the sharp brambles to stand at the fireside. As she approached, Cormac and Rónán smiled at her, words bitten behind bright teeth, and Fergal Ó Fuinseog with his rotund belly and his metal arm bowed with a bard's assuredness.

'When I approach a gathering of men,' Orlaith said, 'and their words cease at my appearance, I fear it is one of only two reasons—that I was the topic of conversation, or that I am so divinely beautiful that all men falter as their tongues are tied.'

'Perhaps both those reasons are true, Lady,' Fergal said. The firelight glinted in his flame-warmed eyes and a smile stretched the corners of his lips.

'I shall choose to believe it, my lord.'

Rónán held a wineskin towards her. 'We were discussing tactics. I fear we do not have enough curraghs for all of us to cross the sea successfully.'

'Should we double up? How many men would one curragh hold?'

'Before it would sink under the weight?' Cormac said. 'They are designed for ten men. They could hold thirteen, fourteen at a stretch, but conditions would be cramped.'

'And how far is this island from the mainland?' Orlaith asked.

'Five thousand rods, give or take,' Rónán said. 'It would take us a quarter day to make the journey; longer if the curraghs are overloaded or if the seas are rough and the winds are against us.'

'The gods will have our backs,' Fergal said.

'The gods,' Rónán told him, 'are far too busy with every other disaster that has befallen us since last Yule.'

'Busy or not,' Orlaith said, 'I am hopeful that they can see all and help all. What are the gods if we do not have belief in them?'

'I'll drink to that,' Fergal said, draining the last of a wineskin and smacking his lips.

They spoke at length as they warmed themselves by the flames, and alternative options to overfilling their boats were spoken plainly. They did not have the time to cut limbs from trees and tether them together to make rafts. They could not leave half the men on the mainland in case Muirgel had bolstered her small island with additional warriors. And there were no magic bridges or winged horses that could carry them across the sea.

'We have no choice,' Rónán said. 'We leave our provisions behind. Each man takes his sword and shield and each curragh will be equipped with seven spears, and three skins of coal-tar pitch for burning. Without the excess weight, we can fit fifteen men per boat. The current will be at its calmest just before dawn. We will divide our men—those with the strongest arms—and they can take turns to row as hard as they can. If the winds do not shift, we will be rowing against them, but we do not have the luxury of waiting for change.'

As the dawn broke, Orlaith found herself yawning and stretching her eyes from their tiredness. It had not rained through the night and, though the air was frosty, and their breath plumed in clouds of vapour when they spoke, the ground had not yet been hardened by winter. The green kalpasi moss at the base of the trees did not crunch when she peeled it from the bark and chewed it raw.

They ate the dawn meal with keen hunger and Etain rounded up Orlaith's women for a short practice with the sword. When they were assembled, Orlaith stood before them and instructed them as she had done daily in the fields that surrounded Banan MacColm's clanship. They swung their blades and rotated their bodies in unison and Rónán's men came to watch. A woman in possession of a sword was no rare sight, but over forty of them, each perfectly timed, must have looked more like a druid's dance of worship than a warrior's training exercise.

When the women were distracted by the men's attentions, Orlaith smacked the flat of her blade against her shield to refocus them. At her side, Etain, who had assumed the position as Orlaith's second in command with an unspoken willingness, barked orders in repetition when Orlaith made her demands.

In five rows, the women practiced, and when the sun dazzled the tops of the trees, Rónán called for his army to fall in.

Cormac embraced his sister. 'I always knew you to be quick with a blade, but you terrify me as much as I am enamoured of your skill.'

'My force is great, Cormac. We would not exist if not to terrify you.'

'I must apologise for eating your honeyed bread when I was six winters old.'

'I have not forgotten it. You have much to apologise for, little brother. My sword is sharp, and my memory keen.'

'Would one all-encompassing apology do for now?'

The men were forming lines three abreast with Rónán and Fergal at their head. 'It will have to,' Orlaith said. 'But when we have rescued young Áed and are returned home, I expect to be greeted with such profuse apologies for being the brattiest little brother in the history of brothers, to the point that your voice will break when you have finished.' She winked at him and he laughed.

'You have too much of Mother in you for me to argue, Orlaith. I will prepare my apology speech as we march.'

'As well you should,' she grinned. She took to the head of her women, Etain at her side, and she nodded to them. This time tomorrow, they would be scrambling into curraghs and riding a choppy sea, and she was certain many of her girls had never seen the coast let alone sat on the wet floor of a boat whose only purpose was to carry them away from dry land. 'Lift your spirits,' she said. 'We will soon be home.'

The morning progressed with slow determination as they picked their way over the brambles and rocks of the forest floor. When they crossed a narrow gulley, whose frothy waters bubbled with winter exuberance, Orlaith cupped her hands and drank from it and felt the chill of life easing down her throat.

Etain said, 'Save some water for the rest of us, Lady.'

Orlaith patted her rose-coloured cheeks and grinned. But before she could reply, a shout came from the head of the column.

They were under attack.

Orlaith leapt over the gulley and drew her sword. 'Formations,' she called. She did not look behind her; her women would be quick to follow orders.

She rushed forward, hampered by the trees that, until now, had provided warmth against the northerly winds. Now she cursed their existence for a lack of striking range.

She watched as the men fanned out among the boles. 'Where?' she shouted to her brother.

'Everywhere,' was his reply.

She turned when a flash of colour caught her attention. A man barrelled towards her, and she ducked under his sword. She came up beside him and swept her blade into his back. His cloak was brown, and his tunic was green, as though his intention had been to hide among the trees. When he fell, she turned her sword and plunged it into him, withdrawing the blade in time to block the sword-thrust of another man.

After her fourth kill, she said, 'Does this queen have an unlimited source of warriors? Do they seep from cracks in the earth like ants?'

Etain rolled over her kill and was quick to her feet. 'Stop

revelling in fun.'

'The only fun in war,' Orlaith told her, pausing to swipe her blade across the chest of a burly man, 'is the peace that follows it.'

She pushed forward. Somebody up ahead announced the presence of a clearing and the thinning of the trees. If they could reach open ground, they would have better luck. She turned behind a tree bole and flicked her blade out to catch the throat of an assailant. He did not fall until she extracted her sword from his neck.

Somewhere in the dark distance of the trees, she heard her brother grunting as he fought; she had heard it many times in their childhood when he swung a wooden sword with his friends, heard the same grunt when their father wailed on the boy's backside with calloused hands for his disrespect. Cormac would not give their father the satisfaction of tears and the only time she ever saw him cry in his youth was the day he was shipped south to be fostered to Rían Ó Hargon's tribe. Sitting at the back of a small carbad, eight-year-old Cormac had waved at Orlaith, a wide smile on his face, and his eyes glistened not with fear or longing, but with triumphant delight.

Orlaith weaved between two men, turned, knocked one in the back with her shield and struck the other with her sword.

Their father had not been a bad man. He was strict, as all fathers are, and his word was law. The druids and the clan kings can make their demands outside his brú, he told his children, but inside his walls, he was king. She was saddened at his death as equally as at the news of her mother's passing. Though she had never sought to marry or have children, for such homely longings had been alien to her until she met Fionn, she felt sorrow at the inability to present her child to her parents that they could hold him and kiss his blemished cheek.

When her mother died, some years after her father's death in battle, Orlaith knew she was homeless. The Fir Bolg invasion seven winters ago ended the lives of many, but only two had brought Orlaith to tears—Áed the Executioner, and her mother.

Returning to Ailigh with Cormac had given her a home once more. And here she was, fighting for its continued existence.

She parried, sidestepped, thrust. She was wrong; there is fun in war—so long as you are winning.

She could see the trees thinning out a short distance before her. She counted the men who had broken through the ranks of Rónán's warriors and, even as she did so, she was plotting a path between them.

One of the men tore the shield from his arm and hurled it towards her. Although she blocked it with her own shield, the force knocked her from her feet and her shoulder struck the sharp trunk of a tree. The man descended on her, his sword raised, and Orlaith kicked out but missed his leg. As he came down with his sword, she rolled aside, wrapping her ankles around his calf, and when she twisted, the man tumbled with her. She got to her knees with a fistful of wet earth and smashed her fist into his mouth. She scrambled for the dagger at her hip and pushed it through his cheek while she held his head with her other hand.

She tore, and his scream was muffled by soil.

She stood and then dropped her knee down onto his chest, sweeping the short blade across his throat.

By the time she had retrieved her sword that had tumbled from her when she fell, another goon was upon her. She swung her sword and caught his cloak—a foolish thing to wear in war——and as she twisted the blade free, she turned so that her back was to him. Tangled with her, she reached over her shoulder and gripped the back of his neck. He had no room to parry.

Orlaith heaved, bowing towards the trees before her, and lugged him over her shoulder as she screamed with effort.

As he landed, his sword flailed wide and nicked her thigh. She felt the blood dampen her short dress as she went to her knees. She had dropped her dagger during the manoeuvre and her sword was too long to be of any use. The man's hand gripped her dress, and she punched his wrist. Her hand felt through the sharp brambles and, despite the agony, she gripped the thorns and tore them free from the ground. She took the length and wrapped it around his neck, twisting as the thorns dug into his flesh and her palms.

She smacked his head into the ground, and she could see the moment his spirit left his eyes.

A hand took her armpit and brought her to her feet. 'Are you hurt?' Rónán asked.

She shook her head.

Rónán turned from her, swinging his sword that glinted as the sun broke the treetops, and he was gone into the fray.

She limped forward, her dress soaked and heavy with blood against her thigh. The clearing was close.

But something smacked the back of her head. She fell, dirt blinding her, and she reached to feel the pain that spread a radiant chill down her neck. Whatever hit her, it did not break the skin, but her head was numb from the blow and her vision blurred.

She rolled onto her back, readying her sword for attack.

And at the edge of the clearing, she caught a glimpse of a man, tall and proud and smiling.

She sat up.

'Fionn?'

She shook her head, and the world swam in multiple directions. She dug the point of her sword into the earth for leverage. She did not consider Fionn's presence to be an impossibility; he loved the battlefield, and she was certain that he watched over her from his seat at the table of the gods.

She staggered forward. The blood at the hem of her short dress soaked her exposed knee and ran to the leather boot that was black with mud.

One of Muirgel's warriors came at her and she severed his arm from his shoulder with one sweep of her sword.

Fionn was smiling.

She advanced, staggering. Her blood seeped inside her boot to squelch beneath her toes.

A bastard's shield struck her chest and she fell, the breath taken from her lips. At close range, the man discarded his sword and flipped a dagger from his belt. The blade struck her below the collarbone by her shoulder and she felt the pain only as a warmth that infuriated her muscles.

She opened her mouth to scream in his face, but she could not hear her cries.

She gripped his hand, twisted, and drew her dagger along his forearm. When he stooped in pain, she jabbed the blade into his groin, and when he came to his knees, she grinned at him, face to face, and ran her blade the length of his stomach. He fell against her, and she held him for a moment, like an embrace, before releasing his body.

Orlaith struggled to her feet. At the edge of the clearing by the slow-moving stream, Fionn's face was all she could see.

Blood washed her leg and her breast. She put her fingers to the wound at her shoulder and the flesh moved when she touched it. She could feel the bone beneath. On the ground below her, the blood from her thigh was dark and viscous.

Her vision curled and she stumbled forward.

She looked for Fionn, lost him. Turned her head, found him.

She lurched.

Another of Muirgel's men took a swing at her. His sword sliced into her side and lodged above her hip. The iron blade was wedged in her body like the teeth of a saw through a tree. She spun, her arms thrashing, and her blade cut his face in half.

Fionn appeared before her.

He smiled.

Orlaith fell to her knees, the sword still in her side.

Her vision darkened at the corners, and the throbbing at the back of her head intensified. She knew she was swaying on her knees, because Fionn would not be dancing, but she could not hold herself upright.

She coughed and blood spat from her lips.

Looking down, she gripped the hilt of the enemy's sword that protruded from her hip, but she did not have the strength to pull it free. She blinked. Lifted her eyes back to Fionn's face.

And the ground came up behind her. She reached out to him, and he took her hand. She felt the sheen of blood between their flesh as their fingers laced together. She blinked, and for a moment, it was Etain who knelt before her, eyes wide, lips parted in screaming pain. But she shook her head and Fionn was there again, his hand in hers, his smile broad and gentle.

She smeared his face with the blood from her fingertips. And she could smell him, that scent that she had longed for all these years, the headiness she would never forget.

She smiled but knew the muscles in her face would not allow her lips to curl. When she looked at her body, she saw more blood than dress. Her vision was a pinpoint.

She turned her attention back to Fionn. She tried to raise her hand to his face again, but the strength was leaving her. Her arm dropped and her fingers curled at the edge of the stream.

There was blood in the water.

She closed her eyes as Fionn leaned down to kiss her.

She felt his lips, warm against hers.

'Fionn,' she whispered.

And he called her to him.

Chapter 36

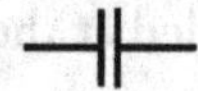

She is dead.

Chapter 37

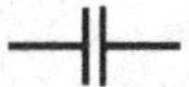

The sunlight sparkled over the still lough.

The women and children of Ailigh, and those men who had been left behind to defend its walls, gathered on the ceremonial hill to welcome their new archdruid.

Grainne felt foolish. The brown robe she wore was ill-fitting, and the gold torc at her neck was heavy on her collarbone. She carried the staff that still smelled of fresh yew, and her bare feet were red from the cold as she climbed the hillside with the deliberate slowness that the gathered people expected of a druid leader.

A strong wind blew the dawn towards them, but Grainne had divined that the winds would turn northerly before long, and the snows would be quick to follow. She had not slept during the night. Following the ceremony of her ascension to archdruid, wine was passed around in cups and then the druids took to Ailigh to visit the sick children, ensuring they were recovering. None were so weak as to be in danger, though some of the younger children maintained a grating cough that pained their throats. Grainne offered them honey and strained willow tea to soothe them.

By dawn, her druids had told Ailigh's women of her promotion, and it fell to Gallen to inform her that they expected Grainne to be paraded among them for their awe and for her blessings upon them.

'Must I?'

'Unless you seek their wrath, it would be wise,' he told her.

'I will stumble in my blessings, and they will see me for the fraud that I am.'

With a smirk that belied the sternness of his voice, Gallen said, 'Hush your lips. You have bemoaned your elevated status since yesterday and your people are tired of it.'

She slapped his shoulder. 'My first act as archdruid may be your demotion. Gather the people on the ceremonial hill for the sun's zenith. I will do as you bid me, though know that I do so with an embarrassment that I will never forget.'

He bowed his forehead to her hands. 'You have already assumed the former master's self-effacing wit.'

When he stood upright, she cupped his warm cheeks in her hands. 'Gallen, you are without question my closest friend. I hope always to hear the truth from you, regardless of my supposed status.'

Gallen held her shoulders. 'I have respected you since the day we met, Grainne. To those we respect, we cannot lie. You are a friend and a mentor and, though I know it cannot be, I would wish always to be your acolyte.'

'You are destined for greatness, Gallen. When you graduate, it will be a wondrous affair. And I will be your mentor no matter the distance that stretches between us.' The gleam in his eyes shone bright from the firelight of her hearth.

'Will you take your seat at the northern compound?'

'I have not decided,' she told him. 'I will be true to my word.

When our dark days have subsided to memory, we will gather all remaining druids and hold a new election. Others are far more suited to the role, whereas I have much to learn.'

'You cannot learn intuition,' Gallen said.

He still held her shoulders and his strong grip was comforting. 'Life is in constant change. Yesterday, you were as a child, today you are a man.'

'I have been a man for many years. You simply did not see it.'

'I have been blind to so many things, Gallen. I am comforted by your presence and your friendship.'

'I had hoped, in days best left to memory, for more than friendship. I had looked upon you in the past as a woman, not a mentor.'

'And only now I see you as a man,' she said. She studied his face, the square jaw that framed his lips, the red curls that spilled over his forehead. When they had met five years ago, she was more than a head taller than him, now she had to tilt her face to look at him. She could lay her head on his chest without bowing. 'What has become of the boy whose violent charms coloured the cheeks of little girls?'

He smiled and took her hand, placing it upon his chest. 'He is here, locked inside. The boy has grown up and no longer seeks the attentions of immature girls.'

'Hush, Gallen. I fear the meaning in your words.'

'Why should it be feared?'

She closed her eyes, a smile creasing her cheeks. 'There is that questioning boy full of bravado. And that is why I fear it.'

'It is not bravado if it is truth.'

'You are young; you will learn.'

'I am four winters into adulthood, and I am yet unmarried.'

Grainne feigned surprise. 'They will call you an outcast, for certain.'

'Can we not be outcasts together?'

She turned her face from him, though her hand still felt the beating of his heart in his chest. 'I am beyond romantic entanglements, Gallen. At least for now. I am acting archdruid—thanks to your insistence—and I must ensure that my priorities remain focused.'

Gallen's fingertips touched her cheek and turned her face to him. 'What archdruid commands her people at night? The darkness is built for a warm embrace.'

'The darkness is built for prayer and contemplation,' she laughed.

'And sleep.'

'Sleep, yes. But not as you would have it.'

'I am rejected, then.'

Grainne removed her hand from his chest and touched his temple. 'If circumstances were changed, perhaps my priorities would differ.'

'Is it too late to refuse you as archdruid?'

She laughed and took him into her arms. 'It is too late for many things. Go, now. Assemble the people that I may walk among them with my superior wisdoms and powerful blessings.'

Gallen kissed her cheek. 'You say it with laughter in your voice, but you know it is true. You may not feel like the archdruid, but you are now, and always will be, my master.' He bowed and left her quarters.

Now, as she mounted the hillside, she saw him standing among the druids on her left. They bowed as she approached, and it gave the gathered women and children the impetus to do likewise when she moved among them.

She did not know how she had missed his growth from skinny child to wise adult. She was so focused on his education that she failed to notice his maturity.

The women applauded her. She took her place by the burning fire and raised her arms for silence. In the east, she saw the storm clouds gather.

She took a deep breath before speaking. 'I do not have the words you seek from me. It is with reticence that I assume the role of archdruid, following the premature departure of my beloved master. I can only ever walk in the shadow cast by his legacy. He was the greatest man I know, and I cannot begin to pretend that I will measure up to his excellence. I take this role not with self-righteousness but with a view to restoring the honour of my fellow druids among the people of Éirinn. We have seen dark times and they are not yet behind us. In time, it is my prayer that Éirinn's fortunes become favourable. Though we divide ourselves among tribes and clanships, we are each governed by the laws of our gods. We are one people, united in brotherhood. I hope for a future where we no longer squabble like hungry dogs, but we share our supper with one another in kindness and truth. We lack trust with our neighbours, but one day I beg the gods for unity among our clans. If we are united in anything, may it be the gods that bring us together. In the hearts of man resides the compassion for strangers. Be not an enemy to your neighbour, but a brother. A sister. It is not my place to rebuild our future; it is ours.'

From the bottom of the hill, towards the east, a tribe of warriors emerged from among the trees.

Gallen took to Grainne's side. 'It is Mac Fachtna's men, come to demand their chieftain's killer.'

'Ardal Ó Ainmire—has his body been cremated yet?'

'No, my lady.'

'Hurry, Gallen,' Grainne said as a member of the Mac Fachtna tribe mounted the hill towards them. 'Fetch his body to me.'

Gallen hurried away and the tall warrior approached. His sword was at his hip, but his hands were held aloft, empty of intent. 'I do not know which druid ceremony happens here, but I am Anlon Mac Fachtna. Where is your king that we may have words?'

'You are welcome among us, Anlon Mac Fachtna. I am the archdruid, Grainne Ní Airic, and a daughter of Mordha.'

Anlon bowed his deference.

'I know why you have come. My acolyte will bring to you the body of the man you seek.'

Anlon squinted. 'You have slaughtered the man whose head belongs upon my spike?'

'He came against the Ó Mordha overking. He failed, though not before kidnapping Rónán's son. The Ó Mordha overking would be here to greet you had he not journeyed west to Thúr Rí in search of his child. It is heartfelt sorrow that I offer to you for the loss of your chieftain.'

They stood in silence as Gallen approached with a dead man in his arms. Lacking ceremony, he dropped the body at Anlon's feet.

'What proof do you have that this pathetic body is the one who murdered my predecessor, Seanach Mac Fachtna?'

'You have my word as archdruid,' Grainne said.

Anlon considered this. Then he drew his sword, stooped, and cut Ardal's head from his shoulders. 'Your king has my sympathies. I hope his son is returned to him.'

When Anlon turned to walk away, the dead man's hair gripped in his fist, Grainne said, 'My lord. I have met Seanach on many occasions. He was a good man, as I am sure you are a worthy successor. With his murderer's head in your hands, I hope that you will rest easy. As Rónán journeys to Thúr Rí, I would wish perhaps that you could join his fight—you hope that his son is returned to him, but that hope could become a promise if you marched your men to join his cause.'

Anlon regarded her. 'I have no ill will towards your king and Rónán Ó Mordha is an admirable man. But I have my own battles to fight. It is with the greatest of respects that I must decline.' He nodded, hoisted Ardal's head over his shoulder, and walked back to his tribe at the foot of the hill.

It was some time before the sound of their cheers disappeared beyond the forest.

Grainne buried her face in her hands and whispered, 'Cáer, strengthen my legs that they do not buckle.' She turned back to the women and children. Again, her druids bowed to her as though finally she accepted her position as archdruid.

She could not recall the words she had spoken to her people before Anlon's arrival. She glanced at Gallen, but rather than offer her words of comfort, he pointed across the hilltop.

From Ailigh's gates, Grainne saw a lone figure walk towards them. She was huddled against the wind with a winter fur held tight around her shoulders. She came among the crowd, and they parted for her.

Achall raised her head, and the wind swept her thick hair from her stark features. 'Have you seen my son?' she asked.

Grainne handed her staff to one of the druids who stood near her, and she walked towards the former queen whose mind had been disturbed by the disappearance of her child.

'Where is my son?' Achall asked.

Grainne embraced the former queen, who allowed herself to be enveloped in her arms, and then Grainne turned to the crowd.

'This is the future we need to embrace. The children. This woman's child has been taken and our king, our men, they have gone to retrieve him. One child; that is all it takes. One child can be the future. The king's son should be our concern. We are women and children—and some warriors whom the king has entrusted with our care. But are we not all people? Can we not all fight for our future? This is our duty. When our men are at war, we are not wives but mothers. Who among you would not fight for her child?' She sought the face of Bec among the children and beckoned her to come. When the darkhaired girl came forward, she took her niece's hand and that of her former queen. 'We have no threat from neighbours when the men are away. You heard Anlon Mac Fachtna's words. He has no intention of coming to Rónán's aid. It is time we stepped up. If we can fight for our children, we can do so for another's child—for Achall's child. Thúr Rí is not far. I propose we gather our might, the might of women, and we race to our king's side. Who will deny my wish?'

Silence swept the hilltop with its icy maws.

Grainne worried that she spoke against the gods. She had come here to dispense blessings at the coronation of her promotion to archdruid, but she incited violence, a call to arms among women and children.

One of the warriors that Rónán had ordered to remain at

Ailigh to protect the women in his absence stepped forward. He planted his spear in the ground. 'Though it pains me not to be in battle, and your words stir my heart, we are under orders to remain at Ailigh until the overking's return.'

Grainne faced him. 'I am archdruid over all the northern tribes. Do you seek to disobey me?'

The man took a knee and bowed his head. 'I will always respect your wisdoms, Lady.'

'I can fight,' a voice called from the crowd. A woman, plump but strong, stepped forward. Grainne recognised her as Aoibhinn, the cook. 'The Lady Orlaith taught me and many others. The armoury is stocked with weapons the king did not take with him. In the years of Orlaith's absence, we continued our studies. We may not be as good as men, but I am a cook. I can skin a hide and boil a broth. I will follow you west towards Thúr Rí and I will cook the head of any bastard who stands in my way. Pardon my language, your ladyship.'

Grainne nodded. 'I cannot force any of you to join me, but I am certain that without our help, our king and his men will face great difficulties.' She remembered Breasal's words at her ceremony. Death is close. If she could will it otherwise, she would do all she can to stop such a thing from happening. 'We seek unity,' she said. 'But we cannot find it if we do not fight for a united cause.'

'Bring back the child,' someone shouted.

'I will fight,' another said.

Breasal and Anú came to her, his boots sinking in the winter mud and her dress dragging behind her. 'My mother has trained me,' the boy said. 'Though I am young, I can fight.'

Grainne crouched before them. 'You children are brave,' she

said, loud enough for everybody to hear. 'Why is it that all children have more bravery than adults?'

'I will fight,' many voices shouted.

The women, children, and warriors took a knee. Only the druids remained standing.

Gallen stepped forward. He withdrew the sword that hung at his hip, and he planted it in the ground before her.

'You are my master,' he declared. 'I will follow you into the bowels of the earth.'

When he knelt, the remaining druids did likewise, and a cheer rang across the hilltop.

Grainne turned to Achall who was searching through the faces of each child in the crowd. 'Shall we go and fetch your child?'

'Áed?'

'Yes, Achall. We will help Rónán bring him home.'

By mid-afternoon, they had packed enough supplies to last them a fortnight, and they hitched the horses to every available carbad they could find. Rónán and his men had set off on foot, carrying their curraghs over their heads. If they were swift, Grainne and the others could catch up to them before her king reached the coastline.

They skirted south around the lough and forded the river at its lowest point. Though they lost half a day from the journey, they could make up for Rónán's haste by the speed of their horses.

Gallen, Bec, Breasal and Anú shared Grainne's carbad. Her acolyte took the reins and spurred the horses forward. A druid's place was at her king's side, especially in times of war. An archdruid's place was at the head of life. She smelled samphire as they journeyed towards the western hills and knew that Cáer was beside her, willing her horses to travel faster. Pushing the wind at their backs.

By nightfall, when they set camp, Grainne entered the tent that had been erected for her and she collapsed on the pallet bed. A small fire, ringed with stones, brought warmth to her skin and she relaxed the muscles in her shoulders that had been tensed all day.

'My most gracious lady Cáer,' she whispered. 'You, who have been known to me for so long, who guides my path, who turns my head to peaceful endeavours—I trust that you are with me as I take your people into battle. Are we not all equal in your eyes? And, if equal, can we not all strike our enemy with force? Your enemy is my enemy, my most gracious goddess. Tell me—am I doing your will? I want to help the king and not harm his chances of success.'

The goddess did not answer her with direct words.

Grainne heard the tent flap open and when she turned, she saw Breasal and Anú standing in the entrance, hands clasped as if melded together.

Anú said, 'Your will is all wills.'

Grainne bowed her head.

It was all the answer she needed.

Chapter 38

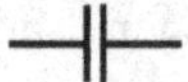

She looked across the shifting sea. White foam ate at the rocks and a black seal slipped from the basalt stone into the water's edge. Éirinn was shrouded in mist and its thick greyness washed the horizon of all colour.

The boy had been brought to her that morning, a wailing, wide-eyed child so similar in appearance to his mother that Muirgel wanted to smack the countenance from his face. She had not seen Achall since she was a child, no more than twelve winters old, when Donal, Muirgel's husband and the chieftain of his lands, had dispatched her north to Ailigh as Rónán Ó Mordha's intended bride. Though he was already Rónán's foster father, he had grand intentions of securing the boy as overking and pledging his loyalty through marriage.

They had not counted on the boy's wilful betrayal.

Rónán's son, who occupied the sterile corner of Muirgel's great hall, had cried when he was brought ashore. 'Why do you cry, child?' she asked him. 'Crying is for infants, and I dare say it has been years since you were nursed at your mother's teat.'

A line of mucus dripped from his nose onto the tunic that had been given to him when his own was stripped from his body as evidence for Ailigh's overking. There were two clean tracks on his cheeks where his tears had washed his filthy face. Dásan had not bothered to bind the boy's wrists. When they were far enough away from Ailigh, if the boy escaped, he would perish in the cold countryside.

'You and I are kin,' she told the boy. 'And no kin of mine will cry.' She watched as Dásan gripped the back of the boy's tunic and dragged him through the gates of her compound. When the door of the ironsmith's cage was locked and the boy knelt on the floor, Muirgel told everybody to leave. She took a stool, whose seat had been padded with furs cut to measure, and she placed it before the boy's prison gate. She stared at him and, in time, when his snivelling had ceased and he wiped his nose with the sleeve of his tunic, he watched her, and they did not speak.

His resemblance to Achall pained Muirgel. The girl had been plain, her hair a tangle of curls that could not be tamed, and the smile on her face, when she offered it, could be confused with a snarl. Her voice had droned like a carnyx horn and, even at twelve, Muirgel knew the girl would never have an ample bosom. Had Donal not made the match, Achall would surely have died childless and unwed.

'You should not squint,' Muirgel told the boy in her prison. 'It is your mother's look. Who is your father?'

The boy shied from her words before speaking. 'Rónán Ó Mordha.'

'Who is your real father?'

The boy's eyes fell back into a squint.

Muirgel nodded. It was no surprise that his mother had withheld the truth of his parentage. The boy was to be raised in the image of the king. 'Tell me,' she asked the child, 'what kind of woman is your mother? Does she rain kisses upon your tiny face, or does she smack your spindly legs when you act not as a king's son but as a bastard boy?'

'Why am I here?' he asked.

'That is not your concern. Why were you named after Áed the Executioner? Do you not know that he was defeated at Knockdhu by a man half his size? I was there. I watched him bleed his essence into the soil. He was no executioner. He was no powerful figure of legend. Do you seek to die in a similar fashion?'

When he did not answer her, she rose and kicked the stool. It skittered against the bars of his cell, and he flinched, cowering into the dark corner behind him.

'I do not intend to kill you, child. Your life is worthless to me. Had you been the king's real son, that matter might change. I will keep you fed until such times as you are no longer needed. I have provided you with a fur for comfort, and you have a pot to piss in. I expect little boys need nothing more. When I conduct my business, you will remain quiet. I will not suffer your waywardness, so do not tempt my nature. If you speak, I will throw you to the dogs, and I assure you they are exceptionally hungry.'

She left the hall, and the door was closed behind her by the guard stationed outside. She ordered one of her cumal girls to fetch Dásan and she waited for his arrival in her private quarters.

When he came to her, he bowed. 'My queen. The boy's father will not be far behind us. A day or two at most.'

'Have your finest men keep watch over the approach from Éirinn. He will come with his army—what is left of it—and I do not intend for him to reach these shores. Do you have news from our distant cousins?'

'No, my lady, but I am assured they will set sail before the Yule. Their crossing will be dangerous this time of year and they demanded additional payment. I have dispatched forty extra slave girls for their uses.'

'Can we spare them?'

'We will acquire more as soon as Ailigh is yours, my queen.'

'Prepare your defences, Dásan. The Ó Mordha king may come with few men, but he is a hardy bastard. His thirst for blood will not easily be quenched.'

'Does my lady require anything further?'

Muirgel untied the string that secured the neck of her dress. 'Make it quick,' she said.

They lay together on her comfortable bed until she was satisfied, and when he rose to dress, Muirgel said, 'If the Ó Mordha king reaches my cliffs, you will remove his head and hand it to me before his child.'

Dásan bowed.

Outside, the sleet of early winter battered the rocks and grasses. As the sun set, not ten nights before the beginning of Yule, Muirgel slipped into a heated bath to ease her joints. The water had been prepared with a solution of aloe vera leaves that had been brought on a trade ship some years before from the distant east. Thúr Rí island did not get much trade beyond the shores of Éirinn, so it was with some excitement that her people greeted the foreign traders who brought medicinal plants and spiced herbs, glass trinkets and odd-shaped weaponry. In return, her people traded Thúr Rí wool, iron ingots, and the occasional cumal girl.

Immersed to the ears in the warm water, Muirgel dismissed her girls and allowed her limbs to float. In the great hall beyond her chambers, she could hear the boy crying for his mother. The corner of the hall in which he was caged would be in darkness, for she had ensured the sconces were unlit. She hoped he feared the dark.

She emptied her lungs of breath and submerged her head, sinking to the floor of the bath that had been inlaid in the ground. Under water, her joints ceased to ache. She envied the fish who did not have knuckles. When she rose from the water, inhaling the scents of her quarters, she felt like a girl again, agile and supple. Her hair clung to her back in thick cords, and her fingers—slender, age-blemished, with sharpened nails—could be straightened without pain. The water was slick on her skin from the oil of the aloe vera plant. She did not know how many leaves her druid had remaining; when her stock was running low, she would dispatch her east to locate the traders or find the plant in its natural wilderness. A leaf of such properties should belong to a queen.

In the great hall, the child's crying had risen to a wail. If he was not afraid of the dark, he feared the loneliness.

Muirgel glared at the solid-wood door between them as though she could will him to silence, but his weeping was louder than the sleet that hammered her thatching. Her quarters glowed yellow from the central hearth and dappled her loose skin. If she did not need the boy alive, she would drag him from his cage and hold his face into the flames of her fire until he ceased his pathetic whining.

She rose from the bath and called for her cumal girls to dry her body. When her hair fell damp upon the back of her dress, and one of the girls was easing Muirgel's feet into shoes, the boy's cries grew into a desperate plea for his freedom.

'If he does not shut his mouth,' Muirgel said, 'I will tear the flesh from his cheeks and rip his jaw apart.'

The cumal girls did not respond.

When the boy's screams stopped with an unnatural suddenness, Muirgel dismissed the girls and threw open the door of her quarters. In the far corner, steeped in darkness, she heard whispered voices.

'Who is there?' She lifted a lit candle in a bronze holder and stepped forward.

As the dim light seeped across the floor, Muirgel saw the ironsmith by the gate of the cage.

'Forgive me, my queen.'

'What are you doing?'

'My lady, please. My cage was built for an animal, not a child.'

'Your cage was built for any purpose I see fit.' She could see the fear in his eyes. 'I ask again—what are you doing?'

'I could hear his screams from my home, Lady. At first, I thought it was a wounded dog, his screams were so piteous.'

'So, you thought to free him?'

'No, my lady.' His words faltered as his eyes circled the room, glancing at anything but her.

'Put down your keys,' she said.

He dropped them at his feet. 'My lady. He is just a boy.'

Muirgel whipped the candleholder across his face and, in the swift movement, the flame sputtered and died. The ironsmith stumbled away from her but did not fall. She lashed the bronze holder out a second time.

The ironsmith raised his arms to protect his face but, even as he was being beaten, he would not defend himself against the queen.

When she struck him a third time, he fell to his knees and she lunged upon him, the candleholder gripped in both hands, and she beat his flesh until she could hear the cracking of his bones.

She beat him still. Her shoulders ached from the effort and her fingers, tight around the ornamental holder, had locked themselves closed. The man's blood sparked her face.

His breath rattled in his throat.

She dropped the candleholder and gripped his neck. If he had intended to plead with her, he could not do so. She squeezed, ignoring the pain in her knuckles, the crying of muscles in her back.

When the skin around his clenched eyes loosened in death, she released him.

Muirgel stood, wiping his blood from her cheeks, and she spat on him.

The boy whimpered in his cell.

She inhaled and smoothed the front of her stained dress. 'Stop snivelling.'

He continued to cry.

'Damn it, child, be quiet or I will bludgeon you just as easily.'

'Let me go,' he shouted.

Muirgel picked up the keys that the ironsmith had dropped, and she unlocked the boy's cell. When she threw the gate wide, he backed away from her, and she could see his fists balled in defiance.

Though his voice was quiet, it was laced with anger. 'Let me go.'

'You may be kin, child, but do not tempt me. I will kill you still.'

'I know we are kin. You have the same scar as my mother.'

Muirgel brought a hand to the scar at her cheek. If Achall was likewise scarred, it would have been given to her by Rónán

Ó Mordha.

'You have the same face,' the boy said.

She whipped the back of her hand across his cheek, and he sprawled across the stone floor. With the keys in her fist, she stooped and swiped them across the boy's face. The cut to his cheek was deep, and it wept blood. And it would scar just like hers.

'Get up,' she said. The boy's limbs twitched. She saw his eyes roll up in their sockets to expose the whites, and when his body convulsed, flopping on the ground like the fish she had not long ago envied, she said, 'Stop this. Get up, boy.'

The jerking of his limbs continued, and then stopped. He sat up and stared at her.

His eyes were not his own, she could tell.

'The gods have turned their back on you, Muirgel of Thúr Rí.'

He stood with an ease of young limbs not ravaged by time.

'The gods have turned their back on you. Dian Cécht says this.'

Muirgel raised her hand to strike him, but the boy turned from her, giving her his back.

When she stepped from his cell and locked the gate, she called for her druid. The boy could not be speaking on behalf of the gods. He was a bastard child, a nobody.

Her druid would fix it.

She always did.

Chapter 39

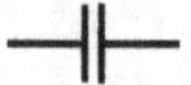

Silver moonlight fractured the frost-covered hillside.

The keening cries of men and women for the warrior's wife were loud and the aggressive heat of their bodies made the rime cower from the area. Thin grains of snow drifted down among the trees but died as they settled, vanishing from life's cruelty.

Rónán dug the point of his spear in the winter ground, and he took the sheepskin *cocholl* cape from his shoulders to drape across his consort's back. Cormac had been kneeling by Orlaith's side since the battle was won, his eyes unblinking, fists balled at his sides. He did not shed tears. If he had, they would have frozen on his cheeks from the chill beneath his skin.

'Cormac,' Rónán said. 'Get some sleep. I will take the watch over her.'

Cormac did not acknowledge him, and when Rónán knelt by his side, reaching out in reverence to touch the shroud that covered Orlaith's body, Cormac's breath caught in his chest, but he cleared his throat to mask the wound that ate at him. Rónán's fingers were blue from the icy air that circled them.

At the other side of her body, Orlaith's warriors—Etain and the others—keened their death wails as one. They knelt before her in full battle garb, sword-points in the ground, two hands gripping the hilts with whitened knuckles. They rocked their heads and wept.

Rónán looked at Orlaith, remembering her features though they were covered by her shroud. Small tallow candles on bronze plates ringed her body and browned autumn leaves had been brushed into a bed for her. From breast to knee, her sword gleamed wet with tears, and a jug of ale had been left with her to give to Manandán when he came to collect her spirit.

Cormac nodded once as though responding to a question that had not been asked.

Rónán touched his arm. 'Will you sleep now?'

He did not answer, and so Rónán adjusted his knees to ease the awkwardness of his position. He would wait with him for as long as it took. He bowed his head and recited the names of those gods he could recall, and he was reminded of a time he renounced them, when his father had been killed by Muirgel's husband and son.

Though Áed was now in Muirgel's captivity, Rónán knew the vile woman would not harm him; not until she was certain that Rónán would come. She was evil, but he could not allow himself to believe that she would murder a child.

As the splintered moon weaved among the dark clouds, the keening of Orlaith's women lessened in its intensity, and Rónán looked up to see that many of them had curled up on the ground where they knelt, taken to slumber against their will. Etain, he saw, was no longer present.

Diarmuid took a knee beside him and said, 'I will take watch, Lord.'

Rónán nodded. He placed his hand on the back of Cormac's head, his thumb stroking the cold flesh behind his ear, and then he stood, patting Diarmuid on the back before he stepped away.

In the din of a camp that was fighting off the gods of sleep, Rónán listened to the crackling of small fires whose damp wood offered tendrils of black smoke to the sky, and he heard the quiet singing of boys and the chattering of drinking cups being knocked together in solidarity. There was a stark divide in emotion—a sadness that surrounded Orlaith's wake, and the triumphant joy of another battle won that emanated further across the hillside and down towards the distant shoreline where men had already made camp. They understood the pain of suffering, the darkness that follows any encounter as a result of death, but Rónán knew they felt warranted relief that they had not succumbed to a violent end. It is the uneasy reprieve of all warriors who lay their heads on cold earth to sleep at the end of day.

Sitting alone, some distance from the warmth of the fires, he saw Etain as she stroked her blade with a small whetstone. When he approached her and asked if he could sit in her company, she nodded and offered him a guttural acceptance of his request. He sat cross-legged on the frosted grass and felt the back of his tunic dampen at once.

He did not beg her with conversation. He watched as she drew strokes along the edge of her blade, raising the iron to inspect its sharpness before running the whetstone across its edge again.

'She was my queen,' Etain said at length, 'even though she did not hold a title.'

Rónán exhaled through his nose, his lips pursed. 'She was everyone's queen.'

'She is with the warrior now.'

'Fionn.'

Etain nodded. 'It is as the gods wish it. Husband and

wife—together. I did not know him. Was he a good man?'

'The greatest.'

'As I knew he would be.'

They sat in silence for a time. Etain's hands had stopped sharpening her blade, and Rónán pushed his fingers beneath his legs to succour warmth. He had heard that the dead return for their loved ones when it is their time to make their final journey, and he hoped it to be true. He stared over his shoulder at Cormac, who knelt with unwavering resolution at Orlaith's side, and he knew that were he to die first, he would stand outside the gates of Ailigh, ignoring the pleas of Manandán mac Lir to board his spectral ship, and he would remain there until Cormac's time.

When his mind snapped back from their wanderings, he turned to Etain and asked, 'Will you lead her warriors now?'

'She did not have a tanist. We were equal, she and us; equal in battle if not in life.'

'I can see you were close friends. Would it not be her wish that you took charge of her women?'

'I will organise them into battle when we are set to war, but I cannot lead them as she would. There is no replacement.'

'Great leaders cannot be replaced. They can only be succeeded. It is our desire that we live up to a portion of their magnitude.'

'And as each succeeder brings a smaller portion of greatness,' Etain said, 'one day there will be no great leaders left.'

'I will weep when that day comes.'

'All eyes will weep. And then humanity will be forgotten.'

The wind stirred frozen blades of grass and a snow shower—thin and mournful—settled around them before fading against the frost.

'Your man Cormac,' Etain said, 'when at last he opens his throat to cry, he will be heard across the world.'

Rónán turned his head to look at his consort. Cormac's upright kneeling was steadfast. 'I do not believe he will cry until she has been avenged.'

'We cannot move him from her side, Lord. He will know when it is time to avenge her death and retrieve your son. When he moves, he will not falter. When he kills, it will be with grief in the tips of his fingers.'

He nodded. The gods had a price, and grief could not be hurried.

He returned to Cormac's side and knelt with him.

By dawn, when Orlaith's warriors had awoken, they renewed their keening cries, as was proper for the death of a leader. They redoubled their moans, for they understood they did not have seven days to mourn her.

Cormac had remained at her side through the night. He had spoken once, turning sunken eyes towards Rónán. 'This is my burden. You should sleep. We will not delay much longer.' Rónán understood—though the pain was an open sore, Cormac was working through a process that would allow him to stand up and continue their fight.

He kissed Cormac's cheek and squeezed his shoulder. 'I will have men rotate a watch alongside you. It may be your burden, but you will not carry it alone.'

As the sun clutched at the western hills, Cormac leaned forward, kissed Orlaith's shroud, and at last rose from his knees. He adjusted the scabbard at his side and came to Rónán.

'It is time.'

They carried her body on a makeshift litter down to the

shoreline where Éirinn broke for the ocean. The silver moon, waxing towards fullness, took residence above the dark stain on the watery horizon that Rónán knew to be Thúr Rí island, and it watched over them as they built a pyre.

Battle songs were sung, for the warriors knew no other melodies, and with quiet movement, Orlaith's body was laid upon the pyre. Diarmuid lit a fire on the leeward side of a small hillock, and a procession, led by Cormac and Etain, fed torches from the fire before returning to Orlaith's side.

A silence washed across the beach, broken only by the longing of the waves to consume her eternal ashes.

Manandán's jug of ale had been repositioned at the foot of the pyre, and with it had been placed bronze trinkets offered for her journey by her warriors and those of Rónán's men who knew and respected her.

Cormac led the mourners three times around her pyre, and when he bowed to her, he touched his torch to the kindling that raised her aloft for the gods to bear witness to her life. The flames were slow to spread. Smoke eddied in a dizzying dance and the clouds parted to receive her.

The light of other torches was given to her, and she took them. When the shoreline brightened with her flame, Cormac knelt, raised a cup, and poured wine upon the sandy earth.

The crackle of a funeral pyre is not easily forgotten, for it does not sound the same as a fire whose sole purpose is to issue warmth or light. It spits as equally as it cracks, and the flames dance to a more erratic tune.

Rónán came to his side, and they watched the fire build and die as the moon skidded overhead. When there was more smoke than flame, Cormac stood and Rónán embraced him.

'I am sorry,' Cormac said. 'I have delayed you. We must retrieve your son at once.'

Rónán did not release him, his arms wrapped around Cormac's broad shoulders. 'You must eat and sleep. We will set sail at first light.'

A jar was filled with the cooling ashes of Orlaith's remains and would be carried back to Ailigh to be buried alongside her husband, Fionn. One torch remained lit, and it too would be brought back to Ailigh in her honour. Rónán knew that songs would be sung for their love.

A tent had been erected for them and they retired to its warmth. Rónán bathed Cormac's hands and chest and scrubbed his back. When he drew a fur over them and pulled himself closer to Cormac's side, he knew that he was already asleep.

His night was uneasy, but when dawn came cold and windless, he splashed water on his face, warmed his chest with a cup of wine, and ordered his men to push their curraghs into the water's edge. He would have Áed back in his arms by nightfall.

Diarmuid issued his commands to the army and they rowed into the murky gloom of a morning shore. In the bow seat of each curragh, a warrior drummed a beat to which the men set their oars, and when they were far enough from Éirinn's edge, small sails were unfurled and positioned to catch the breeze that followed in their wake. Orlaith's torch, held by one of the warriors in Rónán's curragh, lit the area around them more than the rising sun.

To clear his mind of the inevitabilities of life, Rónán took the seat next to Cormac and aided the efforts to row. His warriors were not seafaring men, but they were making sure progress, and when Rónán looked up to see the direction in which they journeyed, he saw that the stain of Thúr Rí had increased in mass. With the sun still behind her, the island was a dark shadow that felt impenetrable.

When the sun rose above the island and they had rowed a third of the distance, a shout came from the foremost curragh boat. 'All hands,' the warrior shouted. 'We have company.'

Rónán turned. From the island, a flotilla of curragh was coming in their direction.

Cormac stood, the ten-man boat rocking, and he drew his sword. 'That is not a welcome party.'

'We cannot fight them on open water,' Diarmuid said from the neighbouring curragh.

'That is clearly what they seek.'

'We are too far out to turn back, Lord.'

Rónán took to his feet and steadied himself against Cormac. Two of the men in his boat looked sea-green with ocean sickness. 'Slow your oars,' he shouted. The order whipped from boat to boat. 'Let them do the hard work. If they tire themselves out, they will be easier pickings. Furl the sails and shore up. We need to unify in defence.'

Forty curragh boats eased together in an attempt at forming a wall.

Their quarry was still some distance away but gaining fast. An island of such size needed assured sailors, or they could not survive. The sea, high and rough, pushed at Rónán's fleet from behind, willing them towards the enemy. Three crows circled overhead.

'The Morrígan,' Cormac said. 'She comes to watch the show.'

'Then let us give her something to squawk about,' Rónán said. 'Spears at the ready.'

Men knelt on the plank benches and hoisted their spears.

'Steady,' Diarmuid shouted.

The enemy slowed when they were within firing range, and Diarmuid screamed his battle cry. The sky darkened with spear and javelin and, as one, their warriors ducked and raised their shields overhead.

Rónán worried that their hide-skinned curraghs would not need a second hit if their hulls were penetrated.

Spears rained on both sides and the screaming of men was excruciating.

When the clatter ceased, Rónán raised his head over his shield and shouted a new order to row. He was right to let the enemy boats approach for he could see that they tired. But as they came close, he found that they were men of great strength.

The first boats at the fore clashed, and one of the enemy warriors jumped with sword outstretched. He was butted in mid-air and fell into the freezing ocean.

Iron sounded against shield and sword as both sides fought to maintain their balance in their boats. Within minutes, the muddy water was black with blood.

As Rónán's boat drew alongside the enemy, he braced his foot against the bow and readied his sword arm. The brute who bore down on him swung a wide arc and Rónán blocked him with ease, but as their boats collided, he stumbled off balance and Cormac stopped him from tumbling into the sea. As he pulled Rónán back, he thrust forward and pierced the enemy.

Aided by Cormac's support, Rónán kicked out to push the brute off Cormac's sword and his body fell back into his fellow sailors.

Rónán jumped the small divide and landed in the enemy

curragh. The impact made him fall to his knees as the boat rocked, and two of Muirgel's men went overboard. Rónán came up with a powerful lunge that shore the arm from his closest foe. He pushed him away to give his sword swinging room and, as he brought it around, his foot caught beneath the bow seat and he went to his knees. His sword penetrated the cured boat-hide, and his fingers lost their grip.

An enemy warrior clambered over the tangle of bodies that had fallen as the boat swayed and Rónán raised his shield arm. Without his blade, he dipped his body away from the onslaught and swung his shield wide to connect with the man's face. He punched him, using one knee to pin the enemy's arm down, and he drove the shield into his face again. When the man slipped overboard, Rónán turned for his sword. He pulled the blade free from the hull and jumped to his feet. Water penetrated from the fracture beside the keel.

With Cormac's help, he crossed back into his own curragh, and they pushed the enemy boat away. Those men who remained in her were battling against the rising water at their feet.

'The pitch,' Cormac shouted. 'Pass me the pitch.' The torch from Orlaith's pyre was passed to him, along with a leather sack of coal-tar pitch. He dumped the black flammable liquid against the opposing curragh and swept Orlaith's flame across its bow. It was appropriate that she made their enemies burn. A bright flame flushed across the curragh's prow.

Turning to find his next quarry, Rónán discovered that other boats—his and theirs—were already aflame. The smell of tar pitch was rife.

A warrior, capsized from his boat, broke the surface beside them and reached for the prow. He had both of his arms over the wall, kicking in the water to overturn them, when Rónán sliced his face with his blade. He kicked to release the man's grip on the boat, and beside him Cormac was fighting off another attack.

In the melee, he could not see whose side was winning.

Black smoke shrouded the ocean and men were shouting and screaming with both pain and fury.

He heard Diarmuid's voice nearby. 'We're taking on water.'

Behind him, a shout came—a woman's shout. He looked for Etain, but in the far distance, rowing towards them, a series of smaller curragh was coming up fast.

'They have circled us,' Rónán shouted. He steadied himself against the hull and loosened his shoulder; maintaining his balance while swinging his sword had tired his muscles.

'We're going under,' Diarmuid shouted.

Cormac took the head of an enemy sailor and it splashed in the water beside him.

Rónán butted out, shield raised, and clashed with a brutish warrior who tried to gain access to their curragh. He pushed the man into the water and when his head broke the surface again, Rónán stabbed downward with his blade. He turned back to the advancing column of boats from the rear. They were close.

As they waded through the dark smoke of burning boats, he saw Achall standing upon the prow, her dress hitched to her knees, a long spear clutched in her hands. Had he not recognised the cursed scowl on her face, he would have taken a swing at her. Behind her, Grainne and Gallen, the hoods of their robes pulled back, stood ready with swords.

Achall screamed like the *sidhe* and jabbed her spear forward as her curragh butted between Rónán's and an enemy boat. She was taken from her feet with the force, and she landed in the forward curragh, her spear stuck through her enemy and into the hull.

Rónán leapt to her aid and dragged her back into his boat.

'We timed it well,' Gallen shouted. The sword in his hands looked more a part of him than did his robes.

With renewed strength, Rónán advanced their boats, calling for all to tighten the line and drive forward. As they pushed beyond the wall of smoke, he saw several of the island's boats retreating.

'After them,' he shouted.

Achall punched a fist in the air. 'Attack,' she cried.

Rónán looked behind them and saw Diarmuid and his son, Darragh, swimming towards them. He knelt and stretched out an oar so that they could grip it, and when they were onboard, they pushed forward again, cutting the ocean like a dagger through linen.

The island was close. And there were only seven retreating curragh boats in their way.

Chapter 40

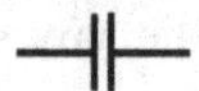

Muirgel paced her long hall.

'Who is your god?' her druid asked the boy.

Áed was turned away from her, facing the wattle wall, and his small back was a vision of defiance.

'On whose authority do you speak?' the druid asked.

Muirgel strode towards them. 'We will beat the truth from him if he does not answer willingly.'

The old druid hushed her, and she spoke in the tongue of the gods. Though Muirgel was convinced the boy could not understand the ancient language, she saw his head cock when the druid stopped talking. From her angle, she could see the fresh scar on his cheek, puckered and pink, dried blood caked in the welt.

'What did you say?' she asked her druid.

'It is a swear that only a god would know.'

'You saw him react. Is he blessed?'

'He is not blessed; he is cursed.'

'Speak, child,' Muirgel shouted. 'Where is your authority?'

Áed shuffled on his feet but he did not turn to them. He brought each fingertip to his thumb in turn, both hands working in tandem as though he was counting or amusing himself with unnatural patience.

Muirgel unlocked the cell gate. 'Bring me a birch whip. I will thrash the answers from him.'

'Lady, you cannot disfigure him further. If he has the druid ways in him, the gods will anger.'

Muirgel scowled at her. 'Are they not angered enough that I have murdered his people in Éirinn? I have new gods on my side, Fir Bolg gods who strengthen me.' She threw the gate wide. 'Bring me a birch whip at once.'

The old druid hurried away.

Muirgel gripped the boy's shoulder and turned him to her. His eyes, half closed, were as dulled of life as any dead man's countenance. She ran her thumb across the fresh scar on his cheek. It was her mark. A family mark. Three generations now bore it and Rónán, when he looks upon his child, would not forget. A thin line of puss oozed from its edge.

'It will get infected if left untreated. Do you want that? Speak to me the truth and I will have my druid tend you.'

Áed closed his eyes.

Muirgel smacked his swollen cheek.

He stumbled, but when he righted himself, he returned to his slackened stance and touched his fingers to his thumbs.

She gripped his narrow throat. 'I am not a patient woman.'

Áed opened his eyes. When he looked up at her, she could see the cloudy apparition of herself in his features.

She took his shoulder and pushed him from the cell as the old druid returned, a fresh birch switch in her hands.

'I warn you, my lady. Killing druids on Éirinn's soil is one matter. Killing one on your own will be unforgivable.'

Muirgel yanked the switch from the woman's hands. 'He is no druid. He is a child.'

She advanced on him and he did not cower from her. He looked beyond her at the old druid.

'Who is your god?' Muirgel asked. She whipped his leg, and she could hear the sting of it.

The boy flinched and reached to ease the pain of his wound.

'See? A boy, like all others. You test me, and I promised pain. You have no god. You are nobody.' She whipped him again, across his arm. He fell back onto his rump, and she raised the switch.

Áed drew his hands up over his face and she whipped him again, drawing blood from his palms.

'Get up. A powerful god-child should be able to suffer for his cause.'

'My lady, do not thrash him to death.'

'Get up, child.'

She heard him weeping behind his bloodied hands.

'Stand up.' She brought the switch down on him again. He shuffled back from her.

Again, she struck him.

'Where is your godly wisdom now?'

When he turned on his side, Muirgel brought the birch across his back, tearing the linen of his tunic.

The boy screamed.

She kicked him. 'Stand up, druid boy. Stand up and face me.'

He curled into a foetal ball, and she struck him repeatedly, drawing blood from his back and legs. His tunic was tattered and red.

'My lady,' her druid screamed. 'He is a child.'

Muirgel lashed the switch around to her druid. 'Stay back.'

Her flame hair had come loose from its ornate leather barrette, and she pushed it back from her face before striking the child again.

His screams had ceased, and he was unmoving.

'You have killed him,' the old druid cried. She buried her face in her hands. 'The boy is dead.'

Muirgel brought the switch down on his back. 'If he was godly, he would not be dead.'

Áed lay on the cold stone floor. Blood cried from his body. She kicked him and rolled him onto his ravaged back.

'Get up,' she said, her breath ragged. 'Stand before me.' She thrashed the switch across his stomach, and he did not move.

When the door of her great hall opened, and footfalls hurried towards her, Muirgel turned in rage. The man who approached stopped in his tracks. He backed away with his hands raised.

'What?' she commanded.

'Warriors approach by sea, my lady.'

'Then get out there and stop them.'

He bowed to her and left.

Muirgel turned back to Áed, but the anger had fled from her limbs. She dropped the birch switch and stooped before his wounded face.

'He is dead,' the druid cried.

When Áed opened his eyes, Muirgel staggered back from him.

He sat up, his face a mess of blood, one eye swollen shut, the scar on his cheek reopened and bleeding, and he turned his open eye to her.

'Donal did not make it to Tír Tairngire,' Áed said, referencing the Land of Promise. His voice was lacklustre, monotone. 'His soul wanders aimless without respite.' He got to his knees as Muirgel backed away from him. 'He begs entry at Mag Mell, but they refuse him. He has been turned away from Tír na nÓg. In time, your soul will find him in the stark darkness of death. But that time is not today.'

'Put him in his cell,' Muirgel said, turning her eyes from the child. 'I am done with him.'

Chapter 41

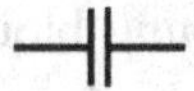

They skirted the coastline of Thúr Rí and drew their curraghs onto a rocky landing. With the sun now behind them as the day wore closer to its dreary end, the hillside above was dazzling with jewels of frost. Rónán's scouts climbed the rocky shelf towards the grasslands for a better look at the area.

Diarmuid spat on the rocks before his feet touched the ground. 'I spit in Balor's eye,' he said. In ancient tales, the Fomorian king, Balor of the Evil Eye, was said to have resided here.

Those who heard him, spat likewise to blind the evil king. You cannot harm what you cannot see.

Grainne came to Rónán's side and they embraced. 'Where is Cormac?' she asked.

'Mooring the curragh. You have heard the news?'

'We saw the remains of her funeral pyre on the beach. It was Achall who recognised the charred hilt of her blade in the ocean's edge.'

'It was gifted to the gods.'

She touched his shoulder. 'We did not remove it.'

'How did you convince Achall to come with you into battle?'

'Her mind is not what it should be. But the moment we took to the ocean, she changed. I think she can sense Áed nearby. Put a sword in her hand. She will be an asset.' She looked behind her at Anú and Breasal. 'I have not the heart to tell the child of his mother's passing.'

'Look at him,' Rónán said. 'I suspect he already knows.'

Grainne walked away from him to embrace Cormac in his grief, and Rónán filled is lungs before approaching the young boy. He stood with the young blonde druid girl whose name Rónán had forgotten, and Bec, Grainne's niece, was nearby.

'Breasal,' Rónán said, crouching before the boy.

'You can call me Fionn if you wish,' Breasal said.

'A heavy hand has been dealt to you, child. But I believe you already know the thing that pains me so.'

Breasal's eyes met Rónán's for a brief second before he studied the wet rocks beneath his feet.

Rónán felt his throat constrict. 'Your mother——'

'*Mamaí* is gone to the man who makes her heart smile.'

He touched the boy's shoulder and when Breasal looked at him again, he pulled the child into his arms. 'It is sad that she is gone,' he said, 'but it is where she will be happiest.'

He felt Breasal nod against his chest.

Rónán mounted the hillside, away from the boy, away from the misery in his eyes. Cairbre, one of his scouts, approached him. 'Lord. There is not much daylight left. The hillfort is about eighty or ninety rods that way,' he said, pointing north towards the peninsula. 'It is rocky terrain, with a narrow pass between us and it, and another hill to scale. Her walls are thick with men. She is well fortified. We should wait for the cover of nightfall, or they will see our approach.'

'Let them watch us march towards them. We do not have time to wait.'

Cairbre bowed and returned to the line of men who came up behind them.

When Cormac and Grainne joined him, followed by Diarmuid and Fergal, Rónán said, 'One last fight. If we can get to her gates, we can break them down with force.'

'If you can pick me up,' Fergal said, 'you can use me as a battering ram. I love the smell of blood in the evening.'

The druid girl, whose long blonde hair whipped across her face as she picked her way over the swept grasses, came to Grainne and tugged on her robes. 'There is sadness here.'

Grainne hunkered and stroked the girl's cheek. 'There is sadness everywhere, Anú.'

Anú looked at Rónán. 'Blood is spilled, but more will follow. The swan told me.'

'I know it.' Rónán glanced at his companions before turning to stare north towards Muirgel's hillfort. 'Leave the children by the curraghs. Place two men to guard them. More blood is coming, but I will not lose a child today.'

Grainne lifted the young girl into her arms and said to Rónán, 'He will be pleased to see you.'

'If he still lives.'

As those who remained of his army—less than two hundred—assembled into rows, alongside Grainne's armed and frightened druids, Rónán raised his sword. An eighty-rod dash was all that stood between him and the gates of Muirgel's fortress. But as he stared north, a wrath of warriors spilled from her walls.

They had been spotted.

Rónán did not have to give a command. As one, his men surged forward. Cormac, at his side, drew his sword and charged with a battle cry that echoed above all others.

When the two sides clashed on the narrow pass, the sound of the roaring waves was lost in the din of war. Those who were not on the frontline threw spears towards the back of the enemy rank, and men were wading into the water on either side to find a way forward.

Rónán rushed into the melee, colliding shield against shield with a massive warrior who opposed him. His feet found purchase against a crack in the earth, and he pushed, flicking his sword under his shield but finding no flesh. He spat in the warrior's face and pushed again. When the enemy shook his face, Rónán sidestepped him and brought his blade in an arc into the man's shoulder. The sword wedged in thick flesh and he butted the warrior's face with the edge of his shield and kicked his knee. When the man's leg buckled, Rónán pulled his sword free and plunged it through his chest. He raised his shield to block the blow of another enemy even as the first one was dying.

The first kill is only something a child would dwell on. Rónán turned to thrust his sword again.

Across the pass, he could hear Fergal singing as he cut through an enemy warrior. 'If you are not singing while swinging, where's the fun?' The old former king had once told him.

Etain barrelled into a man twice her size and as he fell, she jumped upon him like a savage dog. Her women—Orlaith's warriors—were at the frontline, cutting a path through the enemy.

Achall, short on experience but riled into action, thrust the point of a javelin into the belly of an enemy warrior who had broken through the ranks. She ran him through and fell beside him, and Rónán could not tell whose scream was louder—his agonising death wail, or her enraged, guttural battle cry. As Rónán blocked the advances of two opposing men, he saw Achall rise from the ground, tearing the javelin from the man's gut with a vigour he had never seen in her before.

Rónán barrelled into a new enemy, knocking the man from his feet. He fell backwards into the water's edge and Rónán stomped on his neck, forcing the man's face underwater. As he drowned, Rónán pierced a second opponent through his eye with an upward thrust that burst out of the back of his skull, killing him instantly. Rónán's balance waivered on the drowning foe and he stomped his foot back down with renewed enthusiasm.

Fergal's singing continued.

Young Darragh ducked under an enemy sword and rolled on his back, coming up swinging. He was good, but if Diarmuid had not been nearby to pull his son aside, the boy would have been broken in two by the heavyset warrior who tried to fall on him.

Towards the back of the line, Grainne and her untrained druids were picking off the stronger warriors who had broken through the ranks. They worked in tandem, two or three druids amassed together, and when an enemy fell, he did so with multiple stab wounds. The elder druids remained at the rear, swinging short swords with threat but without conviction.

Gallen, who would have stormed the front of the line with force, stood among his brethren as a sentry, protecting his people. His robes whipped behind him as he leapt and thrust at the enemy. His face was as red with blood as it was with effort.

Rónán slashed the stomach of an enemy warrior and spilled his guts on the rocky ground. He turned to face the fore as a new wave of combatants rushed towards their line.

'Tighten up,' Diarmuid called. He had pulled his son behind him, ever the father, but as the line of warriors came together to form a physical shield, Darragh took his place at his father's side.

Fergal raised his voice in song as the fighting renewed.

With his sword dulled and tarnished from the violence, Rónán ordered his men to pull up their shields as one and march forward. They clashed with the men of Thúr Rí and pushed. They had to step over the bodies of the dead—Rónán's men and Muirgel's—to advance, but they succeeded in pushing the enemy back enough to the point where the narrow pass widened.

Diarmuid whistled and the sky darkened with javelin. He issued a command and the centre of their line advanced while those men at the outer edges slowed. They were driving a wedge through the enemy line, separating the warriors to break their cohesion. Muirgel's warriors were ousted towards the water's edge on either side.

They were no more than forty rods from the queen's outer gates, outside the zone of arrow fire from Muirgel's walls, but not by a great distance.

Rónán forced his weight into the wall of oncoming men and jabbed his sword forward. It found flesh. Cormac, at his side, set his jaw and advanced.

When the enemy line was broken in two, Rónán and Cormac parted ways, Rónán to the left, Cormac behind him, and they pounded the enemy into the water on either side of the pass. He cut forward, knee deep in brash ice that formed and broke on the surface of the water as the sun set on their west. He heard the gargling pants of the enemy as he forced him under the water and drove his blade into his chest.

He spun to find his next quarry, but the fighting was drawing to a close.

His warriors cheered.

He took stock, surveying the landscape. The shallow waves

on the landward shore of the pass were littered with bodies. He could not tell which of those submerged men were his or Muirgel's.

Arrows rained from her walls but fell short of their position.

When Rónán called his council members together, Fergal said, 'She will run out of arrows soon enough.'

'We cannot wait her out,' Diarmuid said.

Rónán agreed. 'Can we cover our heads with our shields and advance to the gates?'

'And do what? Pick Fergal up, as he so generously offered, and knock his head against the wood?'

'It is a hard head and has been used for worse,' Fergal smiled.

Rónán shook his head. 'One more thump to that head of yours and you'll forget your own name. But Diarmuid is right—we cannot wait her out. If we step forward, we will be hailed on with arrows.'

'We will flush them out,' Cormac said. He had rinsed his hands in the bloody water and wiped them on his tunic. He took a deep nasal breath. 'Smell that? Dung. If we can set fire to dung and damp straw, we can slingshot it over her walls and smoke them out.'

'Can we take a couple of curraghs and come up from behind?' Rónán asked. 'If the rest of us make a fuss before her gates, she may not notice.'

'It will have to be a big fuss,' Fergal said.

'You can sing to her warriors,' Diarmuid laughed.

'Diarmuid, order the men. Spread out west. Gather as much dung and straw as can be carried.'

Diarmuid nodded and turned to give his commands.

When Grainne, Gallen and Achall approached him, Rónán

was grateful to see they had lived through the battle.

'We lost forty-six men,' Gallen said. 'When we have won, we will mourn them.'

Rónán clasped his arm in solidarity.

'May I have a word, Lord?' Grainne asked. When they stepped away from the others, she said, 'We will retrieve your son; I do not fear it.'

'There is fear in your voice.'

'But it is not for Áed. I fear the loss of good life, and I am fearful for you. I know your intentions. You would seek to destroy her, to end her life.'

'It is as she deserves.'

'She is wicked; I do not deny it. But she is Achall's aunt, for better or worse.'

'There can be no worse.'

'Regardless,' Grainne said, 'as your advisor, and as the archdruid, I must ask you to reconsider.'

Rónán smiled and touched her shoulder. 'You accepted your responsibilities. I know of no better person for the job.'

'I take the role with reluctance, Lord. But please. Capture her. She will be put on trial for her crimes and charged accordingly.'

'She rallied against Éirinn, against your people and mine. Should her charge not be death?'

'That may indeed be the case but give her the trial she needs. Let the people of Éirinn see that you are just and honourable. If she is sentenced to death, it will be carried out by the law.'

'In war,' Rónán said, 'there is only one law—to win.'

'As it is the central law of life. But you can win without mindless slaughter. Get your son back. But if you can do so without driving your sword through every man who stands in your way, do you not still win?'

When Diarmuid and his men returned with their arms full of dung and hay, the sun shielding itself from view behind the landmass of Thúr Rí, Rónán turned his thoughts to an attack on the fortified fort.

He knew Grainne's words to be fair and true.

But he did not like them.

Chapter 42

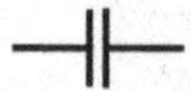

Muirgel stepped outside as a sodden grey smoke billowed under the door of the great hall and clung to the hem of her dress. She was accosted by a horrendous smell that made her gag and cover her mouth and nose with a hand.

Her warriors and cumal girls dashed with frantic energy from one building to another. Missiles of flaming dung fell in the courtyard and steamed when the girls poured pails of water over them. On the south-facing wall, archers sent waves of arrows into the unseen beyond.

'You,' she shouted at a passing cumal girl. 'Where is Dásan? And what is that sickening smell?'

'It is shit, my lady. They are firing burning shit at us.' The girl hurried away without curtsying.

Some of her warriors were vomiting in the western latrine. Smoke eddied between the buildings and burned her eyes as much as the smell choked her. Muirgel ducked back inside the great hall and closed the door, but the fumes had already followed her in. She pinched her nose and tried not to retch.

Áed's quiet voice startled her when he spoke, and she looked at him with squinted, smarting eyes. 'He is here,' the boy said.

He stood by the iron bars of his cage, small fingers wrapped around the dark metal, and his gaze aided the sting in her eyes. Even with one eye swollen and closed from his earlier beating, she felt the strength of his stare. And in that moment, she knew, without doubt, that he was not a child of seven, but a godly one possessed of an ancient spirit.

'He is not here.'

'He has come.'

'Hold your tongue, child, or I will cut it from your miserable mouth.'

'He has brought all the strength of Ailigh with him,' the boy said. 'I can taste the blood. It is like iron ore in my mouth.'

She reached through the bars and punched his face. When he fell backwards, he closed his open eye and she thought he was crying. But she was wrong; he was laughing.

The grey smoke whipped across the hall as it entered from the gap under the door. It dampened the sounds from outside, masking Muirgel and her young prisoner in a sense of isolation. The suffocating stench made even the dried skin of her knuckles weep.

'Get up,' she said, 'or I will give you something to laugh about.'

Áed looked at her. 'He has come.'

When the door opened, Muirgel expected to see Rónán enter, and for the briefest moment, the shadowed figure that loomed in the doorway could have been the overking of Ailigh. But it was Dásan's voice that came to her.

'My lady. We must get you out of here. They are attacking from the south and the north. We must go and see our distant friends.'

'Is it him?'

'He has come,' Áed said.

'Is it him?' Muirgel demanded of her chief warrior.

'It can be no other,' Dásan said.

'But have you seen him?'

'No, Lady. But he is here; he would not send his army without its head.'

'Get out there and find him. I want to know if he is here.'

Dásan bowed and left. Muirgel knew he would not argue with his queen, regardless of her safety.

She walked with a deliberate slowness to her sleeping quarters at the rear of the hall. She soaked a heavy winter dress in the bronze bowl of water, wrung it damp, and carried it back through the hall, dropping it at the foot of the door and kicking it into place along the gap. Though the room was smoky and choking, no more foul-smelling fumes could enter.

She looked at Áed in his cell. He had settled on the stony ground with his hands in his lap. His tunic, torn and bloodied from his earlier beating, draped over his body as though he was little more than a skeletal frame. With one eye swollen and the other closed as if in meditation, he would have appeared dead had he not been sitting upright.

'What silence washes over you?'

He did not respond.

'Answer me.'

Áed opened his working eye and stared at her. When he stood—slow, painfully—his left shoulder hung lower than his right.

'Where is your father now? If he has come for you, why is he not here, breaking down my door to come to your rescue?'

When she took a step towards him, Áed shook his head. 'Stay

back,' he said.

'He cannot come for you because he is defeated.'

'He is here. Do not come any closer.'

Muirgel clenched her fists. She stepped closer.

'Stay away,' Áed said.

'Such insolence from one so young.' She came closer.

Áed raised his hand, as though to ward her off. 'Stop,' he commanded.

Muirgel stopped. Her feet were heavy. Her knees were weak. For a moment, she tried to breathe but the air caught in her chest. Her cheeks flushed and a panic spread through her body as she realised her inability to move. Fear dragged its sharp claw into her gut.

Muirgel gathered her fortitude and breathed.

He could have no influence over her. Such a thing was impossible.

And yet she had stopped walking when he bade her to.

Muirgel shifted her foot and took another step. When she unlocked his cell and entered it, she slapped his already bruised cheek.

Weak, Áed fell to his knees.

'You fear me,' she said. 'And because of that, your trickeries will not work.' She gripped his tunic and pulled him to his feet.

She took him from the cell and threw him towards the door of her hall. She kicked the dampened dress from the floor, opened the door and dragged him out into the smoke-filled, dank air.

'You,' she said, pointing at one of her warriors. 'Gather the men. It is time to end this shameful infraction.'

She walked Áed through the fog of stench towards her compound's gates.

When Dásan came to her side, he said, 'The Ó Mordha king is almost certainly outside.'

'Open the gates,' she said. 'Tell your men to get out there and kill every bastard who carries the Ó Mordha blood in his veins.'

She pulled a dagger from the folds of her dress and took a fistful of Áed's hair.

'It is time,' she told him. 'Now you will see what kind of man your father is.'

Chapter 43

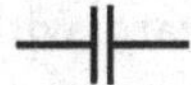

They could hear the retching of Muirgel's warriors inside her walls, and Rónán's men cheered.

Smoke swelled above her stronghold over a ceiling of cloying cries. 'Soon they will be spilling over her walls and begging for death,' Fergal laughed. He tightened the buckle on his metal arm and knocked his fist against it.

A horn blew. Over the din, Rónán heard the immense scraping of wood. The gates were opening. Horses whinnied.

'Call the men to order,' he said.

'Round up,' Diarmuid shouted. Their men took formations and readied themselves.

Rónán touched Cormac's shoulder. 'I suffer for your loss. But I know Orlaith is with us in spirit.'

Cormac's smile, though sad, appeared genuine. 'We will grieve when this is done.' He drew his sword and took his place in formation with the other men.

Rónán closed his eyes and inhaled. It was his last peaceful breath before battle, that final moment of stillness in which his world turned on an axis. When he opened his eyes, his choices would forever seal his future. He would act or react and, in doing so, would determine the fate of his own life, the lives of his warriors, and that of his son. Each movement he made would bring the future closer. The end is inevitable, regardless of the choices we face.

Diarmuid gave the call and Rónán opened his eyes. It was time.

As the gates disappeared into the smoke-filled emptiness beyond, Rónán pushed forward with his men. Behind him, he heard the battle cries of his former wife as she emptied her lungs of fear. If she was not careful, her battle-madness would devour her.

Three carbads, each pulled by two horses, emerged from the eddying fog of smoke, followed by a multitude of warriors on foot.

'Release,' Diarmuid commanded, and the sky darkened with arrows before the men advanced.

Rónán flexed his sword arm and ran. Those warriors who charged towards him were no bigger than any he had faced before. He was reminded of Áed the Executioner's words from a lifetime ago. 'The man you engage with on the battlefield is the only war you will ever fight. Until the next one.'

The carbad drivers spurred their horses towards the remains of Rónán's army. Though the path was rocky and slick with sea spray, the tall horses came with steady power. Rónán saw an opening. He feigned a slice with his sword at the spear-throwing warrior who stood behind the carbad's driver, and as the warrior twisted to avoid the blade, Rónán gripped the hem of the man's tunic when the carbad rolled by. He dug his heels into the stony ground and the force of his stance brought the man off his feet and crashing onto the carbad floor before rolling to the rutted track.

Rónán did not let go. He yanked on the warrior's tunic and brought his back off the ground as the carbad driver reined the horses in to help his companion.

Rónán brought the heel of his foot down on the man's face before turning his attention to the driver. He twisted away from the warrior's sword, jumped, sliced, and cut the driver's neck. His head sagged before the man dropped to his knees and fell from the back of the carbad.

His blood belched onto the rocks.

The spear-thrower had staggered back to his feet when Rónán looked for him. His sword was still in its scabbard at his hip, but he had gripped a rock in one fist. As Rónán swung at him, the man raised the rock and the impact with Rónán's blade made his forearms sing. The sword skittered from his hand.

Rónán kicked. He pounced on the man with his shield raised, using it as a butt, and when the warrior stumbled back, he dropped his rock and Rónán punched his face.

He gripped the man's hair and brought his shield up into his chin. When the warrior's knees gave way beneath him, Rónán turned, his fingers still gripping his hair, and he dragged him to the carbad.

He forced the man's head through the spokes of the carbad wheel, kicked him in the hip, and then he slapped the nearest horse on the rump. Frenzied, the horse bucked and jolted forward. And the wheel turned.

Rónán heard the sickening crunch of the man's neck as it tore between the wheel and the carbad. He did not have the chance to scream. Blood exploded under the carbad, and when the horses carried the body away, the head scowled with sightless eyes at the dull grey sky.

'Go with your gods,' Rónán said.

He turned, found his sword among the bloodied rocks, and looked for his next kill. If he stood still for too long, he was a dead man. Every warrior knew it.

Ahead of him, he saw Cormac slice through two enemy warriors, and Fergal was using his metal arm as both a shield and a ram. The broad man was singing, as he always did in battle. Rónán did not wish to think of a day where he would not hear Fergal's battle songs.

He heard a high-pitched scream behind him and, blocking a blow from the enemy, he severed the man's head and turned to seek out his wife. She swung a spear as though it was a sword, but no man would come close enough to butt it from her hands. Achall was possessed of a power Rónán had seen only once before—in Áed the Executioner. Achall, her dress hitched up around her thighs and her hair tied back, screamed like a *sidhe* demon as she jutted and thrust the spear. When she fell upon an enemy warrior with it, he did not stand a chance. The tip of the spear tore through his neck before Rónán watched Achall pull the spear free and plunge it into his chest.

As Rónán sidestepped another of the enemy and swept him off his feet with the edge of his shield before puncturing the man's chest with his blade, he saw Gallen step up behind Achall and wrap his arms around her, pulling her away from the dead man.

She screamed in the druid's face until he released her and backed away.

Rónán turned. He needed to get inside the gates that remained open. He steadied his mind as others around him choked on the dung-scented smoke. If Muirgel had a plan, he could not fathom it. That she left her gates open was either foolishness or calculated risk. Though his army—what remained of it—was small, they were decimating her men at the threshold of her bastion. She was exposed, and he could not think what games she hoped to win.

A javelin sang over his head and lifted one of the enemy warriors off his feet. As the man landed, Rónán sprinted, gripped the vibrating metal rod that protruded from his stomach, and pulled it free. In the same movement, he turned, whipped his arm, and threw the javelin forward as a trail of blood sprayed from its point. It penetrated the mossy ground just outside the open gates—he was that close to retrieving his son. A spear's throw.

Two warriors set upon Rónán with furore. Their red hair flowed in wild spikes atop their heads, braided moustaches whipped, as though they could be brothers. They mirrored each other in movement, shields raised, swords swinging. Rónán blocked and parried. He jumped back, feeling the ground with his heels, his eyes flicking from one foe to the other, taking in the twists of their limbs as they came. They thrust in time, two swords followed by two shields, and they did not let up. Rónán blocked but could not get an opening. If he drove his blade at one of them, he would be forced to block an assault from the other, leaving him exposed to the first man's sword.

Blow for blow, they matched him, always in time, never faltering. As he raised his shield, they parried. As he flicked his blade, they blocked.

The force of blows against his shield arm sent shocks through his shoulder and chest. His feet tired.

Rónán kept his eyes on what he now considered to be the

twins. They fought as one, their actions imitating each other. Rónán knew his only course of action was to throw them out of sync. One of Fergal's discordant songs would serve him well right now.

He raised his shield closer to the twin on his left and forced an attack on the right-most twin. He hacked and thrust, pushing the man back. Rónán slashed again. He could feel the brutal force of the other twin upon his shield, but he continued his unwavering attack on the second. When the man stumbled and his actions faltered, Rónán twisted and, timing the blows from the first twin, he dipped his shield and swung.

The redheaded warrior's shoulder wept red with blood as his neck opened.

Rónán thumped his shield into the man's chest and braced himself as they tumbled. He turned on his back, kicking himself to his feet, and he charged the remaining twin. He went in swinging, and the man fell beside his brother—real or imagined—in a bleeding heap.

Rónán spun on his heels, shield up, ready for a renewed attack.

When a carnyx horn blasted over the bloodied ground, Rónán could not place its position. The horn blew again, loud and piercing, the sound of day's end, though the battle was not long begun.

Again, the horn droned through the air and, across the narrow peninsula, warriors stopped swinging their blades or throwing their javelin.

With the ensuing silence, a voice cried over the fortified walls. 'Rónán Ó Mordha. Cease or I will slaughter your boy.'

Rónán scanned the top of the wall. When he saw her, he did not at once recognise the woman. She was old, older than he imagined she might be. It had been but seven years since he faced her in a tent outside Knockdhu, close enough that he could slice her cheek with his blade, but even from this distance he could see the unnatural wrinkles that folded her features and buried her eyes.

He could not see below her shoulders, but he knew she would be holding Áed, her fingers gripped around his neck or twisted in his hair to keep him from running. She would have a dagger at his throat, ready to cut him.

'If you have harmed him,' Rónán shouted, 'I will gut you with my bare hands.'

'Stand down,' Muirgel called.

'Release him to me.'

'I have no quarrel with the boy.'

'Release him to me, woman, or I will burn your hovel to the ground and mount your head at my door.'

'You will enter my gates, Rónán Ó Mordha. You and you alone.'

'What do you want?' Rónán called. He adjusted the grip on his sword.

Behind him, he heard Diarmuid shout, 'Archers, prepare.'

Muirgel's laugh echoed between them. 'If I see one bow string pulled taut, I will open your son's neck. Stand your men down.'

Rónán raised his arm to call Diarmuid off. 'Show him to me,' he shouted to Muirgel. 'I do not know if he lives.'

Muirgel looked down beside her and said something Rónán could not hear. Then Áed's voice, strained and weak, said, '*Daidí*. I am here.'

Rónán closed his eyes and gave praise to the gods that his son lived.

Achall screamed. 'Give me back my son, you *bitseach*.'

Muirgel laughed.

'Release him,' Rónán commanded.

'You will drop your sword and enter. Alone.'

'What do you seek from me, woman?'

'I want you to kneel before me.'

'I will not give up my seat to you.'

'I do not want your kingseat,' she said. 'You will kneel before me and let me push my dagger through your heart. You will do this willingly. You will kneel before me and allow me to murder you, and your child will be freed. Your wife, my foolish niece, can take him home and I wish never to hear the Ó Mordha name again. If you do not accept, I will kill him right now and toss him over the wall to you.'

'You would kill an innocent child to taunt me?'

Muirgel spat. 'I would kill a thousand unborn babies if it brought you to your knees.'

'You hold a grudge for so long?' He could not believe that Muirgel harboured such ill intent towards him. Seven years had passed since he murdered her husband. Donal was a man who turned against his own, who had Rónán's father slaughtered in cold blood.

'I grow tired of your tactics,' Muirgel shouted. 'Throw down your sword or I will throw down your son's head.'

'Áed?' Rónán called.

'*Daidí.*'

The boy's soft voice focused Rónán's mind. He turned his sword and dropped it.

'Rónán, no,' Cormac shouted.

Rónán unbuckled the clasp of his shield and let it fall.

'Rónán, stop this.'

He turned, beckoned Cormac towards him, and when he came, they embraced.

'We can take her,' Cormac said.

Rónán shook his head. He cupped Cormac's face in his hands and kissed him. 'For the sake of the boy, I must do this.'

'No. There is another way.'

'I love you.'

'Do not do this.'

He turned from Cormac. To Muirgel, he shouted, 'My life for the boy's. Your word.'

'You have my word.'

'Her word counts for nothing,' Cormac said.

Rónán moved forward.

'Rónán, no.'

He ignored the pleas of his lover. If one more death would end this, let it be his. No one else would die. The war would cease with his fall and his people could return to peace.

As he walked through the gates, he watched Muirgel's men fall away from him, allowing him space.

Muirgel came down from the wall, his son at her side. The boy was bruised and bloody, his tunic torn, but he was alive. 'Release the child,' Rónán said, his arms held wide to show himself without weapon. 'You gave your word.'

'My word is good,' Muirgel said, though she did not release her grip on Áed's hair. 'He can go free when he has witnessed your death.'

'Áed, my son. Close your eyes,' Rónán said. He lowered himself to his knees, keeping his arms spread in acceptance of his fate. 'Count as high as you can before opening them. Will you do that, son?'

'Do not close your eyes,' Muirgel said. 'You will watch as the
Ó Mordha king falls at my hand.'

'Let him go, Muirgel. I have done as you bade. I am here. My
life is in your hands; take it. But do not force my son to watch.'

She came closer with wary steps, her grip on Áed's hair tight
and unforgiving, her dagger at his throat. 'He will watch, or I
will slaughter him too.'

Rónán took the neck of his tunic and tore it, exposing his
chest. He tapped his breast. 'You have one chance, Muirgel. Push
the blade in firm, for if it does not kill me, I will die with my
hands around your neck and I will drag you into the Otherworld
with me.'

'Father,' Áed said. Half of his face was swollen so that one eye
was closed. Rónán ached to hold him, to rock him to sleep at
night as he did when he was a baby.

'My son.'

'The gods have told me—she does not mean to let me go.'

Muirgel's movement was swift. She pulled Áed's hair, forcing
his head back, and her dagger flashed before his face.

Rónán leapt.

Áed twisted.

Muirgel screamed.

As Rónán rose from his knees, he pushed one hand out towards
Áed, knocking him aside. He shouldered into Muirgel's fragile
frame and knocked her to the ground.

She rolled from him, but he pounced on her. Her hands were
empty, and in the dirt, he could not find her dagger. He punched
her face.

Muirgel scratched him. She twisted and clawed at him.

He gripped her hair, banged her head against the muddy

ground.

Her nails dug into his cheeks.

'*Daidí*,' Áed screamed.

'Rónán,' Cormac shouted.

He gripped her neck and squeezed.

Muirgel choked and her tongue flapped in her open mouth as she gasped for air.

When her hand came back to his face, Rónán felt a searing pain, blinding him. He fell away from her and gripped his eye.

Blood squelched between his fingers. He could not see. His eye was gone.

Outside, beyond the gates, he could hear the war renewed.

He reached out, unseeing. As though from a great distance, he could hear Áed crying. He felt Muirgel underneath him, her frail body twisting and turning against him, and he punched her. But there was no force in his fist. He shook his head and he felt blood gushing down his face and neck.

Something touched his back, and he swung his elbow to ward it off. He brought his hands back to Muirgel, gripping her neck though he could not see her. He squeezed and heard her rattled breath as she choked against his fingers. Her hand reached up a second time and he was able to swat it away. Her dagger clattered to the ground.

'*Daidí*,' Áed said. His voice was loud, full of strength. 'Do not kill her.'

'Son?'

'I am here.'

Áed's small hand touched his shoulder and Rónán gripped him.

'I cannot see you,' Rónán said.

The boy's hands covered Rónán's wound. 'I am here.'

Beneath his knees, Muirgel gasped for air.

'Do not kill her, Father,' Áed said. 'The gods are not finished with her yet.'

'What would you have me do with her, son?' Rónán asked. He kissed Áed's temple and held him tight.

'She will go on trial,' the boy said. 'She will stand before the druids and account for her actions.'

Rónán nodded against his son's cheek. The pain in his eye made him feel faint. But he was alive. And so was Áed.

Chapter 44

It was done. Though he could not see from one eye, and the pain inched across his face so that trying to focus his vision was uncomfortable, he carried Áed through the gates, stumbling over dead bodies, and he let Achall's hysterics direct him towards her.

Cormac came to him and held him. A battle raged around them, but Rónán sighed against Cormac's neck.

When the war was won, Grainne tended his wound. Muirgel had pierced him with her dagger and his eye had been destroyed. The skin around his socket had sagged and the eyeball was gone. When healed, the hole would dry, and his vision in that eye would be lost forever.

Nobody said it, not aloud, but he knew that his time as overking of the north was finished. In the quiet clarity that came to him with Grainne's herbal infusion, he understood the magnitude of Muirgel's actions. He would sooner let her kill him than suffer this fate—the fate of a maimed king no longer fit to rule his people.

The remainder of the day passed with relative obscurity. The post-battle lull was dampened further by the druid's medicines. He was taken into Muirgel's great hall where the old woman was now housed in the cage that she had built for Áed. Her druid, a woman who looked older than the most ancient trees that threw shadows across the western horizon, was found dead by her own hand at the rear of the hall. When her slight body was carried outside, Muirgel cursed her.

Her warrior chief was unaccounted for. Those men who surrendered rather than face death said that they had last seen Dásan just before the gates were opened.

'He is a coward,' Rónán told Muirgel. 'He has abandoned you, and when I find him, I will not take any pleasure in gutting him open.'

Having defeated her army, Rónán was now ruler of Thúr Rí island, but he did not sit in Muirgel's seat at the head of the hall. The highbacked chair with its deerskin coverings remained conspicuously empty.

In the furthest corner from Muirgel's cell, Achall clung to her son with arms so tight that he complained she might break his ribs if she squeezed harder.

Rónán sat away from the other men of Ailigh, separated by an immeasurable distance. Cormac, Diarmuid, Fergal and the other advisors to the king huddled in deep reflection. Cormac glanced at Rónán a few times, but although Rónán nodded, he did not otherwise acknowledge him or beckon him closer.

As the sun was setting and tallow candles were lit, Áed prised himself away from Achall's mothering arms and he came to Rónán's side. He tugged on his tunic sleeve and when Rónán opened his arms for him, the boy climbed onto his lap and wrapped his arms around his neck.

He touched the bandage at Rónán's face. 'Your left eye is gone and mine is swollen shut. Though you are not my father, we are both the same.'

'I am sorry,' Rónán said. He was sorry for every hurt the boy
had ever known and every injustice he would suffer at the hands
of other men. The boy had no right to call him father. 'I am not
deserving of a son. It was wrong of me to lie to you.'

Áed kissed Rónán's cheek. 'The evil woman told me what I
already knew. You may not be my father, but I will always call
you *Daidí*.'

Soon, the boy was asleep in his arms and when Achall came
for him, Rónán refused to let him go. 'You will have him all your
years,' Rónán said. 'Let me hold him for one night.'

In the morning, as they climbed into their curraghs and the
oars were lowered into the freezing water, Rónán's successor
had not yet been appointed. Cormac came to him in the night
and lay with him on the fur covered floor of the great hall with
Áed between them. He kissed them both on the cheek, and he
did not say a word. Rónán stared into his eyes in the dimness of
night, until all the colour faded from them and Rónán felt his
body swim into dreams he did not wish to suffer.

Now, sitting beside him in the curragh, Cormac gripped an
oar with one hand and interlaced the fingers of his free hand
with Rónán's. They were pulling into Éirinn's western shoreline
when Rónán said, 'Has Diarmuid accepted his responsibility?'

'He prayed to Cáer last night that your eye would return to
you.' Cormac laughed. 'He would give you one of his own if it
meant he did not have to take the kingseat from you.'

'He is not taking it from me. It has been gifted to him by the
gods.'

Cormac jumped out of the curragh and helped drag in onto
the shore. 'You should be angry that what you built is no longer
yours.'

'Angry, no. The rules are clear.' He allowed Cormac to help him out of the curragh and when he was on dry land, he prodded the bandage where his eye used to be. 'I am no longer whole. Diarmuid is my successor.'

'He was only minding the position of tanist until Áed came of age.'

'Áed will never want it, even if he was of age. That is not his future.'

'Diarmuid does not want it, either.'

Rónán nodded. 'Nor do I. I am tired, Cormac. A king is always tired. I will be moved into one of the outer brú homes and I will sleep until Imbolc. Either Diarmuid takes the kingseat or somebody else will. It is no longer my concern.'

'Why do you relent so easily?'

'Because I will not go against the brehon laws. The kingship is not mine. Why should I cry over it when it is something I did not want in the first place?'

'Your very reluctance is what made you great,' Cormac said as he took Rónán's elbow and guided him into the forest behind the others. 'If I was a bard, my songs would be kind.'

'If you were a bard, I would have killed you years ago; you do not have the voice for it.'

'Your kindness astounds me, my lord.'

Rónán wrapped his arm around Cormac's neck. 'Why do I not repel you with my ugliness?'

'I see no ugliness, Rónán. Love is as blind as you are, correct?'

'I will murder you in your sleep.'

On foot, the journey home was an arduous one. They rested that first night in a clearing not far from Brín Ó Cairbre's tribal lands, and Diarmuid came to Rónán for counsel.

At the far side of the clearing, Muirgel had been chained to a tree. She was forced to march barefoot for her sins against Éirinn, and her soles bled while she sat on the mossy ground beneath the tree under watchful guard of two warriors.

'I will not beg you to take the kingseat,' Rónán told Diarmuid, 'but it is rightfully yours.'

'You know I do not want it, but I will take it regardless—on one condition.'

'I am in no position to grant conditions of office.'

'It is a simple one,' Diarmuid said. 'You will remain as my chief advisor. I do not know what I am doing.'

'No king does. That is the joy.' Rónán thrust his arm out. 'But I accept your terms.'

'I have one more request. This woman, Muirgel—she is yours to do as you wish. Kill her or put her on trial. It is your choice. She is your prisoner, not mine, not Ailigh's. She is not Éirinn's foe, she is yours.'

Rónán nodded. 'She belongs to the druids now. Her fate is in their hands.'

'And if you do not agree with their ruling?'

'It is not our place to disagree, Diarmuid. As overking of Ailigh, you will learn that very soon.'

Rónán fumbled for the gold discs at his breast, the emblem of his station, and he unpinned them from his tunic. 'It is dark, and I have only one eye; I do not have the sight to pin them to you myself. The druids will do what they must when we are home, but for now, pin this to yourself and let me be the first to kiss you and call you King.'

Diarmuid wrapped his fingers around Rónán's fist before taking the gold discs. They were an *ordlach*—a thumb-length—in circumference and they were plain of adornment or imprint. They were hooked on a single clasp that fastened through the fabric of the tunic. He pinned them to his left breast, above the heart, and Rónán leaned in to kiss them. The last time he did so was the day Áed the Executioner had died, all too many years ago. Back when life had been simple.

'My king,' he said when his lips had touched the discs.

'Overking of Ailigh,' a nearby warrior shouted, and the clearing was alive with cheering and praise. Rónán slipped away from the excitement, and he rested his back against a broad tree that would have seen many kings come and go. His words to Cormac earlier that day had been true—he would not miss being king.

And he would sleep until Imbolc.

He did not see Achall or Áed for the rest of their journey home. When he walked through the gates of Ailigh, he went directly to the king's home beyond the inner wall, and he collected his belongings. He presented himself to Diarmuid in the great hall and Diarmuid came down from the kingseat to offer it to Rónán.

'Sit, that I may kneel before you one last time.'

'I require only a bed, my lord,' Rónán said, bowing to his new king.

'I cannot tell you where to live, Rónán. Do not force me. You know which homes lie empty. Take one; whichever one pleases you most. As my chief advisor, I am gifting you free reign of Ailigh. One fifth of Ailigh's wealth is yours. And for all the fucks in the world, never bow to me.'

'You will get used to it,' Rónán laughed.

When he was settled in the outer rampart, in a small home whose hearth had not been lit in many months, he removed the bandage from his face and looked at himself in a bronze mirror. His face was not his own. It belonged to another, someone whose features did not match. The puckering eye socket made him feel ugly and worthless. But when he rewrapped the bandages and stepped out into the fresh evening air, he knew that Ailigh, though no longer his, had been his responsibility for years. He was surrounded by people he considered to be friends. And a man who has friends is more than worthy.

With Diarmuid on the kingseat, Cormac overseeing the tanning of hides that had been left drying in their absence, and Muirgel locked in a hill-cell just outside the walls, Rónán walked through the rampart towards Achall's home. She had been a thorn in his side for years—more years than he cared to count—but she was the mother of his son, parentage be damned. She had been distraught with Áed's taking, and with his return he hoped she had found peace. The least he could do was to see to her needs and ensure they were both well.

As he meandered around the rampart between the homes, Fergal called to him. He raised his metal arm to his face as though he held a cup. 'We should get drunk,' he called.

'I will join you in the barrel hut soon. Warm the beer for me.'

Fergal saluted him and carried on his way. Rónán took a breath and steadied his nerve before knocking on Achall's door.

When he entered, he found his former wife on a stool by their son's bed. The boy was not asleep, but she sang to him as though her voice would lull him into a tired stupor. She applied a damp cloth to his forehead and smoothed his hair with her other hand.

Rónán stood over her, looking down at the child. 'Are you well?'

'He is fine.'

'I cannot sleep,' Áed said.

'They have taken his sleep from him,' Achall said.

'Who have?'

Achall shrugged. 'The gods? The *sidhe*? Someone.'

'He will sleep when he is tired. Are you hungry?'

'He is not.'

'I was asking you, Achall. When did you last eat?'

Rónán looked around her home. The boy's bed was next to his mother's, though hers was unmade and covered in fabric panels that were yet to become dresses or tunics. The outer edges of the hearth were coated in thick, black ash, and the table upon which they ate their meals when the weather outside was too inclement—which, given Éirinn's seasons, was all too often—was buried under broken spindles and wool threads. The fur hides that adorned the floor were ruffled and mushed, and the chest of Achall's dresses was open and its contents scattered.

'I ate,' she said, pausing to consider it, 'recently. Why have you come?' She dipped the cloth in a bowl of cool water, wrung it tight, and dabbed it at Áed's temples.

Rónán pulled a stool across the room and sat beside her. 'I came to see the boy. I may not be his real father, but I am still responsible for him.'

'He is not our son,' Achall said.

'I understand how you feel. But you cannot keep me from him. I have fathered him for seven years, even if he did not come from my seed.'

'You do not understand.'

'Achall, I am too weary to do this. Let me visit with my son for a short time and then I will leave. We can both get some rest. The gods know we deserve it.'

'He is not your son,' she said. 'And I am not sure he is mine.'

Rónán looked at her for the first time since he entered. The skin beneath her eyes sagged and darkened, and her hair, though it had always been untameable, was now a wolf cub's nest. She looked at him, and the green of her eyes was swallowed by the black of her pupils.

'Is he?' she asked.

'What do you mean, Achall? Do you feel well?'

She touched the boy's swollen cheek. 'She gave him my scar. Do you see? The scar you gave me. He has it now. Do you see?'

'I see it.'

'That makes him mine, does it not?'

'Achall?'

'I wish I saw him bleed when she cut him.'

Rónán rose to his feet. 'Achall, what are you saying?'

'Give me your blade. I need to see his blood.'

'What? Why?'

'Is it red? Does he bleed like us?' She reached for Rónán, took his hands. 'Look at him. He is not the boy who left us.'

'Of course not. He has changed. We all have. He has grown up, more than he should have,' Rónán told her. He pulled his hands from hers. 'Why would you say these things?'

She looked at him, blinked, and returned her attention to Áed, mopping his brow with the damp cloth even though he did not sweat. 'What things?'

Rónán narrowed his eyes. 'Why would you want to see him bleed?'

Achall leaned down and kissed Áed's slender nose. 'That is not what I said. He is tired. Are you tired, son? We are all tired. It will be night soon.' She ushered Rónán towards the door. 'You can see him in the morning. You can take him hunting if you do not leave the immediate vicinity. But not until he is well. And not until your bandage is removed.'

'Achall?' Rónán said. 'You are not talking sense.'

She shook her head, then nodded. 'I am quite well. Go home, my lord. You can see the boy in the morning.'

'Why do you call him Boy and not Áed?'

Achall looked over her shoulder at her son and then returned her smile to Rónán. 'He is a boy, is he not?'

'He is your son.'

'And he will still be my son in the morning.'

Rónán allowed her to push him out of her home and into the evening air. A light rain was falling in the breezeless dusk.

Alone, he cursed her. She may not be his wife, but she would always be a pain.

He turned for home, and realised he no longer lived within the inner wall. His life was not sacred. He did not know what would become of him, but he knew that Ailigh would survive.

It had to.

He returned to his new brú on the outer rampart, conscious of the guard tower that rose over his thatched roof. He had entered his home when he remembered Fergal and his offer of getting drunk. But he was tired. And Fergal—who had been a king once—would forgive him. Rónán closed his door and looked at the fire. He did not expect to see Cormac lying in the bed.

'Come to me,' Cormac said.

'I am tired.'

Cormac held the furs aside and beckoned him closer. 'You intend to sleep until Imbolc. And as your consort, it is my job to ensure no one wakes you before then.'

'I am no longer king,' Rónán said. 'You are not my consort.'

'Call me what you will. I aim to hold you until you wake.'

Rónán stripped his clothes off and adjusted the bandage around his face so that his empty eye socket could not break free without him knowing it. He slipped into bed beside Cormac and allowed himself to be encased in his strong arms.

Cormac kissed his neck.

Rónán turned from him, pressing his back into Cormac's chest, and he closed his eyes. He had said he was tired, but until he lay down, he did not realise how tired he was. He yawned.

'Five years,' Cormac said.

'What?'

'Five years and neither of us is dead. Is that a record for a king and his consort?'

'I told you. I am no longer king, and you are not my consort.'

'My point remains. In five years and many battles, we are both still alive. What are the chances?'

'Do not jinx it,' Rónán said, and he cuddled closer.

Wars come and go, and battles are won and lost every day. But he could not think of anything beyond sleep.

By the laws of kings and consorts, life is forever in flux.

For now, Cormac was his king. And sleep was his consort.

Chapter 45

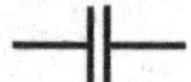

She cast the bones, and when she did not like the answer, she cast them again.

Each time she did, they gave her a different reply, though her question was always the same: does peace return to Ailigh at last?

Yes, the bones said. But also no. The gods could not make up their minds.

She swept the blackened bones back into their pouch and pinned it to her belt. She looked around her private quarters. Since their return from Thúr Rí two days ago, she had met with her fellow druids on two occasions. Grainne had hoped that she could stay at Ailigh and oversee the outreach across Éirinn to locate any remaining druids. She was adamant that her position as archdruid was a temporary one, until those druids who still lived could assemble and elect a replacement.

A fresh cell had been carved into the side of a hillock outside Ailigh's gates, and Muirgel had been thrown into it. Grainne had not yet been to see her. Her trial was set for seven nights hence, under the full moon when the gods would give them their greatest attention. Rónán's people—Diarmuid's people—would cry for her blood. And they had a right to it. Grainne, too, wished to see her dead. The fire-haired woman had decimated the druid-ship across Éirinn, and Grainne still had no idea why. You cannot slaughter the gods' mouthpiece and expect the deities to turn a blind eye.

But the trial was necessary. In the years since Grainne travelled north to begin her training as a child, she had witnessed so much mindless death and destruction. Tribes turn against each other with little reason; brothers fight over cattle; fathers and sons slay each other in petty squabbles. At least with a trial, Muirgel's fate would be accepted by both the people and the gods.

It was Grainne's place to decide that fate. As archdruid, she could only arrive at one outcome for a woman who had her people massacred. If she thought she had it in her, she would gut the women herself, from throat to groin—not for murdering her brethren, but for the act of killing the archdruid, a man whose eyes disappeared when he smiled, whose fingers touched your skin like gentle butterflies. For that one life, Grainne would murder a hundred men in retribution. But the trial would stay her hand. When her verdict is delivered, an executioner would be called and Grainne's hands would not be bloodied.

To take her mind from the impending hearing, she stepped into the afternoon sun, weak and cold as it was, and she watched as a couple of boys carried Diarmuid's belongings towards the overking's brú. She wrapped a fur around her shoulders and picked her way down to the great hall, lifting her robes off the ground as her leather boots squelched in the mud.

When she approached, the guard bowed to her and opened the door. At the far end of the hall, sulking in the kingseat, Diarmuid nursed a cup of beer.

'I have never seen a king so idle,' Grainne said, prostrating herself before him.

'Get up off the floor, Grainne, and tell me what a king should do.'

'What fun would you derive from being told how to act?'

'In all my years as Rónán's tanist, I did not consider the king-ship to be fun.'

Grainne smiled and indicated the table whose eight empty seats had so recently held Rónán's council. Diarmuid joined her there and a cumal topped up his cup and offered one to Grainne. She refused.

'You mean to tell me you are leaving,' Diarmuid said. She knew he meant it as a question, but it did not sound as one.

'As soon as Muirgel's trial is done, and her punishment has been executed. I do not wish to go, but as archdruid, I have a responsibility to my people. As you have to yours.'

Diarmuid picked a splinter on the edge of the table. He had taken Rónán's seat but did not look the part. 'These are not my people. They are Rónán's still.'

'You would do well to change that.'

'And how might I achieve such a thing?'

She shook her head. 'I would say war usually rallies one's peo-ple around their king, but we are not long after war and I do not think your people would look upon you so kindly for it. A wed-ding might lift their spirits.'

'I already have a wife,' he said, 'and I do not need a second woman telling me what to do.'

'You seek my opinion just as readily.' She smiled, but then took a breath and leaned forward in her chair. 'Ailigh has so few people left, and your livestock has been almost annihilated.'

'Thanks to a woman who cannot die swiftly enough.'

'I am loathe to say it, but with dwindled numbers of men and sheep, your limited grain resources will last longer. Your second responsibility as king should be to rebuild your army and your livestock.'

'If that is my second, what is the first?'

Grainne gathered her robes around her. 'Mourn the people you have lost. We should give praise in their honour and make a call of remembrance. Their names will be recited among the gods so that no one will be forgotten.'

Diarmuid walked with her towards the door of the great hall. 'Now I see why Rónán flourished as overking—it was all your doing. Who am I to rely on in your absence?'

'Gallen is ready,' she said. 'He will graduate from acolyte to druid, and he will guide you.'

'You are archdruid. I do not know whether I should kiss your cheek or kiss your feet.'

'We both have new responsibilities, my lord. Take my arm in solidarity and leave your lips untainted for your wife to cherish. Your son—am I to swear him in as your tanist before I leave for the north?'

'Yes. But Darragh is already hungry. Swear him to the role but make it the last thing you do. He could stand to sweat it out for a few nights.'

She laughed. 'You will do well as overking, my lord. I will make arrangements.'

When she returned to her quarters, a heavy rain had darkened the horizon and Ailigh's torches crackled in the wind. Crouching in her doorway, Gallen used the tail of his robes to protect Anú and Breasal from the gathering chill.

'Gallen, son. Why did you not enter and warm the children at the hearth? These rooms will be yours when I am gone.'

'They are not mine yet,' he said. 'And do not call me son.'

She pushed the door open and when they were inside Gallen stoked the fire and he pressed Anú's hands between his own, rubbing the sting of winter from her fingers.

Grainne had seen so little of the children in recent times that she did not know what pain Breasal suffered. He had lost his mother, the most exquisite warrior Grainne had ever known aside from her brother, and the boy's father figure was never known to him. She looked at him now as he stood by the flames of her hearth, his palms raised to the orange glow, knees trembling in the cold, and the red mark of his birth ablaze across his face. He would not look at her, but she could see that his eyes had the glossy sheen of sadness.

She tousled his hair, and he did not react.

'Everyone is sad,' Anú said.

Grainne nodded. 'Everyone has a reason to be sad.'

'Then why do the gods still smile?'

Gallen said, 'Because they know more than we do.'

Grainne had no doubt that he would succeed without her at his side.

Although he bemoaned the fact that these were not his quarters, he set about preparing a meal for the four of them without a word. Grainne watched the children eat with slow, deliberate bites, the actions of tired children who do not wish to chew but will not defy the rules of mealtime.

There were too many words unspoken between them. Gallen poured three cups of warmed wine and let the children share. It would be enough to bring about a drowsiness of mind that lulled them to sleep.

Cormac—the boy's uncle—and Rónán would take Breasal under their care in their new home in the inner rampart. Grainne knew they would do well. And soon, given his unusual, godly insights, she would take stewardship of his soul as a druid's acolyte and prepare him for adulthood.

He lay on the floor, with his head in Anú's lap, and the young girl stroked the outline of his birthmark with a tender finger. Grainne smelled golden samphire in the girl's presence, and she knew that, if a future war did not tear them apart, she and Breasal would grow together in both spirituality and in love. Theirs was a destiny nobody could unwrite.

'*Mamaí*,' Breasal said, in a heavy exhalation that took him closer to sleep.

Anú's finger eased around his left eye and across his cheekbone. She soothed him by rubbing his earlobe between thumb and forefinger. 'She waits for you until seventeen years after your wedding,' the girl whispered. 'She wears her blue and yellow dress with the frilled bodice.'

Soon they were both asleep.

Gallen nursed his empty bowl, running his finger through the powdered oats that remained there, sitting on the floor beside the children whose quiet snores matched the slow beating of Grainne's steady heart.

She looked at him but did not interrupt his musings until she heard his breath, as though he had forgotten to inhale for some time and only drew life within him at the last possible moment, the moment when the gods are most vocal.

'To Ailigh,' Grainne said, 'you are a warrior of the sword. To Mogh Roith, you are a warrior of the gods.'

At the mention of his personal god, he looked up. 'Forgive me. I was a thousand rods from here.'

'Do not apologise for being at the attention of your god.'

'I cannot suffer life away from your side,' Gallen said. His stare was focused.

'Believe in yourself, Gallen. You are more committed than any other.'

He poked the embers of the fire so that they could feel the warmth. 'My commitment is to you, my lady. Not to Ailigh. Not to Rónán or Diarmuid or anyone else.'

'Your commitment is to your god. Remember that.'

'He guides me, but you instruct me. It is you who shaped me, Grainne. What is my life without you in it?' He scraped the scant remains of his meal into the fire.

Grainne rose from her stool and glanced at the sleeping children before coming to him. The flames warmed her shins and, though the smoke was no thicker than usual, it seemed to be trapped by the thatching, swirling around them to dampen the sounds from outside.

'You had a life before me, and you will have one after me.'

'You know the life I had before you, Lady. Nightly, I dream of my mother's face as she lay dying in the rain. Am I to dream of your face also?'

'I hope that you do,' she said, 'though I do not wish it to be a vision of death.'

He turned to her. 'To see you die would be death itself, my lady.'

'I am journeying north, Gallen. I am not travelling to the Otherworld.'

'And you leave me here without you.'

'You will graduate, and you will serve Ailigh well.'

'And who will protect you in the north, Lady?'

'Who will protect Ailigh if you come with me?'

'Ailigh is a tribe of warriors. You are a woman alone.'

'I am not alone.'

'You would not be if I journeyed at your side, my lady.'

'I am not your lady.'

'You are my master.'

'I am your equal.'

Gallen took her shoulders. 'Then kiss me as your equal.'

And she kissed him.

As her lips met with his, he folded her into his arms. His stubble growth grazed her, but the numbing pain was intoxicating. His hands sought solace in the small of her back. Her fingers laced behind his neck, underneath the thick flow of his hair. She could feel the beating of his heart against her breast, and she knew that her own heart was no longer slow and deliberate. It matched the pangs of her longing.

His arms—the strongest arms she knew—picked her up. She could not deny him. He carried her into the adjoining room, and he laid her on the low pallet bed. He stood before her and undid the string of his robes. They fell from him, and Grainne closed her eyes lest she lust for him before he could take her.

She anticipated a certain level of pain for the first time she let a man enter her, but beneath him, she did not feel it.

She felt only joy as his teeth broke the goosepimples over the skin of her neck and his hips fought against the perspiration of her body. Her robes, hitched and pulled aside, were no barrier to his actions.

Grainne's lips were scorched from his unshaven cheeks, but

she relinquished herself to his movement, pulled at his hips to feel closer to him. Closer than was possible.

Closer.

And in the heat of her climax, a rainbow of flashes stole her vision, and her most gracious lady Cáer whispered in her ear a word that Grainne had never felt before. Love.

He lay beside her when their lovemaking was done, his arm around her waist, the children asleep in the room beyond, and when their skin had cooled, he pulled a fur across them and kissed the edge of her jaw, and neither of them spoke because words were inadequate. They were unnecessary.

Grainne's sleep was dreamless and peaceful. Before the dawn she rose, admiring Gallen's naked torso before turning from him. She dressed with her back to him, and she left him in bed, kissed the foreheads of the children who still slept on the floor, and she stepped into the icy morning.

Ailigh would be waking soon. The winter sun was late to rise and early to slumber. In these darker months, Éirinn's people would rise before the sun and half a day's work could be done before the yellow orb was spit from the earth's blue womb.

Grainne had no regrets, for it was the action of fearing the past and failing to meet the future. Regret is the only thing worth regretting.

She adjusted the bronze clasp that secured the fur around her shoulders, and she stared towards Muirgel's hillock. The mound was only big enough for one prisoner when it was excavated. It was inset with an iron gate whose key, at Diarmuid's behest, was chained around Rónán's neck. Rónán was Muirgel's keeper until her trial.

Grainne did not know why her feet carried her toward the

hillock. She did not intend to visit the woman or speak with her, but when she came around the edge of the grasses to face the iron gate, Muirgel's voice was terse. 'A visitor at last. You do me a great honour.'

'It is no honour to be locked within a cell at the cusp of your own funeral.'

'I do not fear death.'

'It is not death you should fear but dying. Dying is the hard part.'

'You cannot imagine a death more painful for me than I have dreamt of yours, Grainne Ní Mordha.'

Grainne looked into the darkness. Muirgel's red hair glowed with a morning brightness unmatched by the dawn's rising sun. Her eyes glinted, cheeks smiling. She did not look directly at Grainne but kept her gaze upon the lough at the bottom of the hill.

'Why did you do it?' Grainne asked.

'Slaughter your people? Because I could. Because I hate you.'

'Hate me? Or hate druids?'

'Does it matter now?'

'Yes.'

In the grey light, Muirgel shrugged and worried with a casual absence at a broken fingernail. 'Both. But mostly it is you that I hate. I have hated you since the day my deceased husband invited you to our lands. It is thanks to you that my family is dead.'

'Your family is dead because of their actions, not mine.'

Muirgel nodded. 'Spoken like a druid who cannot hear the will of the gods for fear of missing the voice of the people.' Her hands gripped the iron bars of her cell and she pulled herself closer so that her cheeks pressed against the gate. Her eyes looked to the distant lough, at the gentle waves that lapped the shoreline below.

'Your own actions did not serve you well, Muirgel.'

The old woman smiled. 'Whose actions ever do?' Still her gaze did not part from the lough to face her accuser.

Grainne felt a chill and she touched the fur at her shoulders to ensure it was still there. She followed Muirgel's stare towards the dark lough. 'Your trial will be swift. There is only one likely outcome, and it is your death. I hope you have prepared yourself for that. I cannot stop the will of the people, for it is also the will of the gods.'

'Of your gods, perhaps,' Muirgel said. Her eyes squinted as the eastern sun rose to dazzle the lough's surface.

Again, Grainne followed the old woman's gaze. 'What do you look for out there? Your druid is dead, and your chief warrior has abandoned you. Your people are gone.'

'Salvation,' Muirgel said.

'You will not find it. Salvation is not something you should seek.'

Muirgel laughed. 'I do not seek it. I expect it.'

Chapter 46

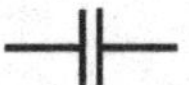

Alaid, son of Beltaid, whose tattooed arms have worked every day since his mother stood atop two milking stools and spat him from her womb, gripped the rope and gave the order to his men.

The lead crew member jumped the halyard as seven of Alaid's warriors heaved. The sail flapped with mocking cries as it furled. A dark storm engulfed the western horizon and, with the sail extended, they would be dashed into the rocks before the songs of the siren could reach them.

'Square the yard,' the captain commanded.

The sky, whose cerulean dawn was being eaten by black clouds, bowed to the storm with willing acceptance. The horizon was fogged with a dense rain that made a mockery of Alaid's perception of distance.

'Heave,' the first mate shouted. 'Heave.'

The brail rings clanked against the thick sail as it was furled. The sea chopped and snaked against the hull as the formidable storm clawed its way closer.

When the sail was stowed, Alaid ordered the starboard steer to bring the ship into the wind. 'And let out the sea-anchor,' he cried. They needed to cancel out the drift or they would capsize the moment the storm hit. He could see the waves breaking twice a man's height and coming in fast. The sea-anchor, a conical sack attached to the bow of the ship and dropped into the water, caught the current and aided their drag.

When the first wave hit, they were still turning into the wind and the massive warship rocked. The hull groaned louder than the men. The spray soaked the deck, but the ship did not go over. 'Hard port,' Alaid shouted.

They righted themselves and the rain lashed their faces. The crash of the second wave, coming in from port, caused the man nearest him to empty his stomach. Vomit whipped over the bulwark and into the darkness, and Alaid punched him in the throat. 'Spew your guts *away* from the wind, you useless maggot. Grab the line before I throw you overboard.'

The ship's hatches were battened with sailcloth and, below deck, the oarsmen had drawn in the oars. Now it was all about luck. If his men could keep the bronze prow trimmed to the wind, they would survive.

He had commandeered the *triêrês*—a massive warship in which 170 oars were once pulled by paid freemen but were now manned by Alaid's fierce warriors—five weeks ago and their voyage was just over half complete. If the storm did not let up, they may not make their destination.

The wind whipped against him. Alaid wrapped a rigging rope around his fist, and he watched the deck crew perform their duties. He had sailed before, but he was not a sailor. He knew who the quartermaster was, where the piper would be, but he did not know enough to weather the ship through a storm. He was a warrior by birth, a smith by trade, and a king to his people. But he was no sailor.

And yet he called himself captain—because he could. Because

these men, all two hundred of them, were his tribal brothers. And he would stand through the storm because he knew, at his journey's end, he would be rewarded with riches beyond imagining. He would own a country.

He would rule the world.

And man would bow to him.

The storm beat upon his ship. Men screamed. One of his warriors, caught unaware, slipped over the bulwark and disappeared. Alaid cursed as the rain stung his face and his arms. He crouched against the bow and uttered the names of his gods.

When the storm passed later that day, it left as quick as it had come. The sky brightened along with his warriors' spirits. He had lost only three men to the sea, which to Alaid was a good thing. He could stand to lose three men if he would win the world.

With the clouds passing and the waves easing, Alaid released himself from the rigging and checked for signs of damage. His ship took the lead path. Behind him, an additional twenty-seven warships cut the waters with exacting precision. Below deck, he could hear the muster of his men as they drew their oars.

Twenty-eight *trièrês* on route from Hellas. Over five and a half thousand men. Hibernia was his for the taking.

Alaid took to his trierarch's chair to oversee the smooth running of his ship now that the storm was behind them. They had weathered the worst of it. His oarsmen would see him through the journey.

Though they had not seen a single bird since they passed through the precarious strait between *Tenga* and *Givraltár* last night, before the storm had hit, he could hear them somewhere on the eastern horizon above the flapping of the sails and the

creaking of the rigging. Birds, Alaid knew, would be the ultimate ruination of humankind. All men fight, but as each one
dies, fewer remain. When the world is reduced to two warring
populations and all others are gone, it is the birds that will super-
vise man's demise. Their claws will take to tree limbs and their
darkened eyes will gaze upon man's final blow. Fires consume
a warrior's flesh, but it is the birds who will pick at his useless
bones as they crumble to the earth.

When those final warring nations are reduced to two men,
Alaid will be the victor, the last man alive. He will stand atop a
mountain of remains as the world burns around him and he will
call to the birds to pluck at his eyes. Sightless, he will not see the
empty world that has become his private domain.

This was Alaid's only fear—that a victorious warrior is destined to become a lonely one. And a warrior who has no one left
to fight may just as well kill himself as go on living with nothing
more to do. Falling on his sword when he is the last man alive
will be his final battle. And when the time comes, he decided,
he will make a sport of it. He would slice his arms and dive into
the ocean so that his swirling blood would force the six heads of
Scylla to fight against each other and devour him. And once in
her belly, no bird could get to his bones.

That will be his ultimate peace.

Alaid barked an order at his men when he noticed the sail
slacken at starboard. Now that they had navigated the narrow
strait and were sailing into open waters beside Ophiussa, they
could increase their speed and shorten their journey time to
Hibernia. Storms be damned.

The messenger who had come to him last year, through
the sweltering heat of a Hellas summer, called himself Dásan,

warrior chief of Queen Muirgel, ruler of Thúr Rí.

Dásan, a man whose broad chest was white with aged fur that glistened against his pale skin, had come with many gifts. His journey, he told Alaid, had been a long and laborious one, paying passage on trade ships with no concept that his destination would be hotter than the arse of a burnt cauldron. He spoke with a thick accent, and Alaid laughed when he gave Dásan some strong wine and could no longer understand his slurred speech.

'We have no collective ruler; not the way you say your people have over many tribes. Why did you come to me?' Alaid asked the foreigner when he had sobered up and opened the chests of gold and iron ingots, jewellery and fine linens.

'I sought only the biggest warrior I could find,' Dásan said. 'You stood taller than the others when I docked in your lands.'

Alaid's teeth had flashed as he puffed his chest and considered how tall he was. The foreign man was also tall, but Alaid towered over him, much as he did over his own people.

He had known, of course, about the war in Hibernia——the place the foreigner had called Éirinn. His own brothers had journeyed there some years before and they did not return. That meant they either met with their death as brave warriors or had seized enough land as to be profitable. Alaid was not a man given to promises of wealth. But when Dásan came to him and offered him a personal fortune, a world in which to rule, he could not refuse.

'Your queen,' Alaid said, handing the pale foreigner another cup of sweet wine and biting into the succulent flesh of a plump fig. 'Why does she fight against her own kind?'

Dásan nodded as though he had expected the question. 'She calls your people her cousins. She aligns herself to your gods.

She offers you riches immeasurable. Her actions are her own. This is not your concern.'

Alaid was impressed. A ruler should never justify his or herself to another.

'She looks like a Hibernian but acts,' Alaid told Dásan before the man departed for home, 'like a Hellas woman. For these gifts and the riches that you have promised me, I will gather my men and my neighbouring tribes, and we will set sail for your green shores. I will take your world from your queen, and I will rule over even her. She will come to my bed when I call for her and I will populate your lands with my seed. This is my promise to your queen—I will do as she asks; I will slaughter her enemies. But I will gut her friends as fast as her foes. Will she agree to this?'

Dásan bowed his head. 'My queen has no friends, only enemies. She will be pleased with your words. Kill them all.' He knocked his cup against Alaid's, and he drank himself into a stupor. In the morning, he gathered his things to leave.

That was almost a year ago. And now, halfway around the world, Alaid's men pulled their oars and sang their songs. And although the storm had passed, the air was growing colder. They were going north, away from the sun, into a cold land, a land whose hills were greener than envy.

And Alaid recalled his final words with Queen Muirgel's chief warrior.

'What shall I tell my queen?' Dásan had asked when he was ready to leave.

Alaid had taken the man's hand and said, 'When we come, we will remember the centuries of our oppression. Hibernia— Éirinn—call it any name you choose. It will be ours. It is mine to take with hands that are owed it.'

Alaid watched as Dásan climbed into the back of a chariot.

'Tell her the Fir Bolg are coming.'

COMING SOON

Book 4 in the Ailigh Wars Saga

**Be the first to read the conclusion
to Merrigan's epic Celtic saga**

Head to:
peterjmerrigan.com
for updates